08/16

KT-215-123

Susan Crawford is a four-time winner of the ~~~
Club award for her short fiction and poetry. Her first nov~,
Pocket Wife, was published in 2015, and her work has appeared
in *Loves Lost and Found*, *Long Story Short* and *The Sun*. A
long-time teacher in the field of Adult Education, Susan is now
a full-time author.

9030 00005 1896 9

ALSO BY SUSAN CRAWFORD

The Pocket Wife

THE OTHER WIDOW

SUSAN CRAWFORD

FABER & FABER

First published in 2016 by Faber & Faber Limited
Bloomsbury House,
74–77 Great Russell Street
London WC1B 3DA

First published in the United States in 2015
by William Morrow,
an imprint of HarperCollins Publishers
195 Broadway, New York, NY 10007

Printed in England by CPI Group (UK) Ltd, Croydon, CR0 4YY
Typeset by DIX

All rights reserved
© Susan Crawford, 2016

The right of Susan Crawford to be identified as author of this work has been asserted in
accordance with Section 77 of the Copyright, Designs and Patents Act 1988

*This book is sold subject to the condition that it shall not, by way of trade or
otherwise, be lent, resold, hired out or otherwise circulated without the publisher's
prior consent in any form of binding or cover other than that in which it is published
and without a similar condition including this condition being imposed on the
subsequent purchaser*

A CIP record for this book is available from the British Library

ISBN 978–0–571–32192–6

FSC
www.fsc.org
MIX
Paper from
responsible sources
FSC® C101712

LONDON BOROUGH OF WANDSWORTH	
9030 00005 1896 9	
Askews & Holts	22-Aug-2016
AF THR	£7.99
	WW16008596

2 4 6 8 10 9 7 5 3

For Linda, a fellow dreamer

ACKNOWLEDGMENTS

I am deeply grateful to my brilliant agent, Jenny Bent, for nudging me to make this a better book. I'm equally grateful to my amazing editor, Carrie Feron, for her vision and suggestions. Thanks to Victoria Lowes and Charlee Hoffman at the Bent Agency for answering my countless questions, to Nicole Fischer for her numerous calming explanations, and to Ashley Marudas, Kelly Rudolph, Paul Lamb, and the rest of the team at HarperCollins, both in New York and Canada, for their help and ingenuity. Heartfelt thanks to UK agent Nicola Barr for her support, and to Hannah Griffiths at Faber & Faber for her thoughtful editorial suggestions.

Thanks to my critique group members who are, as always, remarkably helpful. Special thanks to Bethany Armstrong for her insightful advice as we munched our way through markups and omelets at the Galaxy Diner and to Kimberly Nave, for fielding middle-of-the-night questions and for reading my manuscript with the eye of a thriller aficionado.

Thanks to Ginger Collins for her feedback on these characters in their first stages and to Nancy Blum for the early reading. Thanks to Deborah Mantella for her patience and camaraderie, to Peggy Skolnick for her confidence and common sense, and to both of them for dropping everything to "just please take a quick look" at countless blogs and chapters.

Thanks to Jill Evans for setting up my web page, Stephe Koontz for midnight computer saves, and to Katie Crawford for all her generous help with social media. I'm grateful to Stuart Anderson and Thomas Hart for their expertise in all matters of car engines, to Dan Crawford for his insurance knowledge, Lily Iglehart for sharing the particulars of Boston and Jamaica Plain, to Bob Angles for his support through the years, and to John Angles, who always has the answer. Thanks to Jonny and Amy Davis and to other family members and friends for putting up with my writing-oriented absences. And of course I am so very grateful to all my readers!

Lastly, thank you, Ben and my beautiful girls.

Love is a shadow.

How you lie and cry after it.

Listen: these are its hooves: it has gone off, like a horse.

—*"Elm," Sylvia Plath*

THE OTHER WIDOW

I

DORRIE

The Audi skids on a slick street. Black ice. Dorrie bends to sip hot chocolate from a Starbucks cup. Too hot, it burns her tongue, and she jerks the cup back, sloshing several drops across her coat. "Sorry!" She feels around his seat, wipes the spilled drink with her sleeve, glancing at Joe with his hands tight around the steering wheel. He looks angry, his jaw rigid in the disjointed, nearly absent light, the scraps from streetlights hazy and distorted as snow starts to fall sideways on the wind. She keeps her face a blank, determined not to break, no matter what he says. An actress since the age of five, she's learned to handle almost everything that comes her way, or at least appear to. Even this.

She nearly hadn't met him. She'd let his message go to voice mail—his un-Joe-like, desperate voice on the burner phone he'd bought her when he bought his own—insisting that she catch a train to Back Bay. *Please, sweetheart. I wouldn't ask you if it wasn't an emergency.*

And then his text, *That Starbucks on Boylston.*

Fine, she'd texted him. *You're the boss.*

She'd grabbed an old coat from the back of the hall closet—a heavy, ugly, too-large coat, discovered at Goodwill some years before, picked up as an afterthought and tossed on the pile of things her daughter had stacked on the counter. She'd meant to buy it for the coat drive at the school. But somehow it got lost in the closet. An extra, Samuel said, but no one ever wore it. Until tonight. She'd stuck one black leather glove in the pocket and felt through all her other coats for its mate but hadn't found it. She always seems to have only one of things—gloves, socks, earrings. She'd scribbled *Gone to grab a bite with Jeananne—Emergency* and taped the note to the front door for Samuel and Lily. It was a lie, but at least Jeananne worked at the office. *My boss called me back in,* Dorrie might have written, which would have been the truth. *Emergency, he said,* she could have added for the urgency, but she'd felt safer with a lie.

She pulls her knitted hat over her ears to ward off the cruel Boston cold that jabs its way inside the front seat through tiny lines around the windows, unnoticed gaps at the doors. The hat is silly, blue-and-white striped, her daughter's hat, Lily's, frivolous and whimsical, the opposite of this outrageous coat that makes her feel as if she's in a bad play. Still, it serves its purpose—enormous, heavy; it blocks the cold. And it disguises her, cloaks her betrayal. She reaches in her pocket, touching the one glove with the tips of her cold fingers. She takes it out, sets it on the seat beside her and silence hugs the car, crouches in the cracked leather of the seat.

She rolls up her too-long, bulky sleeves and three bright bangle bracelets slide up her thin arm.

Joe sighs. She gazes at the side of his face, watches as he squints through the windshield at a road vague and fading, like a dream. Even with the car lurching, sliding, even with the gray murk that envelopes them, he seems preoccupied. He has been for weeks. Dorrie raises the hot chocolate to her lips, the cup from Starbucks, where earlier they'd sat and sipped their drinks, like strangers, barely speaking. His gait had been rigid as he'd squeezed past the inviting velvet chairs to simple wooden tables in the back. He'd looked distracted, rumpled, in his work clothes, his starched white shirt untucked in places, his heavy wool coat slightly atilt.

What? she'd said, but he'd just shaken his head. *Not here.* And she'd babbled on about the weather, the coffee, drowning out the voice at the back of her head—her mother's voice, cautionary, clear, even after all these years.

She turns to look out the car window, seeing only a great swirl of white with the night behind it. She flinches, shrinking back against the seat as the car pitches forward. Her mother died in snow like this, when her car collided with a hurtling van. Killed instantly, she'd taken part of Dorrie's father with her, changed him in some basic and essential way, left him sobbing, lost at the kitchen table, a wall phone swinging by his knees, the policeman's words shooting through the mouthpiece like bullets. It was then that Dorrie learned to be an actress, a happy child, a smiling face stuck to her father's thick black wall of grief.

Later, starring in a handful of her high school plays and summer theater, a short run at the Charles Playhouse, she'd found that acting was as natural to her as breathing. She nearly always gets the parts at her auditions and turned down the one understudy role she was offered. Ironic, because with Joe she's only ever been an understudy. *Understudyfork,* her screen name when she e-mails him. Understudy for Karen.

She sets her drink in a cup holder on the console, glances around for the dropped lid, and sticks her hand over the hot chocolate. The car lurches along, sliding, as the tires seek out tracks imprinted on the icy road. "So." She puts her palm down on the seat to steady herself. Her bracelets jangle and clang. She wishes now she'd listened to her mother.

"There isn't any easy way to do this, Dorrie." Joe doesn't look at her. He stares through the windshield at the stormy night. "We have to stop seeing each other, at least for now," and even though she'd sensed this was coming, for a second Dorrie can't speak. She wants to cry, to scream, to grab the wheel.

"Karen?"

"No," he says. His voice is hoarse. "It isn't safe. For *us.*" He turns toward her, and even in the darkened car she sees his fear. It's in his eyes—in the lines across his forehead. "Not now. I've started digging around, but until I figure out exactly what's going on—"

"With *what*? Going on with *what*?" She turns to face him. She doesn't shout. She takes a breath and then another and she musters all her acting skills to make her face a blank. Curious, nothing more. "I don't understand."

Joe shakes his head. "I know," he says, and he speeds up. Too fast, she thinks. He stares back at the blur of road as he turns onto Newbury Street, and Dorrie glances toward the white-capped outdoor seating she can barely see, the banisters collecting snow. "It's dangerous. For both of us. Believe me, if there was any other—"

4

Before he finishes, a bright light catches in the air and spreads out like a blanket as a car crosses over into their lane, swerves back, and disappears. Joe clutches the wheel. He brakes. The old Audi slides sideways as he struggles for control. "Jesus! I can't—"

Dorrie digs her nails into the seat and wills the car to stay on the road. She can't breathe. The tires squeal, staining the air with an ugly shrieking sound that cuts the night in two. Before and after. Sliced clean like a melon. The car spins, pulling forward to the left, flying sideways. Dorrie grabs at air, grabs for Joe, her screams stopped in her throat as the car pitches finally off the road into a tree. Her airbag smacks her like a punch above the eye, the windshield crackles, her glove flies out through broken glass.

For a second there's no sound. No place. No life. For a second the world stops on its axis and there is only snow and night stretched to its limit. A white hand reaches back inside the shattered window—a woman's hand—her mother's hand. A wisp of thick dark hair, a trick of light, a glittering shawl, her mother, who is always there when Dorrie needs her most. And then she knows. *No,* she whispers. *No, Mama. Please,* but her mother only nods and reaches for her daughter in the ruined car.

Blood lies splattered on the dashboard clock, three drops above the nine, four more across the twelve; hot chocolate stains the seats. Everything is strangely soft, the dark, falling fast and hard, a velvet curtain. Dorrie hears the sounds of her own breathing, quick, frantic, and then she hears thin sounds, strange hums and murmurs, real or not, inside her head or from rooms above the shops along the street, her mother's voice whispering *Leave! Leave, Dorrie!* Sleet slams down sideways and a piece of newsprint dances in the air before it falls in through the broken window. One black glove lies faceup in a bank of snow.

The world snaps back in focus. Dorrie grabs her burner phone and shouts their whereabouts to 911. "Hurry!" she screams. "Please!"

She slides across the seat to Joe and even in her foggy, panicked state, she notices his airbag hasn't opened. She touches his face. Blood seeps from his ear and trickles down his cheek. *"Joe."* She tugs at his arm. "Just breathe," she whispers. "Just breathe," and suddenly he does—a gasp, a gurgling, drowning sound—but only once.

Leave, her mother says again, and this time when she reaches in the car, her fingers grasp the heavy coat and tug at the thick sleeve. *Go,* she says. *I'll take care of Joe,* and Dorrie bends to kiss him this last time. He's so cold. Everything is so cold. The wind howls in through fractured glass, and Dorrie slips across the seat to the passenger side. Blood oozes down her forehead and she touches it, feels the gummy heat of her insides. She bangs her elbow hard against the jammed door and slides onto the frozen ground. "I love you, Joe," she says aloud and her words blow back to her.

She hesitates. Torn, before she turns away. She has no choice. To be found like this—with her—is the last thing Joe would want. He'd told her as much—the scandal, the embarrassment for Karen, for their sons. Dorrie tugs her knitted hat down over her forehead to hide the cut, to cover the blood, and her feet slip slightly on the icy ground as she backs up the dark street.

People spill from buildings, from apartments, bars, and restaurants. They dribble down from rented rooms, shouting, struggling into coats and pulling hats from pockets. The empty street buzzes with movement. Lights go on in buildings, silhouettes pass in front of windows, a closed shop opens suddenly, lighting up a mannequin with naked legs, a thin summer dress, ghoulish in the cold and death and dark. Large brick buildings loom like spectators around a grisly stage; tall windows come alive with winter coats on eerie faceless forms.

Voices bark. Sirens blare. People reach the sidewalks and hesitate, but only for a second, before they push on toward the car. When they are almost alongside her, Dorrie slips inside the crowd and moves with them toward the Audi, abandoned there against the tree. Snow collects on its roof, gathers in the broken windshield. But there's something odd. She takes a small step forward. A siren screams around the corner. She backs away, still staring at the car, at the driver's side, barely scratched.

When the ambulance and cops arrive, when the EMTs are there with Joe, when she hears one of them call to the others that he can't get a pulse, and then call out again that Joe is gone, Dorrie turns and staggers through the mounds of dirty slush, the ugly, wicked ice. She stumbles down a street cramped with people, with EMTs and cops, their cars pulled up against the wide, snow-covered sidewalks; others sprawl across the slick roadway. Headlights blast light in sharp, rude waves that bounce off bits of glass and stone and metal, corners of signs, the hem of a skirt against a boot.

Dorrie rounds the corner, watching until the ambulance is nothing but a blur, its shriek a thin sound on the night. She stops in front of a closed bakery—she can see its vibrant bright red awning even through the snow, in the faint scattered light

7

of a streetlamp. Vague outlines of pies fill the window, and she squeezes close beneath the awning, blotting out the pastries with her reflection, pokes at the knit hat, at the blood painting dark red lines across the rows of cheery blue.

She waits. And then she picks her way back along the slick sidewalk to Newbury. A car lurks on the other side of the street, its engine huffing in the snow. It has only one headlight. Bright, like a beacon. Blinding. She can hear the tow truck coming up from Berkeley, the straining, grinding gears, and then the large, rough shape of it bumbling up the street. She listens to the shouts, the "Over here!" and "Back in! Back in!" and "Hook it up!" The clanging, thudding sounds of Joe's beloved Audi being chained. The one headlight from the lurking car winks as people cross in front of it, the make and model unclear in all the snow. She raises her hand to shade her eyes against the cloud of light as the car moves forward toward her and stops, catching her in its one blinding eye. Then, like a large and angry beast, it rolls out to the center of the street, turns, and grumbles off. A sedan, she thinks, dark—blue or black or gray. The taillights shed only a wobbly light. The tag is a blur.

She shivers. Joe is dead. She was there. She wants to lie across the stones of ice, to close her eyes and never open them again. But there is Lily. Her sweet Lily. She takes a deep breath, stares across the blinding snow. She'll get through this; she hasn't any choice. She *didn't* die. She has to find a way to glue herself together somehow, soldier on. She has a daughter she adores, a husband, a job. She has a life. Flawed, to be sure. Huge, gaping shocking flaws, but she'll do everything she can to hold on to it, even if that means walking away from a wrecked car, from this

8

man she loved, even if it means putting on the most challenging performance of her life.

She glances at the lit shops, the slick street, and then she pulls her daughter's ruined hat down tight over her hair and rushes toward the train. Frigid winds snap at her gashed forehead, so strong they nearly knock her down. She feels for her glove in her coat pocket, has a vague memory of it flying through the windshield.

She drops her burner phone in a trash can, but nearly right away she hears its ringtone echoing behind her. She turns around and takes a step back toward the bin.

At first the car is just a blob of light. And suddenly it's coming toward her, swerving up from Arlington. The engine roars; the one bright headlight finds her in the haze, pins her in its sites as the car veers across three empty lanes, straight at her. The tires spin, whirring behind her as she runs across the street. Her feet in snow boots smash across crusts of snow. She slips and nearly falls, but she keeps running, moving—she keeps pushing forward, the knit cap plowing like a bullet through the night.

II

KAREN

Karen Lindsay takes a quick look at the sky. She and Alice have just finished a late dinner at a restaurant near Alice's small bookstore, Bound for Glory, where for years Karen has worked with her best friend. Originally a joint venture with her ex, the running of the shop fell to Alice several years before, when the husband moved to Vermont with his twenty-nine-year-old personal assistant. So unoriginal, Alice says, if she speaks of it at all. She prefers not to.

Karen, who started working at the bookstore to help out, had stayed on, and, although she loves Alice, loves books, it's the sales she really loves. She misses working at her husband's company—chatting up potential customers, popping in to see how jobs were going, all the things she gave up years ago to stay home and raise the boys—all the things Joe does now.

"I don't know." Karen squints out the window at the night sky. "Looks pretty ominous out there. We'd better wrap this up."

"Probably so." Alice takes a sip of tea, glances at the glass. "I'm close. Come stay at my place till the storm blows over." She gestures in the general direction of Beacon Hill, toward the small brick building where she lives on Joy Street, with its cozy furniture, its grow-light plants, its two plump cats lolling on a futon in the bedroom.

"Antoine would have the house in shreds."

Alice rolls her eyes. "You really should trade him in for a cat. They're much less trouble."

"Careful. Antoine just might sic the ASPCA on you for being such a speciesist."

"Sic! I love it. So Joe isn't back yet?"

Karen shakes her head.

"Rounding up clients?"

Karen folds her napkin, runs her palm along the crease. "He's in Rhode Island. Some kind of conference. After what happened last month—or was it the month before? Anyway, lately, he's a man possessed. I never see him. Even when I do, he's got his nose stuck in something to do with the company."

"Wait. After *what* happened?"

"That fire in Jamaica Plain. Remember? Home Runs did renovations on it? About a year ago?"

"Wait. I don't— Oh! No. I *do* remember. That article you were reading at work. A couple died? The woman was pregnant? That horrible fire in the old two-story?"

Karen nods. "Joe was devastated. He knew them. At least he'd met them a few times. Our guys did the work on the house, so he was really— He is incredibly upset."

"Was it arson?"

Karen takes a sip of decaf. "No. They investigated it pretty thoroughly, declared it a total accident, but you know Joe. He had to make sure it had nothing to do with Home Runs, the workmanship, supplies, any part of the renovation."

"You can take the man out of the altar boy . . . No! *Wait!* God! What was that saying again?"

"It's the *church*," Karen says. "'You can take the *girl* out of the *church*, but you can't take' . . . Speaking of Joe—" She stops.

"What?"

Karen stares at her friend across the littered table. Her hand grazes a dessert plate, bumps a coffee cup. She leans forward as, behind her, snow flies across the window. "This might be nothing, but I found some e-mails," she says, "written to him weeks ago. Several weeks."

"What kind of e-mails?"

"I was snooping," she says. "Joe was out of town, and I was, well, snooping, like I said. I logged on to his laptop and read through his e-mails. I was just trying to see where he was, actually. I couldn't remember if he said he was coming home that night or staying over. I kept calling him and he wasn't picking up, so—"

"Wasn't it locked?" Alice dabs her napkin against her lips and looks out the window at the storm, and, for a second, even she looks alarmed. "Password protected? Alan always—of course we're *divorced*—but he had everything protected. He was always so damn secretive, which is *why* we're divorced, probably, now that I think about it. So you found an e-mail . . ."

"Two. And it *was* password protected, but I figured it out. There were two e-mails."

"From a woman?"

Karen nods. "In the middle of the night. She sent them while her husband was sleeping."

"She said that in her *e-mail*?"

Karen nods again. "She also said she missed Joe."

"Oh." Alice grabs her glasses and takes a minute putting them back in her purse. She closes her bag with a definitive click and leans across the small two-topper. "I'm so sorry, Karen," she says, and the look of pity on her face makes Karen wish she'd never brought it up, this crap about Joe's e-mails. "Is there anything I can do?"

"Don't be silly." Karen moves around, gathering her things before she slides into her coat. "I'm sure it's nothing. I just thought I'd liven things up, toss a little intrigue into all this gloom." She forces a laugh. "Really, Alice. It was probably some bored client. Joe isn't the philandering type. He's too disorganized. And he can't keep a secret. I've always known when he was lying—his whole thought process is right there on his face. I mean, it took me five seconds to figure out his *password*!"

"Karen . . . They're writing *e*-mails in the middle of the *night*!"

"No," Karen says. "*She* is. *Was.* It was ages ago. I don't even know if she's still—"

"Don't be *naïve*!"

"I'm not. I'm many things, but naïve isn't one of them." Karen stares at the frosty glass. She can barely see anything; snow is everywhere, blowing on the wind. The roads are empty, slick with ice. "You go," she says. "I'll get this. It's my turn."

"You sure you don't want to come stay with me until the storm—?"

"No," she says. "But thanks."

"Call me, then." Alice gives her a tiny hug and their bulky coats bounce off each other as they stand beside the table. "Call me as soon as you get home so I'll know you made it back safe. Okay?"

Karen nods. "I will." She sticks a wad of bills beside the tab, the scrawled total, trying to forget the night she'd found the e-mails, the night she'd tossed out so casually to Alice, as if it were a review of a dull movie. Really, she still sees the four typed lines every single time she closes her eyes, feels the glass of Pinot Noir in her hand, a chill in the air. That night is seared into her brain, the slight tear in the curtain behind the computer, Antoine thumping around downstairs, the smell of incense burning somewhere in the house, the e-mail. *Hi! I can't sleep. Lily's down the hall, wrapped in her dreams, and I'm here, sitting at the dining room table, staring at Samuel's empty cigarette pack and thinking of you.*

She'd scrolled up, puzzled, to the address: *understudyfork@gmail .com*, and then she'd checked back through his messages, found another one from five days earlier.

Sometimes when Lily looks at me I think she knows. It's in her eyes, the way everything always has been, like some small part of my DNA lets her see what's in my head.

She'd read it again and again. She'd read it nine times, racking her brain. Who the hell was *Samuel*? *Lily*? Who were these people, shooting themselves into her life like a virus through a dirty needle? Clearly, Lily was the writer's daughter. And Samuel must be the husband, tucked away somewhere in a back bedroom. No wonder the poor guy smokes.

Karen pushes through the door. The wind is so strong that for a second she can only stand on the sidewalk, trying to get her balance — awkward, swaying in her bulky coat. She takes a few steps, vaguely aware of some commotion up ahead. She reaches for her gloves and sticks them over hands already red and half numb from the frigid air.

The street is dark; she's stayed much longer than she'd planned, and she wishes she'd taken Alice up on her offer. She still could. She could take the train to Beacon Hill. She ponders this as, somewhere several blocks away, a siren wails—a wisp on the strong wind. She heads for the station. The police are redirecting traffic, and Karen is grateful she took the train to work instead of driving in. She'd be tied up forever in this mess. An accident, she guesses, and, a minute later, she sees its silhouette ahead. She sees it only dimly through the snow—a dark sedan, a branch.

The car could be Joe's. It looks, through all the white and haze, like his old Audi smashed into a tree. No. It can't be Joe. He's in Rhode Island. She starts to take a step or two up the street to get a better look, but then she stops. She huddles in her coat and turns away to trek through the snow, her lips cracking in the corners, her face numb in all the bare, uncovered spots. She hears shouting, the close shriek of the ambulance as it rounds the corner and turns down Newbury.

The siren stops. Karen pushes on, relieved to reach the station, happy to stumble into the first car. She slumps across the seat, turns off her phone, watching as the B train plows through the snow as deftly as a knife might pierce the delicate white frosting of a cake.

When she stands on her front porch, rifling through her bag— when at last she manages to fit her key in the lock with frozen fumbling fingers and fall through the heavy wooden door to her foyer, Karen's house phone is already ringing.

I I I

DORRIE

Dorrie prays the front door won't squeak. The house is silent except for the white cat purring loudly on the sofa. Dorrie creeps into the downstairs bathroom to wash the cut on her forehead, sealing it together with a bandage she finds in the back of the cabinet. Butterfly. Such a happy name for what it is. She will probably regret not getting stitches when the cut begins to heal into a scar, but for tonight she's happy to be home, far from Joe's body lying still and gray in a hospital morgue. She takes off her bracelets, glittery, incongruous in the dim light oozing from the porch. She strips off her coat and jeans, buries Lily's bloody ruined hat in the trash. She moves the white cat gently to the end of the couch and drops onto the sofa with a quilt pulled over her eyes. Her sweater still smells faintly of Joe, a hint of his cologne clings to the threads. She lies in the black room until somewhere near dawn, when she falls into a fitful, dreamless sleep, waking later to her husband tugging at the blanket. She opens one eye, surveys the room through the ribboned edges of the quilt. The sun tilts in at the window. In the kitchen, Purrl stares pointedly at her empty dish.

"Where's Lily?"

"Spent the night at Mia's," Samuel says, and Dorrie feels a small surge of relief that Lily's at her best friend's house. Samuel's voice is gruff, impatient. His hair sticks up in tufts. "So where *were* you?" He plunges his hands in his jeans pockets and looks around until his eyes light on a pack of cigarettes on the dining room table.

He's angry. She can see it in the way he walks across the room, his short sharp strides. She gets up, wraps the quilt around her in the cold house, and slides behind him in her stocking feet. "I guess it was a lot later than I thought."

She reaches out to touch him, but he takes a step away, leaving her hand stuck in the air like a small chapped flag. She pumps up the thermostat and tucks her hands back inside the quilt. "It's freezing in here," she says, but Samuel doesn't answer. He sits down at the dining room table with a coffee cup that used to say One Great Dad, but, after all these years of heavy coffee drinking, it says, O eat Dad. Smoke from his cigarette drifts out a window he's cracked open to the bleakness of the yard, and Latin music from next door flies in on the wind. "I called you all night."

"Oh," Dorrie says. "I guess my phone was off. Sorry. Jeananne was upset," she tells him, "so I took her out for a drink. I left you a note. Didn't you see it? On the door?" She's babbling, nervous. She wills herself to stop before she says too much. Dorrie's often thought that restlessness and Catholicism are a dangerous mix, that she's always been a little too forthcoming, a little too contrite for her own good.

In the glass on the cupboard door, she watches Samuel staring at her back. His lips are tight over his teeth. He still looks furious and she doesn't really blame him. He shakes his head, glances away from her to the backyard. He's actually something of a mystery to her lately, this man she's been with over twenty years. She pries her thoughts away from the night before, from Joe, from the car driving straight at her. She tries to concentrate on this one minute of this one morning in her living room with an angry husband, a failing marriage she has no idea how to save.

As far as she knows, her husband's never been truly unfaithful to her, at least not with another woman. She doesn't count the bottle, but sometimes she thinks she should. Other times she looks at him and wonders why she couldn't just be satisfied with what she had, even if Samuel is unquestionably an alcoholic like his father, dead at sixty three from cirrhosis, never mind the euphemistic "liver troubles." You're the love of my life, Dorrie, Samuel always says. Why couldn't that just be enough?

Certainly her husband is no saint, with his riveting gray eyes, his tousled good looks. And there was all that flirting with a neighbor right around the time he and Dorrie had a row. He'd packed a bag and vanished for the next few days, insisting later that he'd moved himself into a cheap hotel, but Dorrie always wondered if that was true. She thought the flirtatious neighbor looked at Samuel differently after his three nights away, as if they shared a secret, and once she caught the woman smirking at her in the grocery store. "You have trust issues," Samuel said when she mentioned the encounter at the market, and Dorrie couldn't argue with him there.

Men are just really stupid, her best friend, Viv, said when Dorrie told her about Samuel disappearing at a dinner party given by friends— *She wanted me to help her fix the toilet in the upstairs bathroom. What did you expect me to do?* Or the time he spent on a backyard deck in semi-darkness with yet another attractive neighbor. *Mapping out a summer garden,* he told her on the way home, as she sat smoldering beside him. Maybe Samuel's strayed and maybe his flirtations never went beyond a backyard garden or a running toilet. Maybe he's an innocent or maybe he's just really good at hiding what he does. In either case, she isn't innocent at all. Dorrie is the one who's strayed.

She sighs. She won't tell him the truth about the accident. She can't. Not even part of it. She's on her own—to understand what really happened, to figure out if someone truly tried to run her down, and if so, why? And who? It's up to her to save herself.

She takes a deep breath, puts on her best Mariska Hargitay on *Law & Order* face. Strong. Focused. Calm. She clears her throat. "I guess I had too much to drink," she tells Samuel's reflection in the cupboard door. "I tripped over a barstool and cut my head on the counter." She turns around, shows him the butterfly bandage, looks him in the eye. "See?" She tells him how she went with Jeananne to a bar on Charles Street and about the man at the table next to theirs who ordered drinks for all of them. She tells her husband how Jeananne stopped sniffling over her ex to smile at this man with the blond hair and the dark eyes and the scar on his left cheek, elaborates on Jeananne dancing in the tiny aisle of the bar, going home, eventually, in a cab, and how Dorrie sat alone, sipping her drink and waiting for the snow to let up, not realizing how tipsy she was until she stood and lost her balance, hit her head.

When he's had enough, Samuel puts on his coat and steps outside, closing the door behind him. Smoke flies up from his cigarette and blows off into the sky. He coughs a raspy cough into the cold morning, and Dorrie knows he hasn't believed a single word she's said; she just doesn't know why.

She looks behind him at the door popped back open by the wind. It stands ajar. She stops. Panic sends a chill along her spine beneath her heavy sweater, beneath the quilt that used to lie across the bed she shares with Samuel. She feels as if she's sliding, plummeting, that there is no one anywhere to catch her. And then she remembers staring through the snow at Joe's wrecked Audi, the clumps of people pointing, shouting, as she took small steps back toward the car. There was something different then from the way she'd left it only a moment or two before, but at the time she couldn't put her finger on what it was. And now she can. Crossing the small foyer to the door that Samuel has neglected to close properly, she knows. The driver's-side door—*Joe's* door—the one that had been tightly shut right after the accident, was open when she came back with the crowd. And the car with only one headlight—it was there, she thinks, across the street. Lurking. So whoever was inside the waiting car had likely seen her slip away. She takes a breath, and Joe's last words come back to her. *It isn't safe. For* us.

I V

DORRIE

They'll bury Joe today. Dorrie touches the cut on her forehead, puckered and healing, an ugly train-track lie leading backward to the night he died. She tugs at her bangs, covering the naked scar, runs her hands down her straight black skirt, pencil thin, demure, adjusts her stockings. Her blouse is black brocade beneath a black silk sweater, a plaid wool scarf the only touch of color.

She stands at the kitchen window, staring at the small backyard, where an old elm shivers. Behind it remnants of the autumn garden rot into patchy ground and Dorrie lets her eyes go out of focus, hoping for some sign of Joe. Nothing comes. The sky that started out a pastel blue has grown much darker through the morning and the same clouds that were thin and white at breakfast have turned gray by early afternoon.

"So is it a wake or a funeral or what?" Samuel squats in front of the nearly empty fridge and grabs a carton of milk. She looks away.

"A funeral. It's so . . . It's so awful. I really don't want to go." If there were any way at all she could stay home, she would. But her absence would raise questions, the last thing Dorrie wants.

"For his wife especially," Samuel says. He's staring at her. Dorrie feels her cheeks burning underneath a heavy layer of foundation. "Are you okay? You look a little—pale or something. A little green around the gills. You should probably eat something before you go."

Dorrie nods. "I will. You know how I hate funerals."

"I know." Samuel squints at the date on the milk carton. "This can't be easy for his wife. Unless they weren't really—"

"They were," Dorrie says. She straightens her skirt, puts on a bland face, a bland concerned voice. Sedate. Calm. "*Extremely* close," she says. "And I'm sure this must all be *unbearable* for Karen. I can't even imagine." She sticks her daughter's cereal bowl in the sink and pictures Karen reaching for a plate in her own kitchen with a graceful, fragile arm, imagines her holding a cigarette, tilting her head back to blow out the smoke, can almost hear the echo of her footsteps on the stairs, her voice bouncing off the open empty spaces of the house she'd shared with Joe. A character in a Greek tragedy.

"What if it'd been me?" Samuel says.

"Oh! God, Samuel! I'd be devastated. Don't even talk like—"

"Would you?"

"Yes," she says, moving closer to her husband as, again, he takes a tiny step away. "Of course!" And she would be. Even with the lies between them, even with his nights at the corner bar, even though she yearns for Joe. Even if her husband lately takes a step away when she moves toward him. Even so, she'd be distraught if something happened to him. She loves Samuel. She knows he loves her, too; she's never doubted that. She knows that if, at the end of his life, he's standing in some mystical place between worlds and someone asks him to name his one great love, Samuel will breathe out her name without the slightest hesitation.

Dorrie might have a harder time with that question. She would have to weigh all the moments, hours, years, spent with Samuel—Lily's birth, the times they cried together, all the meals and fights, the rants and silences, the blankness they share now. She'd have to weigh it all against the time she had with Joe, exciting, perfect moments that left her always wanting more.

They are two entirely different things. Husbands. Lovers. One is for the long haul, and the other—well, the other probably isn't, although she's only had this one experience, and she'd never really meant to sleep with Joe. But it was like a drug, their love. It forced her to wake up. It saved her.

"Dad?" Lily stands in the kitchen doorway, an overnight bag in her hand. She's going on a ski trip with her best friend, Mia, and Mia's thrill-seeking, fun, athletic parents. "Ready? You look pretty, Mom," she says, crossing the new kitchen floor to give Dorrie a kiss. "See you in a couple days."

"Thanks, honey. Do I look— Is my makeup okay?" Her voice is high-pitched, squeaky.

"Yes," Lily says. "It's fine."

"Be careful." Dorrie hugs her daughter and continues to hold on until Lily pulls away. "Stay on the beginner slopes. Okay?"

"Right." Lily rolls her eyes. "I left my gloves on your dresser," she says. "I need them back, though. You never did return my hat . . ." She's already opening the door, already stepping out to the front porch, and Dorrie makes a mental note to replace Lily's hat. Something artsy, she thinks, something festive.

"Nasty weather rolling in." Samuel turns back to the kitchen. "Bet they'll change their minds about going." He looks at Dorrie. "You should be fine," he says. "Just take your time."

Dorrie listens to the slam of the kitchen door, the two sets of boot heels stomping down the steps. A moment later, Samuel's old Toyota starts up in the garage, moving slowly through the stacks of junk. One of these days the whole shaky mess is going to fall in on him, she thinks. And there he'll be, pinned into his own car by a bunch of silly random things like Lily's broken ski from a ninth grade field trip or a cardboard box full of The Complete Works of Shakespeare or the cartons of clothes for St. Vincent de Paul they never got around to donating.

She scrambles two eggs, dropping one of the yolks into Purrl's dish, where it stares up at her like a large eyeball. Dorrie thinks her husband would have made a great mechanic; he's good with cars—brake jobs, sparkplugs, tires. His current car is one he cobbled together, an old Corolla he picked up for a song. Most weekends, now, he goes to his friend's garage to work on a Volvo he'll give Lily when she turns sixteen. It looks like a little tank. White, and Lily will hate it, of course. She'll want a sexy sleek car like Mia's.

Samuel could have even been a carpenter, considering the great job he did last summer on the kitchen, but he's actually a computer programmer, a very good one. He's brilliantly creative, gifted with his hands. Samuel could make anything beautiful if he tried. He just doesn't usually try.

Sometimes, Dorrie regrets confronting him about his drinking. Maybe he needs to drink. Maybe it keeps his demons at bay or maybe it creates more—demons that block Dorrie out and build a wall between them

"Look," she'd said one night, as Samuel rolled over to his side of the bed, his breath sour with cigarettes and beer. "I can't go on like this." And then, in a sudden and ill-timed attempt to lighten things, she'd pulled the top of her nightgown low and said in a husky, Scarlett Johansson voice, "What've you done with the sweet guy I married?"

"Funny," he'd said. "That's really funny, coming from you. Where were you, sweet *gal*? Where were *you* three nights ago? You really think I don't notice when you're not home, Dorrie? *Really?*" He'd gotten out of bed, stepped into his jeans, and pulled a T-shirt over his head. A second later, she'd heard him in the living room, the jingle jangle of his keys in the front lock, and then the angry rumbling of his car peeling out of the driveway.

When he came back he didn't mention their conversation. All he said was, "I don't know, Dorrie." He stood across the bedroom, glaring at her as she sat on the window ledge in her white summer nightgown, the hum of the AC throbbing underneath his words. "I'm not sure we'll make it," he said. "And you know what? I don't even think I care anymore."

Their sex life all but disappeared after that, the rare attempts at lovemaking awkward and strained, with Samuel disappearing afterward to smoke a cigarette on the back porch. Their approaching anniversary has become a deadline of sorts. "Let's see where we are then," he's said from time to time over the past months. "We'll take stock and decide where to go from there." They still sleep together every night, still share a bed, but they are separated now by heaps of blankets and hurt feelings.

She runs a comb through her hair, unknots a snarl with her fingers, swipes a makeup brush across a square of brown eye shadow and runs it over the few gray hairs near her part line. Samuel, Lily—they're her life. The humdrum moments, the husband in a ripped T-shirt, the daughter laughing on a phone, the messy bedrooms and flat tires, the ordinary, everyday events that singly are forgettable but strung together constitute a life—these things she's gambled she will fight to keep with everything she's got.

By the time she starts her car, the day has grown still darker and more ominous. Dorrie turns off the expressway and glances at the GPS. The clouds dip suddenly, closer to the ground, like cheesy props in a play. Beside the highway, pale buildings hunch together in the cold, the faded brick, the mix of old and new. Naked trees lean forward toward her car, and she speeds up. Their branches look like bones. Dorrie almost never goes to funerals. They bring back her mother's death, her wrecked and ruined car on the six o'clock news, a can of peas rolling down the street, and a size-six shoe at the side of a snowy road. Her mother's funeral, too, was on a freezing winter day. Standing at the cemetery, Dorrie held her father's hand and watched her mother's ghost perched on the hood of the Kellys' old Pontiac in a sleeveless summer dress that billowed out around her in the February cold. *Mom!* Dorrie started to say. *You came back,* but her mother only touched her finger to her lips and smiled before she floated off and disappeared into the sky.

The church is crowded, stuffy with bodies and heat. Dorrie stands in the doorway for a minute, lost in the ambience of incense, flowers, and ancient stained glass, dull and unbright in the sunless day, the muffled, shuffling sounds of heavy coats and boots.

She slides in beside Jeananne and the others from work who sit in a rigid little clump in a back pew. Joe's longtime partner, Edward, stands in front beside Karen, the two sons, the daughter-in-law, his family Dorrie doesn't want to see, the one that contradicts everything Joe was to her. The priest drones on, the service hums and buzzes in the air, the day grows darker through the colored glass, and Dorrie closes her eyes, hears herself in some amorphous hotel room. *I feel so free when I'm with you.*

The procession wends its way to the Mount Feake Cemetery, passes between two stone walls that edge the entrance. The wind blows hard off the river, scrapes across the naked trees, the crusty snow. Dorrie parks at the outer fringe of cars and stares through the windshield as tiny shards of ice begin to fall.

Her phone beeps. A new message. She reaches over to play it back, noticing the caller comes up as unknown. She panics, pushes at the button, hoping nothing has gone wrong on Lily's ski trip—impassable roads, difficult, dangerous slopes.

But it isn't Lily. *"Luck,"* she hears, and, *"yours."* The voice is shrill, tinny, neither male nor female. Not human. Goose bumps stand out on Dorrie's arms. The two words hang in the front seat. She plays it again, and in the silence of the car, the voice is harsh and personal, as if the speaker is right there beside her; the eerie voice scratches at her brain. *"Everybody's luck runs out,"* it says. *"Next time it might be yours."* She plays it one last time, listens as it rips through her and steals her breath, a cold, cruel hand around her throat. It could be anyone. It could be someone at the grave or sitting in a parked car only feet away, or standing in a clump of mourners, watching her. Observing her. She looks around through windows fogged with cold. She stares at a plot of trees behind her car and a shiver runs along her spine.

Was this about the other night—that she was lucky, then, to get away, but next time she might not be? Was this a threat? Her hands shake. Her teeth chatter. She blasts the heater, but she can't get warm. She opens the car door and steps out into the heaviness of looming clouds to make her way across the slippery ground. Her breath is raspy as she hurries past parked cars and huddled trees to stand beside Jeananne, where gravestones are lined up like short, grim soldiers keeping guard, where granite angels wait. She stands at the fringes of Joe's relatives and friends, huddled resolutely in the cold, their heels sinking in bitter ground. The wind howls over the Charles, through the barren trees, crackles through the twiggy bits of branches. Sleet comes down and sticks like needles to their clothes, making an odd sound, like seeds falling through a chute.

Beside the casket, a young priest leans forward to say something to Joe's family and Karen nods. A few blond strands of hair peep out from under her large scarf, and then she turns around, quickly, unexpectedly, before Dorrie has a chance to look away, to run her hand along her coat, or fix her hat, or clear the look of naked anguish from her face. For a second, Karen seems to stare straight at her. She looks lovely and fragile. Lost. She doesn't smile. She lifts her gaze and focuses on something behind Dorrie, her eyes intense and frightened. Blue, like Joe's, and Dorrie can't quite get her breath because the terror that she feels is mirrored there in Karen's eyes. Then, just as suddenly, Karen turns back to the priest and lowers her head. Dorrie turns around, too. She squints to see what Karen saw. There is a shift, a movement in the trees and again a chill slices up her spine because there's something there at the edge of her eye. A figure or maybe just the raw and blustery wind. The service ends. People stand in line to say their last good-byes; people walk among the headstones to their cars.

"Dorreen?"

"Yes." She jumps. "Edward. Sorry. Didn't see you there."

His face is bright pink in the cold. "We'll really have to pull together now." His eyes skate sideways off her face. "Without Joe, it'll be rough. No way around it."

Dorrie's heart gives a little lurch, but she stares at Edward, and it occurs to her that she is not the only actor here. The solemn gaze, the hearty hugs and glad-handing, the support. Edward is a virtual fortress. But maybe not. She nods.

"I need you and Jeananne on board. Both of you." His eyes dart here and there and come up empty, since Jeananne and the others from the office have already gone.

"Right," she says. Her voice is light. Airy. Bright. "I'll tell Jeananne." Dorrie leans in to give Edward an awkward little hug, which he does not return, and then she pulls her hat down nearly to her nose and walks away, trails her gloved hand out behind her in a small, desultory wave.

When she reaches her car, Dorrie turns to take one last look at the disbanding group of family and friends, at the gaping hole that will soon hold the man she once held in her arms, the man who didn't care if she was a little odd, or if she didn't always think before she spoke. For a moment she can almost see him walking toward her, smiling. She can almost feel his warmth again, can almost hear his breathing, almost catch the moments whistling by, quick, shimmering, like skirts on a dance floor, or wind blowing through a jacket in a field. Joe, with his voice like music. *Kiss me*, like the words to an old song or a curtain flapping in a breeze or sun on a tiled floor. Like a memory just out of reach.

People are beginning to move toward her, talking among themselves, shaking drops out of their hair, brushing tiny bits of ice from their coats with the tips of their fingers, and Dorrie fumbles with her keys. *I love you, Joe,* she says to the sky outside the window, and then she sticks on her dark glasses and sets her GPS for home.

She starts the car and picks up her phone from where she'd left it on the front seat. Missed calls. She looks again. She tosses her sunglasses on the dash and stares hard at the last number as she sits, trembling, inside the freezing front seat of her car. There's no mistake. The number from Joe's burner phone stares up at her from the Night Sky background of her cell.

V

MAGGIE

Maggie Brennan opens her eyes. She glances up at a small skylight, like the one in the book about Heidi and the grandfather on the mountain. The illustrations in the book intrigued her as a child, especially the picture of a makeshift bed where Heidi slept beneath a window in the roof. It's what sold Maggie on this place. The skylight. "Yes," the landlord said when she'd remarked on it. "A renovation. Costly, but it adds so much light to what could otherwise be a little dreary."

It's still a little dreary.

But Maggie likes it. She likes to monitor the light herself—how much comes in, how much doesn't. She yawns, switches on a small flat-screen TV across the room. A home remodel burbles in the silence of early morning as Maggie lies buried under multicolored quilts, coveting the claw-foot tub, the large black and white square tiles of a bathroom renovation on HGTV.

The skylight turns a lighter gray. A cough slides through the wall. Maggie rolls out of bed and heads for the shower as, on TV, a couple walks across newly installed laminate.

She'd left her car at work the night before and taken the train home. The main roads are clear, the small ones soon will be. Still, she was nervous about driving in the storm, made a snap decision she regrets now. She'll have to take the train in.

She slips on a sweater from the Loft and sticks an English muffin in the toaster. Nearly everything is within arm's reach of everything else. Her apartment is a closet. "But just look, darling! A skylight!" her mother said when she first saw it, even though she almost never comes to visit. *Four flights of stairs!* Maggie stuffs the remnants of her breakfast in the garbage disposal and flips the switch for a few seconds, rattling cups and spoons on the counter. She leans across the bed for the remote—the skylight is an odd cream color where the sun slants in, where the glass isn't covered in snow. She sticks on leather gloves and steps into her boots, unbolts the door, and slips into the hall.

She'd stayed home the night of that last bad storm, brought in dinner from the deli down the street. With her job at the insurance company, she at least has regular, daytime hours, unlike before, so she can decide things like this, when to stay in, when to go out. Although most people opted to stay off the streets that Friday night, far too many were out driving when they should have stayed at home. Inside. The phones at Mass Casualty and Life have been ringing off the hook ever since; the office is drowning in claims. She pulls up her coat collar and picks her way across the mounds of white. Two girls lie in a patch of perfect snow, moving their arms, making angels before it's all a dirty brown, covered with boot prints. A woman stands in the doorway, shouting, shivering in a pink robe. Maggie waves—it's a neighbor she sees sometimes at the corner market, with its granite steps, its bananas and fresh fish in summer. The woman gestures at the snowy street, raises her hands, and shakes her head as the girls run toward her, laughing, pushing at each other, their angel selves left in the snow.

After she came back to the States, Maggie could have stayed much longer with her mother, but she chose to come here where she has no past, where she waves to people she knows only from the corner market. The house in Southie where she grew up was confining after only a few weeks. She felt like a butterfly trapped too long in its cocoon, her wings pinned to her sides.

Her train whizzes into the station, stops with a loud squeal. She waits. Finally, the train sighs, the doors begin to close, and Maggie steps into one of the last cars. She likes to not be stuck behind hordes of commuters, afraid she'll miss her stop. Especially in weather like this, she likes to be close to the doors.

The train jerks forward, the smell of mothballs and perfume heavy in the air. A woman grabs for a pole and misses, catches herself against a nearby seat as the train bobs down the track. Maggie stares at a window, the black of the tunnel, the reflection of a mother with her baby in a Snugli, fastened like a sling across her chest. The baby sleeps, oblivious to smells and jostling, the heat and screeching of the brakes as they approach the station.

A sudden noise explodes somewhere behind her. Maggie jumps. She ducks. There's no way off the train, no room to even squat on the packed floor. Was it a gunshot? Jesus. She turns— she'll throw herself over the baby and its mother, but the car is crammed with bodies. She looks back at the window. The baby is still sleeping. The mother looks annoyed, starts to gather up her things.

"Hey!" a voice yells. "Cut it out!" Maggie turns around. People on all sides of her tap at their phones, thumb through today's edition of the *Globe,* oblivious. "Scare people," someone else says. "... make a noise like that." Maggie's eyes scan the crowd. Her insides churn. Her heart races. Sweat covers her forehead and she struggles to control her panic in the crowded car. Across the aisle, near the door, a boy stands shamefaced with a plastic bag. Broken. Ripped. A popped bag. A woman stands beside him, wagging her finger in his small round face. The train jerks to a stop, and Maggie pushes through to the outside and hurries up the stairs to the safety of her boring job.

When her computer red-flags the accident on Newbury Street, Maggie's reaction is mixed. At first glance the facts are disturbing and the claim promises to be more of a hassle than the routine settlement. Still, she can't help feeling a slight stab of excitement, a throwback to her days on the police force. "Interest," she tells herself, considering the circumstances, that a man is dead. "Excitement" would be crass.

Lucky for her, a little digging shows that her old partner was the responding officer, and Hank is known for his diligence. She has always liked that about him. Admired that. Misses it. She misses a lot of things about being a cop, and she picks up the small stack of papers, thumbs through it. Her hand shakes, making the papers rattle loudly in the quiet room. She sticks both palms down flat against the cheap veneer of her desk.

The wife took out a substantial life insurance policy on the deceased just weeks before, and her signature stares up at Maggie from a policy dated November 16. Karen Louise Lindsay. It isn't an uncommon situation, not since the economic downturn, but there's enough money involved to warrant a little probing. If it is a suicide, there's no payout. What better smoke screen than to have your wife take out the policy?

Maggie gets up to close the door. Her office is barely more than a cubicle, but these days, in this place, having an office at all is a big deal. There is a door, but no real privacy; the walls are papery and thin. It's a decent company, reputable enough, but to Maggie it seems very bare-bones. Cheap. There's always that initial knee-jerk inclination not to pay out claims, to find a loophole, which Maggie might just have.

At thirty-four, she's one of the youngest investigators at the company. "Probably the sharpest of the lot," her boss has told her more than once, attributing this to Maggie's time with the Boston PD, and that had helped, but she has always been good with people. "My family was dysfunctional," she says if someone mentions her ability to flush out facts. "That's key," and then she always laughs, but, really, Maggie thinks, there is some truth to this. She's learned to think outside the box, to be alert, adaptable, to understand that things are not exactly what they seem. There's always more, there's always the crap lying just below the surface that can mess you up or worse if you're not ready for it. There's always that next trip wire—

She scrolls through her scant contacts and finds Hank's number. "Hi," she says into his voice mail. "It's Maggie. Call me when you have a minute." Her voice sounds much more glib than she actually feels. It's this job. She sounds phony, even to herself. Superficial, which she attributes to being here too long—she's beginning to not know how to turn it off, this work identity. She pushes back from her desk, and the flimsy swivel chair scoots on the bumpy fake wood floor, a little wavy if she looks across the room. The wheels make a strange, scratching sound against a layer of blond wood. The walls are beige. The shade at the one small window is also beige. She's put up posters from the Coop down at Harvard Square. Three van Goghs and a Gustav Klimt she found one weekend, but the atmosphere is mostly beige. The job is beige. Life is a trade.

But being a soldier was not her first choice, either. In fact, it was the last thing Maggie Brennan ever thought she'd do. It was a surprise, being called away. Deployed—an odd word. To be deployed. Like a missile. Like a bullet. Blown away, like a dandelion in the wind, like a thought or a whisper, like the girl she was before they sent her to Iraq. She's different, now, from who she used to be, heading out with her friends to the beach on days too nice to waste in class, smoking weed in the bedroom with the window open, batting the smoke toward the screen with the backs of her hands, giggling on the way to the refrigerator, she and her best friend. Lucy. Lucy in the sky.

She finishes her Coke and nearly gags. It's flat from sitting open on her desk. "Hey, Hank," she says, when he calls her back. "Can you ditch Johnson for an hour at lunch?" Johnson is Hank's new rookie partner. Needy, from what Hank's told her, "And meet me on Newbury? Noon? And, Hank," she says when her old partner says fine; he'll be there. "Bring a copy of your report on that accident in Back Bay. The fatality on Friday, the, um, the ninth?"

She looks back at the claim. "Male. Forty-nine years old. Businessman. Lindsay, Joseph Dylan."

"Sure," he says. "There must've been a hundred accidents that night. No kiddin'. Calls coming in every minute or two. Jeez."

"I don't doubt it. You should see the claims." Maggie leans back. The chair squeaks. "Just call me on my cell when you get to Newbury and we'll decide where to go from there. Oh, and Hank," she says, just before he clicks off. "Lunch is on me."

She buttons her coat and pushes through the back door to the parking lot. It's icy still, but not as bad as the week before. The snowplows and sand trucks have been busy, at least on Commonwealth, and she heads downtown to the company Joe Lindsay and his partner owned. On the way she glances at the few facts she jotted down before she left her office. Edward. The partner was Edward Wells. Home Runs Renovations. Summer Street. She eases her foot on the brake. She's barely moving anyway. Traffic is at a crawl. The inside of her car is cold, even though the heater's up as high as it will go and she makes a mental note to take it in to get it worked on. Soon.

She looks around, taps her fingers on the steering wheel. Okay. The office is here on Summer. Joseph Lindsay lived in Waltham. So what was he doing in Back Bay on a night when everyone else in the city was trying to stay off the streets? She remembers the storm, remembers unwrapping her pastrami sandwich as the wind howled outside the window, her mother calling to make sure she was in for the night. *Bad storm coming.*

She runs her fingers through her dark hair and fluffs it out a little, glancing in the rearview mirror. It's a good hair day. At a traffic light she puts on lipstick, digs around for a small plastic Clinique compact, and brushes blush across her cheeks, looks up at the glass storefronts that line the road, at people walking swiftly down the sidewalk, chins tucked into coats, intent on getting quickly to their destinations.

Maggie parks and locks her car door, reaching down to straighten her boot. It's a new pair; they pinch her toes, but who knew she'd be doing so much walking? Most days she sits behind a desk. Restless. Today she's grateful for the change. The air is fresh, cleaned by the snow the night before. She limps up the steps to Home Runs, stopping to adjust her boot again once she's inside. "Edward Wells?" she says to a woman with red hair. "Insurance matter," when the woman hesitates, when she tells Maggie that her boss just lost his partner.

"I won't stay long," Maggie promises. She smiles. "A couple of quick questions so we can settle on this claim. I'm Maggie, by the way."

"Jeananne." The woman sighs, delivers her to the partner's office, and Maggie follows silently, her boots sinking in the plush and pricey carpeting.

She nods a thank-you to Jeananne and steps inside the doorway, but just barely. "Mr. Wells?" She takes another step into the large, imposing room. "Maggie Brennan." She extends her hand. "From Mass Casualty and Life. I'm sorry." She tries to meet his eyes. "So sorry about your partner. I won't take up much of your time."

Edward nods. He turns his back, leaving Maggie standing in the doorway. She clears her throat.

"What is it?" Edward asks her reflection in a tall glass window.

She clears her throat again, coughs a light little cough. "Is there anything you know that might shed light on Mr. Lindsay's accident?"

He shrugs. "It was an accident. What more is there to say?"

"Why would your partner be in Back Bay on a night like that Friday? In the middle of a snowstorm?"

"I have no idea, Ms. Brennan." He turns around finally.

"Was he having problems?"

Edward looks away. Not fast enough, though. There's something in his eyes. He seems to consider her question for a second or two, and then he shrugs, "Well," he says. "The company was losing money. Still is. Joe was doing everything—we were both doing everything we could to keep the place running, but . . . Yes, Ms. Brennan. There were problems." He stops. "Exactly why are you here?" Edward turns and really looks at Maggie for the first time, at the coat from Urban Outfitters, the new boots, the rakish, flowered scarf, a Christmas present from her mother, and suddenly Maggie sees herself the way Edward Wells must see her, as intrusive and blasé. Wet behind the ears.

"Checking on the claim," she says. "Actually two claims. And it's standard in a situation like this, Mr. Wells."

"On a *traffic* accident?" Edward shakes his head. "Why are you *really* here?"

"Looking for answers." Maggie knits her eyebrows together, tries to look official. "Was he depressed?" she says, before Edward can ask her exactly what *kind* of answers. "Was Mr. Lindsay depressed?"

"Do I look like a psychiatrist, Ms. Brennan?"

"You were partners," she says. "Friends, no doubt. In your *opinion*, was Mr. Lindsay depressed lately?"

Edward shrugs. "I wouldn't necessarily—*know* that, but I suppose it's possible. Likely, under the circumstances. I suggest you ask his wife." Edward turns back to the window. "Karen. Any help you need to settle things for her, just let me know. The poor woman must be . . ."

"Thanks," Maggie says. "Again, I am sorry for your loss."

Edward shifts, half-turns—a nod to civility, before he goes back to staring at the white world outside the pricey window.

"I like the name," Maggie says in the doorway. "Home Runs Renovations." She glances at a Red Sox banner on the wall above Wells's desk.

"Thanks." Edward half-turns again. "We used to go to games a lot, back in the day. Joe and I. He loved Fenway Park."

In the hall Maggie looks at her watch. "Ladies' room?" she asks the red-haired woman. Jeananne appears to be the office gossip, flitting up and down the hall, and Maggie watches as she talks with a small, thin woman wearing yellow snow boots. The woman smiles, but her eyes are large and dark, her face noticeably pale. She reaches to touch Jeananne on the arm and they both laugh. She's vibrant, dazzling, even, but her eyes drift here and there as if she's looking for something. Some*one*, maybe.

Maggie hesitates. Questioning these women now might give her some idea who Joe Lindsay was. No. She hobbles on, the boots stabbing at her toes. They both seem very emotional, still raw. She roots around in her bag for a small notebook, jots down *Yellow Boots and Jeananne,* so she'll remember to catch up with them later—preferably when they're not together.

She finds the ladies' room at the end of the hall and grabs a wad of toilet paper to stick between her throbbing toes. An empty office stands off the main hallway with its door ajar and Maggie nudges it open but doesn't go inside. Lindsay's, she guesses. A woman with blond hair stares out accusingly from a photo in a thin gold frame on a desk beneath the window.

"I'll walk you out." Edward Wells stands behind her in the hallway, and Maggie smiles.

"Thanks," she says. "Got a little turned around there for a minute. Was this Mr. Lindsay's office?"

Edward nods. He gestures for her to go ahead of him on the plushy carpeting, and together they glide toward the lobby. The receptionist nods. She's on the phone. "I guess you haven't heard," she's saying to the caller, and then she lowers her voice. "Mr. Lindsay has just died. Yes," she says. "It was. A great shock. A horrible accident . . . the ice . . . Yes," she says again, after a few seconds. "Dorrie. Dorreen Keating. She can answer your questions. Probably knows as much as Joe did about the— Right. The two of them were working closely just before he— Of course," she says. "Is that with two t's or one, Mr. Androtti? Got it. I'll make sure to give this to Dorreen. You have a nice day." Edward stops.

"I assume you can find your way from here," he says to Maggie, and then to the receptionist, "Never mind, Lola. I'll take that to Dorreen. I'm headed up her way."

"Sure," Maggie says, "I'll be fine. Thanks for giving me your ti—" But Edward turns his back as if she has already gone. He does not shake her hand.

VI

MAGGIE

Maggie pulls up her coat collar and steps outside to brave the cold, hurries to her car. Snow blurs the harsh, sharp edges of the newly renovated area as she makes her way through it to Back Bay. She slows down at Newbury. Her cell blares out a rap song. It's Hank, standing on Newbury and Berkeley. "Johnson's gone off on his own," he tells her. "I'm all yours for the next hour."

She pulls over. Hank opens the passenger side door and slides in quickly, pushes the seat back to accommodate his long legs, his lanky body. He closes the car door behind him, but the cold comes in, drifts up from his clothes. "Hey, Maggie," he says. He smiles. "Like old times, eh?" He blows on his hands. His hair is grayer than Maggie remembers, a little thinner on top.

"Yeah." She smiles. "Yeah. Just like."

"So, here's a copy of that accident report," Hank says, dropping three stapled sheets of paper on the seat and reaching over to tilt the heater vent straight on him. His face is red. Snow clings to his shoulders and drips onto the front seat.

"Anything?"

He shrugs. "The car slid on black ice, hit a tree at nine twelve P.M. Likely death on impact from a blow to the head. The airbag on the passenger side opened but not the one on the driver's side. It was a hard hit, but nothing the airbag couldn't have absorbed. It was an Audi. Old, but still an Audi. Not too shabby, right? Wonder why the airbag didn't open."

"Me, too." Maggie glances at the stapled papers. "I'll take a look. Where've they got it?"

"O'Brien's in Southie," Hank says. "Oh. Something else." He leans back and stretches his legs out under the dash. "There were two Starbucks cups in the front seat, contents splashed across the dash, the airbag, the upholstery. Smelled of coffee and hot chocolate, both."

"Okay. So there was someone else in the car. Or Lindsay was bringing a cup back to the office. Was there a lid?"

"Nope. No lid. Lotsa blood on the steering wheel, the seat, running down the driver's arm. A few drops in the fabric."

"Who called it in?"

Hank shrugs. "No telling. A woman, but she didn't give her name. 'Very upset,' it says in the report. But there were people crawling out of the woodwork by the time we got there, so it could've been anyone."

Maggie nods. "I'm thinking there might be footage from the shops on Newbury and around the corner. Maybe something from that night. So . . . since you're a cop and I'm not . . ."

"There was mention of a lunch?"

"Right," she says. "It was a total bribe."

"Then I'm your man," Hank says, and they head for the sidewalk in front of a café. "How about we start here?"

Some of the shop owners on Newbury don't have security cameras, and most of the ones that do didn't have them turned on that Friday night. Or they bought a camera and never figured out how to run the thing, or the sister's son's friend meant to come over to set it up and never did. One young guy the next street over says his uncle has a security camera and it was turned on, but the uncle's in Florida and won't be back until sometime next week. The nephew takes both their cards, sticks them behind the register, where, Maggie figures, the uncle will find them months from now and toss them in the trash.

Hank manages to wolf down lunch, two coffees, and a doughnut in various eateries. When his hour is almost up, they hit pay dirt at a clothing store displaying summer clothes—go figure—and two or three nearly naked mannequins in the window, their long legs white against the backdrop of a dark blue curtain. Yes, the owner tells them. Yes, his camera is fully operational. Yes, it was turned on the night of the bad storm. "Just in case," he says, shaking his head. "When things shut down. That's when the serious crimes occur," which Maggie doesn't think is actually true, since criminals don't like snowstorms any more than anyone else. Besides, she thinks, this guy's display window wouldn't bring someone in the front door on a good day, let alone through a window with a hammer on a bad one.

"Great," Hank says. He's got his coat unbuttoned, his hat off. "Mind if I take a look?"

They stand, leaning their elbows on the glass counter in

front while the store owner pulls up the footage from January 9 on his iPad. There's a lot of snow, so much that nothing else is really visible. Every once in a while, someone scurries down the sidewalk—a vague blob, or, occasionally, two blobs together. Only a small wedge of street is covered by the camera and even this, the owner says, is just a glitch. "The wind," he tells them. "It knocked the awning, the camera. Everything."

And then there it is, the Audi, spinning for a second in the milky night. They can't see the tree. They don't see it hit. There is only the absence of motion. Nothing, for a stretched-out second, and then things flying. Like an explosion. Debris fills the screen.

After that, there's nothing but white, and, behind it, the passenger-side door, part of the right front tire, turned outward at an ugly angle. Seconds pass. The storm seems to pick up, so much so they nearly miss the movement of the door. And then it opens slightly and closes, as if it's being pushed hard from the inside, jammed shut from the wreck. Finally, the door flies open and a figure slides out to the ground, makes its way through the debris, a figure with a heavy coat, a covered head, a female, judging by the size. Together the three of them watch a small blurry figure hurry from the wrecked car down the street and quickly out of sight.

This is what Maggie had hoped to find. It's why she's here, although she isn't sure what it all means. Not yet. "Thanks," she says and the shop owner nods. Hank glances at his watch and then out at the street, where a squad car is just pulling up a few doors down. Maggie reaches over, pats Hank on the arm, and tells him they should get together, Hank and his wife and Maggie. Or a double date, she says, although she hasn't dated anyone for months. The shop owner is still glued to his iPad. He barely knows they're there; his eyes are watery from staring at the screen, from straining to make things out through all the gray and haze.

"Wait," he says. "You might want to see this," but Hank's already running out the door. "Let me know," he calls back, "how it comes out, or if you need me on this."

Maggie looks at the screen, where a crowd moves through the snow toward the car. The owner rewinds. "Wait," he says again. "This is weird," and he hits PAUSE and then PLAY and Maggie can just barely see the driver's-side door opening as a figure reaches inside and then backs quickly away.

"Damn."

"I know, right? Thought you might find that interesting," he says. "After that, there's nothing. At least nothing I could make out. I think the wind knocked the camera totally out of focus. Want me to play it anyway?"

"No," Maggie says. "That's okay. Listen, thanks. We really appreciate you doing this. Could you possibly—that one shot there. The driver's-side door—could you replay that one more time?"

"Sure thing." The owner fiddles with his iPad. "Here," he says.

Maggie squints at the frame.

VII

KAREN

K aren jumps when her phone rings in her house in Waltham. Despite seeing Alice's name across the tiny screen, she brings the cell up to her ear with trepidation. "I'm leaving in an hour," she says. "Call you when I get off the train." She doesn't wait for an answer. She's running late. She's having trouble doing anything these days—sleeping, and getting out of bed, or off the couch—she hasn't been back to work since the day Joe died. Her lovely turn-of-the-century house, spotless until recently, is now a mass of dirty dishes and half-filled teacups, wineglasses caked with film. Grease from fast-food wrappers seeps into antique tables where she's set things and forgotten they were there. Antoine, their Papillon, has gulped them down, adding his eager slobber to the mix.

He'd spoiled the dog. Antoine only ever really liked Joe.

A prescription bottle from CVS sits beside a stack of mixing bowls in a white kitchen cabinet, Xanax, left over from a dental procedure Karen had weeks before. *You'll be needing these,* the dentist told her, but she hadn't. Not then. She's good with pain. Excellent with pain. Tough it out, she always told her sons when they were little, when they whined over minor injuries or tattled on each other. But it's a different kind of pain that lately has her padding to the kitchen in the wee hours, reaching for the pills that lurk behind flowered cups she bought at Anthropologie on a whim, the one on Newbury, the street where Joe died.

If details from the accident report are painful and maddening—the second Starbucks cup, the spilled hot chocolate—they make her husband no less dead. Nor do they make Karen less alone or empty, and certainly no happier. The insurance payout is apt to be delayed, a claims adjuster told her when she'd called the day before. Standard, she'd said, on a claim this size. And it is large. A million-dollar claim. Karen took it out herself a few weeks before the accident. The business was losing money; Joe was acting crazy, totally obsessed with a tragic house fire—heartbreaking—but in reality it had only the slightest, most tangential connection to his life. And then there were the e-mails, this understudyfork. With all the drama, all the intrigue, who knew what might happen? And then it had! Before the ink was even dry on the insurance policy—just that quickly, Joe was gone.

"We'll have to sort through this a bit," the adjuster told her, and it is unsettling, but only in a vague, unreal way. Money is the last thing on Karen's mind, and, anyway, she has a little tucked away for the moment. That's all she can handle now. Just this one day, this hour, this smallest, most colorless and unexciting step. Later, when it matters what she eats or what she wears, she'll have Joe's half of the company. Home Runs is her future.

She sets the new alarm in the foyer, this plastic, white-rimmed thing that clashes with both the trim paint and her nature. *You're gone so much,* is what she'd told her husband, lobbying for the damn thing weeks before. She hadn't told him that sometimes when she walked Antoine, or stopped for groceries, she felt a presence, someone there, just out of sight, watching her. She might have. If Joe hadn't died, she might have.

She hurries through the door. The cold hits her as she scans the driveway, the street in front of the house, the droopy naked trees and salt-covered asphalt, the bright red of a neighbor's newly painted door. She hits the button on her key ring and slides into her car, hears the locks click behind her as she starts the engine and fiddles with the radio, glances at the rearview, the side mirrors. The house.

"Breathe," she mutters, settling on a soothing classical music station. "Just breathe." Instead of meeting Alice, she should probably be on her way to see a shrink, something she last considered the summer she turned nine and read *The Three Faces of Eve*, plucked from their parents' bookshelf by her older sister Lydia. Eve, with her headaches and three personalities packed inside her nervous southern body, made Karen wonder if there might be a daring alternate inside her, too, waiting to leap out and break all the bottles in her father's gin collection or saunter down to the OK drugstore slathered in Lydia's perfume. Still, aside from that one summer, seeing a shrink never even entered Karen's mind until Joe ended up dead across his steering wheel in Back Bay, leaving her with a boxcar full of sorrow and regret for how things could have turned out and did not, and, worse, this feeling that she's being stalked.

"How are you, sweetie?" Alice stands up to give her a hug.

"I'm okay." Karen pulls out a high-backed wooden chair, sets down her tea and pastry.

Alice's bookstore is a short walk from the Queen of Cups, where the two friends have been meeting here on Wednesday afternoons for years. If Karen's working at the shop, they close and walk up here together. If she isn't, she comes in on the train. It's tradition. Rain or shine, no matter what, Wednesday afternoons belong to Alice. The little tea shop, filled with an eclectic mix of furniture and teas, has chocolate everything. Éclairs, truffles, cakes to die for. "Listen." Alice leans across the table. "Why don't you come stay with me for a while? Just until you—"

Karen throws her coat over the back of a funky, bright blue chair and stares at her croissant. Alice has lived with her cats in a tiny place on Beacon Hill ever since her marriage ended years ago, and at this point there is a definite allure—of course, at this point a cardboard box has appeal. "I just might take you up on that," Karen says. "Thanks. And thanks for all your help with the funeral. With everything. I'll be back to work as soon as I can get myself—"

Alice bites into a chocolate almond scone and waves her hand in the air. "Take as much time as you need. And, Karen. You know I'm always here. You know that. Anything. A place to stay, more hours at the bookstore, a shoulder to— Just let me know."

Karen nods. "It's all a blur." She fiddles with her teacup. "Especially the funeral—all those people, Alice! And they all loved Joe. 'Your husband was the nicest guy.' I thought I'd go mad, I heard that so many times at his—at the church. After. You know. After the service." She picks up her pastry, but then she sets it down again without actually tasting it.

"And at the cemetery. God. The cemetery. I was afraid they wouldn't do the burial and we'd have to put it off until spring, but they were really . . ." Karen sighs, remembering that ancient, eerie place, with the wind wailing off the water, the cold damp ground, such an unfitting place for Joe. She closes her eyes, sees her husband laughing with his head thrown back. So alive. Warm. So unlike Karen, with her inability to open up, her reserve, her handful of people she really cares about, her sons and Alice and Joe, Lydia, taken far too soon by cancer, and, for a little while, Tomas.

"Everybody loved Joe," Alice says. "Definitely one of the good guys."

Karen butters her croissant, rips open her Earl Grey, and dips the tea bag in her cup. "He was. People used to come up to me all the time—Christmas parties, grocery stores, PTA meetings, back when the boys were still—you know—in school, on the soccer team. Complete strangers would come up and tell me what a good boss Joe was, what a great dad—all the coats he collected, all the toys, the mountains of canned beans. 'Such a kind man,' they always said. Of course, they didn't *live* with him. They weren't *married* to him."

Alice starts in on a bear claw. "It's always different for the wife," she says. "You don't have to tell *me*." And for a minute neither of them speaks.

"Alice." Karen leans over the small table, so lacquered it reflects the light from a lamp hanging above it. "I was there. The night Joe died, I was there."

"You were where?"

"Where Joe hit that tree. Where he *died*. You were, too, actually. We might have both—I'm not sure exactly when we left the—" Her voice trails off.

Alice looks horrified. "God!" She glances at the window, takes a swallow of green tea.

"When *they* hit the tree," Karen says. "She was with him—the girlfriend. It was in the accident report—not *who* she was, just that there was someone—you know—someone else . . . an extra Starbucks cup or something. Anyway, I guess you were right." Karen clears her throat, plays with her napkin.

"Wait. I don't— Did you see her? Did you see Joe's car or—?"

"I did *sort* of see the car. But . . . it was snowing so hard, and, I mean, Joe wasn't even in *town* as far as I knew— I didn't see *her*— but I didn't look, really. I just made my way to the station to catch my train. I could barely even see the car, but I— It did cross my mind. It looked like the Audi and I even took a couple steps toward the—but then I just took off in the other direction, caught the train. Sometimes, I wonder if I knew it was Joe. On some level, you know? Subconsciously. That I couldn't deal with it, so—" *I did what I do,* she almost says. She stops.

"If so, you were probably in shock." Alice tsk-tsks, takes Karen's hand in both of hers. "Or blocked it out. Did you tell the police you were right there? Did you mention it when you went down to . . . ?"

Karen clears her throat. "To identify Joe's body? No," she says, and her eyes blur with tears. "I went to the hospital when they called me—but I never told them. It didn't seem important." Karen dabs at her eyes with a napkin and gulps down her tea. For a few seconds, other people's conversations fill the space between them. She starts to tell Alice someone's spying on her. Stalking her. She starts to say that even at the cemetery, even when she stood beside Joe's grave, she'd felt this strange and disconcerting presence. That when she turned around, she'd seen someone—she could have sworn it—a figure in the trees. She sweeps a few random crumbs into a tiny mound. "I've got to get back," she says. She wraps her croissant in a napkin, sticks it in her purse, and pokes at the running mascara at the corners of her eyes. "Antoine gets a little nuts when he can't get out to pee."

"Antoine's always nuts," Alice points out.

Karen hesitates. "Thanks," she says, "for listening." She stands up, puts on her coat, and leans over in the cramped aisle to give Alice a hug before she hurries to the doorway. Once there, she hesitates. For a second, she thinks about boarding Antoine and taking Alice up on her offer, staying in her tiny place, hemmed in by neighbors, surrounded by solid brick, the houseplants thriving under lamps. Although Karen has always felt a little claustrophobic there, it seems incredibly safe now, as if all of Beacon Hill were a scene inside a shoebox, with its up and down streets, the insulated feeling of this coveted and bustling area. She leans her shoulder hard against the heavy door and looks both up and down the sidewalk before walking quickly to her car.

Nearly an hour later, she pulls into her driveway, stares at a yard stretched like a sheet of cotton batting. Pure. Pristine. She walks up her front steps and unlocks the dead bolt, glances at the note she tries to remember to leave beside the alarm now every time she sets it—she's learned the hard way just how quickly the company responds. She punches in the code. Antoine raises his head with a little snort and stares at a thin, black studded leash hanging near a kitchen door in dire need of paint. The portion underneath the knob is jagged from Antoine's constant scratching and other paint shows through, a hopeful avocado from ten years before. Karen perches on a kitchen stool and stares at a stack of unpaid bills on the counter. She should have told Alice about her stalker, should have picked her brain. Karen eventually tells her best friend everything, so maybe Alice could have fit the pieces together, or at least had an objective opinion.

She fiddles with a plastic water bottle. No. She'd dumped enough on Alice for one day, admitting that she'd walked away from the unpleasantness of her husband's messy death. It didn't really happen that way but that was how it must have sounded to Alice. More than enough for one lunch, but that isn't the real reason Karen doesn't want to talk about this feeling that she's not alone. She's afraid if she does, it will become more real. She grabs a heavy flashlight on her way out to walk the dog, not so much for light, but as a weapon. Just in case.

The wind picks up. Antoine chases everything he sees, piddling, finally, at the edge of a neighbor's snowy lawn, which, in the waning light, shows up her dog's poor manners. Hers, really. "You need to drink more water," Karen tells him, glancing at the patch of yellow snow. "Or maybe *less*." She tugs on the leash and Antoine howls. The neighbor's door flies open, and Karen sticks the yelping dog under her arm and heads for home, the flashlight banging against her hip. Antoine wails. Night drops suddenly and Karen picks up her pace as Antoine sinks his little razor teeth into her jacket. "Damn!" It's slippery on the sidewalk going to the house, and Karen teeters, struggles to keep her balance. She grabs the flashlight from her pocket and shines it on the snowy path in front of her, where fresh footprints are scattered like fall leaves across the lawn. She shines the light along a trail of sunken spots marring the pristine blanket of thick snow.

On the front porch, Karen unlocks the front door and drops Antoine inside, pushes back to the yard. She finds the first footprint at the edge of the lawn near the street and follows the trail to the bay window in front, where the tracks turn right, heading for a small gate in the side yard. She stops, stands on tiptoe, aims the flashlight over the wood fence. In the backyard, tracks lead to yet another window and then back to the front, and finally to the street.

Snow picks up, filling the footprints, sucking them back into the night, the yard. Karen shivers. She turns and hurries back inside, sets the alarm, and stands at the edge of the window in the dark of the unlit living room. She could call the police, but by the time they arrive, the footprints will be invisible, with all this snow. They'll tell her it was just a neighbor checking on her to make sure she's all right—her car parked in the driveway, the darkened house, her husband's recent death. Why doesn't she ask around? they might suggest, their radios spluttering from their belts. Why doesn't she check, see if it wasn't just a well-meaning neighbor?

She walks through every room in the house. Checking. Finally, she pours a glass of Pinot Noir and drinks it quickly, pours another glass, and the theory of the worried neighbor seems more likely.

She slumps across the couch under an afghan. The house is far too large and empty with her husband gone. Creepy, now. Even with all his absences, there had always been the ambience of Joe, the knowledge that no matter how long he was gone, he would eventually come back. When he was home, she had his body there beside her. Even if they curled away from one another like burning papers, if she listened, she could hear his breath, and if she moved just so, she felt the pounding of his heart. Since his death, she lies awake, remembering silly things, like standing in the automatic doors at Target, watching as he disappeared, bit by bit, running across a rainy lot to get the car, the blinking lights, the careless, swishing sound of the glass doors. She misses him a hundred times a day, laments the shocking death—the snow, that fucking ice. Cruel of him, she thinks, to die the way he did, with another woman there beside him in the car. Who was she? The question plagues her. Whose arms held him as he died or called his name for the last time? Who was there to say good-bye? Regret and anger bubble up through the wine. Somewhere at the back of the house, a curtain makes a rustling sound, like a sail, and she wonders if it's Joe's ghost come back to haunt her.

And the boys. She can't even deal with that right now. They've taken on their father's death in such completely different ways. Jon calls every day, comes by more often than he ever has before. He keeps it in, whatever he's feeling. Not surprising—he and Joe always had a complicated relationship. Too much alike, she used to say. "Your son is just like you, so you have the same Achilles' heel, the same temper." And now, without the chance to set things right— "Give him time," Alice always says. "He'll sort it out. He just needs time."

Robbie, on the other hand, deals with his father's death like he deals with everything. Straight on. He cries, he drinks too much, he calls his mother twice a day. He'd sleep there on her couch if she let him, but, tempting as that sometimes seems, Karen keeps him at arm's length. She needs her space and, even if he doesn't know it, Robbie needs his, too.

She finishes the wine and hopes it keeps at bay the raw, wild grief that rakes through her late at night, fingers from the past that reach inside her bones to wrench from her all the moments of her marriage and toss them out into the spotlight, sorrow that leaves her wailing in a blue robe on a splintered wooden step at 3 A.M.

Her phone rings and Karen closes her eyes, waits for it to stop—Robbie, she thinks, or Jon. Vigilant. Kind. Worried—her little sentries, like guardian angels, these two. The ringing stops and then starts up again, insistent and unnerving. She won't worry the boys. Not now. Antoine barks, runs in circles at the edges of a dusty Persian rug. Karen sighs, forces herself up from the couch, and digs around inside her purse until she finds her cell. "Hello?"

"Karen," a familiar voice says. "It's Edward. We need to talk." She notices his lack of—something. Tact? Humanity? *Edwardness?* He is usually so calming—kind, really. "It's important," he says. "It's about the company."

"Were you here?" Of *course*. It must have been Edward, barging over unannounced, leaving tracks across the lawn, trying to get her attention through the window after driving all the way out here. Inappropriate, but still a lot less scary than the thought of some stranger. She tries to remember Edward's shoe size, match it to the footprints in the snow. The size of someone's feet was supposed to mean something—the size of their feet and hands, was it?

"No," he says. "*Your house?* Why would I? Jeez. Drive all the way out there without letting you know I was *com—*?"

"How 'bout now?" she says. "Where are you right now?"

"Still at the office." He sounds grumpy, and she pictures Edward, sitting Scrooge-like in his office as the snow pelts down outside. "Meet me for lunch?" he says. "Tomorrow? I can come there if you don't feel up to driving. I could pick up something to go and swing by your—"

"No! God!" She looks around at the plates in piles on counters and the rug coated in dog hairs, the dining room table stacked with mail. "I'll meet you in town."

"Even better." Edward sounds like himself again. "Legal's on the wharf at twelve? That work?"

"Fine," she says. "Legal's at twelve." She hangs up. For a fraction of a second, she thinks about stopping in to see Tomas.

VIII

KAREN

On the way to meet Edward, Karen taps the brake in front of Mass General. She could just park and run inside, visit her old friend Tomas in the ER, or wherever he is now, just to feel there's something concrete in her life. Someone concrete, some kind of anchor. She can't stay, she'll explain—she has this business lunch. Joe is gone—her husband. Dead. She'll take a breath or two, get herself under control before she mentions that her engine sounds a little off. That place in Waltham—that place Tomas worked for a while. Hoods? Does he still recommend it?

She stops, but only for a look, a quick glance at the building, and then she heads to Summer Street. She'd gotten only two texts from Tomas when he came back from Honduras months before. *I'm in Boston*, he'd said in the first one, which Karen had instantly deleted. *Working at Mass General again. Would love to see you.* There'd been another sort of half text. *Karen? Where are you????* And the question marks had added urgency, passion, but, again, she'd not responded.

Would love to get a coffee and catch up, she might have said, but she hadn't. Tomas made it clear before he left the country that he had wanted more than she. He was certainly attractive, with his soft brown eyes, his sexy smile. No argument there. Still, when Karen weighed the pros and cons of taking that next step with Tomas, she'd decided not to. He wasn't married. He might turn out to be a little needy, show up at their front door in the middle of the night, drunk and demanding. Latin lovers were known for their passion, something Karen sensed in him that both attracted her and gave her pause.

She turns on her iPod and drifts into the music. She could have loved Tomas, with his seductive accent, the way he said her name. Karen, the way he breathed it, like a poem, the way, no matter what was going on in his life, he always seemed to have time for her. She'd met him on the train, going home from a symphony when he'd got on at the same stop. Their legs touched as the train left the station. Lightly. A brush. He smelled of coconut and musk.

"I saw you at the concert," he'd said. "I was behind you walking out. It was very nice, although Wagner is not my favorite."

"Nor mine," she'd said.

"What is?"

"I don't know," she'd told him. "Anything with a glass of wine." And he laughed.

If anyone had asked her if she'd meant to see this stranger again, she would have said no. Absolutely not. It was only after two more times chatting on the train after symphonies that she'd begun to wish they'd sat together, yawning through the performance, leaving together afterward, crossing through the lobby, side by side, to the blanched, leftover heat of evening.

He worked in a garage near Waltham. Hoods, and she'd made a

point to take both her car and Joe's in for anything, no matter how trivial—a hesitation in the starter, a worn-out wiper blade. He never charged her for labor. "My friend, Karen," Tomas would introduce her whenever she came in. "Primo treatment on her car, guys." And he would wink at her.

"We're friends," she'd told Alice at the time. "We're only friends. We sometimes get a lunch together, grab a coffee in town. He's fixed my car a couple times when he was working at his friends' garage, but that's it, really. Simply platonic." And it was. Eventually he found a job at Mass General, where he worked as an orderly—he'd been a nurse in Honduras—and after that she saw him less and less. A good thing. Karen loved her husband, and even if they'd grown apart, even if he was out of town too much and brought home a dog that hated her, Joe was still the man she married. She'd understood even though he never pressed the matter that Tomas had wanted more than she could give.

In the end, he'd gone back to Honduras. "My mother is very ill, Karen," he'd told her on a lush, green day two years before, sitting on a bench in the Public Garden. Spring hung like perfume in the air.

"Oh," she'd said. "My God! How long will you be gone?" But he shook his head.

"I don't know."

She could have loved Tomas. But Karen's always known passion isn't everything. She understood that, watching her parents wrestle through their lives in their cardboard house with hard blue rugs, where their daughters learned to live on their toes, dancing, edgy, like birds on a hot wire, always ready to break and run. No. For love. For passion. For Tomas, Karen would not leave her husband.

She parks. She checks her makeup in the rearview mirror and looks around before unlocking her car door. Is she getting paranoid, living all alone the way she is now? Maybe she should sell the house and get a place in Boston, an apartment downtown, somewhere close to Alice.

Is that all this is? Nerves? But there were the footprints, the figure in the trees at the cemetery. Maybe she'll confide in Edward. She opens her car door and turns to lock it before walking quickly toward the restaurant. The wind howls off the water and she pulls her scarf over her head, tucks her chin down, against the icy gusts. And then Edward is there, puffing up behind her; steam flies from his mouth and lingers in the air.

He hugs her. A lengthy hug, she thinks, but they're both grieving, after all. Edward's bulk lends some protection, but still the wind flings her hair across her cheeks, steals their words, their breath. After a few short stabs at conversation, they walk in silence, pushing through the door into the welcome warmth of Legal's.

Edward raises two fingers and they are immediately escorted to a table near a window, where a waiter takes their orders, leaning down to straighten a coaster before he hurries to the kitchen, pad in hand.

"Are you all right?" Edward is himself again—solicitous and attentive. He leans back and looks hard at her face. A rock, she thinks. Edward is a rock, but then she notices his bloodshot eyes, remembers that he's ordered a martini, extra dry, and that it's barely noon.

"Yes," she says. "I'm okay." She looks at Edward's face and decides not to mention the footprints after all. He might feel duty-bound to stay there at the house. For her. For Joe. *He'd want me to*, he might tell her, and then she'd be stuck with Edward draped across her grief. Worse yet, across her living room. "Actually." She sticks her napkin on her lap. "I'm not *fine* at all. I miss Joe. I keep expecting him to come through the front door. He was gone so much, it seems as if he's only away on business, that he'll be coming back."

Edward clears his throat. "I get that," he says. "Same at the office." His voice is tired, brittle; it cracks on the last word. "Quiet as a tomb down there without him," which Karen thinks is a poor choice of words, all things considered.

The waiter brings their food, but neither of them seems to notice. The waiter smiles, nearly bows before he trots back to the kitchen.

"An insurance investigator came by the office earlier this week." Edward takes a swallow of his drink. "A woman. Brennan, I think she said. Maggie Brennan. Used to be a cop. She'll probably be calling you at some point. Asking you some questions."

"What kind of questions?" Karen feels her anxiety level ratchet up a notch.

Edward shrugs. "My guess is they'll try to pass Joe's death off as a suicide. That way they don't have to pay out on your claim. I could be wrong." Edward is already halfway through his second drink. He's barely touched his food. "Just wanted to give you a heads-up."

Karen picks at her salad and glances back at Edward. He looks a little vintage in the suit he's wearing, like a character from an F. Scott Fitzgerald novel. His eyes skip here and there around the room before settling on Karen. Gatsby, she decides. She takes a sip of water.

"I don't know quite how to put this." Edward looks away. His eyes follow the waiter as he moves with expertise among the tables. "Delicately."

"What?" Karen says, and Edward clears his throat again. He looks outside the window. The sky is so light blue, it's nearly white. "Did Joe ever mention anything to you about money?"

"We were *married*, Edward. What kind of question is—?"

"About the company, the downturn of the—"

"Well," she says. "He told me Home Runs had a dip in the road. Hardly an anomaly these days with the economy the way it is." She chews on a radish. The restaurant is filling up. People puff in from outside. The door opens and closes, letting in the cold; banter lingers in the air. At the next table, someone laughs too loudly, falls into a fit of coughing.

"It's a lot more than that, Karen." Edward sounds uncomfortable. Desperate, maybe. "A lot more than a dip in the road."

She leans away from the table, watches as Edward takes a small bite of trout.

"Did Joe ever tell you he'd withdrawn some money from the company?" He doesn't look straight at her. He watches the waiter and chews.

"I think that's called embezzling, Edward, and no. Of course not. This is Joe, the ex–*altar* boy. This is maddeningly honest *Joe*, who once drove all the way across town to return a five-dollar bill to a kid at a convenience store when he got too much change." Of course, she sees him a little differently now. It can't be helped. There is the girlfriend. Not so much integrity in that.

Edward nods. He finishes his drink and wipes his mouth, tosses the napkin on the table. "I loved Joe like a brother. You know that. Still do. Always."

Karen glares at him over her glasses. "You used to *rave* about Joe's honesty," she says. "Have you forgotten? *Honest as the day is long*, you used to say. If something's wrong, you'd better take a look at your accountant. Or Francine, or whoever's handling the finances these days, because you and I both know Joe was no thief! I think I need a drink," she says, and she looks around for the waiter.

Edward squints at her. His skin is dull and faintly gray in the light from the windows. "I should have kept a better eye on things. Hindsight's twenty-twenty and all that. Meanwhile, these discrepancies—fairly well hidden, but there, nonetheless. I just wondered if Joe—if he said anything to you that might help me figure—"

"Well." Karen drums her fingernails against her water glass. "There you go. If things were well hidden, that proves it wasn't Joe. He wasn't good enough with money to *hide* whatever you're accusing him of. Brilliant, but mathematically . . . a little challenged."

"Karen," Edward says. "I'm not accusing Joe of anything. I've only mentioned this in case it comes out. If this Maggie Brennan digs around as much as I think she's going to, it probably will. And if it looks as if Home Runs is floundering, it could mean a delay in your settlement. That's all."

"How so? You've lost me."

He lowers his voice. He covers Karen's hand with his. His eyes are puffy, his pupils pinpoints in the brightness of the sunshine flooding in. "I know Joe would never take his own life. He loved you. He loved Robbie and Jon. Hell, he loved the *company*! But people do, Karen. They jump out of windows, lock themselves in garages with their cars running. People do all *kinds* of crazy things when they think they've lost what they spent their entire lives building. And the insurance companies are totally aware of this. They pursue this sort of thing, especially when there's a big payout involved. They'll take a look in that direction. That's all. Just keep this under your hat until I figure out what's going on."

"No worries there." Karen fumbles around under the table for her bag and starts to stand. She no longer wants a drink. She only wants to leave. "No worries at all, Edward, since this is total bullshit and you know it."

"Excuse me, miss." Their waiter is back, his hair impeccable, despite the noon rush. He sets a drink in the exact center of a flower-print napkin. "The bartender asked me to bring this over. Apparently, a gentleman ordered it for you on his way out. Chocolate Café Noir Cocktail with strawberries instead of raspberries."

Karen digs her nails into her palms. "Strawberries. Why did you— Why not raspberries? Doesn't it always come with rasp—?"

Their waiter smiles; his hair is glossy in the bright light. "The gentleman was very adamant, according to the bartender. 'With strawberries,' he said. 'Make sure.'"

Karen stands up, alarmed. She looks around the restaurant. Only she and Joe knew about her aversion to raspberries—she couldn't stand their texture, the squishiness—so she always ordered the cock-tail with strawberries instead. It was a private joke between them. She glances at Edward, looking up at her, one eyebrow raised. Edward might know. They used to go out together all the time, the four of them, back when he was married to one or another of his flock of silly wives. But he's sitting right here with her, clearly not the "gentle-man" who ordered her a drink on his way out.

"Who?" she says. "Where is he?"

The waiter shrugs. "I didn't see him. As I said, the bartender asked me to bring you the drink and whoever it was"—he looks around the restaurant—"well, whoever it was has apparently left."

"When?"

"Probably just a minute ago."

"Karen." Edward reaches for her hand again, but this time he doesn't quite touch her. "There's something else we need to talk about." But Karen shakes her head. She glances at the front of the restaurant, at the closing door.

"Not now, Edward. I've got to go find— Thanks, though. Thanks for the lunch. It was great," she says, already slipping into her coat. She grabs her bag.

"Wait!" Karen has a vague impression of Edward standing up and hurrying across the room behind her, but she doesn't stop. She doesn't turn around. She runs across the restaurant and through the door to the street.

IX

DORRIE

Dorrie stares at the unfamiliar number in her cell, left the day they buried Joe, left while she huddled with the others, her feet stuck in slush, sleet sticking to her hair. Possibly, the call is from the insurance investigator who came to the office a day or two later. Brennan, Dorrie thinks. She'd seen the woman hesitating in the hall outside her office, heard Edward escort her loudly to the lobby while Lola the receptionist chatted on the phone—mentioned her name, actually. "Dorreen," she'd said to someone on the phone, but Dorrie couldn't hear the rest, and Lola's not been back. Emergency at home, Edward said. Back on the farm. Wisconsin or Minnesota, one of those cold Midwestern states. *Something about her parents,* he'd said, waving his hand in the air.

Dorrie thinks she'll be proactive. She'll phone this number back, this possibly Brennan's number, preempt the strike. The other number—Joe's—she'll not call back. Not ever.

She leans against the kitchen counter near the window. Her eyes blur out of focus at a backyard strewn with branches, brown and dead, like skeletons across the snow. Sometimes she hears Joe's voice, feels him, like a buzzing underneath her skin. A background noise, like trains near the apartment she and Samuel had downtown when they first lived together. They were such a constant sound that almost right away she'd stopped hearing them. She only noticed late at night when they stopped running. She heard the absence of the trains, the silence, and Dorrie wonders if that's what will happen when she stops hearing Joe.

Lily was home, sulking on the couch when she got back from the funeral. The weather had turned too icy for skiing after all, and Dorrie stood in the doorway, secretly relieved, not only that Lily was safe and sound and not careening down a mountain on two strips of wood, but grateful, too, for the presence of her grumpy daughter, the dirty dishes in the sink, the dinner waiting to be made, these things that left no time or space to mourn. No time to worry about the threatening robotic call she'd gotten on the way to the cemetery or to ponder the strange number in her cell that she'd forgotten until now.

She calls it back. Her hand shakes as she pours hot milk into a cup with cocoa clinging to its sides. "I can do this," she says aloud. And then again, "I can do this! I am brave." She hopes her brain believes what she does not believe, as she's lately read it does. She's tried to cut out phrases like *I'm dying for a grilled cheese sandwich,* since she's also read the brain is very literal.

"Hello?" A woman's voice. A familiar voice.

"Viv?"

"Yep. I'm back," her friend says. "I got a job in Boston. I tried to call you this weekend, but I wasn't sure I had the right number. Your message doesn't actually say who you are."

"I know. I've got to fix that." The generic message is because of Karen, really—so she wouldn't know who Dorrie was if she stumbled across Joe's burner phone.

Viv relocated to Vermont months before, and they had barely spoken after she left. There were two or three faint phone calls, with Viv shouting something about living in a dead zone with spotty cell connection before she'd faded off into a round of static. Her name is actually Vivian, but with her New Orleans childhood, her huge violet eyes, and background in theater, Viv suits her better. "I have some clients in the city," she says now. "Four on Beacon Hill. Living rooms." Viv works in interior design.

"I am really glad you're back!" Dorrie says. "And so glad you weren't—" She takes a sip of her hot chocolate.

"What?"

"It's a long story. There was an accident," she says. "I was involved in a terrible, horrendous accident, and someone died."

"Oh my God! Who?"

"Joe," Dorrie says, "but I don't really want to talk about it. At least not right now."

"Okay," Viv says. "But, my God, Dorrie. Are you all right?"

"Not really. In fact, I've never actually *been* less all right."

"Can you meet for dinner? Tomorrow? I'm staying at the Copley Square Hotel—courtesy of my clients, can you believe it?—so we could just eat there if you can get away."

"Seven?"

"Perfect," Viv says. "See you in the lobby."

Dorrie glances at her watch. "Shit. I'm really late. Can we continue this on my—?"

"Go," Viv says. "I'll see you at the Copley." And with a tiny click, she's gone.

Dorrie opens the front door and glances out at the sky. She'll take the train if it looks like snow, but there is only wind, the clop-clop of pinecones rolling down the drive. Somewhere a dog barks.

She pulls her coat out of the hall closet and on impulse grabs the ugly coat she'd worn the night Joe died. She'll take it to the office and leave it there on the last hook. She doesn't want it in her house, can't bear to have it here, a constant reminder. Every time she opens the closet door, a part of her is catapulted back to the night of the accident.

She pulls her hat down over her forehead—a new hat she picked up for the funeral to hide her healing cut, the telltale scar. A jaunty, velvet one that sets off the dark green of her eyes and totally belies her mood. She locks the front door behind her and half-walks, half-slides down the slick driveway. Safely in her front seat, she scans the street for a dark car with one headlight before she eases her foot off the brake and rolls down the driveway. She straightens her hat in the rearview mirror and wonders if that night on Newbury will dictate all her future actions and reactions. Or will it fade? Will it, like the gash on her forehead, fold itself back inside the skin of her former life?

There's no hurry, now, to get to work. The atmosphere is gloomy at the office, dark since Joe's death, despite Jeananne's constant chatter and Lola's temp replacement, who never even met Joe, despite being overwhelmed with trying to catch up with clients and training with Francine. Despite all this, Joe's absence is a constant ache. His voice, his laughter haunt the halls and linger in the doorways. Without his booming voice, his humor, the atmosphere of gaiety he brought to work, the office is a hushed and dreary place. He's taken all the lightness with him. There's only Edward now.

She pulls up at a long red light on Boylston. Cars are lined along the street, and Dorrie's mind wanders back to the first time she ever saw Joe, when he took her hand in the lobby of Home Runs and held on just a second longer than he had to. He was standing in the doorway with water dripping from his trench coat when she came in, shaking a large van Gogh umbrella that nearly always jammed.

"Joe Lindsay." He'd walked toward her with his hand extended, and she'd noticed he had striking eyes. Blue. An odd blue. Like the sky. "Welcome to Home Runs, Dorreen." He'd held on to her hand, as if he'd forgotten he had it, and she'd pulled it back, finally.

"Oh," he'd said. "Sorry."

Dorrie punched at her stubborn umbrella, got it closed. "It's fine," she said. "I have two. And it's Dorrie, by the way," she'd said as her umbrella popped back open, filling the small entryway.

"Dorrie then." He'd smiled at the huge sunflowers, the broken metal ribs. "Nice umbrella."

Often days or weeks went by without her seeing him. She found she was a little disappointed when he wasn't at the office, that she was painfully aware of both his presence and his absence, and that she found a reason to walk down the hall whenever he was there.

When she'd been working at Home Runs for a few months, he'd

asked her to lunch—a basement tea shop on Charles near Tremont. Its windows were like flat cat's eyes that peered across the sidewalk at street level and Dorrie passed it three times in her nervousness, pushing finally through the door to find Joe already inside. She'd watched him for a minute from the doorway, watched the slouched, spent look of him, the way his hands sat empty on the table.

"Sorry." She sat down across from him.

He glanced at his watch. "I thought maybe you'd forgotten."

They'd ordered, chatted about work, but it was stilted, strained. The waiter arrived at last, set their orders down with a smile. The place was filling up with customers; a small line formed near the door.

"Sorry again to be so late. I couldn't actually—" She'd made a little dismissive gesture. Her bangle bracelets clinked and clanged.

"I guess it is a little out of the way." His eyes were dark in the faint light slanting in from the window.

"It's just that it's a little underground. And the sign was— I didn't see the sign."

"They are discreet," he told her, smiling.

"There is a thin line," Dorrie said, "between discretion and bankruptcy."

"Ah, but discretion is the better part of valor."

"Or marriage?"

He didn't answer.

"Wow," she'd said, picking at her salad. "This tuna is really good!"

He smiled.

"I've heard good things about you," he said when they'd nearly finished with their food. He'd wiped his mouth and leaned back from the table. "You have a flair for dealing with people. The few times I've heard you on the phone with customers . . . You're really good."

She'd nodded. A piece of lettuce lodged between her teeth. "Thanks," she'd managed, finally. "I'm a trained actress, so . . ." She'd made a flip-flop gesture with her hand. "Selling . . . acting."

He looked at her, squinted. "I can see that," he said. "I can see you on a stage." He'd sighed, a long, deep sigh. "I very much wanted to be an actor myself when I was young." He stared out toward the window. "Even went to acting school for a while." His voice shook slightly. "Had to drop out, though, to support—to support my . . ." He'd stopped, cleared his throat.

"I'm so sorry." Dorrie had leaned forward. "I didn't mean to upset you by bringing back—"

He'd grinned. "Gotcha."

"You were acting? Just *then*?"

"Couldn't resist."

"Not bad," she'd said. "Not bad at all. *Mean,* but not *bad.*"

"Anyway," he said, serious again. "You'd be dealing much more with the clients. Sometimes you'd meet with them, give them suggestions. I can show you how to do virtual renovations. Tuesdays you'll do on-site visits—sit in their living rooms, drink their coffee, meet their kids, try to get a feel for who they are, what might work for them. A little traveling from time to time, but I'll try to keep you in the Boston area. When you're done, you're finished for the day. Doable?"

She hadn't answered. She'd turned to look at a slitted window, a thin line of light. "I'm sorry, but I don't think so, Mr. Lindsay," she'd said in a voice barely above a whisper. "I appreciate your thinking of me . . ." She'd begun to move around in her seat, collecting her bag. She'd run her fingers through her hair and managed a small smile. Her bottom lip trembled, but only slightly. "Really. I do thank you. And thank you so much for this." She'd nodded toward the table. "Lunch. It was delicious. Really." She'd begun to stand up. He'd looked at her. Shocked.

"Touché," she'd said, tossing her head sideways in a dramatic gesture, throwing her silky scarf across her shoulder. "Seriously. "Yes. It's doable. At least I think so."

"Damn," he said. "You *are* good!"

For dessert, the waiter wheeled a tray of pastries to their table—pies and cakes and croissants and puffy, cream-filled things. "We'll have this," Joe said, "and one of those." She remembers how his fingers shook, the silence filled with air, the waiter's footsteps light as snow, the scents of teas, the flowered cups, the easy way he spoke. She could have stayed for hours.

His hand was light against her back, steering her as they left. She heard the scrape of her chair across the wood grains of the floor, noticed the bright light coming in the window, the clatter of dishes at the nearby tables, the sharp edges of Tremont. She remembers the bones in his face, the lines, the small, flat, broken spot at the top of his nose, the fierce blue of his eyes. They'd stood in the doorway, half in, half out.

Somewhere, she thinks, there's a picture of the two of them. It was in the spring at a street festival in Cambridge. A beautiful day, warm and breezy, after a long winter. It was on a Tuesday. She hopes he ripped it up, but she knows he didn't. It was too perfect—the picture, the day.

Dorrie turns slowly onto Summer Street. Vigilant, on edge, she pulls her car in to the garage. The renovated building has its issues—an outdated radiator that gasps like an iron lung, the huge, high spaces that, in winter, stop the offices from ever really getting warm—but at least there's a garage.

She gets out of her car and the closing of the door booms in the silence. She walks quickly toward the elevator. Even here out of the wind, the air stings her face, numbs her skin. She stops in front of Joe's old parking space with his name still on the sign. *Joe Lindsay, Owner.* She touches his name with her fingertips, a ritual she performs on days she drives in to work, out of reverence or regret.

Joe was traveling a lot after that first lunch, and when he came back, she thought he seemed more distant than before. Weeks passed before they went to lunch again—a month, nearly to the day. They met at a seafood restaurant, where pictures of fishermen dotted the walls. Dorrie ordered clam chowder, dabbed at it, feeling more nervous this time than the last. There was more at stake. "So." She'd slurped down a spoonful of the chowder. Delicious. Fresh. "Would your wife mind you having lunch with me?"

"Not sure," he said. "Probably."

"Do you have— Are you very . . . close?"

"Not extraordinarily close. Why?"

"No reason. I just thought if she was still *jealous* of you after all these years—that's a good sign, isn't it? I mean, that level of emotional involvement. That's a *good* thing, right, in a marriage?"

He shrugged. "Is it?"

"Probably."

They ate in silence.

"Would you be?" she asked. "Jealous, I mean. Of your wife."

He stopped eating, his fork poised in the air in front of him, lobster and butter dripping from the tines. "Yes," he said, and he frowned. "But not about a lunch."

"So," Dorrie had said after a few seconds. "She might think there was something fishy going on?"

Joe looked up. "What? Sorry?"

"Fishy? The lobster? The clams?"

"Oh," he said. "Very funny."

"You're not so good at this. I'd better scale down."

"Ouch. Can you stop now?"

"Not *reel*-y."

"Okay," he'd said. "You got me. Hook, line, and sinker."

She sighs, glances at her watch. She's late. *I love you, Joe,* she says inside her head, and looks down at the level cement. Something stains the gray dullness of the parking spot, making it darker in one place than the others. She squats down. She scrubs at it with a Kleenex, but it's sunk inside the concrete like blood, this puddle of oil.

She feels someone behind her, watching her. There is something out of place, a footstep or the tiniest disturbance of air. She stands up and nearly sprints across the garage to the elevator. The light is bad here. It's almost dark—a huge shadowy space with flickering, erratic lights. She pushes the elevator button with a shaking hand, pushes it again and again, stabbing at it with her fingers, as, on the other side of the garage, the exit door opens and closes with the raucous echo of a squeaky hinge.

X

DORRIE

Dorrie isn't ready for the insurance investigator when the woman knocks on the outside of her open office door. "Got a minute?" She takes a small step over the threshold.

No, Dorrie feels like saying. *Afraid I don't have time for you today. Maybe tomorrow afternoon. Maybe next month.* "Of course," she says. She stands up and a pile of papers slides to the edge of her desk. She catches them, makes it a point to look the woman straight in the eye. She vaguely remembers reading somewhere that it's a sign of guilt not to. Or was it weakness? Or maybe it had to do with dogs.

"Maggie Brennan," the woman says, and she extends her hand. She's young. She looks a little like Lily with her long dark hair, her brown eyes.

"I know." Dorrie shakes her hand, a firm shake, which she has also read is a sign of openness or honesty or something. "I heard you in with Edward the other day."

Brennan nods. "I won't take up much of your time. I just have a couple of questions."

"Sure." Dorrie gestures toward a chair. "Please," she says. "Sit."

"Thanks." Brennan perches on a wooden, straight-backed chair. "Nice office," she says, although it isn't, really. It has large windows and an interesting poster, but otherwise it's kind of bare and clammy. Brennan takes out a little notepad. "These old buildings have character," she says, and Dorrie nods.

"Character, wheezy heat, leaky windows . . . creaky floors."

"Comes with the territory, I guess." Brennan smiles. "So. I'll get right to it. Anything unusual going on with your boss the last few weeks?"

She's pulled her chair up square with Dorrie's, so they're sitting face-to-face, like speed daters or contestants on a game show. Dorrie squints out the window and cocks her head as if she's concentrating very hard. *Well, let's seeee. Someone's trying to kill me?* she's tempted to say, and she worries, suddenly, that she'll start babbling all her secrets. "I think he was upset."

"Why was that?" Brennan takes out a pen, snaps it open, and jots something down.

"There were financial issues. I think they were going to have to lay some of us off."

"How about on a personal level?" she says. "Any problems?"

Dorrie squints at a gray cloud. She can feel Brennan studying her face. She shifts her gaze to a poster Jeananne bought and tacked onto the wall above her desk back when they shared the office. *Believe!* it says. "Well, that." Dorrie forces herself to turn and look at Brennan. "*That* I wouldn't know, Ms. Brennan."

"Maggie," Brennan says. "Please. That's a nasty cut." She tosses this out into the room, bending to pick up a dropped pen as it rolls across the newly waxed floor. Her hand trembles, giving Dorrie a little shot of courage.

"Excuse me?"

"On your forehead there. Under your bangs." Brennan push-buttons the pen point in and out a few times and her hand stops shaking. The clicks echo in the silence of the room. "What happened?"

"I slipped." Dorrie tries to meet her eyes again, but ends up looking at the left side of Brennan's bottom lip. She knows her limitations. She's a terrible liar. Too much Catholic school. "On the ice," she says. "I slipped in my driveway." Her office seems unbearably hot suddenly, as if someone's turned up the heat in the usually icy building, and Dorrie wonders if she's spun into menopause.

"Did you go in?" Brennan leans forward for a better look. Her face is not unfriendly. She actually looks a tiny bit concerned. "To the hospital?"

Dorrie shakes her head. "Mass General is such a— It was so icy," she says, "that night. I just put on a bandage and—"

Brennan scribbles some more notes. "It must be hard," she says, "being here without your boss. Sounds like everybody really liked him."

Dorrie sighs. "He was great. We all miss Joe."

"So you do virtual design, I hear. Like on HGTV."

"Just like." Dorrie smiles. "I follow up, make sure the clients are happy. Plus, I was being trained to take Francine's place in finance when she retires. I'd just started when Joe—when Mr. Lindsay . . . Actually, Maggie, I really need to get back to my—"

"Of course." Brennan stands up. "Thanks. And good luck, Dorrie."

"You, too." Dorrie stares at a stack of papers, runs her thumb along the edges.

"You think of anything, give me a call." Brennan places a card, face up, on the desk. "Anything at all. Oh," she says from the doorway. "You've got some—"

Dorrie's heart stops.

"You've got some oil or something on your boot there."

"Oh." Dorrie rubs at the greasy blob with a tissue, blurs it into a large mess across her boot. "Right. For some reason there was a puddle of oil in Joe's old parking space. I must've stepped in it this morning on my way to the elevator. Actually—" She's babbling, relieved it wasn't something else Brennan had noticed—*you've got some fingerprints there that look like a match for the ones in your boss's car, you've got blood that's the same exact color as some drops they found in the front seat, and the glove we found at the scene—huh—looks like the size you'd take.* "Actually, there was someone in the garage this morning when I got here," Dorrie says. "It was probably nothing, but—it just felt strange. Eerie, you know?"

"Noted. Oh." Brennan says from the hall. "You might try some Goop. For your boot. They sell it in auto parts stores. Stuff's like magic. Both my brothers work on cars, so I learned a few things over the years."

A moment later a chair grates across the floor in Jeananne's office on the other side of the wall. The popinjay, Joe used to call Jeananne—small and chatty. Maggie Brennan has just hit the mother lode.

Dorrie makes three more phone calls. She stretches. There's been a little burst of business—a couple of teardowns and renovations in Chelsea, and three kitchens, two in Jamaica Plain, and one in Martha's Vineyard. On paper, at least, the company seems pretty solid. She yawns. She turns on her computer and scrolls through her e-mails. She's been so backlogged, she hasn't even glanced at any of her e-mails since Joe's death.

A few messages pop up. Most of the company e-mails went directly to either Edward or Joe, and the few clients whose messages went unanswered have already phoned her at the office. Her eyes scan the names. Joe. She looks at the date: January 9. He sent this on the day he died. She takes a deep breath before she clicks it open. A name and a phone number jump on the screen along with a link. Only that.

Tears of disappointment blur her vision, even though she knows this is her business e-mail and that Joe would never send a personal message to her here. Even so. She wipes her eyes and looks back at the screen at a name she doesn't recognize. *Paulo Androtti.* The number must be his. The link is probably to this guy's website, and she promises herself she'll look at it. Later. She closes out and grabs her purse, searching for a tissue to repair her blotched mascara just as Jeananne says, "I wonder. Do people ever really get over something like that? Like his wife and his—"

"And his—?"

Dorrie runs her index finger under her eyes and scrunches her chair over a few inches closer to the wall. Like tissue paper, these walls. Jeananne's voice drifts through.

"Oh. Yes. His wife and his—and his sons, I was going to say."

"Joe had a girlfriend." Brennan's voice is flat, but Dorrie knows she's bluffing. Of course, she's bluffing. *Please, please, please, Jeananne. Just keep your stupid mouth sh—*

"I think so," Jeananne says. "I heard him talking a few times. Two or three. He was meeting somebody '. . . only an hour,' he said this one time, 'but I'll do my best to make it . . . '" She stops. Dorrie lets out a long breath and Jeananne pipes up again. "And then another time, he said he loved her, whoever it was."

"Could have been his wife, no?"

"Yeah," Jeananne says. "Sure. Maybe. Except he said it like he meant it, you know?"

Dorrie rubs at her mascara with her fingers as Jeananne's chatter flutters through the wall. After a minute or two, Brennan leaves to talk to Len in the back, and Dorrie blows her nose, pulls up Joe's e-mail for the second time. She sighs. She touches his name with the tips of her fingers and clicks on the link beneath Paulo Androtti's name, but it doesn't take her to his website as she'd thought; it takes her to a news story. She turns down the volume and leans in toward the computer screen, where a young newswoman is reporting a house fire in Jamaica Plain. "Tragic," the anchorwoman says. She looks excited. Eager. A couple trapped inside, the woman pregnant, in her last trimester. Awful. Horrific. Investigating for arson or any foul play, she goes on to say, and then the newscast cuts to the weather.

Dorrie replays the clip. The couple's last name was Robbins. Sheryl and Alex Robbins. Curious, she looks them up on Google, finds two short articles and their obituaries, a sad and poignant picture of the couple walking a small dog.

The name is vaguely familiar. Jeananne must have mentioned

them—mentioned *this*. Or, no. It wasn't Jeananne; it was Lola. Lola from the front desk. So horrible, she'd said. So senseless. Such a sweet couple.

Dorrie pulls up the Home Runs file on renovations and scrolls down to the R's. Alex and Sheryl Robbins. And then their address is typed in, along with three contact numbers and an e-mail address for Alex.

She closes her door and copies the entire page, saves it on her desktop in her Upcoming Auditions file—empty now except for this. She's tried to keep up with her acting over the years, but lately, these past weeks, she's let it go. Lately, she feels as if her whole life is a play. She prints a copy of the page and zips it into a small compartment in her purse.

At exactly five, Dorrie grabs her coat and walks to the garage, still buttoning it when she hears Jeananne's voice behind her. "Wait!"

She's wearing the ugly coat Dorrie brought in to the office, and it hangs down off her arms. "I just saw that insurance woman again." Jeananne's voice echoes in the empty garage. "I'm working late tonight, so I ran up to Mug Me for some coffee, and when I got back, she was just standing in front of a parking space, staring at the cement."

"Where?"

"There." Jeananne shuffles her coffee around to point. "In front of Joe's old space. She even squatted down to stick her finger in that—what?—gunk there, that little puddle of—"

"Huh." Edward *had* mentioned at some point that Brennan used to be a cop. Old habits die hard, apparently. "Interesting,"

Dorrie says, and even though she's still slightly annoyed with her gossipy co-worker, she watches from her car until Jeananne is safely in the elevator.

Dorrie inches home along slushy roads and pulls up in the driveway, holds her naked hands in front of the heater vent before she hurries inside. Cold sticks to her clothes and she shivers in the hallway, sorts through hefty stacks of mail, separating bills from ads and catalogs. Newspapers still in their bags are piled up on the desk. She'll stick them in with the recyclables. Later. *I'll think about it tomorrow!* she says in her best Scarlett voice and she takes off her coat, shakes the snow onto the round bright rug in the small entryway. She turns on a desk lamp.

"Lily?"

The house is silent. The air is thick with odors from the kitchen. Burnt bread or toasted Eggo waffles.

"Up here," Lily calls from her room. "On the phone."

"Finish your homework first," Dorrie yells, but her heart's not really in it. She can't concentrate; lately, her brain is in a fog.

"I am," Lily assures her. "*We* are. *Math*." Dorrie adds a bill from Boston Gas to a hefty pile of mail. She smiles, remembering Lily mentioning a new guy at school—a math and science geek, she'd said and rolled her eyes.

Dorrie stands at the foot of the stairs, leans forward toward her daughter's room. "Did you find the cobbler?" Clearly not. If she had, the house wouldn't smell like burnt toast. A second later, Lily sails down the stairs.

"Raspberry?" she mouths, her cell phone tight against her ear. Raspberry is her favorite. Raspberry anything—When Lily was three and deathly sick with strep throat, Dorrie, hovering over her daughter's tiny bed with the heart-shaped headboard, asked her if there was anything at all she felt like eating. Lily's voice was such a tiny fevered wheeze, she couldn't hear. *Only . . .*

Dorrie had pushed closer. *What, sweetie. Anything at all you think you could—* Lily whispered "raspberry sorbet."

"It's almost dinnertime," Dorrie says now. "Just take a bite."

Lily gives her a hug. "Thanks, Mom," she whispers. She points at Dorrie with the hand not holding her cell. *Awesome,* she mouths again, sliding back upstairs, plate in hand with not so much as a hiccup in her conversation.

Dorrie makes herself a cup of tea and glances down at her boot, the smear of grease. Goop, Brennan had suggested. She sticks her coat back on and heads out to the garage. If Goop has even the slightest connection to cars, Samuel will most likely have a jar of it out here somewhere. He's methodical. He'll have it on a shelf with other cleaners. She yawns again. Tired. She never seems to really sleep. She sees it in her dreams, that car sliding over into their lane, the tree, Joe's eyes, staring toward the window, seeing nothing. Or did he? The look of surprise on his face. She wonders, sometimes, if he saw her mother in that last instant, her hand, white in the dark car, soft against the hard edges of death, leading him carefully from the wreckage.

The garage is a mess, but somehow Samuel's shelves are in some kind of order. Jars. Cans. Combustibles. She sorts through. There it is. Goop! She grabs it, reads the directions. Toxic, of course. Samuel's big on toxins. She opens it and takes a little whiff, decides to stick her boot outside on the front porch after she's Gooped it.

She never comes out here. It's Samuel's space. She looks around, takes in the photographs of Lily—in her soccer uniform and graduating from sixth grade, Lily standing proudly in her skis—a shot of Samuel's mother in her old Victorian two-family in Chelsea, and a few nice black-and-whites of Dorrie performing on stage. Samuel is an excellent photographer.

She turns toward the door and something catches her eye in all the mess and chaos of her husband's automotive lair, a baggie on the second shelf beside a box of nails. She reaches for it but then she stops, stares at a piece of black cloth on the back of the workbench, sticking out from behind a stack of books on engines and a jar with pens and cutting tools. She walks across the room and gives a little tug, and there it is. A black glove—the one she lost the night Joe died. The lined leather Bloomingdale's purchase she thought she'd never see again lies boldly on the bench. What the *hell*? Or maybe it's the mate, she tells herself, the one she lost earlier. But if so, why would Samuel hide it?

She sticks it behind the books where Samuel had it hidden. She backs away as if the glove is some wild creature she has inadvertently awakened, and slips through the garage door into the kitchen. Suddenly she's back inside her nightmare, but this time she's awake.

XI

MAGGIE

Maggie steps out of her heels and pulls a pair of boots from under her desk. Sometimes she feels as if she's in a strange sort of play, here in this office of beige, her desk a small, unsturdy fortress on a plastic-feeling floor. Not that she's particularly knowledgeable about such things, but she once had a boyfriend who was an actor. Daryl. He'd taken her to a few off-Broadway shows that Maggie didn't understand and suspected Daryl didn't, either. "It was a little esoteric," he might say afterward, as they hunched over their coffees in some earnest little café he'd discovered, or "He takes some getting used to," of a screenwriter with an unpronounceable last name.

She reaches down to tie her boots and heads out to Southie to check on Joseph Lindsay's old Audi, which has been down at the O'Brien brother's place since the night of the accident. She won't bother Hank with this. It's not as if they're partners at this point.

She drives the long way to South Boston, avoiding Chinatown.

It makes her skittish. Edgy. Makes her remember that night with the kid in the slouchy jeans. She makes a wide loop and keeps her eyes on the road. She hasn't done anything even remotely like police work in months. Hasn't had to, not since she left the force. Maggie plays it safe these days, sticks to the forms and sticky notes, some investigations. She stays on her beige stage, alone, except for the occasional phone call to a client—*Your husband, Mrs. Randolph, was he seventy-eight or seventy-nine? I can't quite read the writing on page three*—and sporadic conversations with the agents, the greetings and leave-takings, the swapping of vital information. Aside from these brief contacts, she usually has very little interaction at work, which Maggie thinks might be a good thing. At least for now.

She glances at the street. Shops are less expensive here than downtown; it's a mix of old and new. Southie's up-and-coming, but the people are more casually dressed, the sidewalks far less crowded. She pulls into the lot at O'Brien's and takes out her notepad. A car backfire echoes against the hollow insides of the building and Maggie shudders. It's almost imperceptible. She's gotten good at not reacting visibly. She's better now, she tells herself, but when she's honest with herself, she knows she's only managed to suppress her feelings, that her nerves are raw and that open wounds run along her bones and veins and skin. She knows that fear goes somewhere, shock and guilt and fear. It doesn't simply go away.

She waits for her heart to slow down, takes a couple of deep breaths, and then she walks over to the garage, shakes hands with Ian, one of the O'Brien brothers, tells him why she's there, and Ian points her to the Audi, out back in an old shed. "All this snow and ice." He shrugs, makes a sideways motion with the flats of his hands. "Hell. If the car was outside, there'd be nothin' left of it to see, let alone sell. Parts'd be ruined."

"Mind if I take a look?"

"Have at it." Ian nods his head, walks back to the heated garage to work on something worth saving, something that the Audi, Maggie sees the second she opens the shed door, is definitely not. She's surprised at how hard the car hit. Newbury's not a main thoroughfare, so even if Lindsay was skidding on ice, the brakes should have slowed it down enough to avoid the kind of damage she's looking at here. She snags an old crate with the toe of her boot and pulls it closer to the car, glances around her at the building that was probably a warehouse before O'Brien Towing bought it with the land decades ago. She sits against the wall and squints at the car. Wind drifts in through spaces between boards and Maggie wonders if it was always this drafty or if all the winters have together warped the wood, made the gaps. She remembers coming here with Hank to check on cars involved in robberies, jackings, hit-and-runs. She leans back. The floor smells like straw.

She'd left the Boston Police Department on her own. There'd been no sanctions from on high, no slap on the hand. No one really knew the truth of it except Hank, and even that was because Maggie finally told him. It was just after her fourth-year anniversary, not that anyone besides her mother and her sister actually kept track. Summertime. July. Middle of a heat wave, lots of people on the street. A shop owner in Chinatown hit a silent alarm in the middle of a robbery, and Hank and Maggie got the call.

They'd maneuvered through the cramped, tight neighborhood

and turned on Hunter Street, with its vibrant sounds and colors, the glut of signs and people, the lack of space. They'd turned off the engine and coasted to the front of the store. There was a kid with a hoodie, slouchy pants, the usual, but when Hank and Maggie got inside, the place was a mess. It looked like someone had gone crazy in there—bags all over, food spilled everywhere, and the owner hunkered down on the floor against the wall, looking scared to death.

"Put your hands behind your head and turn around real slow," Maggie told the kid. "*Real* slow." But the boy reached inside his pocket, grabbed something, and whirled toward them, pointing it at Maggie.

"Fuck!" Hank was right behind her in the doorway, and Maggie aimed her gun at the kid, but she couldn't pull the trigger. She froze.

It turned out all right. In truth, it was the best possible outcome. The weapon the boy pulled on them was just a pipe he'd picked up from the street, a construction site, his own *house,* maybe, but it wasn't a gun like they'd both thought.

"Good call as it happens," the chief told her and Hank the next night when they came in. "But sheer luck it went down the way it did. You don't ever wanna take that kind of chance. He could easily have killed you. Either that or messed you up for life. The both of yous." And Maggie knew it wasn't a good call, even if Hank didn't, even if he thought she'd seen the kid only had a pipe. It was something else that rendered her unable to react, froze her like a statue in the doorway to that shop on Hunter Street, that put her somewhere else for those few crucial seconds, put her in a jeep in Iraq, as snipers fired out of a window in a building somewhere down the road. For that small space of time she was every bit as helpless as she was the day several rounds of bullets killed three friends behind her in the Humvee she was driving into Baghdad.

She'd given her notice four days later. She'd stayed on for a couple of weeks, rode with Hank the same as always, but things were different after that night. Maggie was different. She couldn't trust herself to not screw up when it really mattered. She wasn't sure she'd act in the best interest of the ones around her, protect the lives she was supposed to save. "I need my eight hours of beauty sleep," she'd told her partner. "This night shift's killing me." And it was only months later, when she'd been at the insurance company for a while, that she told Hank the real reason she had left the force.

For a second, Maggie wonders if that's why she's here—if it has nothing to do with Joseph Lindsay's life insurance policy or an extra Starbucks cup rolling around the front seat of his car. Did seeing Hank the other day spark something, make her miss the old days, when she felt connected, alive? Was this her chance to put things right, to prove that she's got what it takes, not only to the chief and the department, but to herself?

She starts to get up. She takes a last look at the Audi and shakes her head. What a waste. And then she sees something, a piece of plastic. She squats down and then she lies on her back and pulls herself under the wrecked front end of the car.

It looks like a tie wrap.

What the fuck?

She looks closer, touches the thing. She knows about cars. She takes a few shots with her iPhone before she stands up, and then she takes more photos of the outside and the inside of the car, where she finds a lid jammed down beside the seat. She grew up in that kind of family, the kind that pieced together junkers and kept them on the road—jalopies they'd've scrapped if they weren't so broke all the time, eking out a living, making engines run way past their prime. She stoops down again, fiddles with the tie wrap pulled against the scuffed brake line. She grins. All those afternoons spent helping out her brothers paid off every now and then. It made sense to come here after all. Now, with this goddamn tie wrap fastening a damaged line. Someone tied the brake line to a rough piece of the suspension and over time, the scraping of the line would cause the brake to fail. On a night like that Friday night Joe Lindsay died, the swerving of the steering wheel, his sudden desperate jamming on the brakes just might do it.

XII

KAREN

aren double-bolts the door behind her and tosses her coat across the arm of the living room sofa. She takes off her boots and lets the dog out in the snowy backyard—she doesn't have the energy to take him for a walk. Anyway, it's nearly dark and she won't chance coming home to a bunch of footprints or some stranger with his nose pressed up against her windows. She lets Antoine inside again, locks the doors, and heads to the back of the house. There are so many questions. They make her head throb, all these questions—that and her abysmal lunch with Edward. She rummages through her purse for a bottle of aspirin.

Edward is mistaken. He must be. Joe was many things—a procrastinator, a womanizer. But not a thief. Besides, Joe lived and breathed Home Runs. He kept the company impeccable, beyond reproach, and, despite his philandering, Karen will do anything she can to defend his legacy. Her future—her life—is inextricably tied to Home Runs Renovations. If the company goes under, so does she.

It isn't only the money, her livelihood, her husband's legacy, but the chance it offers her to do again what she did for years, the one thing she was really good at—the one job she really loved.

She crosses her arms and looks around at the small back room, her husband's makeshift office, sprinkled with doggie beds and toys. Antoine preferred him to her, spending hours on end sprawled at Joe's feet with a chew toy lying, damp and gummy, between his sturdy little paws.

It should all be here. Joe spent half his life on the road—surely what she needs will be on his computer. Doubtless, he's made copies too. "Covering all the bases," he used to say, so it must be here in this mishmash. She'll find it. Even though she isn't sure exactly what she's looking for, she'll find it and prove Edward wrong. She'll stay up all night if she has to, see for herself if Joe has tampered with the finances. And if he has, she'll figure out how deep a hole they're actually in. She'll look for clues about his girlfriend, too. If there is anything about her here, Karen will find it.

She puts in Joe's password and pulls up the spreadsheets on the company accounts, the invoices, the payments. Thankfully, they're recent, the ones from farther back are saved in separate files. Karen grabs three aspirins and swallows them dry.

She scans the screen in front of her and then she studies it more closely. Confusing. The dearth of clients she'd expected is not what's here in front of her, unfolding like graphed witnesses across the monitor. She compares the latest pricing to matching invoices from previous years and finds little change. In fact, the most recent invoices show slightly elevated pricing, so, clearly, the company has not been forced to lower their charges to keep customers. She scrolls back through the cost sheets, the invoices, scrutinizing each line to see if people simply haven't paid. But according to the spreadsheet, they have. All of them. Some were late, but even they paid eventually. And there were several more accounts last year than the year before.

So, what's Edward talking about?

She stretches, makes herself a salad. The excruciating headache is receding, but it's still there, lurking, reminding her she's let her body get completely out of whack since Joe's death. Her face, when she looks in the mirror, is thin and puffy at the same time. Too much wine, too much chocolate, too much Xanax, no protein to speak of, and it's difficult to even picture vegetables, she's ignored them for so long. She takes a deep breath, spears an artichoke from a jar, and adds it to a giant wedge of lettuce. She'll get herself on track. She needs her wits about her now.

Back in Joe's old office, she fumbles through her husband's briefcase and comes up with a small day planner filled with lines, crammed with details. Maybe she'll find something here about the company or maybe he'll have penciled in his trysts. Bastard. She gives it a cursory look and finds that it is basically a travel log. Nothing shocking here. Not a word about understudyfork. At least not at first glance. She sits; she studies every boring word. Nothing. Not until she reaches the loose papers Joe's stuck in the back of the planner. "Meet with Arthur Reinfeld," he's scrawled across the first sheet. She flips through the rest of the loose papers and there's another small scrawl at the corner of a blank page. "Met with A.R." Reinfeld, Karen supposes. The company accountant. She's never met him, but she knows the name.

She walks back to the kitchen and sticks the Arthur Reinfeld note on the fridge with a magnet. She'll investigate at some point; she'll call him. She grabs a cup of decaf and heads back to Joe's office, shakes out all the papers from the back of the day planner, and puts them in a tiny pile. No dates, so she isn't sure of the order; there's no cohesion, really. They're like little random upchuckings that he's jotted on the pages, often just one line.

Brakes pulling. Ask Karen to take car in.

Vagrant in garage at work this morning. Sketchy guy. Talk with security.

Antoine to vet if Karen can't. (*Wouldn't* was more like it. She had trouble with Antoine on a fun frolic—forget about trying to get him in the car.)

Airbag light on. Check this.

She sips the cooling decaf. She had taken Joe's car in, but Hoods is only mediocre now. *Take it back in,* Joe had said, after the brake job. *You got rooked.* But she didn't take it back. It was only the memories of Tomas, of the happy times with him that made her go back there at all.

This glimpse of her late husband's thoughts has made her hungry for more. Karen tugs at all the drawers in the file cabinet, rifling through them quickly, coming up with nothing but some old bank statements. She sticks the last of the files in the drawer—tries to, anyway. There's something jammed at the back, stopping them from fitting. A box. She tugs it loose—a gift she'd given Joe three Christmases before. A stocking stuffer, something she'd imagined he could use at work, or in his car, or his files, as he apparently has. She stares at it. He's locked the silly lock on the outside—a lock like the one Lydia had on her diary in the fifth grade, designed to keep out snoopy little sisters, which it had not done. Karen remembers popping the thing open with a paperclip, spilling Lydia's secrets out into her eager, eight-year-old hands. She does this now, picking the lock with a hairpin. Deftly, but with care and much anticipation, she pulls up the lid. Other people's secrets are intoxicating.

She breathes in the cedar odor of the box and thumbs through its contents, feels a stab of guilt as she glances down at ancient letters from Joe's mother, now long dead, the occasional short note from his father, also dead. Pictures slide from a frail envelope into her hand— old photos from Joe's childhood, his mother, young in shorts, his father stern, in white trousers and a jaunty sport coat—a grim man, the opposite of Joe.

She tugs at a newer, far less fragile envelope, stuffed full of pictures from their life together. Joe, shaggy-haired in Miami the year they lived down near the bay—Karen with her hair tied back, her shoulders tan in a sundress, her feet in handmade sandals from the Grove.

She stares at the pictures and forgotten moments float up from their curling edges—laughter from the docks, the creaking of a ship's rigging, Joe's crumbling old apartment on Loquat Street, the first time they slept together, the bumpy bus with stuck-open windows, cold air puffing in as she rode to his place in winter, the jalousies in his apartment that never really closed or opened all the way, the cold and heat that seeped in through the glass. She remembers music playing, her foot tapping, bare, tanned toes, remembers touching, skin to skin, the passion, the lovemaking, waking to the smell of salt air drifting through the bedroom window. At night the wind blew through the flapping screen door, caught them where they lay, their naked legs dark in the moonlight. Sometimes, in summer, it was so still, the sound of crickets roared in the side yard and pot smoke hung thick and sweet in the air. *Who said punning is the lowest form of humor?* Joe asked once, stretched out across a straw mat on her sister's porch, and she'd said he was only jealous—he felt left out when they launched into their routine. It was an acquired taste in their family, Lydia told him, "like opening veins," and they'd laughed, and Joe stared out through the screen as if he weren't even there.

Is that when it started, she wonders now—the space between them? Where does it go, the falling into each other's arms, the passion, the lovemaking? And afterward—lying together talking, dredging up all your stuff from the past and breathing it into the other person, while his pores are still open from making love, like you can, in some way, make him know you, how you've come to be what you are at that moment, with your hair piled on top of your head and your nineteen-year-old hands lying palms up on tangled sheets?

She sighs. Tears trickle down her cheeks. And here's their marriage license, the bill from that little restaurant where they had their reception. A small one. Intimate, with poetry on fancy place cards, hand-dipped candles on the tables, Edith Piaf warbling from speakers on the walls.

And then another envelope with nothing in it but a solitary picture, a special little niche for this photograph she would never have known to look for. She coughs. She holds the picture out, away from her body, as if it were on fire, this photo of her husband with another woman. She stares at the photograph and her hand shakes with rage, with disbelief. She knows her, recognizes the face, something about the face, the expression. Who *is* it? She closes her eyes. This woman was at the funeral, at the cemetery. Karen saw her when she turned around, when she thought she saw someone in the trees. Even then, she hadn't quite remembered where she'd seen her . . . Was it a neighbor? Someone at the company? Yes. Karen stares at the picture. She'd seen her at a Christmas party at the office. Last year's party. Joe introduced them. Darlene, she thinks, or, no. Dorreen.

She sits down on the daybed. The springs give under her weight. An old daybed, a junk-shop find. She should really throw it out. She'll phone the people from St. Vincent's. Dorreen. But they called her something else. Dorrie. Of course. Dorrie. She was married. Karen remembers meeting the husband at the same Christmas party. The smoker, obliviously inhaling nicotine while his wife was in a hotel room with her boss, with Joe. And if Karen needed any more proof, the look on Dorrie's face at the cemetery—the raw expression in her eyes when Karen turned around—*that*, if she had stopped to think about it at the time, if it had registered in her distracted brain, would have been proof enough.

She forces herself to look at her husband's face in the picture, at the lines across his forehead, the crease between his eyes. She studies his haircut, his clothes, distracts herself with trying to guess exactly when the shot was taken. Really, it doesn't matter now. And yet, in some odd way, it does. *A year ago*, she says out loud in the silence, in the ashes of her husband's life, in the room filled with his things, where he kept his girlfriend's picture in a box his wife gave him. *In the spring*, she says. *I bought this shirt at a Macy's sale. I pulled it off the rack and brought it home a year ago this spring.*

She leans against the wall on the daybed Antoine has completely ruined. She sits on a tattered quilt the dog has twisted into a large swirl from turning around three times before he sits. Or lies.

Lies, Karen says aloud, and she looks back at the photo in her hand. Once, in the waiting room at the doctor's office, she'd read an article on infidelity. Men cheat for different reasons, it said, but, contrary to popular belief, the other woman is usually not all that attractive—that isn't what the straying husband really wants. He wants someone genuine, even plain, according to the article, someone who can offer him a little understanding, validation. Basically, he wants a wife without the kids and dirty dishes—without the years of baggage.

Yet Dorrie is beautiful. At least in this picture. And she loved him. It's in her eyes, how much she loved him, the way her head tilts slightly toward his shoulder, her small, slight figure leaning back against his arm. In the photograph, her hair blows over her shoulder as she turns to look at a group of what look like mimes. A street fair.

For a minute Karen can't get her breath. She's furious. Hurt. Shocked. In her head she knew Joe was seeing someone else, but now, with this tangible and blatant truth, she knows it in her heart. She'd rationalized. Just as she always has, she'd stored away her knowledge, her anger, for later. Really, she knew there was someone else even before she found the e-mails. She knew it from the way her husband touched her—and from the way he didn't, the nights he slipped in bed without a sound, without a whisper. No more "Karen? Are you awake?" No more of that.

She looks back at the picture. It's the eyes she notices. Large and green and slightly sad. The eyes of a victim. Joe has always had a soft spot for victims. But only pretty ones.

She slides down to sit cross-legged on the floor. She feels as if her entire married life has been a lie. And, at the root of it, it was. Their sons, of course, their sons are real and perfect—nothing can take that away from her or from her marriage. But Joe. She drops her head into her hands. He was a lie. She closes her eyes, and sees his face, and then, for just a fraction of a second, she sees her father's face, the round white moon of it, shining through a murky window, her father, ripping through the early fabric of her life. Preparing her. Setting her up. For this. For the lie that was her husband.

Suddenly she wants the photo gone, this testament to Joe's affair. It has no place here in her house, and this she finds to be the most outrageous thing of all—that he would bring this fucking picture *here* to their home, to the place where she cooked dinners, gave Christmas parties, raised their sons. Here! And the Samuel in the e-mail. Of course. His name was *Samuel*! Dorrie's husband. Sam, she thinks was how his wife presented him that night. *This is my husband, Sam.*

She wipes her eyes and rips the photograph in half and then she rips it again and then again, until there's nothing left but tiny slivers, tiny flakes of flesh and hair, of sad green eyes and white lace blouse and Macy's sale-rack, sky-blue shirt. When she's finished, she goes to the basement for a broom, dumps the tiny scraps into a bin she'll wheel out to the street for Wednesday morning pickup.

Joe has managed this last blow. *From the grave,* her mother would have said, with a slight vindictive sneer—she'd never liked him. *I told you so.* For a moment Karen thinks of shredding everything her husband valued, his entire lifetime of collections—the photos he does not deserve. Not now. The letters from the past thirty years—what right has he to any of them? To anything at all? No matter that he's dead. She thinks about burning his things, about not passing them along to either of his sons. She considers going to Dorrie's house and banging on her door, of outing her to her stupid husband who smokes cigarettes and leaves his empty packs on the dining room table.

She grabs the box *she* purchased, the box *she* wrapped and put under the tree one Christmas, the box, polluted now by that one picture. She rifles through the few remaining papers with a careless and exacting hand. She'll throw it out. All of it. Unless it has to do with the company or with her, with Robbie or Jon directly, there's no point in holding on to anything Joe's—

She stops. She leans back on her heels and nearly drops the envelope—second to the last in a stack of letters bound together with a sticky, crumbling rubber band.

She stares at the writing on the envelope addressed to her. Opened, but addressed to her. She flips it over, but even before she does, she knows whose name she'll find there on the back. She knows it's from Tomas.

XIII

DORRIE

Dorrie leaves the glove on Samuel's workbench and slips back through the garage door. By the time she's reached the living room, she's already texting Viv.

We need to meet tonight! She skips the details, gets straight to the point. *Seven? In the lobby?*

Okay, Viv texts her back, *I'll meet you down in the—* But Dorrie doesn't read the rest. She sticks the phone in her purse and glances at the empty cobbler plate on the kitchen counter. A note peeps out from under it. Lily. Damn. *At the library,* she's scrawled, *doing research.* She must have left with Mia. Or maybe with the new boy, the science geek. Dorrie doesn't even know his name. Michael, is it? They—*Lily*—must have left while Dorrie was plowing through her husband's things in search of Goop. She's slipping. She hadn't even heard a car honk in the driveway.

You are in serious trouble, she texts Lily.

Sorry, Mom. I couldn't find you. I'll be back as soon as we're done at school. Study group. Home by nine.

Who is we?

Mia and me. Smiley face. Heart. Smiley face.

She texts Samuel, props Lily's note against his precious Keurig. She'll take the train, avoid the traffic, especially with ice still on the roads, but she is careful, walking to the station. She stays along the lit sidewalk. She keeps her eyes open, watches for approaching cars. She moves quickly, erratically. Once inside the station, she averts her eyes, waiting. Odors stick on the dank thick air, and Dorrie breathes them in, the smell of grease and electricity, of crowded bodies, damp wool, and cold. Lights flicker. Brakes scream, echoing in the hollow space. She scrambles into the first car when the train shrieks to a stop. She sits beside a window, happy when an older man sits down beside her. Hefty as he is, he blocks her from the aisle, makes her almost invisible, and she stares at the black window, so close the glass fogs with her breath.

Dorrie sits in the restaurant at the hotel. She's chosen the bench side, where she feels less exposed, and she fluffs the bright, orangey pillows at her back. Across the table, Viv fidgets with her silverware, moves her glass, twirls up the edges of the tablecloth. She glances around the room as if she's looking for a sniper.

"So?" Dorrie leans back. She feels safe in the warmth sipping wine, surrounded by odors from the hotel kitchen—relaxed here in the plush Copley, at a cozy table with her best friend in the world. "Thanks for getting together tonight," Dorrie says. "I don't think I could have waited until tomorrow. I really *had* to get out of the house."

Viv shrugs. "My schedule's pretty free for the moment," she says. "Work starts next Tuesday, but until then I'm totally— Oh," she says. "I'm auditioning for a play at the Huntington next Thursday. Why don't you come? You could try out for—"

"I might. I saw it online actually." Dorrie takes a swallow of wine. "So that guy? Ralph, was it? The guy whose den you updated."

Viv waves her hand in a dismissive gesture. "Yeah. Good old Ralph. Good old Ralph and *Janice*."

"He was *married*?"

"Who knew?" Viv says. She takes a drink of wine, but she does it with such drama, it could be hemlock.

"Well," Dorrie says. "*He* knew. I mean he could have *mentioned* it." This isn't really a topic she wants to pursue. "Speaking of marriage," she says, "husbands and such . . ."

"What?" Viv fusses with the placemat, lines it up exactly with the edge of the tabletop.

"Samuel." Dorrie sighs. "He's acting so—I don't know—weird, so *estranged* or something. It's a little scary."

Viv leans forward. She looks frantic. Dorrie takes a sip of wine. "There's something I have to tell you." Viv's face is so much paler than when Dorrie first saw her in the lobby, her hair almost black against the pastiness of her skin.

"Are you sick?" Dorrie leans forward "Are you—?"

"No," she says. "But I do have to tell you something about Samuel."

"*Samuel?*"

"Sometimes I wish I still smoked," Viv says. She tosses her head. Ever the diva. "Don't you?"

"Well, no, actually," Dorrie says, "but I never really smoked."

Viv nods. She glances at the waiter, who's just bounced out from the kitchen.

"So?"

"Samuel and I," she says. "We had this—"

"Oh my *God*!"

"Just hold on," Viv says, but she edges her chair back from the table.

"What?"

"Samuel called me one night. Weeks ago when I was in Boston for a few days, a couple days. It was a night or two after you and I got together. Remember? We went to the—what?—that play over in Cambridge. We talked about trying out for a part there—can't remember what the part was—were. There were two that we—"

Dorrie squints across the table at her friend and suddenly she notices how beautiful Viv is. She looks at her from Samuel's perspective, with her perfect alabaster skin. The dark curls. The violet eyes. "I had a contract in town, or, no. It wasn't in town. It was Dedham. Drapes. A short job, a few days."

Dorrie gazes out the window, looking for the health food store where she and Samuel used to buy vitamins and bulk oats and dried apricots the summer he made shelves out of old discarded boards that ran the length of the kitchen. They filled the shelves with large glass jars of rice and barley, beans of every hue, that year—their vegan year.

The waiter swoops back to their table and takes their orders, reaches for their menus, which he snaps shut and sticks under his

108

arm as he hurries to the kitchen. Dorrie takes another sip of wine, tries to focus on Viv's prattling, tries to rein her in. "So? You and *Samuel*?"

"He said you weren't home. 'I never know where Dorrie is these days,' he said. He sounded—I don't know—frustrated, I guess. Kind of pissed, but something else, too. Kind of—"

"Drunk?"

"Huh." Viv looks at her, raises one eyebrow. "Yeah. Probably. I didn't actually think about it at the time, but, now that you mention it . . . Anyway, he insisted I meet him downstairs. 'It's important,' he said. 'It's about Dorrie.'" The waiter comes back with their salads and Viv pauses while he sets them down. For a minute they both pick at the smattering of greens, tossed like a Pollock painting across the plain white, understated plates.

Dorrie chews. Lettuce sticks in her throat; she reaches for her water glass. "And you told him . . . What exactly *did* you tell him, Viv?"

"He said it was about you, so I told him yes, of course. I told him I'd meet him in the lobby. 'One drink. That's it,' I said."

"Was it here?" Dorrie wonders out loud. "Did you meet him here?"

Viv looks around, as if she's just parachuted into the middle of the dining room—as if she's amazed to be here. "Actually," she says, "it was."

"Huh." Dorrie tries to picture Samuel leaning over the spotless tablecloth, drawing a linen napkin across his bourbony lips. "So cut to the chase, Viv. What is it you feel compelled to tell me right *now* as opposed to when it might have been a little more—um—ap*prop*riate? Relevant?"

Viv shrugs. "I wasn't in good shape at that point. Jacques and I had just recently split up. And I was drinking way too much."

"Ah, yes. Jacques. Husband number what? Three? Four? So back to *my* husband . . ."

"Well . . ." Viv's eyes shift away from Dorrie's face. "We chatted for a while."

"And drank for a while?"

"Yes. It got late. One thing led to another . . . He asked me if he could come upstairs for a minute. Just to get himself together."

"And you, being the gracious hostess you are . . ."

"He was really a mess. I tried to send him home, but he had his car and he wouldn't let me call a cab. Plus, he still hadn't told me whatever he was supposedly there to tell me about *you*."

The waiter brings their food, but Dorrie isn't very hungry. She stabs at her pasta, twirls the vermicelli around her fork.

"So did you bring him upstairs?"

"I didn't *bring* him upstairs. I let him use my *bathroom,* Dorrie. I let him lie *down* for a minute, get himself *together.* That's all."

"Did he come on to you?"

Viv shrugs again. "In a bumbling sort of way, I guess. There were a few 'I always thought you were so gorgeous' comments— 'Independent women are so interesting'—some of that, but he wasn't serious. He was just trying to—"

"*Seduce* you?"

"No. Trying to be macho, or something. He was really upset about that guy you were seeing—forgot his name. The one who just—"

"Wait. So he knew about *Joe*?"

Viv nods. "I think so. Not who it was, but that there was some-one. Yeah."

"How? How would he *know*?"

Viv shakes her head. "I thought maybe you told him."

"No. I had no idea Samuel knew about— You didn't tell him anything, did you?"

"Not a word. I acted like the whole idea was ridiculous. And, Dorrie I am so *so* sorry about the accident. I know you must be—"

Dorrie waves her hand in the air. "Go on," she says.

"He just really didn't seem like *Samuel* that night. Maybe it was the booze, but he seemed really—I don't know—like not who I thought he was." Viv stops eating and stares across the table.

"And who exactly *was* he, Viv?"

"Well," she says, totally unfazed, Dorrie thinks, consider-ing they're discussing what her best friend's husband said while stretched out across Viv's bed in a hotel room. "He just seemed really angry, like I said. Reckless."

"I always knew you liked Samuel," Dorrie says. "Since the first time you met him, I knew you—"

"No I didn't, Dorrie. To be honest," Viv says, and Dorrie holds up her hand like a traffic cop, but Viv bulldozes right along. "To be honest, I always envied you. You seemed to have everything—a daughter, a house, a husband who adores y—"

"Oh for—don't even *think* of going there."

"Okay." She chews some more. "But he does."

"Husbands who adore their wives don't try to seduce their wives' best friends," Dorrie says. She wonders fleetingly if Jerry Springer is still on the air.

Viv scoots her chair a little closer to the table. "He said you didn't love *him* anymore. 'She can't even bring herself to look at me half the time,' he said, and then he passed out cold. When he woke up an hour or so later, he seemed like Samuel again. I mean, he was still drunk, but not *as* drunk. He phoned for a cab and took off. 'I'm really sorry, Viv,' he told me. 'I don't know what I was thinking.'"

"And it didn't occur to you to call me at that exact *second* he left the hotel to tell me what happened?"

"I *did,* actually. I called your cell, but you didn't answer and I just hung up. I didn't want to take a chance on Samuel getting the message instead of you."

Dorrie doesn't say anything. There actually were a couple of missed calls from Viv awhile back. She just hadn't bothered to return them. And then Joe . . .

"Of course by then I had a different—I had to change my number. But that's a whole other story."

"You could have called the house. You could have texted me a message. You could have—hell—you could have sent me a message on Facebook," Dorrie says, even though they both know she never even looks at Facebook; she's quit and rejoined several times in the last year.

"Really, I didn't want to face you after that. Not that anything *happened.* It was just that I hadn't told you at the *time,* so then it kind of became a bigger deal than it actually was. And then there was the whole Samuel part of the thing—I didn't want to make things worse between you two." She sighs. "But I couldn't keep not telling you. Anyway, he was— when we were still downstairs, before he got really drunk, he said something about how he didn't know what was going on, but that he'd find out. 'She's never even home,' he told me. 'This has gotta stop.' So, really, I had to tell you. Eventually. When I got back to town, I called you up first thing." Viv wipes her mouth daintily on a flowered napkin and turns her violet eyes on Dorrie. "Can you forgive me?"

"I don't know." Dorrie stares at her friend across the table. "I mean, how could you just not *tell* me something like this?" But then, for a second, she thinks about everything she's kept from Samuel. From Lily. From everyone. She sighs.

"So," Viv says after a minute or two. "This accident you mentioned. Your boss and everything. What happened?"

Dorrie shakes her head. "It can wait."

"Next time, then."

Dorrie doesn't answer. She isn't sure there'll be a next time.

They say good-bye in the lobby. Dorrie doesn't move away when Viv leans forward to give her a little hug, but she doesn't really return the hug, either. She fumbles through her purse for her wallet, drops a five-dollar bill in the guitar case of a kid who's singing on a freezing, treeless spot of ground across the street. "Plaisir d'Amour." Appropriate.

She walks quickly to the train, her breath sharp and shallow. Again she's careful to look around as she heads into the station. She takes a window seat in the nearly empty car and thinks about Samuel. It was so totally out of character for him to go to Viv's hotel the way he did, but Viv did say he wasn't acting like himself that night—not until he woke up and apologized and left. Thank *God,* he left. *She's never home,* he'd whined to Viv, even though it wasn't true at all, even though it was Samuel who was rarely home. And then there was his insistence, upsetting, in light of recent events that *this has gotta stop,* and Dorrie shivers in the overheated subway car because she suddenly has no idea who her husband really is. Or Viv, or, really, who she is. Now. She feels wispy. Stuck. She feels like a question mark that she yearns to pound out straight and flat and strong, into an exclamation point.

XIV

DORRIE

D orrie takes a taxi from the train station and makes it home
before Samuel. Sliding through the kitchen door into the
garage, she averts her eyes, ignores the lone glove, peeking out like a thick black sin. She walks back to Samuel's shelves
of toxins, to the ziplock bag she'd spotted earlier. She tugs it out
from its hiding spot and stares at three neatly rolled joints inside.
Shit. She plunks down on a wooden stool Samuel's pulled up to
the workbench. Lily. She grapples through her bag and pulls out
her phone.

Where are you?

Library, Lily texts her back. *I told you.* Question mark. Confused face.

Come home NOW. Dorrie throws her cell back in her purse
and sighs. Is it this new kid? This boy? The science nerd? Mia?
No. Mia's totally focused on school and college and—God. Is Lily
really even *at* the library, or are she and this stupid pothead *guy*

swerving around stoned? She should have told her daughter to stay there, right where she was—told her not to move an inch, that she'd come pick her up. She still can. She reaches for her phone. But what if Lily isn't really *at* the library? What if they get in a wreck trying to make it there before Dorrie? No. She won't go. She'll wait.

She closes her eyes in the cold of the garage, remembers acting out the casts of characters in Lily's bedtime stories all those years ago. For a while, Samuel would join them, walking over to the little wooden bed he made for Lily that always looked to Dorrie like a box of forty-eight crayons, covered in quilts, Lily in her blue nightgown. All the colors.

"Gonna have a story tonight?" Samuel might ask, and Lily would clap her little hands in delight, scooting over so he could squeeze himself onto the tiny, sloping mattress, flop his legs over the footboard, cross his arms under his head as Dorrie conjured princesses and genies and lamps, flinging them into the room to escort Lily off to sleep. She sighs, wishing she could take a magic carpet ride back there for just a day. A night. An hour, even, that she could shrink her daughter back into that crayon bed, the blue nightgown with the cat embroidered on the pocket.

She fiddles with a box of matches on the scarred wood of the workbench, pulls her coat tightly around her as she props open a small window. Music drifts from a neighbor's house, a clarinet and something else. A trombone, maybe. She strikes a match and sticks one of the joints between her lips, inhales deeply as the sound of the horns merge and blend and dance across the night.

At some point Dorrie hears a car pull up in the driveway, but it takes off too quickly for her to see if it *was* actually Mia in her little butter-colored car. She slips into the house as Lily storms through the front door. *So embarrassing,* she hurls back over her shoulder. Her heavy boots thump loudly on the stairs.

"Wait," Dorrie calls. "We need to talk," but Lily keeps going. "I can't! I have hours more work to do. On my *own* now, since you don't trust me to be at the *library* with a *study* group! Since you forced me to come *home*! What more do you *want*?"

"Tomorrow then." Dorrie decides not to press the point. She feels a little spacey anyway, standing there in the living room in her coat. She tries to remember the last time she smoked pot. Fifteen years ago? Twenty?

Samuel's car pauses in the driveway and then, a moment later, pulls into the garage. Dorrie sighs. Samuel is the last person in the world she wants to see, especially now, after she's just learned he spewed out their life problems, stretched across Viv's hotel bed in a room the size of a postage stamp. Still. Lily is his daughter, too.

She meets him in the doorway. The garage is freezing, but she steps across the threshold and eases the door closed behind her. "Lily's smoking pot," she announces in a stage whisper even before he's all the way out of his car. "I found it. It's probably that guy she likes. The science nerd. Or at least that's what she and Mia call—"

"Found what?" he says, but Dorrie is already squeezing between Samuel's car and several piles of junk. She grabs the baggie from behind the box of nails.

"This," she says. "Lily's stash. Do they still call it that? Stash or—"

"Oh." He stands in the icy garage and stares down at the baggie Dorrie's plunked into his palm.

"Oh? Our daughter's smoking weed *here* at the *house* and all

you can come up with is *oh?*" Her teeth chatter and she clomps them together.

"It isn't Lily's."

"Huh? Well then who . . . ? Oh." She giggles.

Samuel flips the baggie back and forth in his hands and it makes a thin, slithery sound, like a fish. "Wait." He looks at her, his eyebrows knotting in a frown. "I guess she *is* smoking pot."

"Why? I thought you just said it was—well, *implied* it was your—"

"Yeah," Samuel says. "It is, but there were—there's a joint missing. I don't know—should we—maybe we should wake her up, give her the whole Say-No-To-Drugs talk right now. But with me being the one who— Of course, I am an adult, so really . . ."

"Which makes it *legal* for *you*, right?"

"Yeah. That's right." Samuel looks around. He looks trapped. Since his daughter thinks he's basically infallible, Dorrie almost feels sorry for him until she remembers the whole Viv thing.

"Why's the window open? It's cold as a— Wait!" Samuel moves a little closer, sniffing like a bloodhound. "Hey! Jesus, Dorrie!"

She giggles again, relieved. With Lily, there will be a ton of other issues, now that she's tumbled into that dark terrain of adolescence. Still, it won't be this particular one. Not tonight.

"Why?" she says when Samuel's forced the sticky window closed and locked the kitchen door behind them.

He shrugs. "It helps. It takes the edge off."

She doesn't ask him what kind of edge. She doesn't want to know. "Beautiful," she says instead.

"What?"

"The horns."

118

Samuel shakes his head. "I'll drive Lily to school tomorrow." He doesn't look at her. "A little father-daughter time," he mumbles. "Comin' up?" He tosses his coat over a chair in the living room and starts upstairs.

"No," Dorrie says. "I have a headache. I think I'll just stretch out here on the couch for a minute—"

XV

KAREN

And there it is. Karen pours herself a glass of stale Oyster Bay before she even takes the letter out of the envelope that's stuck halfway back together with old damp glue from the flap. It's postmarked two years before. She takes a sip of wine and gently tugs on the thin sheet of paper.

My dearest Karen,

I am here in my mother's town, but I am wishing to be back in the States with you. I so much want to be there in Boston, to be working again at the hospital, and to see you. I close my eyes and see the tulips starting to bloom by the river, and I can almost taste the pastrami at that deli where you took me downtown.

I miss you, beautiful Karen. I hope to soon be back in

Boston, but until then please do not forget me and please
write to me here at my mother's home.

Love always,
Tomas

The writing is overly slanted to the right, and his name is signed
with such a flourish, Karen isn't sure if Joe could even make it out.
Only Tomas's last name is on the back flap, along with his mother's
address in Honduras.

She takes another sip of wine and sits back on her heels. What
must Joe have thought? The letter didn't sound platonic. It was actually extremely personal, romantic, even. Joe would have assumed she
and Tomas were having an affair. Of course he would have because
Joe was a philanderer himself, at least potentially, when he inter-
cepted Tomas's letter. Funny, Karen thinks, how that works. Funny
how she didn't realize Joe was cheating until his little twit literally
spelled things out for her in black and white, because she, Karen,
wouldn't have thrown away her marriage the way Joe did. People,
Karen has decided, can only project what they would do. It's the thief
who worries most that he'll be robbed, the peeping tom who pulls his
shades down tight. In this case, likely the adulterer who imagines his
wife deceiving him. Projection.

She looks back at the date on the postmark. Is that why Joe dis-
tanced himself from her so completely? Was his involvement with
the woman at work the result, rather than the *cause*, of his detach-
ment? God. Karen sits all the way down on the floor, pulls her legs
up under her, and wraps her arms around her knees. Maybe his affair

with Dorrie was payback for what he thought she'd done with Tomas. Initially, at least, which makes what he did a lot more plausible. Not necessarily forgivable, but plausible. If he thought he'd lost his wife, if he thought she had betrayed him, that she loved another man . . .

But how dare he steal a letter meant for her? How dare he grab this small and slightly sad communication from a friend on the other side of the world? It was petty and provincial and really not at all like Joe. She guzzles down the rest of the wine, but she doesn't feel the least bit tipsy. She feels suddenly more grounded than she has in months. He was jealous. Needlessly. Suddenly, she's overcome by sadness, a suffocating grief that sinks inside her bones. She stares at the letter in her hand as if she's seeing it for the first time. And then she sighs and tears it into tiny pieces, marches into the kitchen and burns it to ashes in the sink.

How could she have been so blind? So stupid? So totally oblivious? The failing business, the stolen letter, the photograph of Dorrie, this girlfriend with the smoking husband? How could she have missed all this? She gazes out the window at the snow, so bright, it's visible in the dark, blanketing the street, the yard, her car. Or did she not see any of these things because she didn't *want* to? She gets up, stumbling over Antoine. It doesn't matter. Even if she didn't want to know the details of her husband's life, of their crumbling marriage—even if, like the proverbial ostrich, she'd had her blond head stuck in sand for the past two fucking years, she's got her eyes wide open now, her head straight up, fielding all the truths bombarding her at breakneck speed. Even if she let things get away from her before, she's determined, now, to get them back, to figure out exactly how she came to be where she is, with her husband dead, a thriving business in its death throes, and a stalker marring both her front yard and her sanity.

It's late. Karen checks the locks and the alarm, stands at the broad window, and gazes out across the front yard, glancing across the street, and then as far as she can see in both directions before she heads off to bed. Tonight she'll sleep in the middle of the mattress, not huddled up against the wall, the way she has for the past two years, possibly because her husband misconstrued this stolen letter from a lonely man, uprooted from his life to nurse a dying mother. Apparently Tomas had given up and never written her again. He must have thought she didn't want to hear from him when, or, possibly, *because*, he'd left the country. Drained, but at the same time oddly energized, she falls across the bed in yoga pants and a T-shirt, sends two texts—one to Edward, telling him she's ready to talk about the business, and the other to Tomas. *Would love to have a cup of coffee sometime*, she says. *So glad you're back in Boston*. And then she turns off her cell. Quickly. Before there's any chance of a response.

The next morning Karen wakens to the ringing of the home phone in the kitchen. She rolls over, glancing at the clock, surprised to find it's nearly ten. She yawns. Stretches. Whoever it is can leave a message. Finally, she's slept through the night. Across the house, in the kitchen, Antoine's tags clang against his bowl as Karen reaches into her purse to turn on her cell.

She drags herself out of bed, ties her old blue robe around her on the way to the kitchen. She puts on coffee, lets the dog out and then back in before she picks up her new message. Not Tomas or Edward. She shakes her head. Of course, it wouldn't be Tomas—he'll call her on her cell. Or he won't call at all. She waits. A strange voice identifies herself as Maggie Brennan, from Mass Casualty and Life. "A surprising turn of events," the woman tells her. Could Karen call her back at her earliest convenience? And she's left her number.

Karen sips her coffee and finds her phone, enters Maggie Brennan's number. "Karen Lindsay," she says when Brennan answers. "You left me a message?"

"Yes." Karen hears squeaking, pictures Maggie Brennan swiveling around in a cheap office chair. "Your husband's death." There's a slight pause. "I don't want to alarm you, Mrs. Lindsay, but there are a few irregularities. I wanted to give you a heads-up, let you know I'm still looking into the claim. I'll be in touch," she says, and then she's gone.

Before Karen has a chance to think about the woman's cryptic words, a small ding announces Edward's response to her text the night before. *I'll come there,* he says. *See you early afternoon,* and she sighs, texts him back.

Fine.

She finishes her coffee standing up and makes her way through the house, attacking the visible portions with a short-lived zeal. After an exhausting two hours, the house is presentable, at least presentable enough for Edward. He arrives at one on the dot. "Lunch hour," he informs her. "I won't be staying long. There's so much to get in order down at the office."

"Lunch?" She's put together a little plate of food—veggies and fruit—and Edward scoops up a few stalks of celery, dips them in hummus. He chews. "Drink?" Karen asks, following his gaze to a collection of scotch and bourbon. His eyes narrow in on a particularly good bottle of scotch, but he shakes his head.

"Rain check," Edward says. "I'm—like I said—I'm on a quick

lunch break and then it's back to the old—the old grind. 'Balls to the wall,' as they say."

"Let's at least sit, shall we?" Karen carries the plate of nibbles to the living room and sets it on the coffee table as Antoine leaps out from under a nearby chair and sinks his teeth into Edward's ankle.

"Ow!" Edward kicks at the dog, but lightly, as if it's a game the two of them are playing and not an all-out attack on Antoine's part. "Nice doggie." He reaches down to pat Antoine on the head, and Antoine nips at his hand with a nasty little growl.

"*Antoine!*" Karen makes a grab for the dog but he skitters sideways and hides under the chair. "I'm so sorry, Edward," she says, and she surveys his hand. "At least he didn't break the skin. I think he misses Joe so much—he barely touches his food these days. Ever since the night of the accident, the poor thing has . . ." Antoine marches out from under the chair and trots into the kitchen, gobbles down a few remaining Kibbles pellets from his bowl.

"Seems to be coming around." Edward forces a wry smile and slides forward on the sofa. "I think you should sell me your half of the company," he says, and, even though this comes as no surprise at all, Karen feels shocked. Blindsided. "I can offer you three hundred thousand. Considering the shape we're in at this point, that's more than generous."

"I'm not ready for that yet, Edward," she manages, as Antoine returns from the kitchen, barking loudly at the sofa and leaping forward in tiny increments, on all four legs, toward Edward. A timely if embarrassing disruption.

"I know. And I'm sorry, Karen. I don't mean to rush you. The only reason I'm even suggesting it so soon after Joe's death . . ." Edward stops. He sighs. "It's this insurance investigation—the likelihood they'll try to paint the accident as a suicide, like I said the other day. It's easier for them. No payout that way. Insurance companies always try for suicides. That's their job, and really Maggie Brennan's—a big part of it anyway. I've been doing some research on this company, but it's almost impossible to really see what—" Edward stands up. He's almost yelling over Antoine's barking. The dog jumps backward as Edward tromps toward the kitchen with his empty plate.

"Has she said anything to you about the claim? This Maggie Brennan?"

"No. Nothing. She just—" He glances at the refrigerator and for a few seconds, he doesn't say a word. "I could just see her wheels turning. She was a cop with the Boston PD so—" He shifts his gaze to Karen. "I'm telling you—as your friend—that if you sell, I will do right by you, Karen. You know that. Listen," he says, and he buttons up his coat and hurries to the front door before Antoine can launch a fresh attack. "I've got to get back to the office. Let me know, though, when you've had a chance to think things over. Watch the dog," he says, as Antoine gallops out from the hallway. A second later the door smacks shut behind him as Edward's slick shoes skate across the icy porch.

Karen walks back to the kitchen and stares at the refrigerator. Once there were a variety of things fastened there with multicolored magnets—drawings, postcards, photos of the boys, lists for the market. Now she almost never puts things up—there are only tiny tidbits she jots down from time to time, little reminders she might leave here and there around the house. The only thing on the refrigerator now is the PROSPER magnet, sticking Arthur Reinfeld's name above

126

the handle. Did Edward see it? He did seem to fade out for a second there, staring at the fridge. And then he left. Abruptly, now that she thinks of it. Of course the dog was nipping at his heels. Literally.

Her cell dings in the living room and Karen pours herself a glass of water, runs the tap over the empty plates. She takes a swig of water, and when she's stalled for several seconds, wanders to the living room and dumps out her purse. She glances at the new text on her cell: *Of course,* Tomas has texted back. *Tell me where. I will be there happily. I am off work until the evening.*

XVI

DORRIE

Dorrie still works on her own on Tuesdays. Now she tries to cram in as many calls as possible, as many visits as she can, into this one day of the week she often spent with Joe. When he was in town. When she finished her work early. It wasn't every week, but it was often enough for her to hate Tuesdays now, to waken with a sick feeling, with a knot in her stomach and memories running through her head. Her body knows it's Tuesday, even before she opens her eyes. She's on the sofa. Fully clothed. The cat purrs on the chair arm. "Why am I—?" Purrl yawns, opens one large amber eye and Dorrie shakes away the remnants of her headache, smells the faint sweet smell of weed in the tangled ends of her hair. She groans.

Samuel and Lily have already gone, and Dorrie drags herself off the sofa, feels the Tuesday-ness envelope her. She heads for the bathroom, turns on the water, and reaching for the shampoo, remembers showering with Joe.

It was the day of their third lunch together in an earthy little restaurant in the North End. Italian, it was nearly dark, even in the middle of the day—a rainy, gloomy day. It was noisy in the restaurant and they leaned over the table to talk. Joe lit a candle in a glass lantern that reminded her of the one Samuel stole for her when they were young and barely scraping by—he'd brought it home from Papa Pasta's, where he worked three nights a week around the time Lily was born, and she had felt a sharp, quick stab of guilt. Behind them, the owners argued in Italian, their hands making shadows, like puppets, on the wall.

"My mother was Italian," she'd said. "Half Italian."

"Do you speak it?"

"A little." She tilted her ear toward the kitchen. "I understand it pretty well. Like now. The chef's saying, 'Isn't that an adorable couple out there at table five,' and the waiter's saying, 'Yeah! Especially the woman. What a cutie. Boy is that guy a lucky son of a—'"

"Really?"

"No," she said, and they'd both laughed as Dorrie picked at her lasagna. "Your wife," she'd said. "What's she like?"

"Smart," he'd told her. "Witty. Puns a lot, like you, which I've always hated. Probably because I can't do it."

Dorrie nodded, chewed, forced a smile. "She sounds really—"

"She's great." He drummed his fingers on the table. "And *we* were. We were great." He stuck his hand up for the waitress. "Things change. People change."

"That's life, though, really, isn't it? Change?" Dorrie polished off her wine. "I mean, *we* certainly have. Samuel and I. He hasn't got the slightest idea what's going on in my head most of the time.

Or, really, in my life. I don't think he even cares. Not unless it involves him directly or his job or—"

"You sound like her." He'd caught the waiter's eye, motioned for more wine, and Dorrie let all thoughts of Karen slide back into that vague region of Joe's life, so much less real than the spilled marinara sauce on the checked tablecloth, the aria drifting out through speakers near the entrance.

"Thought I'd show you how to use the design program," Joe said, and he'd pulled out his laptop, set it up on the table, patted the booth beside him. "You'll need to come over here to really see what I'm doing." And she'd scooted in beside him, watched his hands on the mouse, his long fingers, watched the different rooms invented, born, the virtual tubs, the colored walls, the floors, converted with a click.

"Here. *You* try," he'd said after a minute or two.

"I always wanted to have this for our house," she'd told him. "I always loved to watch the transformations on TV, but I didn't know this software was available. For just normal people."

"Normal?" He'd leaned over her shoulder, squinting at the bathroom she'd created, slightly unaligned, walls the color of eggplant.

"Well," she'd said. "People."

"It's okay," he'd said. "Normal is vastly overrated."

"I agree." She'd pointed to the bathroom. "Just look!"

They slept together that day. Maybe it was the wine. Maybe it was the rainy, dreamy weather, or the music in the restaurant or Dorrie wanting to erase Joe's words—*you sound like her*. He'd called ahead, reserved a room at the Harborside Inn, with rosy quilts, a red brick wall behind the bed. She felt his breath, warm on her face, warm against her body, his skin against hers. Warm.

130

Outside the rain pattered down, making splattering sounds, as the world walked by on cracking sidewalks, lumbered past on thick black streets, sloshed by in shiny rubber coats. Across the Charles, a train shuttled down the Red Line and a flock of pigeons flew off, making flapping sounds, like the shuffling of a thousand decks of cards, the swishing of a million gowns. Somewhere Lily whispered with her friends in study hall and Karen ran her hands down her perfect thighs in her perfect house in Waltham, but inside that room, there was only Joe. Afterward, they lay like spoons, his chest against her back, his lips against her hair. She listened to their breathing, listened to the rain. She closed her eyes and clung to that brief moment between passion and the guilt she knew she'd feel for being what she'd told herself she'd never be—the other woman, betraying Samuel. Karen. But she had. And would again. She'd risk everything to be with Joe, to feel him next to her. *Come on out, Dorrie. There's no reason to be all locked up inside like you have been, butting up against your own bones and lies.* She'd risk everything she had to feel alive.

XVII

DORRIE

Dorrie heads to Brookline. Maple Street. A couple with three grown sons wants to open up their house a little more. Eileen and Albert. For entertaining, Eileen said. Mostly for her husband's job—she's been so slack in that department. She's thinking about a sunporch. She's wanted one for years. And since Home Runs did such a fantastic job on their kitchen recently . . .

Dorrie turns off Boylston. Maple is a pretty street, more so in the spring, when the trees aren't bare, when they frame the yards in lush green, when grasses edge the fence that curves along the sidewalk. The houses are diverse, brick and wood. Dorrie parks and Eileen Ramsey lets her in, putters in the kitchen, making coffee. She sets a cup in front of Dorrie. "Sugar?" she says. "Cream?"

Dorrie shakes her head. "Nice kitchen," she quips. "Whoever your designer is, she must be—wait. What's—?" Eileen smiles. A small and unconvincing smile. "Don't you like it?" Dorrie says, surprised. It is nice. The rest of the house is stuffy and airless. Crowded with heavy mahogany. Sealed in by dark long drapes and ancient papered walls.

Eileen Ramsey sighs and sits down on the sofa next to Dorrie. "Of course," she says. "The kitchen is great! It's just that new crew leader . . . at the end of the renovation it was . . ." She shrugs.

Dorrie sets her coffee cup back on the table. "New crew leader?"

"Well," Eileen says. "Yes. I had nothing but respect for the first one, the way he worked with his guys, but that other man, the one who replaced him—"

"What? He—?"

"*Slobs,*" she says. "Their stuff was strewn all over the yard. They left early most days, even when the weather wasn't bad. Got here late. Nothing like the old crew."

"I'm so sorry," Dorrie says. "I had no idea! I don't actually work in that *part* of the company. I'll pass this along, though. I'll see what I can—"

"I don't know." Eileen sits up straight suddenly. "No. Don't say anything. Maybe they were just—getting used to the job or something. They came in at the very end. The last week or so. And I do love the kitchen."

Dorrie turns on her tablet, brings up the back part of the Ramseys' house. "On another, happier note," she says. "How about this for the sunporch? And we can do a teardown here, between the dining and living rooms. That way, you won't feel so . . ." She looks around; the smell of damp is everywhere in the house. Damp and mildew and age. *Depressed* is what she wants to say. *That way you won't feel so depressed.* "Crowded," she says. "The house will feel so much more open!"

"I absolutely *love* it!" Eileen says. "But I don't want that last group here again. I'd rather not have any work done if you can't—"

"I'll tell Edward," Dorrie says. "I'll make sure they send another crew."

"Fine." Eileen picks up their empty coffee cups and sticks them in her new oversized kitchen sink. "I'll talk to Al. See when he wants to . . ." Her voice is lost in the turning on of water, in the clatter of the cups and saucers, a neighbor's car pulling up across the street. She reappears, finally, runs her wet hands down the sides of her jeans as she walks Dorrie through the stuffy entryway to the front door. "I'm so sorry about Mr. Lindsay," she says. "We read it in the papers. Awful. Absolutely horrifying." She tsks, shakes her head.

"It was." Dorrie concentrates on the wallpaper, old and slightly peeling in the upper-right-hand corner, just above the door. "So the crew leader." They stand on the front steps. Snow drips down in tiny flecks and sticks to Eileen's hair. "What was his name? The one you liked?"

"Paulo." Eileen fastens her hair into a clip and a few flakes fall like dandruff onto the front porch. "Paulo something. Italian, I think."

"Androtti?"

"Yeah," she says. "Paulo Androtti. That was it."

When Dorrie gets back to her car, she sits for a few seconds, replaying Eileen's last words in her head. None of this makes sense. Why would Paulo Androtti leave in the middle of a job? And, more important, why did Joe e-mail his name along with the

134

newscast link? Most likely Paulo was the crew leader on the house that burned, but, really, he handled most jobs in Boston. Had handled. He'd not only left Eileen's kitchen project, but the company as well. And very suddenly, according to Jeananne. Some kind of brouhaha with Joe, she'd said when Dorrie asked about him a few days after she'd read Joe's e-mail. Over money, Jeananne thought Edward had said.

Dorrie glances at her beeping cell. Samuel's left a message. He'll be late, he says. He has a meeting in town. But at the moment he's in Amherst, looking at an old Volvo. He might use the parts, he says, for the car he's fixing up for Lily.

If she liked him at the moment, Dorrie wouldn't hesitate to tell him how impressed she is that he's trekked out to Amherst in this freezing weather, but she doesn't. Anyway, she really hasn't got much of a point of reference. Her own father is a blotch, like a Rorschach. He could be anything or anyone—it all depended on the angle. Often working out of town, he drifted through her early childhood, a vague and quiet presence so that, when her mother died, he was of little help to Dorrie, still the awkward, flimsy presence he had always been. When her mother was alive, she always turned on the small glass lamp in the space beneath the stairs. "So he can find his way to us," her mother used to say, but it didn't help him find his way to Dorrie. He remained, until his death, a kind but distant figure, the antithesis of Samuel, with his wild and crazy hair, his boundless energy. Opposites. Or so she'd thought.

She doesn't go straight home. Samuel won't be back for hours and Lily's texted her to say she's going out to eat with Mia and some other friends. The evening stretches out impossibly. Memories of Joe suffocate her. She feels edgy, restless, craving a connection to him. On impulse, she googles his address and programs it into her Garmin. Without stopping to think, she suction-cups the Garmin to her windshield, pushes GO, and turns down the volume, so the sexy British voice won't blare out *ARRIVING AT DESTINA-TION* in front of Karen's house. She heads down Brighton Avenue. She needs the closure, she tells herself. That's all. Joe always kept his home, his family, so removed from her, from the two of them, secure in Waltham. Protected. She speeds up when at last the traffic thins a little. She turns up the radio—an REM special—and stares out at the town, the streets; the Garmin snaps directions.

She makes the turn before Joe's block and sucks in a deep breath. And then she's on his street, the street he navigated all those years, where he put on his brakes or eased off his accelerator. Here's where he might slow down to finish a phone conversation with a client, or to hear the end of a good song before he pulled into his driveway, opened his garage door.

She almost stops. Suddenly, she wants to turn around. The notion of a garage and a yard is all a contradiction of who she'd let herself believe he was. Clearly, Joe was so much more than just her lover, so much more than a boss or a business owner. He had a whole other life. A nice, stable, good life—respectable, with dogs and sons and garages and a wife. For the first time, here, on this street lined with ancient trees and somber, stoic brick, she understands what she did not before—that she was just his way of letting go of Karen—of his marriage.

Dorrie nearly chokes. She no longer wants to see his neat storm shutters, his twiggy hedges. She starts to sail quickly past his house, to ignore the lure of his porch lights, the shimmer of his snowy lawn. The front curtains are closed except for a space where they don't quite meet, where a small brown-and-white dog sits with its nose against the glass. Without thinking, Dorrie pulls over across the street, dims her headlights, twists her hair into a knot beneath her hat, adjusts the brim. She turns the REM special down so low it's nearly off and when she looks up again, a woman walks to the window and stops. Quickly, before Dorrie can either turn off the headlights or turn them up, Karen's face is there against the glass, staring out across the lawn, and then she moves away. As Dorrie backs the car up and struggles with the gears, Karen must be grabbing a coat from somewhere close—a chair, a sofa—because Dorrie glances back to the house just in time to see her fly out the front door as REM whispers "Losing My Religion."

XVIII

DORRIE

When she hears Samuel come in, Dorrie's dying to tell him what she knows, to bombard him with questions—how could you go to my friend's *hotel* room? Or I *knew* you always had a thing for Viv—but she can't afford to open that whole can of worms. And that's exactly what would happen. The real reason for her husband stretching out across her best friend's bed was her own, and unlike Samuel's, *actual* infidelity. She'll have to bite her tongue, at least for now. She concentrates on a small crack on the wall above the stove, remembers, as she sticks leftover tuna casserole in the oven, the first time she'd invited Viv over for dinner—how Samuel had insisted that they'd never met, although they had, in fact, met at a play in Cambridge a few weeks earlier. She remembers how he said, "I never forget a face. Not, anyway, a face like yours"—how Viv had laughed, how she said, "Samuel, honey, I do believe you've kissed the Blarney Stone," her dark hair curled around her face, those eyes, her southern drawl. Dorrie slams the oven door and remembers trying to explain the meaning of a Blarney Stone to Lily.

She gnaws on her lower lip. "Where were you?"

"A meeting," Samuel says. "I told you. I called you from Amherst. The car turned out to be a total junker, but I paid the owner a hundred bucks to hold it for me. I might be able to use some of the parts on Lily's—"

"What sort of *meeting*? At work, you mean?"

He doesn't answer. He shrugs his shoulders, walks across the room toward the coffeemaker.

"The Copley Square *Hotel*?"

"Huh?" He pushes the button on the Keurig and turns around. "No. Why?"

"Just wondered." She turns back to the stove. "So, where?"

"Downtown."

"Where the hell *were* you, Samuel? What *kind* of meeting, exactly?"

"AA," he says. He bends over the Keurig, waiting for his coffee fix.

"Really?" she says. So that explains the pot in the garage. *It takes the edge off*, he'd said. "Wow. That's— Why, now, though?"

"Does it matter why?" he says and he walks out of the room.

"No," she says. "It really doesn't. I'm glad you're— Wait. What about dinner?" But he's out of earshot, and if he answers her at all, she doesn't hear.

Later, when Lily is back home and sleeping, when Samuel slips into his side of the bed, Dorrie inches up against the wall, ignoring him when he puts his arms around her. She doesn't move.

She waits for his snoring to begin, waits for him to roll over to his side of the bed, to fall asleep the way he always does, with his back to hers, but he doesn't move away. He keeps his arms around her; his unshaved face is scratchy up against her skin. Dorrie turns around and they kiss, differently, more passionately, than the usual quick peck. He tugs at her pajama top and she raises her arms over her head as he pulls it off. They make love in the dim light from the mute TV across the room, soft light from a full moon eking in beneath the shade, as Purrl thumps loudly down the stairs to the kitchen for a midnight snack and Dorrie pulls the quilts over their heads to smother sound. It's very different this time from their usual encounters—few and far between and always awkward. This time she doesn't hold her husband at arm's length. She doesn't look over his shoulder at the wall or smell beer heavy on his breath, and, most surprising of all, she doesn't pretend he's Joe.

They don't say much afterward. It isn't a fairy-tale moment— they haven't really fallen back in love—but at least it's a start. She lies beside her husband as he turns away and she wonders how they got here, to this vacant place she thought they'd never ever be—so different from when they were young, running home on their lunch hours to be together, Samuel taking her in his arms, knocking the door shut with his foot as he backed her to their creaky bed—and afterward, flying across the Common to her job, red-faced, her shirt not quite tucked in or with the buttons wrong, her hair frizzed crazily. Time was so much longer then, the hours, the minutes, a song on the radio, waiting for Samuel to come home after work, listening for the sound of the hall door creaking open, his feet bouncing up the five flights of stairs—it seemed like an eternity. Is that the way Viv felt, waiting for him that night? Is that the way Viv *feels*? Maybe they still sneak a drink together at the hotel. No. She's just projecting. Rationalizing, and Dorrie wonders if the time will ever come when she can look her husband in the eye and say nothing happened or everything happened, without that feeling in the pit of her stomach that she's let everyone down.

Her cell phone buzzes across the room. Dorrie finds her pajamas and slips them on as beside her Samuel snores, oblivious.

It isn't really *really* late, but it is late for someone to be calling. She should let the message go to voice mail. All her unexpected phone calls lately are scary, anyway, and the quilts are heavy and warm, calming her into what could finally be a decent night's sleep. She sighs, takes one more look at Samuel and gets up, grabs the phone out of her purse.

Viv. What the *hell?* At least it's not from Joe's old number, and Dorrie sneaks downstairs, muffling the phone against the flannel top of her pajamas.

"Hello?" She sits in the window seat on the slightly peeling wood, the bay window with old thin glass. Icy air drifts in through cracks around the panes, but, despite the cold, she inches closer up against them, speaking in low tones that echo in the silent room.

"Dorrie? Listen, I know it's late. I was planning to just leave you a message."

"Well," she says. "I'm up now. Actually I— We—"

"Look." Viv sounds almost breathless. "There's something I have to tell you."

"Great. What? You're having Samuel's child?"

For a minute, there's just the sound of Viv breathing and then she says, "I told you he was really different that night." In the moonlight streaming in, Dorrie nods, rolls her eyes.

"There was something else."

"What?" Dorrie's only vaguely interested at this point. It's been a long, exhausting day, and after their last conversation, she has no desire to talk to Viv, especially at this hour, especially now, when she's finally feeling almost okay about Samuel. "*What?*"

"He wasn't himself."

"So you've said. And *said.*"

"No, but . . . it was more than that. He was really, really angry. Just be careful, Dorrie. I know you're furious with me, but I still love you. And I'm worried, that's all." She hangs up.

Oh for God's sake.

The sky is sparkly and the street is beautiful, bathed in moonlight with the streetlights looking like stars. It's freezing, though, even with the magic of the snow, and after a minute or two, Dorrie tosses the afghan back on the couch and hops off the window seat.

And then she sees Samuel. He's standing on the stairs, silhouetted by the lamp behind him in the hallway. He stares at her.

"Samuel?"

He doesn't answer, and it crosses Dorrie's mind that Viv was right. The man who has stopped halfway down the stairs does *not* look like her husband.

"Wait!" she says, her hands on her hips. "Samuel, wait!" But he just stands there for a second longer, like he's made of stone.

X I X

KAREN

Karen studies her hair in the bathroom mirror, trying to decide whether to wear it up or down. The first time she saw Tomas it was up in a twist with a few loose wisps. It certainly attracted his attention then. Still, she doesn't want to give him the impression she's spent hours trying to re-create the details of their first meeting. This might well be true, but the purpose is defeated if he knows it.

She turns from side to side in front of the full-length mirror in the bedroom, noting her mushrooming waistline—all those days of lying on the couch, of eating whatever junk food was easiest to heat or pick up from a drive-through window. She sucks in her breath and watches as her stomach nearly disappears. At least it's wintertime. She pulls a sweater out of a drawer and puts it on. Simple, but still nice. Red. Tomas always loved red. "On you," he used to say. "Only on you, I like the color red."

She decides to keep her hair up after all, and she steps into a pair of black jeans from last winter. A little snug, but they'll stretch out by the time she gets to the restaurant. She does a few squats, feeling the material give slightly, and then she checks her makeup on the way out of the bedroom, slides a pair of boots over the skinny jeans. She feeds Antoine, finds her coat in the hall closet, and heads out to her car. She'll take the train. It's more dramatic.

Tomas is already in the station when her train screeches to a stop. He stands in the center, where he can spot the trains coming in and going out, reminding Karen of the times she caught the E line here to meet him. She can't really study him, observe him from her seat— there isn't enough time—but she can see that he looks good. Great, in fact. He's wearing a coat she doesn't remember, and she wonders if it's from Honduras or if he bought it after he arrived. Did he find it here in Boston at the end of autumn or the snowy start of winter? She's not exactly sure how long Tomas has been back in the city, or even in the States.

She reaches up to fix her hair as best she can, tucking a few runaway strands into a hairpin, and then she hurries off the train. She stops. She stands inside the hubbub of the station, and then Tomas is coming toward her, and she finds herself walking faster, nearly running. Anna Karenina. He stretches out his arms and she lets herself slide into him, lets herself be hugged by him for a moment. She pulls away.

"Tomas!"

He moves back a step or two, holds her at arm's length. "You look beautiful," he says.

"Thanks. So do you. Handsome, I mean." She feels a little off balance, almost breathless. Silly. Like a schoolgirl with a crush. It's cold in the station. She pulls her hood over her head and a few hairpins shimmer to the ground, land soundlessly on the concrete. He takes her hand and she feels the cold of his fingers through her glove. His freezing hands. She wonders how long he's been standing here on the platform, how long he's been waiting here. For her. She smiles. Her lips are numb.

"Let's go," he says. "I've found a new restaurant. It's close. The food is very good." His coat is cold. Heavy and coarse. They walk in near silence, their words nipped off at the ends, a quick sideways glance, a light, halfhearted laugh, their faces buried in the fronts of their coats. Snow falls in slivers and collects along their sleeves.

"Do you like it?" They sit near the window. The place is warm. Friendly, with a clamor of dishes and laughter.

"Yes," she says. "It's very cheery." She pulls off her gloves—her fingers are chapped and old-looking from the cold. She sticks them in her lap, leaves her coat on, shivers from the lingering chill.

Tomas glances at the menu, gestures toward the waiter. His mustache is filled with snow that melts and drips onto the table. He orders *té con leche* for them both.

"I've missed you," he says when the waiter has come and gone, when they're sitting face-to-face, their hands around the teacups.

"I missed you, too, Tomas." She says this in a friendly, offhand way, but she looks up finally, meets his eyes before she looks away again to study her fingers on the steaming cup. "When did you get to Boston?"

"I texted you," Tomas says. "Over two months ago." The waiter comes back and Karen loops her hair behind her ear, asks Tomas to order for them both.

"I'm so sorry for your loss, Karen. For Joe."

"Thank you," she says. "How did you know?" She stares at him across the table. "The paper? The *Globe* ran an article—"

"No." He shakes his head, a tiny movement. "I was there. At Mass General. I was there that night in the ER. I wanted to call you, but I didn't wish to intrude," he says. "I know you like space."

Karen nods. "Your mother?"

"She passed away."

"I'm sorry, Tomas."

"Sometimes it is for the best," he says. "She was ill for a long time."

"Unlike my husband."

"Yes," he says. "A very different thing." They both turn to watch the waiter set down plates of steaming food.

"Very. A terrible accident."

"Eat," Tomas says and the two of them bend over the delicious food. For a little while, it feels as if Tomas has never been away.

"Dance with me?" he says, when they have eaten nearly every scrap, and Karen shrugs out of her coat to dance in the back of a large open room, much dimmer here, much more intense. She rests her chin on Tomas's shoulder and they sway among the other dancers. Tomas turns her slowly, dips her nearly to the floor.

"I'm so glad you got in touch with me," he says. His mustache tickles her cheek.

She pulls away. Only a little, but enough. He doesn't try to pull her back, but she remembers how she used to feel with him, faintly suffocated. Will that change, now that she's alone? Now, without Joe?

She feels herself beginning to thaw, her insides, her heart. She leans her head back slightly and looks at Tomas. His eyes are dark and kind. The front door closes with a bang, breaking the spell. He twirls her once, twice, before they walk back to the table.

"I have to go," she says after a few minutes. "The dog," she says. "Antoine . . ."

Tomas nods. "And I, as well." He looks down at his watch. "It was so good to see you, Karen. Are you all right?"

She shrugs. "It's lonely now. The house—" She grabs her coat and Tomas holds it as she slides it on.

He nods again, tosses a few bills on the table. "I'll walk you to the train. And Karen." He stops just inside the door. "Well," he says. "You know. I am here."

It's freezing. They talk very little on the way to the station, and she's happy when they get there, relieved to be inside. "Tomas," she says, when the two of them stand at the entrance. "I never got your letter. I would have answered it, but I never—I just found it. I was going through Joe's things and it was there with his— He must have taken it."

"Oh." Tomas doesn't seem shocked, really, or even surprised. "He's done worse things to you than that, no?"

Karen starts to answer, but her phone rings. Alice. She'll call her back. She'll text her from the train, but Tomas, too, is in a rush, a little harried, pressed for time. He hugs her briefly, plants a quick kiss on her forehead. "Go on," he says. "Really. Answer your phone. I have to leave now, too, or I'll be late for work." He backs away and waves, takes off down the sidewalk.

Work. Karen picks up her call from Alice, but she watches Tomas walk away. Alice's voice is garbled, and Karen keeps the phone up to her ear, catching only dribs and drabs. Her mind wanders. Work, she thinks again. She'll stay at the bookstore until she's back at Home Runs. She misses it anyway—the books, the customers, Alice—not to mention, she's nearly broke. And it is in the city. She'll feel more connected, more a part of things again. The thought that if she's working in town, she'll be closer to Tomas is just there at the corner of her mind, but she dismisses it. "Alice," she says into the bad connection. "We need to talk about me coming back to work. In fact, maybe we could add a few more hours. At least until the insurance settlement comes through or I convince Edward to— My money's running out more quickly than I—" There isn't any answer. The phone's gone dead. She sighs, runs across the station to her train.

It's nearly dark when she gets home, and after taking Antoine out—a fast and frigid walk—night settles in. Her lunch in town has energized her, and she's anxious to get back to going through Joe's things. She grabs a glass of wine and starts across the house to the back bedroom.

Antoine stands at the window, nose pressed up against the glass, his back legs planted on a chair arm. His tiny nails dig into the upholstery. "Antoine!" She claps her hands, but he doesn't budge. He's parted the curtains with his nose, making the entire house visible, and Karen starts toward him to nudge his pudgy body down. She reaches to pull the curtains back together, and sees a car on a side street facing her house with its lights dimmed. She moves closer to the glass, and the car jerks slightly forward and then back as Karen throws her coat around her shoulders and runs through the front door. By the time she's off the porch, her blue slipper coming down on the top step, the car is nothing but a vague bright blur, squealing down the street. Seconds later, someone with one headlight out pulls off from the curb a few doors down and drives away. Half a minute after that, a FedEx truck lumbers by. Karen finishes her glass of wine and thinks she'll make an appointment with a doctor or a counselor—someone who can help her with her nerves. An herbalist, maybe or a Reiki healer. Alice will know someone.

She continues back to Joe's old office, pulls up the spreadsheets on his laptop again. He was meticulous when it came to the company; she can't imagine these aren't right.

She sits on the floor, Joe's computer propped up on her lap, and she leans her back against the daybed. It wasn't only Joe or even Joe and Edward. She was there, too, when the company was in its infancy. Even before that, when it was just a vague idea in her husband's mind, Karen was there. She helped him plan things, cheered him on. She helped him save and, later, it was Karen who found their first small space downtown. It was much more than just a job for Joe, but it was more than that for Karen, too. It broke her heart, giving up her own career to raise the boys, to keep this old house patched together, but even that was an investment in the future of Home Runs, in their future together, hers and Joe's and their sons'.

She spots a piece of paper under the heavy wooden desk across the room. A tiny piece. A corner. She tells herself she really has to clean up the entire house. She needs to streamline—this office, her life—especially with no money coming in. Will she have to sell her home? If so, where will she go?

She scoots across the rug and grabs the paper, a bill of some sort. Joe was usually so careful, filing things away. He must have knocked it off his desk or dropped it from a coat pocket. A Chase bill. Strange.

They've never had a Chase card. She glances at the date—over a year ago. Her eyes scan the list and linger on a charge for the Harborside Inn.

She knows the place, but it's been ages since she stayed there, only one time, when she and Joe were caught in Boston in a heavy snow. They got the room on impulse, and Karen watched the snow fall through the night in thick wet clumps as they made love. Why would he bring this bill here to the house? To flaunt his adultery in her face? To stare at and remember on nights he missed his stupid little twit? She turns it over and stares blankly at a note he's written on the back.

She gets up and walks across the hall to the bathroom. She'll flush it down the john. She sits on the toilet lid and drops her face into her hands, angry. Hurt. Furious. Still, in a way these unexpected finds are comforting—the photograph, the secret credit card. Ironically, these things that tell her Joe was not exactly who she'd thought—not quite the man she'd loved for more than half her life—these things make losing him more bearable, because, clearly, even before the accident her husband was already gone.

She doesn't drop the Chase bill in the toilet. Neither does she rip it into pieces. Instead, Karen stares at the note Joe's written on the back: *Check on building materials returned to Home Depot? Why?* And "why" is underlined three times.

X X

DORRIE

D orrie gets up early and takes a shower before Lily is awake. They really need another bathroom, Dorrie thinks for the millionth time, at least a half bath off the kitchen, a small powder room that Samuel could build over a few weekends. She yawns, listens to his heavy footsteps in the hall.

She slips into the bedroom and dresses while he gropes for his coffee in the kitchen. She avoids him. She isn't sure exactly how she feels about him after last night's chain of contradictory events—the sweet and fairly loving husband in the bedroom, the scary voyeur on the stairs. She fixes her hair and bangs on Lily's bedroom door before she pops frozen waffles in the toaster and retrieves the orange juice from the fridge. "Lily!" she calls into the general morning din, and, seconds later, Lily plops down sleepily at the table. She snarls a greeting, grabs a waffle from the toaster, butters it, and eats it like a piece of toast. Three crumbs fall across the blue paisley of her pullover, and she brushes them off with the backs of her fingers. Samuel comes and goes, a shadow in the bright white light of morning, reaching around her as she stands at the sink, to plant a kiss discreetly on her cheek.

She sticks the last dish in the dishwasher and waves Lily off from the front porch, watching as she slides into the front seat of Mia's shiny butter-colored car. "Be careful!" Dorrie calls. "The roads might still not be very—" Lily cuts her off with a dismissive, embarrassed little wave and Mia's car chugs down the driveway, leaving Dorrie standing like a shrew, her hands on her hips, her apron flapping out around her. Bits of snow blow off the eaves in a sudden puff of wind, and she feels an eerie dread. She tells herself it's only nervousness about Maggie Brennan coming to the office again this morning. There are a couple of employees she still has to talk to, she said when she called. Dorrie unties her apron. All these questions. All this madness with Joe's phone. She wipes her hands and sticks her apron in the kitchen. As she grabs her coat and hurries to her car, her heart flip-flops and her mother's voice inside her head shouts *Watch out, Dorrie.*

Brennan is already inside with Edward when Dorrie opens the door to her office. Did Edward happen to remember something else? she hears Brennan say, anything at all? Did Edward notice the oil in Joe's old parking space?

"No." Edward sounds a little shocked. "It could be anything, though." His voice is calmer suddenly, as if he's sorting this out. He goes on to say it could be someone from the building or even from the street, pulling into the garage to call for a tow. Joe's spot would be the likely place to park, he tells her, and it's clearly empty. Now. His voice breaks on the last two words.

Dorrie hears what sounds like papers being rearranged. Seconds later there's the sound of Brennan crossing the wood floor of Edward's office, and then silence as she hits the plushy carpet on the way to the back room. Dorrie sticks on her coat and slides into her snow boots. "Going up to Mug Me," she stops in Jeananne's doorway to report. "I need to go over some things I jotted down while I still have some vague idea what my notes mean."

"I'll come with you if you can wait a couple minutes," Jeananne calls, but Dorrie's already halfway to the lobby.

"I have this craving for a Mug Me Monster Muff," she calls back, and, anyway, I need to—like I said—I'll forget what I—"

"Fine," Jeananne yells up the hall. "Be that way. I'll just see you up there."

"I'll grab us a table!" Dorrie is now approaching the front desk, her yellow snow boots slogging along the lovely carpeting, her coat unbuttoned, and her hat wobbling on her head. She doesn't slow down until she's at the corner, safely inside the popular little coffee shop. Bits of snow fall from her head and drip across her forehead and she takes off her hat, teases the flakes from her hair.

She orders two Monster Muffins—walnut, one for her, one for Jeananne—and takes her hot chocolate to a table in the back. She stares at her notes. Her feet are killing her. Yellow boots seemed fun when she first bought them, but now she feels as if she's trapped inside a children's book when she wears them, every time she happens to look down at them, a book on ducks or maybe some kind of mystery. The Girl in the Yellow Boots. And then she thinks back to the night Joe died, tries to remember if she wore

153

these same bright boots. She doesn't think she did. She hopes she didn't. *Yes,* she imagines someone saying, someone who was there, the driver of the lurking car, possibly. *That's her all right. I recognize the yellow boots!*

She bites into her muffin. She's managed to avoid Brennan with her endless innuendos, her prying, probing questions. She opens a small steno pad and glances at the notes she's jotted down from clients' phone calls, messages she's picked up. She flips the page and studies the figures she went over with Francine a few days before. Francine kept the books quite neatly, putting all the data in order when Edward e-mailed it to her—income, output, new clients. She never had the details, only bare-bones figures, but somehow Francine managed to balance the books.

Good thing. Dorrie would be totally lost. Francine's spread-sheets aren't at all like the ones Joe used when he was showing her the basics, pushing her to take Francine's place when she leaves. "It's a more secure position," he'd said at the time. "You'll be indis-pensable and so"—he'd smiled—"*indispensed!*" "He wasn't using actual numbers," Francine said when Dorrie pointed out the huge discrepancies between the sets of spreadsheets. "Why *would* he? In *training?*" But that's all moot now anyway. She and Francine are simply putting the quarterly numbers together so Francine can leave with a clear conscience. Edward's taken over completely where the finances are concerned. "Until he gets things straight-ened out,'" Francine reported a few days ago. And then she'd tsk-tsked. "Poor man," she'd said. "Such a mess to sort through," and she'd gone back to filing her nails.

"Mind if I join you?"

"Brennan! Maggie, I mean! No of course not. Please." Dorrie reminds herself that she is an actress. She smiles. A warm, welcoming phony smile. Three toes on her left foot are going numb inside her boot. She swallows the bite of muffin and lifts her mug of cocoa in a little toast as Brennan pulls out a chair and sits down across the table.

For a minute, Brennan fiddles with the napkin dispenser, fumbles out a couple of thin papery wipes. "We match today," she says, and Dorrie notices the bright yellow sweater poking out from Brennan's understated leather coat. "Your boots, and my sweater."

"Yes. Nice—umm—nice sweater." It isn't, really. It's awful. She smiles. She'd pegged Brennan for a fashionista.

"My nephew picked it out," Brennan says, and Dorrie notices she looks a little embarrassed. "It's like staring at the sun. Horrible. He's turning three today. I'm stopping by his party on my lunch break, sooo—" She points to the sweater.

"Careful there," Dorrie says. "You'll start a fad." She looks around behind her. All they need now is for Jeananne to come in and remember something else about Joe's possible affair.

"That what *you're* trying to do?" Brennan stares down at Dorrie's feet.

"Well. No. I just—when I bought them I was in kind of a strange mood. Silly, I guess. A silly mood, and I saw these and I just—"

"No. I meant wearing them on the wrong feet."

"Oh." Shit. "They're a little loose," Dorrie tells her. "I wear them both ways," which makes no sense, but it sounds better than the truth, that she was in such a mad rush to get away from Brennan, she'd stuck her feet in them wrong. "You should get yourself a muffin," she says. "They're really good here. They make them. In the back. In the kitchen. I guess they've got a whole—you know—a whole bakery thing set up in back."

Brennan shakes her head. "Birthday party. Like I said. Cake. Ice cream. The works. Everything I don't need. What's that you're drinking?"

"Hot chocolate." Again Dorrie has a quick stab. Dread and something else. This business about the hot chocolate. Brennan is acting, too, fishing for information.

"It's excellent here," Dorrie says. "It's not my usual choice, hot chocolate. I'd walk through blizzards for a good ginger tea, but it's—well, like I said—they make outstanding cocoa here. You should get yourself a cup."

"Next time," Brennan says.

Dorrie smiles; she slows down, concentrates on breathing, the way she does before she goes onstage. She wraps her muffin in tissue paper, sticks it back in the bag with Jeananne's. She'll have it for lunch while Brennan's gobbling down birthday cake at her nephew's party. "Well." She makes a tiny move to stand. "I'd love to stay and chat . . ."

"Dorrie." Brennan glances at her empty mug. "Your boss's death is looking a little more complicated than I first thought."

Dorrie thinks of the other vehicle, the near collision just before the accident, the lurking car—wonders if a witness has come forward. "Suicide?" She slumps back in her chair.

"No."

"Wait. You're telling me he was—?"

"No," "Brennan says. "I'm not telling you anything. I'm not

a cop. I'm an insurance investigator. What I *am* saying is that Joe Lindsay's death does not *appear* to *me* to have been accidental." She glances down at Dorrie's mug again. "And that there was someone in the car with him the night he died."

Of course, Dorrie thinks. The hot chocolate strewn from one end of the front seat to the other. Brennan must know about it. "His wife, maybe? Karen?"

"I'm telling you this because whoever was in the car with Mr. Lindsay could be in danger. I don't know about the details— *who* it was, *why* it was—and I don't care. I'm just saying whoever was in the car could be in trouble."

Before Dorrie can reply, there's a racket outside on the street. Mug Me comes alive with customers running to windows and grabbing coats, with the baker taking off his apron, hurrying out from behind the counter. Someone overturns a chair, running for the door. Brennan's face goes white. The dread that Dorrie's felt all day intensifies.

"What happened?" She stands up. "What?" she says again, but no one answers. She rushes to the window but there are too many people crowded up against it, blocking it with their bodies. She can't see out. Behind her, Brennan shakes her head, but more as a gesture of confusion than an answer. Dorrie grabs her bag and puts on her coat, leaves Brennan alone at their table, alone in the coffee shop, as she pushes through the door and outside to the street.

There's a huge crowd. Where have they come from, all these people? Dorrie can't see anything at all. A minute or two later, an ambulance rounds the corner with its sirens blaring. Two police cars are parked at an angle across the road. They'll have to move, Dorrie thinks. Fast. They're blocking the ambulance. She feels a hand on her back and whirls around. Brennan stands beside her.

"Are you okay?"

"Yes." Dorrie takes a few steps forward. "Of course. Can you see what—?" But Brennan is already gone, nearly out of sight inside the crowd, talking with the cops. Dorrie pushes forward through the jumble of bodies. And then she sees it.

Her coat.

Oh God no!

The Goodwill coat lies on the street, its sleeves together, as if someone's folded it carefully and set it in a pool of slushy crumbly snow. Red. Red snow. Dorrie's eyes shift slightly to the left, take in the jumbled hair, the small gloved hand. Jeananne.

She pushes past the onlookers and tries to reach her friend, to whisper in her ear, to let her know she's not alone, that everything will be okay. *Jeananne!* She's on her knees. *Jeananne!* But they nudge her away. Someone pulls her, tugs her backward. Brennan. "They need the space," she says, but Dorrie pulls against her, slaps at her. She's screaming; she can barely hear Brennan. Her words are tiny disconnected chunks of sound. Like ice. Like snow. *"I'm here. Jeananne. I'm right here!"*

There's so much noise around her. Dorrie only catches bits and pieces of accounts, of witnesses' reports. *A car,* she hears, *a dark sedan. So fast!* a voice says. *Out of nowhere. Braked at the last second. Too late. Didn't stop. Didn't even slow down.*

Dorrie watches as the paramedics slide the stretcher inside the ambulance and close the door. The police cars are already gone and the ambulance takes off. Its sirens blare. Brennan stands beside her with her hands balled up in fists. Her yellow sweater is a sad and blatant contradiction to the blood that runs along the street beneath her feet; her skin is deathly pale. "Jeananne!" Dorrie screams again, her voice muffled by the sounds of the ambulance, the murmurs of the crowd, "I have to go to the hospital," she says. "I have to let her know I'm there."

Brennan nods. She gestures toward a car pulled against the curb, closer to Home Runs. "I'll drop you." But Dorrie shakes her head, declines the offer.

When they part ways on the sidewalk, when Brennan opens her car door with a trembling hand, Dorrie stops. She turns around. "Brennan," she says. "It was mine. The coat. She was wearing my coat."

XXI

MAGGIE

Maggie does not at first pull away from the curb. Instead she sits with her hands on the steering wheel, the key stuck in the ignition. She doesn't turn it. The inside of the car is silent. Cold. People walk along the sidewalk as if nothing has happened, as if a young woman wasn't run down minutes earlier on this same street. Maggie stares through the windshield where flakes drift down like afterthoughts. She doesn't really see them. She doesn't see the sky, gray and cloudy after such a bright white start, the blue sky, the blazing sun covered now by clouds. She doesn't see any of this. What she sees is Jeananne's body hurled into the air. She sees it even with her eyes closed, the small body being tossed into the sky, landing like a rag doll on the pavement.

She shakes her head. That isn't right. She didn't see it happen. She didn't see the car. She didn't even see Jeananne until she stooped down next to Dorrie to get her out of the way, to give the EMTs a chance to do their jobs.

Her brain is filled with bodies exploding outward toward the sky, with screams and blood and broken people, broken lives, broken minds. She reaches for the key and starts the ignition. She looks at her hands shaking on the steering wheel, takes a deep breath and then another and another. She turns on her iPod, lets the music fill her head, lets Modest Mouse drive out the memory of Iraq, the Humvee—the image of Jeananne lying on the pavement, her eyes closed, her face drained of color, dull in the faded brightness of the day, as if she was already gone.

She glances at her watch. Twelve. The birthday party will be starting. Timmy will be tearing through his presents, his plastic soldiers, horses, blocks, the Fisher-Price piano Maggie's sister bought for him, the paints and drawing table, clothes from Maggie's mom. She looks over her shoulder at her own gift sitting on the backseat, the caterpillar light that projects the galaxy, so Timmy can look up at night and see the universe change colors on the ceiling over his bed. Maggie runs her hand through her hair and sticks on her dark glasses, even though the light outside is dim. She puts the car in gear and slowly pulls away from the curb.

She leaves the party after only an hour. Early but her nephew barely notices. He's busy with a dump truck with a noisy horn. "Who gave him that?" Maggie asked her sister, as the horn beeped endlessly across the living room. "You piss somebody off?" It was uncomfortable being there. She doesn't really get along with Dave, her sister's husband. Even so, the neighbors were nice enough, the kids were cute. It was good to see the family, even though her mother kept an eye on Maggie the whole time. "You okay?" her mother asked her every five minutes or so. "You look a little pale."

She was glad to go. She's glad to be heading back to the flimsy office, the numbers that wait for her in black and white across the page. Today she's grateful for her boring job.

She thumbs through a stack of claims she needs to look into and then she phones Home Runs. "This is Maggie Brennan," she says. "The woman who was hit. Jeananne. Is there any word on her condition?" No, the woman on the other end says. Not that she's heard, anyway. Not so far. She's a temp, she says, so she's not really in the loop, and Dorrie hasn't come back to the office yet. "Shall I have her call you?" she says, but Maggie tells her no. She'll check back later.

She makes a few more phone calls, walks down to talk with a couple of the guys at the end of the hall, and then stares at the two claims on Joseph Lindsay in the file on her desk.

On impulse, Maggie rifles through her purse and finds the number for the bakery near Newbury. "Hey," she says, when a young man answers the phone. "This is Maggie Brennan. I spoke to you about the security tapes from the night of the accident over on—yeah. Right. Your uncle back yet?"

It takes only a minute for the uncle to find footage from the Friday night Joe Lindsay died. "Craig Zant," he says, extending his hand to Maggie and then again to Hank when he ducks in.

Hank's on duty; he comes in only long enough to get the ball rolling before he heads back to the squad car, where his impatient partner waits.

Craig is cordial, but he's anxious to get this over with. He's hung a little CLOSED sign on the front door and a few people have already had their hands on the knob before they noticed the sign. "Nine o'clock on," Maggie says. "That's all I need to see."

There isn't much. Lots of darkness, lots of snow. They stand together at the counter, staring at Craig's iPad, watching snow and night as customers repel off the bakery door. The owner huffs and puffs and fidgets. "What exactly is this all about?" he wants to know, and Maggie tells him there was a fatality that night—"a death over on Newbury."

"We aren't actually *on* Newbury, in case that escaped you, young lady," the owner says, antsy. Grumpy. The nephew was much nicer, but he isn't here, only the uncle. Craig. You get what you get.

"Wait!" Maggie says. "Freeze it!" And just that quickly she is there. Under the awning, right in the light. Damn. Maggie couldn't have posed her any better. She stares straight ahead, and then she reaches up, pulls her hat down low across her forehead, and it's stained with something dark. Blood. No doubt about it. Dorrie stands there staring at herself in Craig Zant's shop-front window in that one square of dusty light. Right onstage, like the actress she is. "Thanks," Maggie says. "Possible to send me a copy?" She writes her e-mail address down on a paper bag, buys a couple of pastries, leaves an extra ten dollars on the counter.

In the car she turns on her iPod, concentrates on Iron and Wine. That damn coat. "It was mine," Dorrie turned around to tell her on the street. "She was wearing my coat." At the time, Maggie hadn't gotten the whole picture. She hadn't known then that the coat Jeananne was wearing was the same coat Dorrie wore the night Joe Lindsay died.

She feels restless. Edgy. She isn't ready to go home, but it's late now to go back in to work. She thinks about driving to Waltham, interviewing Lindsay's widow, but decides against it. Instead she stops in front of Mass General. She'll go in. See how Jeananne's doing. She pulls into the ER parking lot. She gets out of the car and locks it carefully behind her. She even takes a few steps toward the door before she hears the siren, sees Jeananne's body sprawled across the street—and then that day in Baghdad, her friends behind her in the Humvee, when she thought she'd driven them to safety, when she turned around to tell them they were all okay, they'd made it out, and saw they were all dead. Her insides shake. Her stomach feels as if she's being stabbed, as if she's under fire in a combat zone. She doubles over, ducks down. When she gets back to her car, she sits behind the wheel for a minute and sweat covers her forehead, her face. She reaches over to open the glove compartment and pulls out an unopened pint of Absolut she keeps there for emergencies, for panic attacks that hit her sometimes without warning, that terrify her, paralyze her. She twists at the cap and her fingers tremble and slip. She can't get a grip. She leans back against the seat and concentrates on slowing down, on breathing in and breathing out, until her heart stops pounding, until she is exhausted. Drained. She sticks the untouched pint of Absolut back in the glove compartment and stares out the windshield toward the street.

XXII

KAREN

Karen wakes up thinking about Tomas. She smiles. For a moment she is only here, suspended, reaching for the edges of a dream. Before she opens her eyes into the brightness of another day, before the guilt from her indulgent dream settles in, she lets herself drift. She stretches, burrowing deeper under the covers. She forgot to set the thermostat before she went to bed, and it can't be more than fifty-five degrees. She did sleep, though. Maybe it's a good thing, Tomas being back in her life. Even if it's only a fairly loose connection, a friendship, even if he still wants more from her than she can give, although, after yesterday, she's not so sure he does. He tramped off much more eagerly than she'd expected. Of course, he had to get to work. Or maybe he has someone else in his life by now. And Karen can deal with that. Tomas was always so intense—this might be better in the long run. She smiles, gathers the comforter around her as she stumbles to the hall and pumps up the thermostat with Antoine at her heels. "I know," she says, "I know,

Antoine," and together they head for the kitchen. She opens the back door and Antoine streaks outside as her cell buzzes on the counter.

Karen grabs the phone on the second ring. She knew he'd be like this, unable to back off, to give her space. "Tomas?"

"Nope. Sorry. It's Maggie Brennan."

Oops. "Sorry. Thought you were someone else."

"Right," Brennan says. There's a pause, and Karen thinks about telling her what happened the night before, that there was a car parked on a side street with its lights aimed at her living room window. "I thought I'd drop by if it's all right with you."

Karen hesitates, but only for a few seconds. For all she knows, it was Brennan out there snooping around the night before or someone else from the insurance company. Maybe they've got her under surveillance. Maybe they think she had something to do with Joe's death. Maybe they saw her standing in the crowd after the accident. No. She won't say anything.

"Say in an hour?"

"Sure," Karen says. "Do you know how to get here?"

"Yeah," Brennan tells her. "It's a pretty straight shot from Boston."

Brennan's managed to eradicate all thoughts of Tomas, any remnants of lightness leftover from the day before. Karen dresses, grabs a cup of coffee, puts two glasses on a fancy painted tray, heats up a streusel she finds in the freezer, and digs out butter and coconut spread.

An hour later, Brennan knocks on the door. Once inside, she extends her hand. "Maggie," she says. "Nice to meet you," and Karen is surprised at how friendly the woman looks. So young. So unlike what she'd pictured. Antoine yowls from Joe's office, where Karen's stuck him for the moment with his plaid doggie bed, one of several scattered through the house.

"Just coffee," Brennan says, as Karen leans to pour orange juice. "It's cold as—" She doesn't really say what it's cold as, but she doesn't have to. The front yard looks like a tundra. "Black," Maggie says, and she wraps her hands around the large cup to warm them.

Karen gestures toward the streusel. "Please," she says. "Help yourself."

"Can we sit?" Brennan wonders. "I've got a couple things to go over with you." Karen nods, and together they walk to the living room, food in hand. They sit down on the couch.

Brennan clears her throat. "As I told you on the phone, there seem to be some irregularities surrounding this claim. In my opinion, with what I've seen up to now, it appears your husband's death might not have been an accident."

So Edward was right. Karen feels her face turn red, her cheeks burning. "Oh," she says. "My God. I knew he was upset about the business, but I didn't realize . . ."

"You didn't realize what, Mrs. Lindsay?"

"Karen. Please. Call me Karen. That he was really that unhappy. Not unhappy enough to take his own—I mean, Edward *told* me you might decide Joe's death was a suicide, but I didn't believe him."

"Actually, I'm inclined *not* to think it was a suicide at this point."

"Wait." Karen stares at Maggie Brennan, who used to be a cop. "What are you saying?"

"I'm saying *at this point* it looks like what happened wasn't just random. But that's only my opinion. I could be wrong. I tend to see

things in a gloomy light sometimes. I was a cop," she says, "and a—"
She bends over the coffee cake and cuts herself another slice. "Do
you mind? This is really—"

"Please," Karen says. "Finish it! I don't need the calories. What
were you going to say? You were what? A cop and what?"

"A soldier."

"Really." Karen doesn't say this as a question, but as a verification,
an indication that she's heard her. She can so see Brennan as a soldier. "Excuse me," Karen says, and she grabs a couple of plates, heads
for the kitchen, grateful for a moment to herself. *Not just random.*
What the hell? "So where did they send you?"

"Iraq," Brennan says, and Karen barely hears her from the kitchen.
"I joined the reserves in college."

"Was it a surprise, then?" Karen pours another cup of coffee.
"Being called up? Being sent to—?"

"Yeah," Brennan says. "Totally."

Karen takes an extra few seconds leaving the kitchen, still pro-
cessing what Brennan said. Or, really, what she didn't say. Did someone murder Joe? This seems not only unlikely, but unbelievable. Of
course Brennan isn't sure. *Inclined to think,* she'd said. Karen sets
down the coffee and notices that Brennan's hands are shaking when
she picks it up. Coffee sloshes over the sides of the cup and she sets
it back in the saucer.

"Hot," she says. "I'll let it cool down for a minute."

"What makes you think my husband's death wasn't an accident?"

"The brake line. Someone used a tie-wrap to fasten it against
the— basically, it was rubbing against something that would eventually scrape through the line. Which it did. The brakes went
out on that side so when your husband tried to stop, most likely

168

jammed his foot down on the brake, the car went into a spin and out of control."

"How did you happen to notice the, um—?"

Brennan makes another attempt with the coffee and this time her hands aren't shaking quite so much. Still, Karen thinks. She's clearly got some issues, most likely from Iraq. All these kids coming back . . .

"Just happened to spot it," Brennan says. "My family worked on cars all the time. Brothers with old heaps. Boneshakers. Older brothers. I watched them a lot. Would *Joe* have done it? Do you think your husband messed with his own brakes?"

Karen considers. "I don't think so. He was complaining, though, about them not being right. He asked me to take his car back into the shop, but I didn't. I kept meaning to, but . . ."

"So maybe he thought he'd do a quick fix?"

Karen shakes her head. "He wasn't good at all with cars."

Brennan looks at her. "This wasn't exactly a good job." She stands up. "Listen," she says. "Thanks for the coffee cake and everything. The—um—coffee. I'm afraid I won't be able to close the case until I have more information."

"Of course. Just keep me up to date," Karen says, although she isn't sure what she means by this and it appears Brennan doesn't, either.

"You know much about cars?" Brennan turns around suddenly in the doorway.

"Nope. Nothing," Karen says. Antoine barks rowdily from the back bedroom. "I'd better let the dog out before he barks himself into *cat*-atonia. Pardon the pun." She takes a few steps toward the hall.

Brennan laughs. She doesn't move. She just stands there. "What kind of dog?"

169

"Oh. A French Papillon," Karen says, and Brennan still doesn't move.

"Don't know if I've ever seen one," she says, and Karen sighs, tromps up the hall to the back bedroom, throwing the door wide.

"Just be your obnoxious little self," she whispers into the flailing crispness of Antoine's ear. "You know how to clear a room." But when she gets back to the foyer, Brennan is stooped down, scratching Antoine under the chin.

"Did you *drug* him?"

Brennan smiles. "Naw. He's a good boy, right, Antoine?"

"Well," Karen says, "he *can* be. He usually *isn't*, but apparently he *can* be."

After a few seconds, Brennan gets up and heads for the door. "Oh," she says, and Antoine stands at attention in front of her, as if the two of them together have become a little team. "There are a couple of things I didn't mention. It appears someone was with your husband the night he died. Any thoughts on who that might have been? A client, maybe?"

"No idea. He was supposed to be in Rhode Island. Maybe he got back early and the weather was so awful, he decided to stay in town till the storm was over. Maybe he was at the chess club. He goes there quite a lot. Knights on St. James." Karen averts her eyes. Brennan's looking at her with a weird expression. Does she think Karen had something to do with Joe's death? Is that why she's come all the way out here? To gauge the guilt or innocence of her unwitting hostess? Or does she think Karen was the one with Joe that night, careening around with a Starbucks cup?

"One of the women who works at Home Runs," Brennan is saying, "was hit by a car yesterday just up from the office. On Summer Street."

Karen gasps. The air won't come. She can't breathe. "Dorrie?"

Brennan shakes her head. "Jeananne. A hit-and-run."

"*No!* Was it—I mean—it was accidental, though, right?"

"No way of knowing. The car came speeding around the corner, seemed to jam on the brakes at the very last second, but with the slick roads— anyway, it slammed right into her. At least that's what one of the witnesses said."

"Is she—?"

"She's not so good. Broken wrist, broken ankle, head injury. She's hanging in there, though, from what I hear."

"I wonder why Edward didn't—why no one told me." Karen thinks back. The phone had rung. Her home phone, but she hadn't answered it.

"Where were you?" Maggie Brennan has her back turned. Her hand is on the doorknob.

"Here," Karen says. "I was at home. And then in the afternoon I had a late lunch with an old friend. In fact, this morning, when you called, I thought you were—"

"No," Maggie says. "On the night your husband died."

"Oh. Actually, I was in Boston. Right near where he died. Right on Newbury. I was having dinner with a friend and then we got caught in that horrible snowstorm. Me, especially, since I had farther to go. I could barely see a thing. I thought about going back to Beacon Hill, waiting out the storm with my friend, but that hill is so difficult."

Brennan stares at her for a second, but it's a very long second, and then she says she'll be in touch about the claim. She tugs at a front door swollen in place from all the wet and dampness of the last weeks. "Thanks again for breakfast."

"Sure," Karen says. "Anytime." God. "It was nice meeting you, Maggie," she says, and Brennan smiles, takes off down the sidewalk, gets in her Land Rover without a backward glance.

Karen's cell phone jingles on the table next to the couch and she stares at it for a minute. Finally, she thinks. She's finally gone. Brennan really overstayed her visit. All that business with Antoine was a little much. "Brat," she says to the dog, who still stands like a small deputy in the doorway. Antoine barks a small, halfhearted bark and trots out to the kitchen as Karen picks up her phone to check her text.

Maggie Brennan might be headed your way soon, Edward's texted her. Karen looks up quickly, pulls the door open, and steps outside. She looks at the street, the yard, everywhere that's visible from the front porch, where she stands, coatless and shivering, staring out at the sunny, blue-sky day in search of—in search of what? Edward? Or the nameless nemesis who's always at the edges of her life, her neighborhood, her fucking sidewalk? She squints at her untainted lawn. A car door slams across the street.

How did you know? she texts him back.

Didn't. Educated guess.

XXIII

MAGGIE

Maggie drives back to Boston with an eye on her rear-view mirror. She's much more vigilant, more aware of her surroundings, since Iraq. Sometimes she feels like a guitar string tuned a little too tight.

She turns on the radio and listens to some vintage Smashing Pumpkins and thinks about her trip to Waltham. Karen seemed genuinely shocked to hear her husband's death might not have been an accident, obvious not from anything Karen *said*—Maggie learned when she was a cop that people will *say* just about anything. It was clear from her reaction, though, her body language, facial expressions—from the aura, if Maggie believed people *had* auras, which, at this point, she won't discount. Happily, she doesn't see them. Not yet, but there's always tomorrow. Who the hell knows what she'll be seeing tomorrow?

She reaches down to turn the heater up as high as it will go. She needs to get it fixed. Like Joseph Lindsay and his brakes.

According to his wife, he'd noticed there was something wrong. Did he get sick of having to pump the brakes and decide to do a quick fix, not realizing what would happen over time? No. From what Karen said, he knew next to nothing about cars. *He wasn't good with cars*. It was a paradox, though, because anyone who knew enough about cars to tie-wrap the brake line where they did would know not to. They'd know the line would wear through sooner or later. Still. She fiddles with the music, turns it down as she hits Boston traffic. Joe Lindsay traveled a lot for the company. Was he out of town when the brakes got worse? Did he have a mechanic do a Band-Aid fix just until he got back to Boston? *Make sure you get these fixed right,* some mechanic in the boondocks somewhere might have told him. *This is just to get you back to the city.* And Lindsay might have meant to do just that, but put it off. Forgot about it, even. Stranger things have happened.

She thinks back to the conversation she just had with the widow. Karen said she was in town—right near the accident—when her husband died. Having dinner with a friend, she said. But why would she set out for Waltham in the middle of a snow-storm? Or even at the start of one as bad as the one predicted that Friday night? Why not just stay on Beacon Hill with her friend? Sleep on the friend's couch? It wasn't like she still had kids at home. There was the dog, but, clearly, Karen didn't center her life on snappy little Antoine. And, even if she did, would she risk her life to get home to him? *Really?* Or was Karen's friend a guy? Maybe Joe Lindsay wasn't the only one fooling around. Maybe his wife was, too. When Karen answered the phone that morning, she was obviously expecting it to be someone else. A friend, she'd said. *This morning, when you called, I thought you were—*

So who the hell is Tomas?

Back in Boston, Maggie drives straight to Mass Casualty and Life. She's missed a lot of time. There was Jeananne's hit-and-run and now the trip to Waltham this morning. Still, the thought of being cooped up in her claustrophobic little office makes her feel like stepping on the gas and heading straight out of the city and never coming back, catching the closest highway and driving until she's halfway to Canada, far away from all the traffic and the crowds, from the jabbering, demanding clients, from the pitying looks she gets from her family.

She parks her car. The cop part of her is dying to dig into the Lindsay case. Claim, she reminds herself, not case. Not at this point anyway.

She thinks about the paperwork stacked up on her desk, the clients, about Viola Watkins on the phone the day before, the seven messages she left while Maggie was at Mug Me with Dorrie, while the woman in the too-large coat was getting run down by a dark sedan. She thinks about how many messages Viola's had a chance to leave while she was in Waltham.

She eases the Land Rover out of the parking space and into the street. She'll go back to Southie. She'll check out Joseph Lindsay's car again. She'll find out if she's drummed up all this drama just because she hates her job, if she's connecting disconnected things, conjuring ghosts that don't exist. Ghosts she left back on a crappy blown-out street in Baghdad years before.

Ian isn't at the shop. When she asks for him, she's told to talk to a guy named Lucas in the back, a freezing area filled with cars in varying states of disrepair. "Revival," Ian calls the back lot. *If it's got a gasp of life, we can resurrect.* It turns out Lucas is Ian's nephew, something Maggie might have guessed. They have the same tall, skinny build, the same brooding gray eyes. The nephew says yes, the Audi's still out in the shed. He tells her she can go on back. And then he seems to reconsider. "I'll walk you over," he says, and he sticks his tools in a long metal box, wipes his hands on a rag.

"I've got this," Maggie waves her hand in the air. "Really. Don't stop what you're doing on my account."

"Glad to." They walk a minute in silence, tramp through mounds of dirty snow.

"My uncle said you were in Iraq," he says when they're almost to the shed, and Maggie feels a little shock go up her spine. Silently, she curses Ian, his meddling, his big mouth.

"Yeah." This is so the last thing she wants to talk about, or think about, at this point. "Has anyone else been here about the Audi?"

"Not that I know of." Lucas opens the door and steps inside. "I was there, too," he says, "is why I mentioned it."

She squats down, averts her eyes. "I don't really like to talk about Iraq."

"Yeah," he says. "Sorry. I totally get that. Worst time in my life. Listen. I'll just leave you to it then."

"Thanks." She stares at the Audi.

He stops in the doorway. "What's your name? Your first name?"

"Margaret."

"Margaret Brennan. Irish," he says. "Pretty."

"Maggie, really. Everyone just calls me Maggie."

He smiles, holds out his hand. "Nice to meet you, Maggie."

She watches him leave and then she wishes he hadn't left, that he was still there, talking tie-wrapped brakes and whatever else might come up. Although she'd cringed at his remark about Iraq, she liked Ian's nephew. Warm. And he has the most amazing eyes. She smiles. Maybe she'll come back, run into him again if Ian's out for a while. Maybe he finally took that trip to Florida he was always threatening to do. She looks out the small window and smiles. *Promising* to do.

She looks back at the car. Obviously a head-on collision. Even so, Hank said only one of the airbags had gone off—the one on the passenger side, which is what saved Dorrie—no question, now, that it was Dorrie. Maggie moves over to the car and pokes around under the hood. No fuse in the airbag system. Interesting. So, with the fuse out and a sudden forceful stop of the car—like when it slammed up against the tree on Newbury—when the airbag should have been signaled to go off, it wasn't. It didn't.

She backs away from the car. Could it have been knocked loose by mistake or left disconnected after a distracted mechanic did some work under the dashboard? She glances at the sound system. New. So, maybe whoever installed it—some idiot texting his girlfriend or whatever—forgot to stick the fuse back in again when he was finished. Was the caution light on? And, even if it was, would that have been enough to make Joe Lindsay take his car in to get it checked? Would he have even noticed it?

Or did someone purposely remove the fuse? Did the same person who rigged the brakes also disconnect the airbag on the driver's side? Was Lindsay murdered? And, if so, who would want him dead? Edward? Friends or not, he might have wanted the company to himself. Or *will* he be the only owner? Did someone else stand to gain from Lindsay's death? Like Karen? The wronged wife? Hell hath no fury, after all. Maybe Edward's just a jerk, not a murderer. Maybe Karen is a good hostess but has anger issues. Or did Joe Lindsay sabotage *himself*? The company was losing money, his marriage evidently down the drain. Did he decide to kill himself, make it look like an accident, and do right by his widow with the hefty life insurance policy? But if he'd gone to all that trouble, wouldn't he make sure he was alone the night of the accident?

Maggie picks up a rag that's lying near the car and wipes her greasy hands. Or maybe the whole thing *was* actually an accident. Sometimes the simplest explanation is the one that makes the most sense. She takes out her phone and points it at the car, gets a couple of shots of where the missing airbag fuse should be.

She won't turn this over to the police. Not yet. Not until at least *she* is fairly clear on what they're dealing with. This could be her chance to redeem herself. If she can figure out what's happened—if she can hand this over to the BPD with only a few loose threads to tie up . . . Meanwhile, she'll keep her eyes open. If it was a murder, maybe Jeananne's hit-and-run is tied in somehow. She hopes to hell it isn't.

She looks down at her watch. Nearly two. The stack of claims will be a mile high on her desk, her voice mail overflowing with impatient, bristly voices. Out of the corner of her eye, she notices Lucas look up as she slides across the frozen slush. He waves. "Find what you were looking for?"

"I'm not sure," Maggie says. She stops. Makes a little visor with her hand and stares across the stained white of the yard as Lucas walks toward her. "Anybody mess with the car after it came in? Remove any fuses?"

He glances over her shoulder toward the shed. "Nope. Why would they?"

She smiles. "They wouldn't. Just trying to figure out what happened," she says, and Lucas walks along beside her through the snow.

"Once a cop . . ."

"Wow. Is there anything Ian *didn't* tell you about me?"

"Yeah," he says. "Your name. Your first name. And I'm assuming there are a few other things you've kept from my uncle."

"Many," she says.

"We could get a drink sometime. Cover them then."

"I don't think so." She slips through the gate, unlocks her car door. When she looks back, he's still standing in the same spot. He raises his hand in a wave, but he looks embarrassed. Disappointed. "It's your turn," she says. "We can cover *you* when we get that drink."

He smiles. "What's your number?"

She jots it down on a scrap of paper, hands it to him through the metal fence. She starts her car and heads back in to work.

XXIV

DORRIE

D orrie jumps, startled when she sees Samuel standing in the kitchen, staring into space with his coffee and his O eat Dad cup. "You're late," she says, and he nods.

"Overslept." He's looking better these days, since he stopped drinking and started going to 12-step meetings. It's only been two weeks, but Dorrie can see the difference in his face. It isn't puffy, now, the way it's been for years. She wonders, sometimes, why Samuel suddenly changed his life around, but she won't ask him. She'll let well enough alone. She doesn't want to rock that boat. Hurray for AA.

Purrl bolts into the kitchen, meowing as she trots, so it's a weird sound, like a doll that wails when it's turned upside down, but the wails are segmented on account of her moving.

"Have you seen her yet?" Samuel says.

"Maaa aaa aaa." Purrl continues her pilgrimage to the empty bowl and stops in front of it. Dorrie opens the cupboard door over

Samuel's head and takes down a Tupperware bowl that has Meow Mix snapped inside it, so Purrl can't help herself.

"Yes," she says. "She looks bad." Did he mean Jeananne, Dorrie wonders, or did he mean Viv? Is it her best friend he's really thinking about, wondering about? If it is, he doesn't let on—he doesn't even blink.

"I'm sorry." He sets his cup down gently in the sink. "I'll drop Lily. I'm already so late, another few minutes won't—" He walks into the hall, calls upstairs to his daughter, who, Dorrie knows, would so much rather drive to school with Mia.

Dorrie lingers over breakfast, trying to decide whether she should go to work at all today or stay here in her house, where she feels slightly safer, and then take a cab down to the hospital later.

Jeananne isn't doing well. She isn't doing anything, apparently. Her condition is "unchanged." She's neither worse nor better, the doctors told Dorrie the night before. She's heavily sedated, to give her brain a chance to rest. A bit like floating in limbo. The prognosis isn't very good. Dorrie understood this from the expression on the doctor's face as they stood together in the narrow hallway in intensive care and he said, "We'll have to see," with a bright smile, a little pat. She could tell the doctor had assumed the role he'd played a thousand times before with families and friends.

Was it an accident? Some stupid, frightened person rounding a corner too fast? Driving without a license? With a DUI or two under his belt? Panicking? It's quite possible. Did they even notice that they hit someone? Jeananne is small and the day was snowy. No. She isn't *that* small and the day wasn't *that* snowy. Whoever hit Jeananne knew they'd hit her and, for whatever reason, didn't stop.

Something falls upstairs and Dorrie jumps, even though she

knows it's probably only Purrl stepping across her dresser, knocking over nail polishes and framed photos. She shivers. There is no place now that she feels safe, not even here in her own kitchen. The cat, the phone, the creaking of the house, its old bones rattling, groaning, settling. Everything is suspect. Nothing is the way it was before.

She decides to go to work, that she'll be better off there, where there's more than enough to keep her busy, to pry her thoughts away from Jeananne and Joe, from Brennan's dogged probing—where it's at least a little safer. Dorrie stretches, sticks a pot into the sink, and runs cold water on the oatmeal crusted to the bottom.

Her cell rings as she heads down the driveway to her car. A small beep announces a new message as she sits in the front seat, waiting for the engine to warm up, holding her hands against the heater vents, as if she can pull the warmth out with her fingers. The engine is so cold, it chokes. Gasps. She waits. She'll give it a minute longer. She pulls out her cell to see who called, but the number isn't one she knows. She hesitates, her finger poised above delete, but then she shakes her head, puts the phone on speaker, plays the message. At first there's only dead air, not even breathing, and then that robotic-sounding voice again, more muffled this time. "Why are you still here?" She takes the phone off speaker and replays the message with the cell up to her ear. *Why are you still here?* Her heart speeds up; her breath comes fast. She feels as if she's on a tightrope in a high wind. She feels as if each step she takes is terrifying, deadly—that there is no net beneath her.

She saves the message and turns off her phone, tosses it inside her bag. The engine is as warmed up as it's going to get. She looks over her shoulder, up and down the street. What the *hell*? She jams her car into reverse, puts on her dark glasses, and creeps along the streets to the city.

The phone call was jarring to be sure. At the same time, it makes her feel oddly vindicated. She now has something she can hand over, an actual voice, making an actual threat, right there in her phone. But would anyone else consider it a threat, or would they see at as a prank call from a bored teenager, out of school? Or, worse yet, a wrong number—a pissed-off husband, looking for his wife in a crowded mall? "Why are you still here?" as in *Why are you still here in Bloomingdale's and not on the other side of the mall, trolling for that overpriced face cream at Sephora?* Except the malls aren't actually open yet. A restaurant then. Or possibly a rest stop on the road somewhere in Connecticut, the connection weird and robotic, distorted from the weather. And who, exactly, would she hand this over to anyway? Definitely not Samuel. Viv, maybe at some point, but they're not especially chummy at the moment. And Jeananne . . .

She sighs. Maybe she should talk to Brennan. *I don't care about the details,* she'd said. And Dorrie believes her. But it was illegal, walking away, leaving the scene of an accident. Even if she told Brennan she was too afraid at the time to admit she was in the car with Joe, or that she wasn't thinking straight—the shock, her banged head. Even so, she'd had a thousand opportunities to come forward after that. Brennan was a cop for years, an enforcer of the law. She might feel duty bound to turn Dorrie in, and then the whole thing would unravel. Her affair would be out there like a video on YouTube for everyone to see.

Every once in a while, in an off moment, after the unexpected glimpse of Karen darting onto her front porch, Dorrie thinks she might confide in her, but she knows it's an insane idea. Karen would call the cops in the blink of a large blue eye. And really, for all Dorrie knows, it's Karen breathing into the phone, mumbling baffling, scary things through a bath towel, digging up an old toy microphone one of her sons used as a child and making tinny threats.

She slides out of her car and doesn't beep it locked until she's halfway to the elevator, leaving herself an exit if she needs one. Inside, in the lobby, Edward is collecting money for Jeananne. "No flowers in the ICU," he explains to Francine and yet another new temp receptionist; he acknowledges Dorrie with a slight nod and she can see that Edward is certainly not acting now. He's extremely upset, more upset than Dorrie's ever seen him. His eyes are red and watery, his voice quiet in the silent lobby, subdued and unsteady. Jeananne worked primarily for Edward, and a quick and crazy thought that maybe she is more than his assistant floats through Dorrie's mind.

"Thought we might pool our resources," Edward says, "buy an iPod for her room at the hospital, download songs she used to listen to, her favorite groups. It might help her to—" He stops. Dorrie forages through her wallet and comes up with a twenty, which she places on the receptionist's desk.

"It's a wonderful idea, Edward," she says. "Really.

He nods. The phone rings on the desk in the lobby and the new temp presses several buttons with an emerald-polished nail. She looks confused. Phones begin to ring in different rooms.

"Yes," Edward says, although it isn't clear what question he's answering. His eyes rest briefly on Dorrie and his expression surprises her, startles her. He looks upset. But he looks frightened, too, as he turns to walk back to his office. Dorrie hesitates. This might be a good time to make peace, to smooth things over with him, although she isn't sure what, exactly, *to* smooth over. She drops her bag on her desk, drapes her coat over a chair, and heads back up the hall to Edward's office. She'll tell him she'll be glad to get the iPod for Jeananne, happy to download some songs and take the iPod down to ICU. She shakes back her hair and clears her face, puts on a small, beatific social-worker smile.

She takes her time. Edward intimidates her. He's the opposite of Joe, so gruff and abrupt, which is probably the reason Joe worked with the clients. Edward might well frighten them into the arms of the competition. Besides, she isn't sure how much or how little Edward knows about her involvement with Joe. For years the two of them went to the chess club together every Monday night. Knights on St. James, she thinks it was. Maybe, after Joe stopped going, he confided in Edward, some late night, after a few too many beers. *Why did you stop going to the chess club?* Edward might have asked him. *How come I never see you up at Knights anymore? Is it that ditz from work?*

She pauses outside his office. She can hear Edward's voice, loud and strident. Angry. "I don't know why you're bothering me about this now, Lansing. And *here*? He's just—Joe's just *died* for chrissake." Dorrie hesitates. Edward looks at her across his office, shakes his head. He sticks up his hand like a little wall, and Dorrie nods, keeps her expression undisturbed as she backs out. At least she tried.

When she's in her own office, Dorrie closes the door and dials the operator from her cell. She's had a disturbing call, she explains.

A threatening call. Is the operator able to give her the name of her last caller? No, the operator tells her. She's very sorry, but for that Dorrie would need to be with law enforcement, have a court order from a judge.

The exchange from that morning's call is not a Boston one. It starts with a seven, not a six. Interesting. Dorrie writes it down. She'll wait. She'll put in her trainee time with Francine, which is lately limited to poring over pictures of Paris on the Internet, and on her break she'll call the number, find out for herself who it was.

At exactly eleven, she walks to the break room, her heart pounding so hard she hears it in her ears. She uses one of the desk phones, pushes star sixty-seven, and then she push-buttons in the number. She waits as it rings, and, when no one answers, she hangs up and hits redial. She does this three times and, finally, someone does pick up. He sounds slightly annoyed. Not particularly scary, but definitely annoyed. "Geppetto's. Can I help you?"

"Yes," she says with a southern accent, practiced and perfected for a role she had the year before. "You surely can. Where exactly are you located?"

There's a long pause. Dorrie can hear him inhale.

"What city?" she says. She pronounces it "ceety." Lays it on thick. *Cat on a Hot Tin Roof* thick. She won't give anything away. Not at this point.

"Oh." He exhales hard, as if he's smoking a cigarette. A joint maybe. "We're here in Waltham. Where're you?"

XXV

KAREN

Karen locks the door and sets the alarm. She takes off her boots and sticks them side by side beneath the table in the foyer, sticks the plates and glasses from her little brunch with Brennan in the dishwasher.

She glances at the magnet on the fridge and dials the number for the accountant. "It's Karen Lindsay," she says. "I'm a client." She takes a gulp of coffee as the receptionist rings her through to Arthur Reinfeld.

"Mrs. Lindsay." Arthur Reinfeld has a nice voice. Soothing. "I am so awfully sorry about your husband. Horrible shock. Joe was a great guy. A great businessman. Unbelievable. So completely unexpected! I just met with your husband three days before his death."

"Thank you," Karen says. "He was— It's very difficult," she says, and swallows down another gulp of coffee. It won't do to get emotional. Not now. She takes a deep breath. "Thank you," she says again. I was going through Joe's things, Mr. Reinfeld, and I wonder if you would be kind enough to help me. I have some questions. I'm a bit over my head here. I'm sure you can understand."

"I can. And I sympathize with you, Mrs. Lindsay."

"Karen," she says. "Please."

"Karen, then. As I said, I sympathize with you, Karen. I really do, but I'm afraid I can't help you with this."

"I don't understand," she says. "Weren't you Joe's accountant?"

"I was. Yes." Arthur Reinfeld pauses. "But I handle the taxes for the company. That's really all I do. Any specifics, you'll have to get with Mr. Wells." He sighs. "Much as I'd like to help you, I'm afraid I can't."

Karen hooks a kitchen stool with her foot and sits down. "But aren't I, as Joe's wife, as his *heir*, Mr. Wells's partner by default? I will be taking over Joe's half of the company."

There's a pattering sound on the other end of the phone. Karen imagines Arthur Reinfeld tapping a pencil point against his desk, anxious to get off the phone. "But, as yet, you haven't taken over?"

"No." Karen sighs. "Not yet."

"Well, then, I'm afraid there's really nothing I can do."

Karen is stunned. Furious. "I understand," she says. "Actually, I don't at all. You handled my husband's finances for years. Couldn't you just—"

"I really can't." He sounds sincere. The pencil stops tapping. A chair squeaks. "I'm not at liberty to tell you anything at this point," he says. "And, again, as I said, I do only the taxes now. For the past couple of years, actually. It was nice to finally talk with you after all this time, Karen, despite the circumstances, and I do wish you luck getting everything sorted out. It's so difficult after a death. Again, I am so very sorry about Joe." And Arthur Reinfeld politely ends the call.

Fuck Edward. *And* Joe. "And his little dog, too," she says. Antoine snarls.

I just met with your husband three days before his death.

Karen doesn't even take a breath before she calls the company and asks for Edward. She waits while a series of clicks and whirs connects her first to Francine, then to a male voice she doesn't recognize—the enigmatic Len, she guesses—and at last to Edward. She is somehow spared Dorrie.

"Edward?" she says the second he answers. "You want to talk about the company? Let's talk!"

There's the sound of a door closing. "I think we both know that right now is not the best time or place for this discussion."

"Where, then?"

"Shall I come out to Waltham?"

"No," Karen says. "I'll come there. I can be in town in an hour. Where?"

"How about D'Angelo's?" he says. He sounds depressed. "I'll buy you lunch."

Edward is already inside when Karen arrives at D'Angelo's, a cozy little place in the North End. It smells like garlic rolls and red sauce. It smells caloric.

"Sorry," she says, glancing at her watch. She's twenty minutes late. She makes a slight gesture for Edward not to bother getting up. "Traffic," she says. "They're working on the roads."

"Right," he says. "Endlessly." His face is pale. Drawn. His eyes are faintly swollen.

"Are you okay?" She asks this even though she's furious at Edward. He looks that bad.

"My assistant," he says. "Jeananne. I told you. Very upsetting."

Karen nods, although she thinks he hadn't told her. It was actually Brennan. "Horrible. She always seemed like such a nice . . ." She doesn't finish. She has no idea what Jeananne was like. She'd met her at a couple of Christmas parties and she always seemed extremely talkative. Chatty, Joe used to say. "I'm sorry." Karen takes out her reading glasses and scans the menu. "How is she?"

"Not well. But I'd really rather not talk about Jeananne, if you don't mind. As I said it's very . . ." Edward signals for the waiter, a white-haired gentleman, who listens to their orders and repeats them back verbatim without writing them down. She and Edward make small talk for a few minutes, but Karen gets the sense that Edward isn't listening, that he's barely heard a word she's said.

"I'll get to the point," Karen says. "I found something Joe wrote. It was scrawled on an old—" The waiter arrives with her salad and Edward's pasta. She pauses. "An old bill," she says when the waiter has left again for the kitchen. "But first. How did you know Maggie Brennan was at my house this morning?"

"I didn't, really. I hazarded a guess, that's all."

Karen fiddles with her silverware, nibbles at her salad. "Anyway, I found this note Joe wrote to himself."

Edward takes a sip of his drink. "And?"

"*And* . . . he was wondering, Edward, why there were so many supplies being returned to Home Depot."

"*Really?*" Edward looks her straight in the eye across the table.

"Odd, since Joe was the one who *okayed* the orders. That said, there were some questionable—" He clears his throat, sits back in his chair. He pushes his plate to the edge of the table; he's barely touched the food. "I confronted Joe on the phone," he says, "the day before his accident. I told him we had to discuss a few things when he got back—Rhode Island, I think it was—and he agreed. We planned to get together and go over all my questions as soon as he was in town, only . . ."

"Yes," Karen says. "Inconvenient, his accident. So what are you saying, exactly?"

"I'm *saying* that at this point I'm trying to find answers. I've even locked the staff out of the accounting program until I figure out what the hell is going on. I loved Joe, too, Karen. He was my best friend for my entire adult life. Since college. Please remember that."

"I'm aware," Karen says. She folds her napkin into a small triangle and sets it on the table. "I just don't see the problem with the company. We had a profit of nearly two million dollars last year!"

"Those numbers are only the tip of an extremely optimistic iceberg," Edward says. "Dessert?" Karen shakes her head, and Edward wipes his mouth, tosses his napkin on the table. "The costs are barely touched on in those spreadsheets. You don't really understand, and Joe—hell."

He lifts his hand in the air and the waiter hurries toward their table. "You aren't seeing the whole picture here. Check," he says, and Karen's barely grabbed her bag before they're back outside, shivering on the sidewalk. Edward leans over and gives her a little hug. Karen looks at him, his haggard face, and she remembers how much she has always liked him, what a good friend he's been to both her and Joe—to the whole family, recalls the time Jon got arrested for driving without a license at the age of fifteen. He hadn't called home—the first person he had thought to phone was Uncle Edward.

The hug lasts a tiny bit longer than it should; Edward's arms around her are uncomfortably tight. Karen moves back a step or two and notices again that Edward's face is deathly pale, his cheeks sunken—the man looks absolutely haunted.

"I'm here," he says. "I'm here for you, Karen. No matter what. Always loved you. Always will." He smiles, gives her arm a little pat. Friendly, but not romantic. Not Edward. He saw her once with Tomas. "This is Tomas, our mechanic," she'd told Edward. "He's given me a ride to town so I can keep my date with Alice." It was a Wednesday, so she was meeting Alice later, but it was a lie about the ride. Her car was actually up the street in the parking garage. "Joe told me you guys found a good mechanic," Edward had said. "In fact, he's convinced me to switch. Planning to take my car there for a tune-up." But he'd looked uncomfortable. Jealous, maybe, she thinks now. He never mentioned their encounter, but after that, she'd wondered if he believed her or if he thought she and Tomas were having an affair. Did Edward tell Joe about their chance meeting, validate Joe's hiding Tomas's letter?

"Take care of yourself, Ed." She reaches up, gives him a little peck on the cheek.

"You, too," he says. "It isn't easy for either of us. Joe was such a big part of—" His voice breaks. He puts up his hand in a halfhearted wave, and walks away.

"Wait," she calls, and Edward stops. "That twit Dorrie," Karen says. "Fire her!"

Edward stares at her across the squares of pavement between them. "No," he says, finally. "This sounds personal, Karen. She's good at her job, and without Joe, we need everyone we've . . . No, Karen," he says again, and he turns on his heel and heads off down the sidewalk.

Well, shit.

On the way to her car, Karen hears the little dinging sound of a text message. She looks at her phone. Alice. For a second she allows herself to feel a pang of disappointment that it's not Tomas, a pang of regret that he's decided to back away, even if that's what she wanted, even if she's told him this a thousand times. "Hello?" she says. "Hello, Alice?" Sometimes Karen thinks the chance for anything to happen with Tomas has come and gone, or maybe wasn't ever there at all. He came into her life when she needed something, anything to keep her from disappearing, from being sucked inside the backdrop of her boring suburban neighborhood or the cold concrete of Boston—to make her feel, for that moment, that she sparkled, that she, too, could shine. And maybe that was all it was. And maybe that's enough.

XXVI

DORRIE

The new receptionist is out, and, considering her obvious difficulties with the phones, it occurs to Dorrie that Molly—or is it Maureen?—might never come back. Francine, too, has taken the day off, or at least the morning. "I might pop in for a few hours in the afternoon," she said, phoning Dorrie on her cell. "Nothing much for me to do at work these days, aside from tweaking my Parisian itinerary, what with Edward's takeover."

Dorrie has been left to answer calls. No promises, she's told Francine; she'll do her best.

"It isn't rocket science," Francine snorted, "despite the new temp's issues."

"I guess not," she said. "It's just the whole logistics of the thing." But there haven't been many calls at all this morning, and those that have come in she's managed to reroute to her own office. It's productive, if extremely boring, being in the office on her own.

Len, from IT, is somewhere in back, but he's such a misanthrope, she barely knows him, even after all this time. It's boring, but she's managed to make headway with her backlog of paperwork, returned most of her clients' calls.

When the phone rings at ten thirty, it feels as if she's been at work alone for days, and Dorrie nearly jogs up the plushy hall to the front desk. She starts to answer in a businessy, generic voice, but then she puts on a thick British accent—another role, just before Christmas at the Colonial on Boylston. "Yes. Hello," she says. "Might I be of service?" It's still a part of her, the accent. When a play ends, Dorrie can call up the character for ages afterward.

"Who is this?" Edward sounds confused.

"Dorrie," she says. "Sorry, Edward. I was just—I was practicing. For a play I'm in. *Will* be in. At the—"

"I have news," he says, and he sounds almost gleeful. "Jeananne's hit-and-run? The driver has come forward. Turned himself in."

Dorrie sinks into the receptionist's chair. "Oh my. *Really?* That is so—that's—I am so glad to hear that. When?" she says. "Who was it?"

"This morning. And it was a teenager. Some fifteen-year-old kid. Took his mother's car without her permission. Grabbed the extra key and stole her car from the parking garage where she worked. Right near the office as a matter of fact. Rounded the corner too fast—waayyyy too fast—put on the brake, but it was too late. Smacked right into Jeananne. Said his conscience got to him in the end, but my bets are on the mother finding out and making him turn himself in to the—"

"Still. I am—*so* relieved, Edward. Thank you for calling."

"Spread the word," he says, "and hold the fort!" He hangs up, leaving Dorrie with an earful of bad clichés.

So it wouldn't have mattered what coat Jeananne was wearing. *Thank you, God!*

Back at her desk, Dorrie sits for a minute, letting it sink in, this new information about what happened to Jeananne. If she was wrong about the hit-and-run, could she be wrong about what happened on the night of Joe's accident? Did she only *think* she was being followed? Did she just imagine, in her fragile state, that someone tried to run her down? Her lover had just died in front of her. And who knew what shape her brain was in at that point, after the damn airbag whacked her in the head. And the cold. Was she even fully aware of what was going on around her or was she bordering on shock? If so, how accurate was her take on what happened?

But there were the phone calls. There were the texts. There isn't any question about that.

And there were Joe's last words to her. *It isn't safe.*

No. She is both grateful and relieved that Jeananne's accident was just that—a random hit-and-run, a stupid, frightened teenager unused to navigating corners—but this knowledge doesn't change what happened on the night Joe died. It doesn't make Dorrie any safer.

She brings her e-mail up on her computer and looks again at Joe's last message, the e-mail he sent on the day he died. Is that why he dragged her out on a night when everyone else was huddled inside, stretched across their couches, watching old movies on Turner? He was trying to tell her something as they rounded that corner, as he struggled to keep the Audi on the road. Did it have something to do with this? With this baffling e-mail?

She pulls up the company's site and tries to remember Joe's password. He'd changed it on a Tuesday afternoon while they were together somewhere in town. A pub. It was months ago and he'd just begun to train her on an updated design program Home Runs purchased. He changed his company password every few months, he'd told her, and the new one, it was something to do with her, with the perfect afternoon they spent together that last spring. She clears her mind, closes her eyes. Cambridgestreetfestival05. Or, no. Cambridgestreet*fair*05. That was it. The day he took the photo—a day in May, the fifth month, that gorgeous day—they'd strolled through Cambridge, so different, on that festive afternoon, so opposite the staid reserve of Boston, just across the Charles. Harvard Square was packed with students, the sun dripped down on mimes and clowns, musicians—stores were crowded with newcomers, with shoppers in bright clothes, with lovers holding hands, emerging from a harsh and bitter winter. Spring. A perfect day. She types in Cambridgestreetfair05 and hits ENTER.

What comes up is more than spreadsheets. What comes up is far more detailed—the company's expenditures, a list of charges. She gets up, makes herself a cup of tea even though she doesn't want it, really. She walks up and down the hall a few times, stalling, trying to shake her feelings of unease, of disgust at herself for spying. Still, whatever Joe was trying to tell her, whatever was important enough to end their relationship . . . it might be here. It might be somewhere in the files, a hint, a glimpse. She has to try. She brings the tea back to her desk and sits down in front of her computer.

There are columns of withdrawals, deposits. Something is wrong. Off. There are numerous purchases made at various Home Depot stores in the Boston area. And . . . She stares at the screen—almost as many returns, usually the next day or the day after. Was this standard? Did the contractors buy different versions of the same item to give the customers a choice and then return the options that weren't picked? Possibly. She jots down their account number and closes out, deletes this last visit from her computer's history.

She calls Home Depot's 800 number, relays the company's account number, and requests a copy of bills covering the last four months. "I'm tidying up our finances," she explains. She puts on Francine's no-nonsense voice, her controlled and skillful tone. "I've lost my copies somehow," she says, and gives her private e-mail address to the pleasant, eager agent on the other end of the line. It will be sent within the hour, the friendly voice assures her. "Thank you for your patronage."

On the floor beneath the desk, her cell phone beeps, and Dorrie fumbles through her bag to pull it out. A text message. From Samuel, she hopes, and she thinks about suggesting they meet for dinner, all of them, Lily, too. She'll get her mind off things. They could go somewhere they've never been—the new Mediterranean place near her office or that bistro in Jamaica Plain their neighbors were talking about at the Christmas potluck that they'd been meaning to try. In fact, that would be best in this iffy weather, keep it close to home.

Meet me, the text says, but then she inhales, a sharp intake of air; it isn't from Samuel. It's from Joe's old phone. Again. Her first thought is to delete the text and forget she ever saw it. *Tonight,* it says. *8:00. Meet me at the Starbucks. That last place.* That last place! How would anyone but Dorrie even know that? Dorrie and Joe? He must not have deleted his final text to her from his burner phone and whoever this is, whatever sadistic creepy person has it . . . She shivers. Her heart pounds and skips. She really has to calm herself down, figure all this out. She takes a few deep breaths before she reaches for a bottled water and guzzles it down.

She wants to leave. She wants to slip out of the building and into her car. She wants to be as far away from Summer Street as she can get. She looks up the hall. Francine hasn't come in yet. Besides the useless Len, there's no one else here. *Hold the fort,* Edward said, so she has no choice. She fidgets, makes a few more phone calls, preemptive ones this time. Follow-ups, to keep herself busy, to keep her mind off ghostly phones and Home Depot returns. She hangs up the phone and glances at her watch. Three nos, a maybe, and two yeses. She jots down the names, the numbers, the addresses. *Sunporch in the spring,* she scribbles next to the first address and then, beneath the second, *Reno on upstairs bathroom.*

She checks her e-mail, finds a brief message from Home Depot. They've sent her four attachments—October, November, December, and January. She opens them, one at a time, and there they are again, the plethora of items purchased and returned almost immediately. She stares at the articles. Electrical supplies and tools. But not in January. In January there were only three returns: two faucets, a sink, and a light fixture, which sounds fairly standard.

The front door opens and Francine hurries in. Her coat rustles across the lobby. "Dorrie?" she calls. "Good *gawd* it's cold out. Dorrie? Are you here?"

"Yes," Dorrie calls back. "Be right there. Just let me—" She saves the e-mail to her Upcoming Auditions file and closes out, just as Francine appears in her doorway; her face is pink, her nose a fiery red.

Why all these returns?

XXVII

KAREN

Karen wakes up to Antoine nibbling at her hand. She forgot to stick him in his little room the night before, or maybe she just wanted the company. At any rate, he's wakened her before she was ready to wake up. He's waked her in the middle of a dream. About *Edward*, of all people. "Thanks, Antoine," she says. "You got here just in the nick of time!"

There was a short period, back in college in Miami, when Karen and Edward were closer. It was before she'd actually met Joe—long before the languid days in his old crumbly apartment.

Edward was in one of her classes. She closes her eyes and drifts, tries to remember which one. English Lit, she thinks. Or, no. Humanities. He sat behind her in the dome-shaped auditorium, watching slides—a whirlwind trip through the history of art—Leonardo to Georgia O'Keeffe in six weeks' time. A taste, the professor said, to whet their appetites. They'd shared a table in the cafeteria once or twice, had a few Cokes together, a couple of talks about Degas or

Bosch, wending their way through throngs of students to sit down. Her hair was long and bright. Edward was tall and kind. Who knows what might have happened? Karen had wondered once or twice over the years, during one or another of Joe's endless trips, or sitting in traffic on the way to the ER to treat Jon's sprained ankle or Robbie's broken arm. It might have crossed her mind as she sat alone on the back porch, her husband dozing in front of the TV, that things might have turned out differently if Joe hadn't come along when he did. It turned out they were friends—the poli sci major and the budding engineer—a perfect match, the two of them, so opposite they rounded one another out. "You complete him," Karen used to tell her husband, laughing. And it was a better match by far than she and Edward would have been. The man went through wives as quickly as a bottle of scotch, and then paid lavishly to be rid of them. Edward's Expensive Exes, Joe called them. All four of them.

Still, there was that one time. Edward's second wife had left him in a huff. Her spiky heels had barely clicked out of his life, her plane was barely off the tarmac before Edward turned up at their door. "She's gone," he had announced. "She isn't coming back." And Karen let him in, fixed him a drink, fixed him another, and, before she realized it, the three of them were wasted. Joe staggered up to bed, and Edward stayed the night, too drunk to drive. They talked for a while longer, just the two of them and Karen made some coffee, made it very strong, a cup for each of them, because she'd felt attracted to him then. That one time. That one night, tucking in the sheets on the couch in the den.

And now she's had a dream about him. *Always loved you. Always will.*

God!

"Okay, okay." She lets Antoine lead her to the kitchen, watches as he runs in circles between her and his empty bowl. The dream was so vivid. So sexual! She pours Antoine's kibbles in his bowl and makes herself a cup of coffee, but she doesn't sit down. She paces. She tells herself the dream of Edward was only misplaced longing for her husband—it would be too painful to dream of him, his death too fresh a wound, too recent, still. It was Edward in the dream because he'd held on to her a tiny bit too long outside the restaurant; it stuck in her subconscious. That was all. That and his offhand remark about always loving her. She tells herself these things, and then she reaches for her phone and texts Tomas. *Can you get away?*

Yes, Tomas texts back. *Of course. Where?*

Lunch, she says, but in her heart she knows it won't be only lunch. She lets Tomas pick where they'll meet—a little ethnic place on Boylston. She reads his text directions, slathers raspberry jam over her toast, and washes it down with her coffee. Outside, Antoine runs across the snowy yard and she opens the back door. He bounds inside, shakes off the cold. Trees sway in the wind. It's a sunny day. A yellow day. The sky is clear. Snow sparkles on the tree limbs. As she watches, a blue jay lands on a large oak branch and makes a raucous sound before it flies to a rickety bird feeder that she keeps stocked with seeds. Karen looks back at her phone. *Yes*, she texts Tomas. *Twelve thirty is perfect.*

At lunch she barely tastes the food. Chilean, she thinks, or Peruvian—something South American, and she's not even sure of this. Afterward she can't remember what she ate. The conversation is stilted, halfhearted. Tomas drones on about Honduras, his job at the hospital.

"How are you?" he says. "Are you doing all right? Is there anything you need?"

Karen nods. She looks up at him. "Yes."

They play with their food. They speak of the weather, what a pretty day it is, how glad Tomas is that he doesn't go to work until the evening. Usually. "Not always, though," he says. "If they need me at another time, they call me in. I am the last one hired. I am the new one."

Karen pokes at her food, asks him how his family's holding up after the mother's death. Polite, a little distant, as if they are friends who know each other slightly, co-workers grabbing a quick bite before a meeting.

"Fine," he says. "It was expected. No one was surprised. Sad, of course, but we were prepared. My brothers and I were with her at the end."

Karen stares at her hands. "And after? When you got back? Do you have your old apartment?"

"No," he says, "but the one I live in now is near to the old building. Would you like to see it sometime?"

"Yes," she says. "I'd like that very much. Is it far? Can we walk there?"

He looks away, somewhere over her head. "Yes," he says. "Not in this weather, but it isn't far. A short train ride from here. Would you like to see it?"

She nods. "Yes."

It's a tiny fourth-floor walk-up. No elevator; the stairs are poorly lit. Even in the daylight, even on a day as bright as this, it's difficult to see the stairs.

"Be careful," Tomas says. "The owner is a crook. He doesn't care about these things." He cups her elbow lightly in his hand, steers her in the dark stairway, and Karen finds she's breathing very hard by the time they get to the fourth floor.

"Out of shape," she says and laughs. "I didn't realize quite how much." Tomas fumbles in his pocket for his keys. The door is old— dark brown paint is chipped away in spots, exposing other colors. A rainbow door. The lock is also old and Tomas jiggles the key until it catches, finally, in the tumblers. Odors from apartments downstairs drift in the air between them, beef and garlic and rich sauces. Karen inhales. "Guatemalan," Tomas says. "Sometimes the women bring me food to try."

"It smells heavenly." Karen inhales again. "I've gained five pounds just breathing in your doorway." For a second, she has the craziest thought that she could leave her life in Waltham in a heartbeat and live here in this quiet, unassuming place, at least for a little while. A transition period—that she could slide inside Tomas's life without a backward glance. She's lived in places like this—that room off Boylston, before she moved in with Joe, and the place in South Miami with the landlord's grumpy dog, its leash clipped to a clothesline in the yard.

The place is tiny. Dark, again, despite the yellow day. The window is small, dirty with smoke from the stove. A huge cat sits on the fire escape, turning when he hears Tomas's voice. He thumps against the window with his massive head.

"Spike," Tomas explains. He wrenches the window open a few inches and the cat slinks in. "One day I was sleeping between shifts, and I woke up to a commotion on the fire escape. I looked out and saw this scruffy old guy fighting with a tom on the third floor. I believe a female house cat was involved. Attractive. Fluffy. I sometimes see her sitting in a window on the second floor. Spike will come inside to eat now, to visit, but he's an alley cat at heart. 'I could never live indoors,' he tells me. 'It is much too boring.'" Tomas tugs at the stuck window and it slams shut with a noisy thud.

Karen looks around. Tomas flicks on a light, rummages in a cabinet for a bag of cat food, and pours the pellets in a chipped yellow bowl in the kitchen, an alcove off the only real room.

There is a large brass bed that he explains came from a junk shop two or three stops up from his. He tells her about lugging it onto the train in pieces. "Three trips," he says. "One for the headboard, one for the footboard, and one for the—what—the raves?"

"Rails," she says. "The rails."

She perches on the bed. There isn't any other place to sit, really. It's the bed or the straight-backed chair pulled up to the table near the kitchen. She takes off her boots. They both know why they are here. Tomas sits beside her but not too close. He looks at the fire escape, at the small opening at the bottom of the window, and for a few seconds, neither of them speaks. There is only the crunching sounds of Spike at his bowl, voices floating down the hall, up and down, a cadence, words she doesn't understand, the clang of dishes. Somewhere there's a delicate, faint sound, a teaspoon on a china cup.

Tomas leans toward her. He cups her face in his hands, and she moves her head slightly, kisses his rough palm. He touches her hair, light, tentative, and it comes undone, drops around her shoulders; hairpins fall across the blanket and he kisses her. Soft. The bed sinks down in the middle; the springs are worn, the mattress falls inward slightly, forms a valley when they make love. He is gentle, whispering her name and other words that Karen can't quite hear or doesn't want to, endearing things, sweet things, fragments. The mattress puffs up around them. She closes her eyes and sees the print of a chenille bedspread, Tomas's. Or was it somewhere else? Was it another time? Another room? Joe's, or someone else's? Through the wall she hears a radio or maybe a TV, the news in Spanish, mixing with the oddly distant sounds of her own climax.

She opens her eyes. Sunlight leaks through the smudged window. Spike watches her from the bureau; his eyes are yellow in the near dark of the kitchen.

"Come here, Spike." She pulls her hair back from her face, feels the bones of Tomas's arm against her back. "Here kitty-kitty." Spike yawns. He jumps down from the bureau and Tomas gets up, opens the window, closes it again as the cat slinks out to the fire escape.

"He is going for a smoke," Tomas says.

They lie together, not speaking. Tomas lights a candle, pulls a cigarette from a pack on the bedside table, leans to light it from the flame, a votive candle in a glass. Like in a church, she thinks, like candles for the dead.

"I have to go." She leans up on her elbow. In the darkness of the room, Tomas is gray. His cigarette burns orange, crackles. His body underneath the sheets looks shrouded. Sacred.

He nods. "I love you," he says. At least she thinks so. He says it so quietly, she isn't sure. She doesn't answer. She isn't certain what he's said. She shifts her body slightly. And in that second Karen knows that she does not love him. He's lovely and exotic and a little enigmatic. He's patient, kind; he's gentle, and he's waited all this time for her. For this. But she does not love him. Maybe before he went away. Maybe on a beautiful spring day with a bright blue sky. Or maybe sometime in the future, when Joe's death is not so fresh, when anger, pain, and guilt aren't all mixed up together and fear isn't so much a part of her life. But not now.

She sits up. "Your apartment is wonderful," she says. "I wish I could stay here forever." And it's true. She loves the place, the cat; it's just Tomas she doesn't love.

"You could." He snubs out his cigarette. "You can."

She laughs. "Antoine has probably eaten half the living room by now."

He looks at her in the dull light from the dirty window and the tiny flame of the votive candle. He doesn't speak. He reaches out to touch her hair. Just a touch, and then he gets up. "I'm going to jump in the shower," he says. "Join me?"

"In a minute." She lies back down until she hears the water coming on, and then she gets up, too, slips into the tiny bathroom and washes at the sink. She doesn't join Tomas in the shower. Instead she pulls on her jeans and sweater, slides into her heavy coat, tugs on her boots.

Across the room, Tomas's cell phone jingles; it bounces on the wooden table near the bed. She starts to knock on the bathroom door, to tell him that he has a call, but she doesn't. "WORK," it says. She scribbles down a note for him. *Had to go. Thank you for an incredible day. The hospital called while you were in the shower. Xoxo K.* And then, as an afterthought, just because it's there, she programs his work number in her phone. Just in case. She props the note against the pillow on the sagging bed and slips out through the rainbow door.

XXVIII

DORRIE

Dorrie knows she'll end up going to the Starbucks. It's both unsettling and frightening that whoever texted her from Joe's phone knew where they had their last rendezvous, their last cups of coffee and hot chocolate, their last chance to look into each other's eyes. A chance they'd squandered. What she wouldn't give to get it back, but she doesn't want to go there now. She shouldn't go. *It isn't safe.* She will, though. She can't not go.

Waltham, the man had said. She's googled the name and found that Geppetto's is a bar. They serve food, but it's primarily a bar. Waltham. Did *Karen* call her from there? Did she have Joe's throwaway phone? Did someone else find it and give it to the dead man's wife along with the rest of his personal belongings? The police? The EMTs? Did Karen call the only person whose two numbers Joe had logged into his phone? Is she intent on drawing Dorrie out? On seeing who was with her husband on the night he died?

Was Karen sufficiently fueled on hate and fury to start running people down in the streets?

No. That's crazy. From the few things Joe said about his wife, she didn't sound at all the type to suddenly go mad over—anything, really. *Passion was never Karen's strong suit,* Joe said once. He'd gone on to say that this was probably a good thing, that Karen was definitely the grounded one in the family. *She keeps us all on track.*

Of course, there could be more than one thing going on here. Karen could have her husband's phone and someone else could be careening around on the streets.

She'll go to the Starbucks where she last saw Joe. She'll go and watch without being seen. Even if the trap is being set for her. She'll skip right over it, leave its sharp metallic jaws to clamp down on the one who placed it there.

But first . . . For a few seconds, Dorrie stares at the renovations still waiting for design. She's made a huge dent. Still, with Jeananne gone, the work is overwhelming. She gauges the few remaining jobs and looks for design ideas in the files. One of the kitchen renovations has her stumped. An odd shape. Cramped. The owners want to add a pantry, remove two walls, but even with the walls out, the space is still extremely small. She scrolls through kitchen renovations from the year before. A job from last October gives her some ideas and she scrolls through the attached documents. As she's closing out, the inspector's name catches her eye. *Everett L. Lansing.* Lansing. The name of the caller Edward was arguing with on the phone the other day. She scrolls up. Everett Lansing has signed off on several jobs. On a hunch, Dorrie organizes the jobs by location and finds that Everett Lansing has signed off on nearly all the downtown Boston renovations. Or was Edward talking with another Lansing? Hardly an unusual name.

Huh.

And even if the Lansing here and the Lansing on the phone with Edward are the same, so what, really? People can have arguments, misunderstandings. It's hardly remarkable. Still. Why wouldn't Edward want him calling the office? Dorrie gets up and closes her door. She retrieves Joe's e-mail from her Upcoming Auditions file and jots down Paulo's number, keeping one eye on her office door. She'll call him later. From the house or from her car—from anywhere but here.

Samuel is home early, his car already in the driveway next to Mia's when Dorrie gets home. Mia's parents are out of town, so she's spending the night. Upstairs, she and Lily are catching up on homework they've left until the last possible minute, or, more likely, are trying on all Lily's clothes. They share outfits since they take exactly the same size. Dorrie glances at her watch.

She can hear Samuel in the kitchen, opening the refrigerator door, sorting through the contents. Her nerves jangle. Her insides vibrate like an electrical wire. After a minute or two, she walks out to the kitchen and crosses the glossy new wood floor, sliding a little in her stocking feet. She tugs a box out of the freezer.

"What's that?" Samuel comes up behind her at the stove.

"Veggie burgers."

"Is that *it*? That's dinner?"

"Well," Dorrie says. "Kind of. Mia's here and she's a vegetarian. There's other stuff though. There's some Brussels sprouts and peas and—"

Samuel raises one eyebrow. "I'll just make myself an omelet," he says, and he reaches into the fridge for the egg carton. "Where's the whisk?"

"In the dishwasher. But really—you should watch your cholesterol," Dorrie says. "It wouldn't kill you to eat what we're eating. It's unhealthy, all those eggs." She stares at the five eggs he's broken into a large blue bowl. He reaches for the cheese. "And cheese," she adds.

"I'm kind of a dead man walking anyway," Samuel says. "I smoke. I drink. *Drank*. Eggs and cheese are the least of my worries. In fact, they're sort of the superheroes of my health regimen."

"Don't say that, Samuel." Dorrie turns away from the microwave, where black bean burgers rotate on a bright orange plate. She looks Samuel in the eye. "Don't joke about dying."

Samuel shrugs. "Who'd care anyway?"

"Lily would. I would. *Lots* of people would." She doesn't say Viv would, but she thinks it. All this stuff about Samuel being scary is probably Viv's way of keeping the conversation on him, feeding her obsession. Samuel's "dangerous" to Viv because her feelings for him threaten her self-image, to say nothing of her friendship with Dorrie. She hasn't actually said this to Viv, but neither has she spoken to her since the late-night phone call.

"*Would* you care?" The microwave beeps. Samuel's eyes are bright in the recessed kitchen lighting.

"Yes."

He looks relieved. Just for a second.

"I'm going out," she says, dumping organic peas into a pot of boiling water. "There's this audition."

"That's—broad." Samuel flips the omelet expertly without losing the tomatoes and green peppers he's added, as a nod to health, apparently. Dorrie shrugs.

"It's in town," she says. "For a play that starts next month. I'm meeting Viv."

Samuel doesn't answer. He reaches over his eggs for the paprika.

"You know she's back in Boston."

"Uh-huh," he says. "Good. Great. You two can—"

"You've always liked her, too, though, haven't you?"

"Yeah." He keeps his back turned. "Yeah. She's okay. I mean, she's your friend."

"Right. *My* friend." She stops herself. "Girls!" She yells in the general direction of Lily's room. "Dinner! So have you seen her?"

"Viv? Uh-uh. You should invite her over for—"

"*I* have," Dorrie says. She stares at his back, but Samuel doesn't turn around. "I saw her down at the Copley. The Copley Square Hotel? You know it, right?"

He still doesn't turn around.

"You remember the Copley Square Hotel, don't you, Samuel? Right in the heart of—"

"What kind of a question is—of course I know the—what are you trying to—?"

Okay, Dorrie thinks. Okay. So we both know that we both know. She hesitates, but only for a second. "Nothing," she says, as the girls appear in the kitchen doorway. "Could you set the table, honey," she says. "Love the outfits, by the way. You both look totally—I love the drama. The flair."

"Of course, this from an actress." Across the room, Samuel eases the omelet onto a large yellow plate. "Talk about divas!"

"Wait. So you don't— What do *you* think, Dad?"

Samuel squints across the kitchen. Tilts his head. Pensive. Scrutinizing. "I have to agree with your mom on this one," he says. "You girls are definitely rocking those outfits."

"You should try a black bean burger." At the table, Lily glances at Samuel's omelet. "They're awesome when you add avocado and salsa." She cuts off a large chunk of her burger, passes him her plate. "Just try it," she says, and all eyes are on Samuel, whose daughter hung the moon, as he digs into the black bean burger with all the gusto he can manage. "Wow," he says. "This is really—"

Dorrie feels a pang of guilt. Bad enough she's cuckolded him with Joe—now she's lying to him. Again. But she has to go. She has to find out who's threatening her. She clears the table, loads the dishwasher, and glances at her watch. She has time. She has nearly an hour. The girls are upstairs again, wending their way through Lily's eclectic stash of clothes, and Samuel's in the backyard smoking—the tip of his cigarette glows orange in the black air. She grabs her cell and calls the number she jotted down at work. "Hello," she says when a woman answers. An older woman. Dorrie puts on a voice that drips authority. "May I speak to Paulo please?"

"They've gone," the woman says.

"They?"

"Paulo and *Elizabeth*," the woman says. "His *wife!*"

"I'm with Home Runs Renovations." Dorrie's voice is quick, sharp, the voice of an executive totally consumed by her job. "I just need to ask him a quick question about some work he did for us last—"

"He isn't with your company anymore. Surprised you wouldn't know something like that. He hasn't worked at Home Runs Renovations for quite some time." The woman bangs the phone back on the hook.

"Jeez." Dorrie pulls the phone away. Too late; her ear rings from the clatter of the woman's disconnect. Why did Paulo Androtti leave the company? Judging by his mother's attitude—it had to be his mother—it wasn't a simple parting of ways. Dorrie tugs at her ear. Or maybe his mother is just really mean.

"When will you be back?" Lily calls from the living room, but she doesn't look up. It's a rhetorical sort of question.

"I'm not sure," Dorrie says. "It depends on how long it all lasts." Not exactly a lie—she draws the line at lying to her daughter, and happily the English language leaves a lot of room for interpretation. Nuance.

Lily nods, her eyes glued to the TV. "Good luck," she says, and Mia raises her crossed fingers, smiles. From somewhere upstairs Samuel yells, "Break a leg!" An unfortunate choice, Dorrie thinks, and she pushes through the door onto the icy front porch.

She takes the train in and browses through shops until a quarter of eight, and then she strolls up the street to Starbucks. She's taken care to grab a different coat from the one she generally wears to work, doesn't remember buying it, this old woolen black thing from the back of the closet. She's not exactly sure it's even hers. She's wearing a large hat that must have been Samuel's at some point, since it's way too big, nearly covers her face down to her nose, and an old pair of boots.

She crosses the street. It's a frigid evening, the sort of night that people choose to be inside, not wandering along sidewalks, not if they have a choice. After a minute or two, Dorrie takes a breath and walks up to look directly through the Starbucks window. She can see nearly the entire inside of the coffee shop, and she studies the customers. No one looks suspicious in the least— a handful of couples, two groups of women chattering over pastries. A few people sit alone with their laptops, but they don't even glance toward the door, so they seem innocent enough. At least oblivious enough. *Inept* enough, if one of them is her stalker. She glances at her watch. A wasted trip.

Dorrie! Her mother's voice is in her ear, in her head. *Run, Dorrie! Quick! Run!* She turns slightly, away from the Starbucks window and steps backward, toward the street, scanning it.

"Dorrie!" This time the voice is loud. Different. A woman's voice, but not her mother's, and Dorrie whirls around as a figure darts off to lose itself in a clump of people—someone in a black coat—a jacket, maybe—and a knit hat covering the top part of his face. *Her* face?

"Dorrie?" a woman's voice calls again from a collection of cars parked along the curb, and, for a moment, Dorrie doesn't see a thing. For a moment, she thinks she's lost her mind.

XXIX

MAGGIE

When Lucas texts her, Maggie hesitates. What had seemed like a good idea at the junkyard earlier that day feels suddenly like an encroachment—a little overwhelming, suffocating. It's all happening too fast, she tells herself. He should have waited a few days before he got in touch. A week or so. She would have been more ready for a date if he had. Anyway, she's already agreed to meet Hank. *Some news about work,* he'd said in a voice-mail message earlier. *Meet me at seven. That diner on Boylston where we used to grab dinner.*

For a few minutes, she ignores Lucas's text. She takes her hair out of a braid and lets it fall to her shoulders, winds it around her fingers, making it curl slightly at the ends. It's been a long time. She glances back at the text and knows it wouldn't matter if Lucas waited for a day or a month. She still wouldn't feel ready. It's the way she is now. Shy. She's begun to analyze her actions, every step, as if she isn't certain of the ground beneath her feet.

She often feels like she's fifteen again, self-conscious and cautious around strangers, co-workers, even the handful of people she calls friends. When she does go out now, it's almost always for a reason, a trip to the market or a family gathering she feels pressured to attend.

In high school Maggie was the one who took the biggest risks. She was tough, a tomboy. *All those brothers*, her mother used to say. *It comes with the territory.* But she is different now. She isn't the same person she was, the daredevil. Magpie, her friends called her back then—her old friends. But now she finds it hard to even talk with them. They've pretty much stopped calling her. They've given up.

She thinks about that first time she went drinking after Iraq—how the friends she'd known forever seemed like strangers, how she'd panicked, felt as if she couldn't breathe, couldn't slow the pounding of her heart.

"You okay?" one of her friends, Marian, she thinks it was, had asked, leaning in for a better look.

"I have a headache," Maggie told her. "I get them a lot now."

Marian had nodded. "The explosion?"

"Yeah. Probably." There hadn't actually been an explosion, but her friends seemed not to know particulars, or, really, want to know. They were glad she was home. Iraq was far away. They wanted her to be the way she was before. They wanted Magpie.

She pinches her cheeks and glances at herself in the mirror in the ladies' room. She takes a deep breath and texts Lucas back quickly, before she can change her mind. *Yes*, she says, and he answers her in seconds. *In town*, he says. *But let's make it dinner. Yoblansky's Tavern on Dalton. Is that okay? Dive bar. Laid-back.*

Sure, she texts back. *Eight o'clock?* And he says yes. *Perfect.* Maggie sticks her phone in her bag. *You can do this*, she tells herself. *Hell. You made it back from Iraq in one piece, more or less. You can handle a quick drink with a cute guy.*

She'll head home early to change clothes and come to work first thing in the morning, try to make a dent in the claims stacked up on her desk. She's spent so much time on the Lindsay death. And then today, at Ian's shop—dawdling, her mother would say. *You were dawdling, Maggie. Dawdling with that boy.*

She takes her time getting ready, putting her hair up and then down, changing outfits, changing lipsticks. She looks in the mirror, leans in close, her lips pouted, turns up the radio to cancel out unbidden thoughts that cross her mind. *Those poor boys. Those poor boys, dead.*

She glances at her watch. She hasn't much time. She's running a little late—all this obsessing on her hair. She turns off the radio, slides into her coat, and triple-locks the front door on her way out.

Hank is already at the diner when Maggie scrunches into the booth across from him.

"Ordering?" He reaches for the menu on the table.

"Naw," she says. "You go ahead, though. I've got somewhere to go after."

"Yeah? A date? You really got it goin' on there, girl."

"Thanks," she says. "So why'm I here?"

"So Carlos," Hank says. "He's leaving to be a state trooper in Vermont. Go figure, eh? His wife's family wants her closer, now she's got the baby."

"They looking to replace him?"

"I'm thinking they might," Hank says. "And that's just in our district. Word is the whole department's hiring."

"So when's Carlos leaving?"

Hank shakes his head. "I'm not sure. It's soon, though. That's why I wanted to give you a heads-up. Just in case you've had enough of the insurance business. I know you love your job and all." He stretches, leans back in the booth, winks.

"Right." Maggie looks at her watch. "Listen," she says. "I gotta go, Hank. Thanks for the heads-up." She grabs her purse and slides out of the booth as Hank turns his attention back to the open menu on the table.

"Hey, Mag," he says. "You look great. Seriously."

"Thanks. And thanks again for the—you know—the heads-up." Maggie straightens her coat. She will definitely put in for Carlos's job. She'll download an application and fill it out when she gets home tonight. She'll keep it to herself. But she will do it.

She starts her car and pulls off the curb to the street. Decides to take a different route. If she's lucky—if she hurries—she could still be on time. She checks her face in the rearview mirror, her pale face, her smoky-lidded eyes, forces a smile. "Yeah," she says. "You still got it."

Traffic is bad but she's seen it worse. She shouldn't be more than a few minutes late. She knows the place—been there once or twice. Not recently, but recently enough to know how to get there, where to park. She noses along Boylston and it crosses her mind they should have planned to meet somewhere besides a bar. Coffee instead of beer. Or, no. Not coffee. Tea. Hot chocolate. She smiles. Right. She's just pulling alongside Starbucks when she sees her. The clothes are weird. Still, there's something in the way she stands, the way she moves toward the window, the way she peeks inside. It looks like—*Dorrie?* What the hell is she doing, slinking around, peeking inside windows?

She laughs. Dorrie. How did she ever pull off having an affair? And with her *boss*, no less? Maggie feels herself relax a little. Some thin, taut string that runs along her bones begins to give. She starts to speed up as the traffic moves ahead, and then she sees him. Him or her. A figure. She sees someone so covered up by clothing, she has no idea what the person looks like. It's a weird match to Dorrie, with the heavy puffy coat, the knit hat covering half the face. Whoever it is stands behind Dorrie, just at the edge of the sidewalk, clearly watching her. Stalking her.

Maggie's passed them now. She's driven too far forward.

"Dorrie!" she yells, and the figure bolts suddenly to the left. "Dorrie!" she yells again, and Dorrie turns, finally, squints into the street as the figure moves back up the sidewalk, farther out of reach, and there is nothing Maggie can do—no place to pull against the curb, no place to even stop, except for just that second. "Hurry!" She beckons Dorrie to her car and unlocks the passenger-side door. "Get in! Quick!"

XXX

DORRIE

orrie climbs into Brennan's old Land Rover and fastens her seat belt. Riding in cars with virtual strangers is not her favorite thing to do, especially since the accident, when getting in the car with anyone makes her grit her teeth and look around for trees.

"Why am I here?"

"Good question," Brennan says, with her usual dry humor. She looks different, though, really pretty.

"Awesome outfit," Dorrie says.

"Thanks." Brennan thumbs a quick text to someone while they're still stuck in the middle of Boylston Street. "So what were you doing back there?"

"Oh." Dorrie glances out the window. "I was meeting a friend," she says. "It wasn't definite, though. She wasn't sure she could make it. Babysitter problems. You know how that is."

"No," Brennan says. "Not really."

Dorrie takes off her hat, runs her hands across her hair. "Anyway, I was just checking. If she wasn't in there, I thought I'd head on home."

"So instead of just calling her, you made a trip all the way back to town to see if your friend was in Starbucks?"

Dorrie forces a jolly little laugh. Waves her arm in the air. Bracelets clang in the cold car. Audrey Hepburn in *Breakfast at Tiffany's*. "No. Of course not. No," she says, and she is both thrilled and disgusted that she's learned to lie so easily. "I was in town anyway. It was a tentative coffee. How about you? What are we—um—doing?"

"There was somebody following you. Puffy sort of coat. Jacket, maybe. I couldn't see the face."

"Oh," Dorrie says. "Shit. Where?"

"Behind you. And to the left."

"In a car or—"

Brennan shakes her head. "On foot."

"Well. Wow. Thanks, Brennan. Lucky you were here," Dorrie says. "Wait. Why *are* you here?"

"Actually," Brennan says, but she doesn't say anything else. Her cheeks are flushed.

"Ohhh. A guy?"

"I have a date."

"Well, what are you waiting for?" Dorrie says. "Go!" She unstraps her seat belt, but the car is moving, so she fastens it again and sits back.

"I can't just leave you," Brennan says. "Whoever was in that lame outfit was clearly stalking you. And speaking of lame outfits, what the hell are you *wearing*?"

224

"What? *This* old thing? Dorrie laughs. "Sometimes we leave extra coats at work. That's why Jeananne was wearing that stupid—" She lets her voice trail off, tries to hide her feet, those awful cowboy boots. "Really, Brennan. Go. Meet your friend!"

"Can't do that. You could be in danger. I told you."

"I'll be careful. Promise. In fact, I'll let you drop me at the train," she says and Brennan's car slows to turn toward the Back Bay station.

"This one work?"

"Perfect." Dorrie leans against the heavy door. It's like a tank, Brennan's car. A fortress. Maybe she should buy a used Land Rover, give her car to Samuel. "Enjoy your date," she says over her shoulder. "And, Brennan. Really. Thank you."

"Keep an eye out," Brennan says, "while you're in the station," and Dorrie nods. She isn't sure exactly what to keep an eye out *for*—whoever was behind her could have ditched the puffy coat. Still, she scans the street, the sidewalks, the nearby storefronts before she heads inside. The train is just pulling in and Dorrie slides into a crowded car, stuffed with bodies that hide her own.

The lights flicker on and off, the car lurches to the side and then back too far the other way before it straightens itself out, rumbles down the track. She reaches up to take off Samuel's old black hat but she decides to leave it on—no reason not to. Around her, people read, swaying against the straps, grabbing for poles when the train lurches suddenly around a corner. No one stands out. She looks at her reflection in the window across the aisle and thinks that in her current outfit she might pass for a man. She hopes so. A very short man, but that happens. Most likely, whoever was behind her couldn't know for certain who she was, although Brennan recognized her right away. But Brennan knows her. And, anyway, Brennan was a cop. In fact, she seems to still be one, at least to think like one, and Dorrie wonders why she ever left the force.

Her mind wanders to the other night, to making love with Samuel. It was like old times, she thinks, almost like, and she remembers all those years ago, their tiny room downtown, the fifth-floor walk-up, making love as dinner burned to ashes on the stove. They can't go back—she knows they can't. She knows it in her mind, but in her heart she wonders sometimes, hopes sometimes.

It's freezing on the street outside the station, and Dorrie hurries along in the mud-colored boots she found buried among other old discarded shoes in the hall closet. She walks as fast as they allow, these clumpy, webby things that pinch her toes.

She fumbles with the key in the front lock and then the new dead bolt that Samuel's just installed, huffs on her fingers, numb and clumsy. She really has to buy some gloves—and she's unpleasantly reminded of the lone black one in the garage. She shakes her head. She'll think about that later, get that sorted out. There has to be an explanation.

"I'm back!" she yells from the doorway, the tiny room they call a foyer, with a coatrack and a square of floor. She crumples up the overcoat and ditches the old boots in the back of the closet, spots the girls in the living room. The TV blares. Finally Lily looks up. Mia waves.

"That was quick." A commercial chirps on and Lily gets up to forage through the kitchen, comes back to the living room with an aging box of chocolate chip cookies from Whole Foods. "How'd it go?"

Dorrie shrugs. "Those cookies might be stale," she points out, but Lily rolls her eyes.

"How would we even know?" she says. "They're so fortified." Mia giggles. Dorrie looks around.

"Where's your dad?"

"He went out, too. He left right after you did."

Dorrie walks over to the window and glances at the driveway. "Huh," she says. "I didn't even notice his car was gone. Did he say where he was going?"

"Yeah." Lily's back in front of the TV. "A meeting, he said."

Dorrie looks at her watch. If he left right after she did, Samuel must have gone to an eight o'clock meeting, which means it would let out at nine. Say fifteen minutes to shoot the breeze with people afterward and then another fifteen minutes to get home. He won't be back until nine thirty at the earliest. She'll wait for him, she thinks. She'll make some decaf, put some stale cookies on a plate. Or, no. Forget the cookies.

So what's he doing pulling up in the driveway now, at five minutes to nine?

She meets him in the foyer and catches him before he reaches the hall closet. She watches him take off his coat, shaking off the bits of snow before he hangs it up and shuts the closet door.

"No hat?" Dorrie stands in front of him. Samuel looks away.

"Hi, girls," he calls. He looks back at his wife, standing with her arms folded over her chest, blocking his path to the living room. "Hat?" He looks confused. "What hat?"

"It's cold," Dorrie says. "It's freezing. Why don't you have a hat?"

Samuel doesn't answer at first. He looks over her shoulder at the TV as if he's watching *Dancing with the Stars.* "Well, Dorrie," he says, "I didn't wear one. But thanks for your concern."

"And why are you home?"

"I happen to *live*—"

"*Now,* I mean. So early."

"Why are *you* home so early?"

"I finished with the rehearsal."

"And I finished with my meeting," Samuel says. "So what's your point?"

"AA meetings last more than half an hour," Dorrie says.

"Not if only two members show up and say everything they have to say in twenty minutes," Samuel mumbles, and he nudges his way past her to the kitchen.

XXXI

MAGGIE

Maggie parks and turns on the inside light so she can fix her hair in the rearview mirror. She feels calmer. The escapade with Dorrie made her almost forget about her first-date jitters. She bends forward, repairs her lipstick, glances at the text from Lucas. *I'm here.*

Client rescue, she texts Lucas back. *Be there ASAP.*

What was Dorrie really doing? Her story about the friend was obviously a lie. A bad one at that. Dorrie seems to be covering up all sorts of things, and, really, Maggie can totally see why she'd want to keep her affair with her boss hidden, the fact that she was with him when he died. Adultery is a tricky thing. Innocent people often get hurt—people on the outskirts, like Dorrie's husband, and—a daughter, Maggie thinks she said. And Karen, of course, although she's probably known for some time about her husband's affair, even if she didn't know exactly who the woman was. Wives always know these things, Maggie thinks, wives and girlfriends. They pick up on subtle differences—a new haircut, a new shirt, a sudden interest in fitness. And then there are the far less subtle things—perfume, or soap, shampoo—something that the husband might not think about or even realize was there. But his wife would.

Maggie knows she's in over her head with this claim. She's not a cop. Not anymore. She's an insurance investigator, she tells herself. She needs to reel herself in. Affairs and tie-wrapped brakes. What is she thinking? Still. She's so close . . .

She eases out to the pavement, careful not to open her door all the way; she's parked too close to the person next to her. No choice, really, since her car's so huge. If someone told her years ago she'd be driving a Land Rover, she'd have laughed. "Are you fucking *kidding* me? Those things are gas guzzlers. They're the *reason* for all these wars," she would have said. Did say, in fact, more times than she could count, zipping along the highway in the cheapest, smallest car she could find.

She hurries into Yoblansky's and spots Lucas sitting at a table not far from the door, but a little out of the way, off the beaten track, offering at least a hint of privacy. "Hi," he says. He stands up, pulls out her chair.

"Gentleman." She smiles.

"Of course. You should see me *before* I've had two beers."

"I *have*," she says. She glances at the menu. "At least I hope so. This morning? At work?"

He leans over, points out a couple of items on the menu. "The chicken's good," he says. "Nothing fancy, but it's good. So your client. Her car break down?"

"Something like that," Maggie says.

He looks gorgeous with his dark blue shirt, his leather jacket, a new haircut, she thinks, since that morning. "Sorry I'm late," she says. "I hate it when people keep me waiting."

He shrugs. "That sort of thing doesn't bother me."

"Yeah?" she says. "I'll leave if someone's really late. I can't stand just sitting, just—waiting."

"Really?" he says. "I'll have to remember that."

"A *wise* gentleman."

When the waitress comes to their table, Lucas orders for them both.

"I'm glad you decided to come." He folds his hands and leans over the table. The people in a booth behind them laugh at something Maggie didn't hear. "I was afraid you wouldn't."

"To be honest," she says, "I came close to canceling on you."

"What changed your mind?"

She shrugs. "Nothing, really. I mean, what's the harm? A drink's a drink."

"Or a drink's a chicken sandwich." He smiles. "How long you been out?"

"A while," she says, and the waitress returns, sets their drinks down too hard on the table. Beer sloshes over the sides. Maggie's fingers close around the mug and she takes a couple of swallows. "So when's your uncle coming back?"

"Monday. Maybe. He isn't sure."

"Listen," Maggie says. "I'm not so good at this. I'm a little out of practice."

"Me, too," he says. "But, hey. We did it, right? We're having a social interaction." And Maggie sees he has it, too, this shyness she has, this fear that makes her want to hole up in her apartment and makes dating such a challenge.

"Yeah."

"So maybe next time . . ." he says.

"Next time?"

"It'll be easier. A piece of cake. And speaking of dessert . . ."

"Totally stuffed," Maggie says. "But I'll have a bite of whatever you order. As long as it's chocolate."

They split a slice of cake. Chocolate. They finish off their beers, poke at the dessert with their forks. They talk—about the uncle, the business, about Maggie's job at the insurance company, her job with the Boston police. They talk about how cold the winter's been, about everything. But not Iraq, not about the way her hands shake sometimes for no reason, the way she's lost touch with her friends, replaced her social life with a TV.

"Hey," Lucas says later, when the dessert is long gone, when they've polished off their beers, when the place is packed to overflowing and the waitress has swatted the check on the table, face-down in front of Maggie. "Do you know that guy?"

Maggie slides the check to the center of the table. "I think she's into you," she says, nodding toward the waitress. "What guy?"

"At that table over there," Lucas says, and he cuts his eyes toward a shadowed booth in a corner near the door.

"No," she says. "I don't think so. I can't really see him. Why?" She bends down to grab her purse, slides into her coat.

"He's been staring at you all night."

"Oh," she says. "*That.* Happens all the time. My beauty, you know." She laughs, but Lucas doesn't.

232

"I can see that," he says, and Maggie feels her cheeks turn red. She's grateful for the darkness of the bar. He stares at her.

"God," she says. "Stop, willya? You're making me self-conscious."

"Sure. Sorry." Lucas sticks a wad of bills under a water glass and the two of them stand up to leave.

"So where's this guy?" Maggie turns around again, hoping for a better look, but the table is empty. "Where'd he go? Maybe we can fix him up with our waitress."

"Gone," Lucas says. "He took off a couple minutes ago."

XXXII

KAREN

Karen closes Tomas's door with a tiny whisper sound and almost runs down the odious dark stairs. She flings herself against the heavy outside door to the sidewalk, but once outside, she doesn't want to go back home. She isn't ready. She'll go see Alice at Bound for Glory.

She takes the train back to the restaurant where she'd left her car hours before and drives straight to the bookstore. The sound of tinkling bells announces her entrance and she stands, for a few seconds, in the doorway, trying to catch her breath.

"Are we alone?" She looks around.

"Sadly." Alice sighs. "January."

"I've done something really stupid." Karen crosses the room and takes off her coat, hangs it on a hook behind the counter.

"What? Oh. Before I forget—" Alice reaches for a little pile of books beside the register. "They're on grief," she says. "I've been meaning to give them to you, but I keep forgetting."

"Thanks," Karen says. "These are great. They're really—I slept with Tomas."

"Wow." Alice raises one eyebrow. "That's kind of—umm—out of character. Sleeping with some guy you haven't seen in—what? A year? Two years? Not a very Karen thing to do."

Karen sighs. "I'll straighten out those shelves," she says, but she doesn't move. She runs her thumb along the pages of her little pile of books. The store is lit completely by the lamps and the smattering of lights across the ceiling. The yellow day is now the color of mud; almost no light comes through the windows, and Karen eyes the reading area, longs for a quick nap. Behind the crowded shelves, two couches and a wooden rocker sit enticingly on a worn Persian rug—Persian to match the cats, Alice said when she bought it. There is always a fresh pot of coffee, nearly always pastries from the Queen of Cups. The ambience is cozy. It is, as Alice always says, her second home.

"Maybe that's exactly why I *did* sleep with him," Karen says. "Maybe I just wanted to feel something. *Anything*. And he was . . . there." Some people can get away with acting on impulse, Karen thinks, but she's never really been one of them. Dorrie probably is. *Definitely* is.

"Maybe." Alice looks up. The bells tinkle. "Hello!" she says, as two women close the door behind them. "Welcome to Bound for Glory," and she squeezes out from behind the counter, walks toward the door. "Is this your first visit?"

Karen helps out, stalling until rush hour is over and even then she takes the long way home. She wishes now she'd joined Tomas in the shower at his place. She feels dirty. No, she thinks. The shower wouldn't help; it's more that she feels tainted, compromised, and she's surprised by sudden overwhelming guilt. She'd thought she could escape for a couple of hours, feel some kind of vindication for what Joe did to her, to their marriage, all those months. *Years*, for all she knows. She'd also hoped that being with Tomas would erase all thoughts of both her dead husband *and* Edward. And it has. She wasn't banking on this, though, this guilt, remorse, almost. It was too soon.

Maybe, she thinks, pondering the afternoon on her way home, she'd wanted to see if the feelings for Tomas that she had up until today ignored, denied, could ever be revived. Like it or not, *ready* or not, she's alone now. There's no husband, good or bad, faithful or philandering. She is totally alone in a drafty old house in the middle of Waltham, sharing a bed that's far too large for only her, with Antoine, who would doubtless go completely nuts if she actually did take up with someone. If nothing else, Antoine is loyal to his rotten, furry, growling little core. But not Karen. Or so she'd thought.

The second she heard the shower come on, dribbly and sparse from the bad pressure on the fourth floor, as soon as she heard Tomas begin to sing, she knew she'd made a terrible mistake. Tomas himself doesn't worry her in the least—she can tell him that she feels disloyal, she needs time. She can say the cops know she was right there when Joe died. She needs to be careful, she can tell him. She looks guilty enough already—the insurance policy, her presence. The fact that she's involved with another man . . . it could destroy her.

No. It isn't really Tomas. It's herself she's worried about—her sanity. Her dignity, maybe. She isn't sure. She only knows that she feels duplicitous, as if she's spit on everything she valued, as if she's spit on Joe. Even if he wasn't the best husband these past months, he was still the love of her life. How could she taint his memory the way she has, demean herself the way she did this afternoon? She doesn't even *love* Tomas. *Never* loved him; she can see that now. It was only lust, maybe a sprinkling of revenge for Joe's philandering, a smattering of longing for Tomas, of course, for their friendship years before. But mostly it was lust.

The odor of his building is inside her pores, the smell of soap and floor cleaner and garlic, of Tomas's hands, his skin, the odor of their lovemaking. She'll wash her clothes when she gets home, her hair. She won't think about today again, at least not for a while. She stares through the windshield. A dark night. Streetlights shine like small round stars against the black.

She turns on her iPod, fast-forwards through the mournful, melancholy songs she's listened to since Joe died, fiddles through to vintage Springsteen. She turns it up. And then she turns it up louder, singing quietly along. She sings louder, pressing her foot down harder on the gas. *Tramps like us, Baby we were born to run.* For the first time in years, she feels like a woman. For the first time since Karen can remember, she feels alive!

When she gets home, she realizes she's forgotten to set the new alarm again. A foreboding, although at first she doesn't see anything out of place. It's only when she's taken off her coat and tossed her hat on the couch.

Antoine shivers in a corner of the kitchen, his fur damp and cold, as if he's just come in from the yard. Antoine doesn't have a doggie door, even though Karen had for years insisted they should get one. Joe hated the idea, thought it was inviting trouble. Rats, he said, or, hell, a break-in. "At the very least he'll bring in all his friends," Joe said one night, shaking his head and walking out of the kitchen, flapping the sports page loudly. "That's ridiculous," Karen had said. "Antoine doesn't have any friends."

"What happened, sweetie?" She stoops to pet him and he doesn't snarl. A bad sign. Antoine must be really off his game. His fur is nearly frozen. Karen grabs a towel from the bathroom and dries him off as best she can, and then she plugs in the hair dryer and aims the warm air at him. Antoine yelps in protest and only then does it occur to Karen that if *he* went *out*, someone *else* must have come *in*. She tiptoes to the back door. It's locked, but Antoine's paw prints are still visible in small wet spots that dot the tiled kitchen floor. There are no larger, footprint-size puddles, which tells her that whoever came in cleaned up the telltale tracks. Did one of the boys stop by? No. Robbie's still at work—she'd spoken to him not an hour ago, and Jon's on Martha's Vineyard with his girlfriend's parents.

This time she doesn't hesitate to call the police.

"Please," she says. "Hurry."

"Anything out of place? The house look different at all?"

"Haven't checked," she says and she hangs up. She only hopes whoever broke in found a way to get back out again. She slinks down the hall to the back bedrooms, barely breathing. The wide-screen TV still sits pompously in the living room; the computer she uses for her writing projects is open on a desk in the den.

She walks to the back of the house. Her jewelry, when she looks in the box, is still there. At least at first glance, everything appears untouched. Outside, a police car whirs to a stop, and she goes quickly to the door to let in the patrolman. Officer Rush. Fitting. He's alone.

"Aren't you supposed to come in pairs?" she says, but Officer Rush just shakes his head.

"Not on something like this," he says, and Karen knows he isn't taking her call seriously. He is here perfunctorily, but she hasn't a faintest hope that Officer Rush will do much about—about what, exactly? A wet dog? She clears her throat.

"So. Anything missing?" Officer Rush wonders. He taps his pen lightly against his pad. He stands inside the doorway, but just barely.

"Not so far. No," Karen says, "but I haven't really had a chance to—you know—really. *Thoroughly.* You arrived so quickly."

"Right." He looks pleased. "Our response time is excellent."

"Do you want a cup of coffee, Officer?" Karen feels nearly at home with this whole situation. Brennan. Officer Rush.

"Been drinking it all day." He waves his large hand in the air between them. "One more cup and you'll be peeling me off the ceiling. Thanks, though." He takes a step or two toward the kitchen. "I'll have a look around. See where they got in. Let me know if something comes up missing."

"Right," Karen says on her way to the back of the house. "I didn't see anything when I came in, but, like I said, I didn't really—" She opens the door to Joe's old office carefully. She's stuck Antoine inside the room so he won't go crazy with Officer Rush in the house since he seems seriously traumatized as it is. She looks around. Joe's laptop. Where is it? She looks everywhere—she starts with where she knows she left the thing, and works her way around the room from there. Gone.

And so is her iPad.

"Got it!" Officer Rush has clearly discovered something.

"What?" She hurries down the hall toward his voice. "Where are you?"

"Here," he says. "In this little room back here. Off the kitchen here. I found where they got in."

Karen joins him in the tiny storage room. Broken glass covers the floor.

"You'll need to get that boarded up till you get the window replaced." He jerks his head toward the broken window.

"I know what he took!"

"Yeah?" He turns around. "What's that?"

"My husband's laptop," Karen says. "He just died. My husband. He's just passed away."

"I'm sorry," Officer Rush says, scrolling around on his cell.

"Yes." She nods. "It was totally—" She stops, takes a breath. "And my iPad. My iPad's gone, too."

"Is that it?" He sticks the phone in his jacket pocket and jots something down. Karen can almost see him stopping at the nearest McDonald's for a coffee, running it through his mind now where the closest one is. Checking it on his phone. Not close at all, actually. *Recalculating.* He snaps the little notebook shut and starts to stick it in his pocket. *Well. That's a wrap. Now for that Double Mac.*

"That's all I noticed. So far," Karen says. "It's an Apple, though, and I have an iPhone, so you can track it."

"'Find' feature enabled?"

"Yep," she says. "Putting in my password now."

"Oh." Out comes the little pad again. "And the laptop?"

"No," Karen says. Damn. She hands her phone to Officer Rush. Both the laptop and her tablet are relatively new. Her iPad was barely out of the box, Joe's laptop only about a year old. Small enough to

240

sneak out under a jacket, get through a window, out of the neighbor-hood without a moving van or a vehicle at all, actually. Perfect for a quick afternoon heist.

"Got the track," the officer says. "You're lucky he didn't turn off the 'find' feature first thing. Happens a lot."

"Whew," she says. "Great. Where is it?" It can't be far. Most likely someone wanting drugs, a quick buck to trot over to a dealer. Some kid. She's got to start turning on the alarm when she goes out.

"In town," he says, surprising her. "I'll call it in to the Boston PD with the location. I can't see what kind of place it is, but, hopefully, it's still with your intruder there and we can grab the laptop at the same time."

"Great!"

"Unless they've already sold it," Officer Rush says, and he heads out the front door.

Karen walks back to Joe's old office and bends down to pat Antoine, who is strangely quiet in the corner. He shivers, even though she's dried him with the hair dryer, and Karen wonders if he's going into shock. "Antoine," she says, "come on, boy!" She trudges up the hall to the kitchen and rattles the bag of dry dog food, but he is stubborn in his misery. She scoops him up. Without all the yipping and snapping, he seems suddenly very small. She carries him into the bedroom and sets him on the bed, covers him with a quilt, and Antoine brightens. Barely. She brings the dog food from the kitchen and hand-feeds him, coaxing him at first. After a few tiny nibbles, Antoine feels up to helping himself, sticking his wet nose inside the bag and even managing a small snarl. Back to normal. Almost.

She would gladly have bought a laptop for the thief, one with-out all the company finances on it. Better yet, just handed him the money. She sorts through Joe's papers. This time she'll go through everything, every file, every cabinet. He must have hard copies somewhere. Or are they at the office? In his car? Joe was careful. Cautious when it came to technology. Almost old-school. "If it fails, nine times out of ten, people are totally lost," he used to say, "unless they backed everything up or have a hard copy."

The phone rings, and Karen looks behind her, trying to remember where she's left it. The bedroom, she thinks, with Antoine. She jumps up to head for the hallway and her heel catches in the plaid doggie bed. She falls forward, grabs at a table to steady herself, knocking a stack of papers to the floor. She glances down. She'll get it later. And then she sees the spreadsheets. Sheets of them. September–December, one of them says, and then May–August. She stops, bends down. January–April. All of it's here! Right here! Thank God! She feels like letting out a little yip of joy herself. "We're okay, Antoine!" she calls out toward the bedroom. "It's all here!"

"Officer Rush," a very masculine-sounding voice informs her, when she grabs the phone on the last ring. "They got your iPad. It's at a restaurant down on Commonwealth. Owner says a waitress turned it in after she found it on a table in back. Weird. Kids," he says, and Karen pictures Officer Rush throwing up his hands. "Anyhow, they're taking it down to the station now for prints. Should be good to go by morning."

"Great," she says. "Thank you, so much! How about the laptop?"

"No laptop. Sorry. Get that back window boarded up and turn on your alarm. Probably a random break-in, but now they know the window's broken and they've got a way in, so be careful, Mrs. Lindsay."

"Right," she says. For a minute she thinks about calling Tomas, about asking him to come by after work and stay the night. She even scrolls to his work number at the hospital. She hesitates. He won't be off for hours. And even if she talked him into ditching work and coming over now, it would only make things more uncomfortable between them. She'd be leading him on. Worse, she'd be using him. And he'd be coming here to her house, which he has never done before. She's feeling guilty enough without adding to it, beating herself up later for having Tomas sleep in her late husband's bed. And he would. At this point, she can hardly ask him to spend the night on the couch.

No. She hurries out to the garage and finds a piece of plywood from some abandoned project—a birdhouse, was it? A backboard for a high-school science project? And then she calls Robbie, tells him what's happened. She can hear his car door beeping open before she's even finished.

"Did they dust for prints?" Robbie stands in the small violated room, and Karen says she doesn't know, actually. She assumes so.

"Not they," she says. "It was just the one guy. Officer Rush."

Robbie nails the plywood over the broken window and checks the yard three times before he leaves. Reluctantly leaves. He offers to spend the night. Insists on it. *Think about what Dad would want*, he says in desperation, but Karen tells him no. She's fine. She's not alone; she has Antoine, but thanks him for his concern. She practically pushes her son out the front door and then she sets the alarm, curls up on the couch with several quilts and the now dry and fluffy Antoine. Robbie calls her back from the highway into town. "So," he says. "You're saying someone went to all that trouble—breaking into a house in a suburban neighborhood, a house with a barking yippy dog—and then just happened to *forget* the iPad in a coffee shop in Boston?"

"I know." Karen yawns. It's been one hell of a long day. "And it's strange they didn't take more."

XXXIII

Dorrie leaves work early and takes a cab to the hospital, even though there's nothing much to be done for Jeananne at this point. Still, she can talk to her. She can sit with her, or, really, stand—ICU is not the place for lengthy visiting. Jeananne's still in there somewhere, just unable to answer at the moment, or open her eyes, apparently. Music from the iPod streams from a metal table beside the hospital bed, playing Jeananne's favorite songs.

Dorrie sits in the lobby on a plastic chair. Sometimes she isn't allowed to see Jeananne at all. Sometimes she sits for an hour or so and leaves without even a glimpse into the room in ICU. It depends on who's on duty. Jeananne has no family nearby, or, as far as Dorrie knows, anywhere at all. She was an only child, father long gone, and her mother died three years ago. A cousin somewhere, but Dorrie has no idea where. It was only the husband—ex-husband now, so most of the nurses let her go in. They've been easing off on the sedation for the past couple of days, and Jeananne is breathing on her own. She has, the nurse called to tell Dorrie earlier this afternoon, even come around for brief periods. She's confused, but that happens. "All the drugs," the nurse explained. They've operated on Jeananne's ankle, her broken wrist, and she's apparently come through like a trouper. Dorrie's not to be too optimistic, she's been cautioned, but she is. She knows Jeananne. "Can't keep a good woman down," she always says, and the nurse smiles, gives Dorrie's arm a depressing little pat. "We'll hope for the best."

Dorrie reaches for her bag. She'll phone home, leave a message for Samuel and Lily. She hadn't known about Jeananne before she left the house this morning. She rummages through her purse. No phone. Damn. With all that's happened, she doesn't like to be without it, not even for a minute. She feels herself start to panic, even though she's sitting in the lobby of the ICU, surrounded by medical personnel and concerned, nail-biting family members. She thinks about taking a cab to the office to grab her cell phone off her desk. It's only a short ride. She could still make it back in time to see Jeananne.

"Dorrie?" The nice nurse stands in the doorway. "Your friend seems to be coming around," she says. "You might want to walk back, see if you can help. She's more likely to respond if you're there."

Jeananne is tiny and pale. She doesn't look any different today than she did the last time Dorrie saw her. She looks like a doll. A shell. Dorrie hesitates.

246

"Come in." The nurse moves over slightly in the cramped space. "Just talk to her," she says. "Try to connect with her. She's still a little disoriented."

"Jeananne?" Dorrie is suddenly self-conscious in this room of beeps and blinking lights, the huffing pumps and monitors. "Jeananne?" she says. "It's Dorrie. Can you hear me?" There is a tiny movement, the flicker of blond eyelashes. "Jeananne?" Dorrie leans over the bed. Her face hovers in the air above Jeananne's. Her breath is fast. Her heart pounds. "Jeananne," she says. "It's Dorrie. Can you open your eyes?"

And she does.

"Nurse!" Dorrie turns around. The nurse stands in the hall, writing on a chart. "Nurse!" Dorrie calls again, but the nurse is already crossing the threshold, already grabbing Jeananne's wrist, fragile as a bird's wing.

"Hey," she says in a soft voice. Bridget, her name tag says. "Welcome back."

Jeananne's lips twitch. In the bright and greenish light, her white face is opaque, like milk glass.

"Do you know who this is?" Bridget gestures toward Dorrie. "Do you recognize your friend?"

Jeananne nods a teensy little nod.

"Can you tell me her name?"

Jeananne's voice is a whisper, a small, light wisp, catching in the cacophony of hospital sounds, but it's still her voice, even though she doesn't actually answer Bridget's question.

"Where am I?" Jeananne squints around the room.

"You're in the hospital. Mass General." Dorrie moves in beside Bridget and the two of them crowd against the metal rails, gazing down at Jeananne as if she is a newborn in a crib, as if they've never seen anything more beautiful. She stirs. Dorrie can see her veins through the skin along her forehead and the white skin of her arms. Darkness pools beneath her lids. She closes her eyes.

"I am so sorry," Dorrie says. "I feel like this is all my fault. If you had just come with me to Mug Me—if I hadn't been in such a hurry . . ."

Jeananne's eyes open again; her forehead creases. "Silly." Jeananne shrugs, a tiny movement underneath the sheet. "Accident."

"I know." Dorrie takes her hand. "I'm so glad you're awake," she says. "So glad you're going to be all right." Would she? Dorrie looks around, but Bridget's gone. "I should let you rest," she says.

Jeananne's lips twitch. Not quite a smile.

Dorrie bends to give her a small hug. "I know. Enough with the resting, but you need to get your strength back. We really miss you at work. Especially Edward. And me, of course."

Jeananne's forehead crinkles again and it occurs to Dorrie that Jeananne might not exactly know at this point who Edward is. The theory that they were passionately involved now seems absurd.

She catches a cab back to work to pick up her car and her cell phone that she's sure she's left somewhere in her office—she probably set it down on her desk after the call from the hospital, when she'd run out to the hall to tell everyone the good news, only to find the place was virtually empty. Only the new temp who barely knew who Jeananne was looked up when Dorrie announced the good news in the hallway. "That's really awesome," she'd said, chewing on an aqua fingernail. The cab turns onto Charles and Dorrie stares out the window at the sidewalks lit by streetlights, and tries to shake off an edgy feeling. In the back of her mind, her mother whispers something Dorrie can't quite hear. She doesn't want to. It's enough that Jeananne's better.

The taxi pulls off I-93 toward South Station and merges onto Purchase Street. As it lurches to a stop against the curb on Summer, Dorrie spots the guard through the large front window. Still on duty. Her edginess recedes a smidgeon; the whispers in her head subside.

Lights are on at Home Runs, and she wonders for a second who could possibly still be there. Jeananne was the one who worked late. *And will again!* She smiles, raises her fists high in the air. *Yes!* She hurries down the hall, spots the lights on in the back office—the tech guy must be here installing the new computer system. She doesn't bother to go back to say hello.

She finds her phone where she'd left it on her desk, sticks it in her purse, and starts to hurry out to the garage, but, on a whim, she goes back and sits at her computer. It's late, way after hours, so there's no one here, only Len, lost somewhere in the bowels of the back office. It's the perfect time to take another look at the customer files and see if there's anything she might have missed the other day when she glanced at the background on the couple that died in the fire. Robbins. She turns on her computer and pulls up the file, scrolls down to the R's, but she doesn't see their name. She scrolls back up. "Remaley . . . Rogers." What the hell? She scrolls through all the R's again, and then she types "Robbins" into the search engine. Nothing. A wave of nausea hits her. Someone's deleted it. She looks around behind her and then up and down the hall. The edginess snakes back along her spine, an eerie feeling as if she's not alone, as if she's being watched. Her heart flip-flops like a trapped bird.

But maybe she did it. Maybe, in her hurry the other day, she deleted the Robbins file. She checks under Upcoming Auditions. The copy she'd made is still there. Good. And she has the hard copy zipped inside her bag. She closes out and takes the elevator down to the garage.

The lights are wonky, casting shadows everywhere on the walls, distorted, stretched-out shadows. She unlocks her car and the beep of the key lock echoes in the huge bare space as Dorrie slides behind the wheel and starts the car. Tries to start the car. It makes a whirring sound and cuts off.

Damn.

She tries again. This time the motor coughs and the car shudders, but the engine still does not turn over. It's very cold. Extremely, maddeningly cold. But the car is only three years old, so it isn't as if she's driving one of her husband's old fixer-uppers that can't handle this kind of weather. She climbs out and looks under the hood. She's learned a few things after all these years with Samuel. She checks the battery connections, all the hoses she can spot— nothing seems loose or disconnected. She shakes the battery and turns the key again. Nothing. This time there's only a click. A dead-engine click. And then the squeak of the outside door. She doesn't move. She's frozen, her hands gripping the steering wheel so hard her knuckles go from pink to white. She stares ahead, through the windshield, terrified to look around her, terrified to look at the side door. She doesn't hear it close; there's only the squeak of the hinge.

The wind, she tells herself. It's only the wind. It's stormy out. Lots of wind. It's caught the door, that's all. It's swung the thing open. Any second now she'll hear it slam back shut.

She waits. The door is either being held open by the wind or someone has been careful, closing it gently to stop the noise. She grabs her purse and this time she looks around, makes sure no one is there beside her car or crouched nearby. Footsteps echo in the silent cold garage, clipped, hurried footsteps, and for once she's glad the light is bad.

She opens the car door without a sound and runs as fast as she can for the entrance, around the lowered arm and back into the building, calling for the security guard who sits, playing games on his cell phone. Oblivious. But at least he's there.

"Help!" she yells. "Please."

"What?" He hurries toward her in the lobby. "What happened? What's wrong, Dorreen?" He remembers her, remembers her name. Dorrie stops running.

"There's someone in the garage!"

He stops. Roland, his name tag says. "Who? Did he—"

"I don't know who, exactly, but I think whoever it is followed me. And my car. It's—it won't start!"

"Did you see him? Can you describe him to me so I can—?"

"No." Dorrie considers. "I didn't—I didn't actually *see* him. I heard him, though. Coming toward me in the garage. The light's so bad I didn't—I couldn't actually *see* him." She remembers the heels, the clicking sounds of someone hurrying away. "Or her." *Or maybe a totally clueless office worker clicking through the garage at the exact right moment scared off the would-be attacker.*

"I'll take a look," Roland says, and he runs out of the building, turns left down the sidewalk.

She'll call a cab, ask the guard to watch her until she's safely inside, until the taxi's pulling into the street. She calls Samuel. "My car," she tells him. "It's stuck here in the garage. Can you come get it?" She leaves this in his voice mail and then she ends the call and waits, but Samuel doesn't phone her back. She texts him, waits again, but, again, nothing. The security guard comes back a few minutes later, shaking his head, throwing his hands up in a gesture that tells Dorrie there was no one there by the time he got to the garage.

"Was the door open?"

"No," he says. "The door was closed. Maybe it was the wind. It's raw out there. Maybe what you heard was just—"

XXXIV

KAREN

When Karen called them, the people from Glass Houses wasted no time coming to repair the broken window, replacing it with double thermal glass—so much better than the old single panes, they told her. She should really have all the windows in the house replaced.

She still hasn't gotten back her iPad, and she scans her memory, trying to recall what she had on the thing. She'd occasionally used it as a sort of journal. Shopping lists, books she heard mentioned on talk shows or on the radio that she wanted to remember to pick up on her next trip to a bookstore. Dribs and drabs of a fairly uneventful life.

She runs the broom across the floor, sweeping tiny bits of glass into a dustpan. She isn't really bothered by the thought of the police skimming the contents of her iPad. Things that people jot down might be annoying or poetic, depending upon one's point of view, but they're certainly not illegal, and not, she thinks, especially interesting to a squad room full of thirtysomethings cops, busy texting their wives or girlfriends on their lunch breaks. It's whoever stole it that she wishes hadn't any access to her thoughts or book preferences or, hell, her shopping list for that matter. She feels as if she's been violated twice. Raped. Exposed. First her house and then her brain. From now on she'll use the ugly white alarm religiously.

Her home phone rings. Edward's name pops up on her caller ID.

"Hello?" she says, answering, finally, on the sixth ring. "Hello, Edward."

"You okay?" She can hear him puffing on the other end of the line, as if he's running a marathon or walking up a steep hill. "Robbie told me about the break-in."

"I'm fine," she says. "I wasn't home, actually."

"Well," he says, "thank God for small favors, eh? Listen. Karen. Can we talk?"

She sighs. "Sure."

"It's about the company," he says. "Have you thought about my offer?"

"Yes," she says. "Well, actually, no. Not seriously, but since you ask. No. I would have to say I have no intention of selling my half of the business to anyone. Not even you, Edward."

There's a brief silence. "Entirely your decision. I'd give it a little more thought, though."

"Why is that, Ed?" She strolls to the back door, lets Antoine out. He looks both ways before he steps tentatively across the threshold to the snowy yard, a little gun-shy after his ordeal.

"All this digging around on account of the insurance policy. That, coupled with the—unpleasantness—with the books and the, um, irregularities. Are you sure you want to be involved?"

Edward. Gloom and doom. "Of course I don't. But how would selling my part of the company change any of that?"

"It wouldn't," Edward says. "But I'd take full responsibility for everything. It's all on me. I'd be the one holding the bag here, and I think that's what Joe would want. I knew him better, probably, than anyone—except you, of course—and I know he'd want me to do everything I possibly can to protect you from this."

"And maybe you're right. But that's kind of moot now, too, isn't it? Joe's dead. Who knows what he would have wanted, and, really, at this point . . ." She stops. *At this point who cares?* "The company is pretty much all I have now, Edward," she says, and she is struck by the poignancy of this truth. "I want to come back to Home Runs—take over Joe's old job."

"You haven't been part of the company for years."

"And just look what happened!"

He laughs. "Point taken," he says. "But my offer stands. Oh, and Karen."

"What?"

"Lock your windows," he says, "and get an alarm if you don't have one. I can help you find a good security—"

"Got one," she says, "but thanks." She hangs up. She stretches, feeds Antoine, who has strolled back inside and seems to be almost up to biting her hand, but not quite. She peruses the entertainment section of the paper, scans plays in the area. She finds one at the Loeb Drama Center that sounds like an excellent escape, certainly a healthier one than sleeping with Tomas. She grimaces. They had gone together to three plays—two at the Loeb. In fact, she'd only ever gone to plays with Tomas, at least in the last few years, doubtless why she's thinking of them now. She sighs. And then she reaches for the

255

phone and calls Alice. "I have to get out of my house," she says. "I've been burgled." For a minute she wonders if that's the right word. It doesn't sound right. "I was thinking of a matinee," she says, "at the Loeb. Can you get away? Can Sally watch the shop while we—?"

"Your *house*, you mean?" Alice says. "Your *house* was burgled?" And Karen says yes. The house. Small electronic items. Alice says she's so sorry, and yes the shop is covered and of course she'd love to see a play. "It'll be fun," she says. "It's been ages! I'll meet you at the Harvard Square Station. What time is the play?"

Karen stands with Alice in the lobby of the Loeb theater. Outside the wind moans, and Karen considers staying over with Alice at her place, but then she thinks of Antoine and sighs. The play was an experimental one. Good but, Karen fears, a little over her head. Maybe she's losing her mind, she thinks, her brain. Maybe she's so rattled by Joe's death that even a simple play is puzzling.

"I didn't really get it," Alice says.

"Oh," Karen says. "Good! I'm so glad! I thought it was just me. My brain or some—"

She feels a hand on her arm and she jumps. "*Tomas?*"

"Yes." He winks. "For some reason, I had the urge to see a play."

"Me, too." Karen smiles. "Did you like it?"

"Yes." He glances around the lobby, takes in all the people. "Very much."

"Did you *get* it?"

He nods. "Of course. You forget I've been in this country most of my life, Karen."

"No. That's not what I really— Never mind. This is my friend,

Alice," she says. "Alice, Tomas." They shake hands and the three of them make small talk for a few minutes, but it's uncomfortable. Awkward.

"I'd better go," Tomas says finally, and everyone is a little relieved. "It's my one night off this week, and I've got things piled up to do."

"I wonder if he really did get it," Karen says when Tomas has disappeared around a corner, "or if he was just trying to impress."

Alice shrugs. "Hopefully, he was just trying to impress us. Well— you. I can see the attraction," she says. *"That* I get. He does seem a little needy, though, and needy men can be really . . . needy. Draining."

"'Methinks thou dost protest too much'?"

"Nope. Not my type." She looks sideways at Karen as they push through the door. "But . . . *yours,* clearly."

"It was just the one time." Karen sighs. "Granted, it was an unforgettable, tempestuous, passionate, orgasmic one time, but still one time. A total anomaly. Anyway, I have to say, it was romantic, Tomas turning up here after the other day."

"Whatever," Alice says. "You sure you want to go all the way back to Waltham?"

"Antoine," Karen says.

Alice rolls her eyes. "Speaking of needy."

Karen gives her a quick hug and runs off toward the train. The wind is strong and she huddles inside her coat, plunges forward through a wall of cold. Before she's reached the corner, a car pulls up beside her.

"Karen?"

She stops. *Tomas?* Was he lurking there? Waiting for Alice to leave? She feels a little thrill. Except Tomas doesn't have a car.

"*Edward?*"

"Hop in," he says. "It's freezing. And it isn't safe for you to be wandering around alone."

"I'm hardly wandering around," she says, sliding into the warm plushness of Edward's front seat. "And not much I can do about the alone part now, unless I never leave my house." She fastens her seat belt. "So *what* are you doing here again?"

"Picking you up. Jon told me you were coming in for a play."

She had told both her sons. Because of the break-in, they've been more vigilant than usual and she didn't want them to worry. *Make sure you set the alarm, Mom! Seriously!* They'd both said exactly the same thing. She loves her sons. They are both kind, attentive. Gregarious. *I really lucked out with my two boys,* she always says. *They have the best parts of Joe and me,* and they do—her reliability and Joe's openness, his trusting nature. Or was he really open? For that matter, was he really trusting or even trustworthy? Joe after death has become a total mystery.

"So why did you call Jon?" she says when they're on the highway to Waltham. "I'm happy for the ride. *Ecstatic* for the ride! But, this is a little weird, isn't it, Edward?"

He shakes his head.

"So are you stalking me?"

"Jesus, Karen. I was worried about you. I called to remind you to set your alarm and you didn't answer, so I phoned Jon. Call me an alarmist."

"Good one!" Karen says, but Edward just looks at her blankly across the front seat. Definitely not a punster. Karen yawns, adjusts her seat belt. The play was strangely restful, far less dramatic than her life at this point—a handful of characters milling around, saying meaningful and esoteric things.

She turns up the music whispering from Edward's dash—an old CD. *"Bringing It All Back Home,"* she says. "Wow. Love it!" In the striped pulse of streetlights, Edward smiles.

He pulls into her driveway and pushes against his heavy door, comes around to walk her inside.

"Thanks, Edward. You saved me." Karen swishes her hand around her purse, fumbles for her keys in the dark of the front porch.

Edward takes a step toward the front door. "Where's Antoine?" he says. "Shouldn't he be yapping his annoying little head off by now?"

"He's had a trauma," Karen says.

"The break-in. Right. Are you okay with being here alone?"

"Well, yeah." She turns the key and Edward tromps right along with her into the foyer. "I guess so. I mean, they only took a couple of things, and I should get the iPad back tomorrow."

Edward nods, but he doesn't look as if he's in a hurry to leave. In fact, he moves a little closer. He moves very close. "Karen," he says, and his voice is low. Soft. For a split second, Karen thinks about her dream. That silly dream. She takes a step backward, but Edward moves along with her, puts his hand on her shoulder, leans forward as she takes a few more steps away.

An earsplitting sound cracks the night. A siren. The alarm. "Oh," she says. "Oh shit!" Antoine runs from the back bedroom, yapping and snarling. The phone rings in her bag. She stands frozen in the doorway.

"Turn it off!" Edward yells into the racket. "Turn the damn thing *off!*"

Her hands shake on the monitor, the tiny screen. Three. Six. Nine. Four. No, she thinks. Wait. Three. Nine. Four. Six. She punches in the code and hits DISARM and the sound stops, leaving only Antoine's barking and the ringing phone. She empties her purse out on the sofa and grabs her cell. "It's okay," she tells the caller. "It's me. I just forgot to punch in the—"

"Password?"

"I just put it in."

"No. Not the code. It's a word. When you set it up, you gave us a password."

"Oh," she says. "I think my husband . . ." What was it? She can't think. Antoine's making so much noise. "*Antoine!*" she yells.

"Right. That's it. You have a nice night, Mrs. Lindsay." The woman hangs up. Antoine whimpers. When Edward moves forward, Antoine snarls and snaps.

"Listen," Karen says. "I'm really tired, Edward. I hate to be rude, but—"

"Sure." He shoots Antoine a scathing look and reaches for the door. "I'd reset this thing before you go to bed," he says. "But do me a favor and wait until I'm long out of here."

"Thanks again," she calls from the doorway, but this time Edward doesn't even turn around. He waves his hand above his head and beeps his car door open, and Karen stands freezing on the front porch for a minute, watching him go. She closes the door and resets the alarm, coaxes Antoine out from under the couch, where he's flattened himself after all the drama in the foyer.

XXXV

DORRIE

Dorrie stands for a second on her front porch, searching the street before she turns to close and lock the door behind her. Lily glances up from the dining room table, where she sits, a pile of books and papers stacked in front of her. "What happened, Mom?" She chews on her pen.

"My car broke down."

"So—all this time?"

"I went to see Jeananne before that," Dorrie tells her. "She's coming around. We even had a conversation. Sort of."

"Wow! That's really awesome, Mom!"

"So did you guys eat?" Dorrie opens a can of vegetable soup and pours it in a pan, switches on the burner.

"I've been munching. Dad wasn't home, either."

"No?"

"Uh-uh." Lily turns back to her papers. "What do you think about global warming?"

"Totally opposed to it." Dorrie grabs a loaf of ciabatta bread. "Could you eat a grilled cheese?" she says, and Lily nods.

"Can I interview you on it? Global warming? We have to interview six people for science, but two can be family members."

"Sure. So did your dad call?"

"Yeah. He called from work to say he'd be late."

"Did he say why?"

"No. He might have said he was going to a meeting," Lily says. "I can't remember." She mumbles this. She has her hands full with global warming.

When Samuel comes in, Lily's gone upstairs to talk to Michael from science class. Very cute, apparently, the science nerd. And, from what her daughter's told her, also something of an authority on global warming.

"Car's in the driveway." Samuel glances at the soup in the pot. "Did you eat?"

"Well, yes, Samuel. It's eight thirty. Where were you?"

"Where *was* I? Fixing your car!"

"Before that, though. Lily was a little worried," she lies.

"I called her. She didn't sound worried."

"So *where* were you?"

"At a meeting," Samuel says. "And, by the way, Dorrie." He stops. He takes his bowl of soup to the table.

"I made an extra sandwich," she says. "It's in the toaster oven."

"Thanks." Samuel grabs a plate and sticks the sandwich on it, tromps back to the dining room.

" 'By the way, Dorrie,' *what*?"

"Your car," he says, but his voice is muffled with grilled cheese sandwich. "Someone messed with one of the ignition wires."

"The . . . wires? I checked them, actually. They all *seemed* to be—"

"They weren't."

"So . . . what? Maybe I went over a bump too fast or something?"

Samuel shakes his head. "It's fixed now," he says. "I taped it back together but it's just an emergency fix. I need to replace the wire."

"Thanks, Samuel." Dorrie slumps down at the table.

"What's going on, Dorrie?" Samuel has stopped eating. He stares at her. His lovely eyes are steely gray, squinting over the grilled cheese sandwich.

Dorrie looks away. "I don't know." She'll give him crumbs, glimpses, state the obvious. "I mean everything is— There's what happened to my boss and then Jeananne's accident. And now my car! It's very . . . *disturbing,* to say the least." Samuel doesn't answer. He sits, watching her as if he thinks she might say more, tell him what's going on. "Could it have happened by accident?" she says, breaking the silence, chipping at the wall of lies between them.

Samuel looks up. "I mean, I guess it's *possible.* Not likely, though. Have you had anyone check your engine lately? Put in oil?"

"No one besides you. Would it be dangerous? The wire being cut?"

He shrugs. "Not really. It would just mean you were stuck wherever you were when it happened."

Dorrie gets up and clears the table, bangs the plates around in the sink.

"So who would want to do that, Dorrie? Who'd want to screw with your car?"

"I don't *know*." She turns to face him, because at least here she's being totally honest. "I have no *idea*, Samuel!"

"Mom?" Lily stands in the doorway.

"What? Sorry, honey. What?"

"The interview." Lily fidgets with a steno pad. "It's due on Thursday."

Dorrie nods. Samuel looks confused.

"Is everything all right?" Lily plunks down next to Samuel at the dining room table.

"Sure. Everything's— It was scary, that's all. Being stuck like that."

"Why don't I interview Dad first then?" Lily clicks her pen. "I can get you after."

"Hey, go for it," Samuel says, and Lily writes his name at the top of a blank sheet of paper and underlines it three times.

Dorrie bumps the dishwasher door closed with her hip and strolls to the living room to sit down, to get her breathing under control. Nothing is safe. Nothing *feels* safe, so nothing is exactly as it was before. Everything looks slightly different, insubstantial, and temporary. Purrl jumps in her lap and Dorrie buries her face in the soft fur, feels the cat's heart beating quickly. At least *she's* the same. Purrl, with her tummy troubles and her penchant for half-and-half from Trader Joe's—possibly the *cause* of her tummy troubles. Purrl jumps down, trots out to the kitchen toward her bowl, ma-a-a-aing as she walks, and Dorrie knows she has to talk to somebody before she goes the rest of the way over the edge. She finds her cell phone in her purse and puts in Brennan's number.

"Hello," she says. "It's Dorrie. I think I really need to talk to you. Tonight." She presses URGENT.

Pick you up at your house? Brennan texts her back within a few seconds.

Yes.

Okay. Fifteen minutes.

I'll be on the porch. Dorrie texts her address, wonders if this will only make things worse. She walks back to the dining room, tells her family she's going out for a quick coffee with a friend from work. "My nerves," she says. "I need to get my mind off this whole business with the car."

Samuel looks up sharply. Lily taps her pen against a steno pad.

"Which friend?" Samuel says, and Dorrie tells him it's one of the temps from the office, from a few months ago. "Maggie," she says. "Her name's Maggie. You can come out and meet her if you want," she adds, but Samuel shakes his head.

"I'll pass." He leans back over the table toward Lily and the interview, and when Brennan pulls into the drive, he doesn't come outside. Still, Dorrie sees him at the window, peering out as she gets in the Land Rover, as the inside light illuminates Brennan for a second before the car door closes—checking, she supposes after what Viv told her—wondering if her friend is male or female.

She and Brennan make halfhearted small talk in the car—the weather, the good news about Jeananne's hit-and-run driver turning himself in. They touch on the other night, Dorrie's stalker, but, although Dorrie asks about her date, Brennan only smiles. "It was fine," she says, and concentrates on pulling in to a diner in Jamaica Plain. "This okay?"

265

Dorrie orders an herb tea from the counter, and together they sit down at a small table under harsh, cheap lights.

"So?" Brennan seems preoccupied. She checks her phone and then she slides it into her bag. "Sorry," she says. "I put it on vibrate so we can talk. Work." She shakes her head and Dorrie knows the call she's looking for has nothing to do with work. She smiles. It must be the guy from the other night. Good for Brennan.

"I didn't know who else to call." Dorrie takes a sip of tea. What she needs is a martini. Or four. "I feel like I'm coming unhinged. My life, really. Crumbling. And I'm in the middle of it, grabbing at all these crumbling, disintegrating things that used to be walls."

"Poetic," Brennan says. "But can you be a little more . . ." She takes off her coat and slings it across a chair. "Direct?"

Dorrie knows she's stalling, trying to sort through what to say and what not to. "Somebody messed with my car today," she says finally.

"Where?"

"At work," Dorrie says. "In the parking garage."

Brennan doesn't look all that surprised. She looks worried. "Was your car locked?"

"I can't swear to it," Dorrie tells her. I always lock it, but I was running late this morning . . . I can't be sure."

"Because if it was locked and the lock wasn't tampered with, then someone would've had to have had your key. Or access to it anyway."

"I'm the only one with a key," she says. "And my husband. Samuel has an extra key." Fuck.

"Does he know about cars?"

"Well," Dorrie says. "Yeah. He just fixed mine. He's the one who told me about the wire being cut."

Brennan takes a swig of her tea. "So who was at work today?"

Dorrie shrugs. "Me, Francine, the new temp—forget her name, Marlene or Maureen—the IT guy, Len. You know; the usual suspects. Or. Wait. Not *suspects*, really. I just meant—"

"Was Edward there?"

Dorrie thinks back. "Part of the time. He was in and out."

"Did anyone have access to your keys?"

"My . . . Sure. I guess so. I mean, I left my purse in my office when I went down the hall to work with Francine."

"Any other times?"

Well, yeah. Every time I went to the ladies room or anything. Yeah. It's in a drawer—I mean, I don't leave it out in plain sight, but. Yeah."

"So, really, anyone at work could have just lifted your keys, messed with your car, and then waited until you went to the ladies room or whatever to stick the keys back in your purse."

"Yes. Edward, you mean."

Brennan takes a gulp of her drink. "Damn," she says. "This stuff tastes like mud." She walks over to the counter and comes back with two half-and-halfs, which she pours into the murky tea. "Did you see anyone? Hear anything? In the garage?"

"I heard someone walking. It sounded like a woman. It sounded like heels clicking against the floor of the garage."

"Well that's— Huh. But I guess it could have been somebody coming back in. Or leaving. The garage is for the whole building, right?"

Dorrie nods.

"Actually, I've been meaning to ask you about Joe." Brennan dumps sugar in her coffee, swirls it around. "Did he lock his car?"

"What? At work you mean?"

"Yeah." She takes a swig of sugary coffee.

"No. Now that you mention it. Every once in a while, we'd pull in at the same time and, actually, I remember noticing he just kind of walked away and didn't bother locking his car door. I even said something to him once—'Don't you lock your door?' or something—but he just shook his head, said nobody'd want his car. It was too old. Why?"

Brennan shrugs. "Just wondering."

"The puddle."

"Yeah," she says. "The puddle. Anything else?"

Dorrie wants to say hell yeah! She wants to say I don't trust anyone at all. My best friend, my co-workers, my boss, not even my own husband. She wants to say the only people in my life I feel like I truly know right now are my daughter, my rotund cat, and, oddly, *you*. She shrugs. "I guess not."

Brennan frowns. "Like I told you before, I don't care about the personal stuff. People do what people do. The heart wants what the heart wants. All of that. Not my business. Got my own problems. Believe me."

"Well," Dorrie says. "There are a couple of things."

Brennan sets the coffee down on the table, taps her fingernails against the side of the cup. "Besides the car?"

"Yeah." Dorrie looks around the little coffee shop as if she half expects someone from work to stroll in. "Joe was showing me how to do the payroll, collections, spreadsheets, everything. I'm good with numbers. Acting and numbers. My two talents."

Brennan smiles. "Handy ones to have."

"Right. So I was working with Joe to take over when Francine retires at the end of the month. She's been wanting to leave since the beginning of last year. 'The second I turn sixty-five,' she always said, 'I am out of here and off to the Left Bank,' although I'm not sure she's ever going to actually—"

"Dorrie." Brennan taps her fingernails a little harder against the heavy cup, a little faster.

"Sorry. Like I said, I have this thing for numbers. So, the ones Joe had on his spreadsheets don't match up with the ones at the office."

"Interesting," Brennan says. She sticks her napkin in her empty cup. "So, you said there were a couple of things." She looks like she's just itching to get to her cell phone, which is humming madly in her purse. She doesn't, though—she just puts her hand on her bag, like that way she can touch whoever's calling her.

"Sorry. I tend to—I'm a little ADD," Dorrie says and Brennan forces a smile.

"Well, let's reel it back in, shall we? It's been kind of a long—"

"Right," Dorrie says. "Joe e-mailed me a name on the day he died. A phone number and a name and a link."

"A link to what?"

Dorrie shrugs. "A news story. That house that burned down a while back. Jamaica Plain? Our company did a huge renovation on it a year or two before."

"I remember that fire. It was in the news. Wealthy couple. The woman was pregnant. The name Joe e-mailed you. Theirs?"

"No," Dorrie says as they stand up to go. "No. The name was Paulo Androtti. No explanation or anything, just his name. He used to work for us. Apparently, he was a really good contractor, but he quit suddenly a couple of months ago. Walked off the job and never came back. I called his house—his mother's house, I'm guessing, but she was no help at all. Also . . ." Dorrie rummages through her purse and zips open the side compartment. She pulls out a folded sheet of paper. "There's this," she says. "All these electrical items returned to Home Depot right after they were purchased. I don't know if it means anything, but it struck me as odd, especially since it just started suddenly, in the past year or so. And then it stopped just as suddenly."

"When?" Brennan glances up from the Home Depot invoices.

"January."

"Oh. Right. I can see— Damn, Dorrie." Brennan lets out a little whistle. "You ever think of being a detective?"

"I played one once." Dorrie smiles. She pulls off her hat, tosses her hair dramatically across her shoulder. "Detective Monique Develier," she says in a thick French accent. "At your service." She folds the paper and zips it back into her purse, glances at her watch. "I'd better get back," she says. "My daughter needs to interview me about global warming."

"Which sounds good on a night like this one," Brennan says, and together they walk outside, their breath making steamy little clouds in front of them. "Listen." Brennan pulls out her keys, unlocks the Land Rover. She slides in and opens the passenger-side door. "Could you forward me that e-mail in the morning? First thing?" Dorrie nods.

"I feel so much better now that I've dumped everything in your lap, Maggie. Appreciate you listening."

Brennan throws up her hands. "Hey," she says. "Once a cop . . . But seriously," she says, as they pull up in front of Dorrie's house. "Be careful. Watch your back, lock your doors, and hold on to your purse. In other words, act like a woman in danger. 'Cause I'm pretty sure you are."

XXXVI

MAGGIE

The next morning Maggie uses the phone number Dorrie included in her e-mail to find Paulo Androtti's former address in Dedham—his mother's address, actually. The mother is unpleasant and unhelpful, a total dead end, but a neighbor walking her dog on their street is far more forthcoming. Paulo and his wife have moved out of the area a month, maybe six weeks ago, the neighbor says. She isn't sure where, but she's heard that Paulo's working again. "A new construction site on State Street," she says, as her huge black Lab tugs at his leash, drags her down the sidewalk. "Good luck."

Maggie takes her time going back to Boston. It's freezing still. The workers might not all show up in weather like this, or they might get down to the site late, and Maggie knows she could scare this guy off if he knows she's looking for him. She'll have to catch him unawares. Likely she'll only have the one shot.

She slides her car in against the curb and follows the fencing to the entrance of the site, where a security guard jogs out to stop her. "Can't go in there, miss." Sunlight catches on his badge and bounces off.

"Sorry," Maggie says. "I need to see the job supervisor about one of his crew members. Got a message for him."

The guard nods and walks back to a trailer near the entrance. WADE & SONS is painted in straight up-and-down letters on its side. Maggie blows on her hands, sticks them in her coat pocket. Her nose is numb.

"Help ya?" The superintendent nudges his hard hat with the back of his hammy hand and it slides away from his forehead, exposing a thick mop of black hair.

"Yes." Maggie smiles. Her lips stick to her teeth. The supervisor puffs on his cigar, and smoke drifts out with his breath, circles his head like a noose. "I'm looking for Paulo," she says. "Paulo Androtti. I heard he's working down here."

"Yeah. He's here. Drywaller. I'll get him. Didn't catch your name?"

Maggie shrugs. "I'd rather surprise him." She smiles, a demure, secretive little smile. The supervisor winks, takes another puff on the cigar before he drops it, squashes it beneath a large booted foot. "Gotcha," he says and walks toward a tall building, a steel framework, rising in the gray air. A construction lift click clacks up the side of the building like a huge bionic roach, and a JLG unfolds, extending up two stories, where a figure stands, welding on a beam; sparks shoot like fireflies into the sky and disappear.

A young man hurries toward the gate, a smallish man. He flips his hard hat back and squints at Maggie, holds his hand up like a visor in the sun. At the gate he stops, his feet wide apart.

With his too-large gloves, he looks like a pitcher. "Who are you?" His voice is cautious, his eyes narrow.

"Maggie Brennan." Maggie extends her hand, but the man simply nods, gestures at his covered fingers.

"Believe me," he says, "you don't want to shake hands with me. Not when I'm on a job as dirty as this one. What can I do you for?"

"I need your help," Maggie says. "It's about the work you did for Home Runs Renovations."

Paulo puts his gloved hands up. "You can stop right there." He moves away a step or two. "*Right there,* lady. I am so outta that place." He turns to look back at the building where soon he will be screwing drywall into metal studs, where Maggie will not be allowed to go. "Sorry I can't help you." He doesn't look at her; he's poised for flight.

"Everything's about to come out," Maggie says. It's a gamble. "Be smart, Paulo. Save yourself. Go to the cops before they come for you."

"Look," he says. "I don't know what the hell you're talking about. I just know I left that place. Couldn't stand one of the owners—Wells—so I quit. That's all there is to it. No big mystery. I quit working there and now I'm working here." He gestures behind him.

"Fine." He looks nervous. She can smell fear and this guy's swimming in it. His face has gone white. His eyes dart here and there. "Tell you what, though, Paulo. I'll give you a card on the off chance you change your mind. This guy Hank—he's great. A really stand-up guy. Used to be my partner. You just tell him I told you to get in touch. Maggie, tell him." She extends the card and

Paulo stares at it for a minute before he removes the bulky glove and takes it from her, sticks it in his wallet. And then he turns and walks back to the half-constructed building. Sparks fly from the welder's hands and shine down like falling stars.

Four hours later, after meeting for her sister's birthday lunch at The Cheesecake Factory, Maggie pulls up to a red light and looks at her cell. A message from Lucas. She's met him several times since their first date at Yoblansky's, and she no longer hesitates about getting together. "Yes," she tells him every time he calls now, looking at her watch, glancing at her hair in her rearview mirror. "What time?"

She loves his messages, the brief, nearly abrupt words, the gritty voice. She presses her thumb down on the message he most likely left while her mother prattled on about the broken tiles, the roof she's suddenly decided might collapse with all this snow.

Hi. *Just checking in,* Lucas says. His voice is slightly blurred as if he's had a few too many beers. *Miss you.* There's a drumroll sound behind him, like a train or a machine or maybe a car starting up. *Call me,* he says. And then there's nothing but the machine sound, as if Lucas forgot about the phone. After several seconds it goes blank.

Maggie looks around when she's parked in front of her apartment. She stops again at the snowy entrance to the hallway as she goes inside, and once more at the top of the stairs. After that time with Lucas at the bar, she won't take any chances. It's made her more careful, that guy in back, staring at her in the dark bar and then disappearing, like something out of an old Gothic novel.

She peels off her new sweater, throws it on a nearby chair. Sometimes Maggie wishes she'd never left the force—if she'd stayed she might have made detective by now. She was up for it, the test anyway. She only had to walk inside that room, pick up a pencil, and take it. "Just show up," the chief had told her. "I'll get you on the list to take it."

She pours herself a glass of Merlot and takes a few sips before she calls Lucas back. He doesn't answer, so she leaves him a voice mail, soft, after the wine, after the waiting, the hunger for his voice, that feeling she's almost forgotten crawling up her spine, that connection she thought she might not ever feel again. In the end she doesn't send the message. She deletes it. She finishes the wine and walks to the tiny niche she calls a bedroom, stripping off the rest of her clothes on the way. She'll phone Hank in the morning. She looks at her watch. No. She'll call him now. This thing at Home Runs is a job for the police, detectives—for people who can do what she gave up to sit behind a desk in a beige office.

"Hank," she says into his voice mail when he doesn't answer. "It's Maggie. I need to talk to you. There's something more I've stumbled into. The accident claim. I need to talk to you," she says again. It sounds lame. *She* sounds lame. She sends the message and turns off her phone.

She lies awake, listening to the sounds of the building, the set-tling, groaning sounds of old wood beams and struggling water pipes, half-closed with rust and age. Somewhere a toilet flushes. Across the wall, someone sneezes, runs water for a bath. It's fairly early. People are still up. It doesn't bother her, this noise, these sounds of life; they make her feel as if she's not alone. Even though she barely knows her neighbors and if she sees them on the street she almost never speaks, even so, they're here, all around her, surrounding her with life.

Maggie gets out of bed and finds her phone. She turns it back on, hoping for another message from Lucas. When there isn't one, she presses the replay button to listen to the one he left earlier that night. *Call me.* She glances at the clock. Ten thirty. Before she has a chance to think, she calls him back. At first he doesn't answer. His phone rings several times and she decides to hang up. She doesn't want to leave a message. It's late; suddenly she's not sure what to say. She's just about to end the call when he picks up.

"Maggie?"

"Yeah," she says. "Did I wake you?"

"No. I was up." She hears a TV in the background, the bland voice of a commentator. The loneliness of his apartment seeps through the phone. "You get my message?"

"Yeah, but I was out. Working," she says. "This is the first chance I had to call you back."

"I was at Yoblansky's. Thought you might meet me for a drink."

"That would have been nice," she says. "That would have been really . . . Rain check?"

"Sure. Any night. You pick."

"Tomorrow?" she says.

"Yeah. Great. I'll text you. Miss you," he says, and he clicks off.

"Miss you, too," Maggie says into the dead phone. Somewhere a door slams, a pot bangs on a stovetop. She smiles.

XXXVII

MAGGIE

When Maggie catches up with Hank it's after dark. She hops off the train and walks the block or so to where he's pulled over on Boylston. She slides in the passenger-side door.

"Sorry," Hank says. "Couldn't get away any sooner."

Maggie shrugs. "Just got here myself. I'm turning this over to you," she says, and she takes a flash drive out of her purse, hands it to him. "It's all the notes I jotted down on this whole thing—everything I got. Plus photos I took at O'Brien's. If the detectives have any questions on this, they can call me."

"Same thing?" he says. "That accident on Newbury?"

She nods. "I'd like to settle on the claim. It wasn't a suicide, but I'm pretty sure it wasn't an accident, either. And one of the women where the guy worked—looks like she's in danger, too."

When Maggie's given him a brief rundown, Hank shifts in his seat, lets out a long whistle. "Yeah. I totally see what you mean. I'll take a look at the flash drive tonight and get this over to Haines's office in the morning, first thing."

"Good," she says. "Haines is good. They as backed up as they used to be down there?"

"Yeah," Hank says. "Always. Worse, maybe. You need to come back, work your way up. You'd make a good detective, Mag."

She doesn't answer. She turns to look out the car window. She doesn't tell him she's put in to come back. She'll save herself embarrassment in case they never call. "Thanks," she says.

She gets out of the car and walks the couple blocks to Yoblansky's to meet Lucas. It's several times they've met now, here and other places, shot the breeze, talked about their families, their friends, about his uncle Ian and the shop, or Maggie's job. Afterward, they've gone home to their separate lives, to their separate apartments only two train stops apart—or back to their jobs after a lunch. It's a nice night. Bitter cold, but still. The trees barely move, their naked branches pasted to the sky.

"Hi." She slips onto a bench across the table from Lucas. "People might start talking, we keep meeting here like this," Maggie says.

"Our place." He smiles. "I ordered you a Heineken."

"Thanks," she says. "I'm impressed you remember."

"I want to know everything there is to know about you, Margaret Brennan. I'll remember all of it," he says, and Maggie sees he's already drunk most of his beer. She wonders how long he's been sitting here waiting for her.

"No," she says. "You really don't. Trust me."

"Yes," he says. "I do."

She shakes her head. "Sometimes I feel like I'll never be who

I was." She isn't sure why she's said this. She isn't even sure it's what she means. She takes a long drink of her beer.

Across the table, Lucas nods, staring toward the window. "I know," he says. "Me, too." He glances back at her, fiddles with his glass. "Maybe that's all right, though," he says after a minute. "Maybe it's like there's something missing. Broken. And after a while it's just a space." He shrugs. "The V.A. sent me to this group I go to sometimes," he says. "You could come with me if you want. Check it out. You don't have to talk or anything. Wouldn't have to go back if you didn't like it."

"Did it help?"

"Yeah," he says. "It did. It does. Some."

"I don't know," she says. "It's really hard to talk about all that, to think about it."

"But we kind of do anyway, right? I mean, isn't that the problem, that it's always just there at the corner of your eye?"

She takes another sip of her Heineken. "Yeah," she says. "I guess." For a minute or two neither of them speaks. Conversation floats from the next table. Behind the counter, someone drops a glass. "I got with my old partner," Maggie says, "on my way here. Gave him all my notes so he can turn the whole thing over to one of the detectives in the morning."

Lucas nods. "Good," he says. "That's really— You relieved?"

"I'm relieved it's out of my hands, but I'm worried they'll bury it under a bunch of other stuff." She fidgets with her napkin. "Since one of the women really is in danger. In my opinion. Of course, I'm just a lowly claims investigator at a company with plastic floors. What do I know?"

"Plenty," Lucas says. "Whoever she is, she's very lucky to have you in her corner."

"Speaking of corners . . ." Maggie never invites anyone to her apartment. She likes to be anonymous. She likes to not have people know where, exactly, she lives. "Over near the Hill," she'll say when people ask, or "Right downtown," or she'll just roll her eyes, talk about how tiny her place is. "I have to turn sideways to walk across it," she'll say, laughing. "Speaking of corners." She looks down at her napkin, fiddles with her glass. "I kind of live in one— this little room on Marlborough. It's not far, though. If you want to come up for a coffee after."

"Sure." Lucas smiles. He looks around the table at their empty plates, their half-drunk beers. "Is it 'after' enough?"

Maggie puts on her coat and together they walk out to the sidewalk. Hand in hand, they slosh up to the crowded train, sit close together on the shifting wobbly ride.

"This is it," she says after the short walk from the station. For a few seconds they just stand there outside the building. She stares at the black paint, peeling on the metal banister, at the heavy brick, the outside door the landlord painted red last summer. Snow collects on a small twiggy bush, and she brushes at it with her fingertips. She looks at Lucas with his hands inside his jacket pockets, at the flecks of snow in his hair. The sky is gray in the streetlight. She hesitates a moment longer, and then she opens the front door. They walk inside, and he is warm beside her; his step is solid on the creaky wooden stairs. She fumbles for her key. Across the hall, a woman laughs, calls out a name, sets a plate down loudly on a table. Music wanders through the wall.

"Nice," he says, when they're inside.

"What little there is." Maggie flicks on a light in the tiny kitchen, starts the coffeemaker. "I have dessert," she says, peering in the fridge. "Blueberry cobbler."

"Think I'll pass," he says. "Next time?"

"I don't know. You might wanna grab it now."

"No next time?"

"No cobbler."

"Got whipped cream?" He puts his arms around her from behind, kisses the top of her hair.

"Yes. But go sit down," she says, sticking the dish inside the oven. "I'm getting sidetracked."

Lucas treads over to a small table at the edge of the only real room. The light is soft. The space is warm. Pillows with yarn stitching lie along a love seat. One plump chair sits in the corner. A woven round rug, orange and gold and red, pulls the room together in amber light from a lamp Maggie picked up at an art show the summer she moved in. A truck screeches somewhere down the block, and she brings coffee in her favorite cups—another find, another summer—cuts a piece of cobbler for the two of them, two forks, one plate, dabs whipped cream along the top. She sits beside him on the braided rug.

"Great," he says. "Beautiful." But he's looking at her. He kisses her.

She dips a blueberry in whipped cream and presses it between his lips.

"Like that old song," he says. "Suzanne by the river . . ."

"It was oranges," she says " 'She feeds you tea and oranges.' "

He kisses her again, sets the plate down on a coffee table, a board on bricks.

"I have a skylight," she says.

"Where?"

"There. Over the bed."

"Can you see the stars?"

"On a clear night."

"Like this?"

"Yes."

XXXVIII

KAREN

Karen's cell phone beeps in her purse on the dining room table. A new message from Tomas. Since they spent the afternoon together, he's texted her nine times. She'd texted back two short, clipped answers, distancing herself, even though she knows what happened was her doing. He'd hardly had to drag her to his place. She feels her face go red. Flutters her fingers through her hair, folds them together as if to keep them from calling him back.

She'll read his message later. Maybe she'll even— No. She shakes her head, drops the cell back in her bag. She can't. Not now, with her feelings in such a muddle. She'll give it a few weeks and reconsider. Even if she isn't in love with him right now, that could always change. She'll read his text later.

She finishes her coffee and calls Home Runs, asks for Francine. She'll take her out before the woman leaves for—where was it Edward said she planned to go? Paris, was it?— A farewell lunch, she tells Francine, when the silly temp manages to connect her to the right office. "Twelve thirty, then," she says. "Can't wait."

Three hours later, Karen sits at a small table at Chips on Charles. Francine looks a lot older than she did the two or three times Karen saw her in the past. "How long has it been, Francine?" she says, when the waiter has taken their orders and scampered off toward the kitchen, pad in hand.

"Oh Lord." Francine fiddles with her silverware, sticks her napkin on her lap. "Years. Wasn't it shortly after the company opened? I'm usually out of town during the Christmas holidays, so I always missed the office parties. Haven't been to one for years."

"I guess it has been ages," Karen says, and for a moment she's amazed at the passing of time. "It seems like just a few years ago a *couple* of years ago and now Joe's whole lifetime has finished. It doesn't seem—"

Francine is not a hands-on kind of person. She isn't motherly. She's reserved and Bostonian. She looks away. Uncomfortable. "Yes," she says. "Such a shame. Are you all right? Financially, I mean. I hate to be crass. None of my business at all, of course. It's just that when my own husband died several years ago, and we hadn't really expected—weren't prepared—and me with a career in finance. 'Physician heal thyself,' eh? Anyway, Mort's passing left me nearly penniless. Our savings were gone, our bank account—in tatters."

"Yes. Well, I'm all right for the moment," Karen says. "But, speaking of finances, I am a little confused about the ones I found on Joe's laptop. They don't seem to match up with what Edward's—"

"Afraid I can't help you there," Francine says. "On the other hand, Dorrie might be able to shed some light."

"*Dorrie?*"

"Yes." Francine butters a biscuit and takes a leisurely bite. "She's got a head for numbers, that one. She remembers everything. Like a flipping savant. Like Dustin Hoffman in that movie. Remember? *Rain Man*? When he rattled off all those— Anyway, Joe had her training for my job. To save hers, I suppose."

Karen spears an olive with her fork and chews. Great. Fucking great. Lover, protector. What the hell *else*?

Francine wipes her mouth, reaches in her purse for a small lipstick and mirror set, silver, with birds etched into the case. "I'm sure this isn't helpful in any way, but there was something a bit odd, I thought."

"Such a pretty mirror set. So what is that, Francine? What was odd?"

"It *is* pretty, isn't it? A gift from my daughter last year on Mother's Day." Francine applies her lipstick and presses her lips together to blot them, making a small popping sound in the quiet room. "A man came in—it's been weeks ago now. Months. Shortly before your husband's accident. Same week, as I recall, just before he—Joe—went out of town. Or. No. He was *already* out of town. That's right. The man was frantic to speak to him. 'He isn't here,' I told him. 'Won't be back until the end of the week, if then. Monday would be better, really.' He said it was pressing—that he was a city inspector and he—Lansing, I believe he said. Edwin Lansing? Earl?—Everett Lansing. It was Everett Lansing. I'm sure of it. Most unpleasant."

"Did he say why he had to talk to Joe? What was so urgent?"

Francine shakes her head. "No. He just threw up his hands and stomped back out. Frightening man. Public official at that. What has this city come to?"

Francine declines dessert, putting up her hands as if she's stopping an onslaught of angry, buzzing bees—and Karen gives her a small hug on the sidewalk. "Best of luck to you, Francine," she says. "Joe thought the world of you," she adds, although, really, he didn't at all. *She's much more Edward's employee than mine*, he used to say. *Acts like I'm intruding when I ask her a simple question*. But the woman has more than paid her dues, put in her time. She certainly deserves this little send-off lunch.

It seems to Karen as if the world is conspiring against her. Even Francine was snooty in a civil sort of way, not at all forthcoming. And here's a new voice mail from Brennan. Karen hits PLAY, listens as she walks back to the car park. "I'm at work," Brennan says, "so I just have a second, but I've turned this whole business over to the Boston Police. I'm a little out of my league with this, way over my head, but you should be getting your check once they finish the investigation and you're cleared. I'll be in touch as soon as I know something. Take care." Karen hears the click of Brennan's cell phone disconnecting.

Good luck, Brennan. And good luck to the Boston PD, sorting through all the lies and cover-ups. "Yeah," she says loudly. "Good luck figuring out about Joe and the fake spreadsheets and his other woman and his trying to save her job and maybe his, too, by sliding the little twit into Francine's position. *A head for numbers, that one*, Francine had said. *Like Dustin Hoffman in* Rain Man. Maybe it's time to pay Dorrie a visit, Karen thinks. Maybe it's way past time.

And the city inspector, this Lansing. What the hell was that all about? What urgent business did he have with Joe? Was Edward right? Was Joe involved in some nefarious dealings with this man who bullied poor Francine? She ponders this, walking to her car in a nearby parking space—a lucky find, a spot just steps from Chips on Charles. She beeps the car door open and slides inside. There's something under the wiper. Oh. God. Will this day never—a ticket? Has she parked illegally? They really need to make it clearer where customers can park and where they can't. She'll call City Hall. She's had enough! Lansing and now this! She slides back out and grabs the paper from her windshield and stares at it. It's not a ticket. It's a note. Handwritten. *Be strong*, it says. *You are not alone.*

She looks around, sticks the note in her purse, and screeches out of the parking space, locking all her doors. Just what she needs to hear, that she is not alone. She laughs, a nervous titter. And then she laughs louder, harder; she laughs until tears stream down her cheeks. She'd give her left arm to be alone, to not feel watched, observed, and now this stupid note. Of course, it's probably just a well-meaning zealot, roaming the streets of Boston with a pad of paper and a pen. *You are not alone*, as in God is with you? *Really?*

At a traffic light she reaches in her bag and pulls out this little missive. She stares at it, the perfect script, the exaggerated slant. The flourish. Tomas!

XXXIX

DORRIE

D orrie wakes up thinking that she has to find Karen. Not necessarily to talk with or even actually approach, but just to—what?- she wonders, lying in bed, wrapped like a mummy in a pile of quilts. Samuel complains constantly about their gas bills, about therms and leaky windows and improper insulation. "Hemorrhaging money," he says. "Just use more covers." And so she does. The heat is somehow better up the hall in Lily's room and the bathroom, but the bedroom she shares with Samuel is icy cold in winter, burning hot in summer. Is the vent even open? She keeps forgetting to check; meanwhile, she sleeps like an entombed queen.

She doesn't really want to talk with Karen, or even deal with her. Maybe it's just nosiness. Dorrie yawns. Or maybe it's her reluctance to let go of Joe. She's handed Brennan all the information she's managed to dig up. Now it's up to Brennan and the cops to decide what, if anything, it means.

Dorrie throws off the covers and swings her legs over the edge of the bed. She shakes her head, trying to clear it. There's something just there at the edge, something she can't quite see. She senses it, though, like a heavy fist poised above her head, the same dread she felt the morning of Jeananne's hit-and-run—dread and fear, mixed with the tinny voice on her cell, the *Why are you still here?*, the texts from Joe's burner phone, the clicking of high heels in the basement garage—a collage of shapes and sounds, of wisps and whispers, of swerving cars and words of caution— her mother's, Brennan's—a black glove flying out a windshield, landing on her husband's workbench, and Jeananne bleeding in the snow. She stretches, lies back down, pulls the quilts over her head, and knocks the alarm button with her sheeted hand when it begins to ring.

A pot bangs on the stovetop in the kitchen and Dorrie drags herself into the bathroom, fixes her hair and carefully applies her makeup, dabs concealer, heavy, in the hollows underneath her eyes. She hesitates for just a second before she gets dressed.

"Mom!" Lily yells from somewhere near the kitchen, and Dorrie grabs a scarf on her way downstairs.

"Wow." She stares at her daughter. "You're already dressed!" Like Dorrie, Lily is not a morning person. *Peas in a pod, you two,* Samuel always says. Used to say. Lately, Lily is pulling away, her life shifting toward boys, toward the guy behind the counter at the corner deli, and now the science nerd. Dorrie sighs.

"I told you last night." Lily gulps down her orange juice and sticks the empty glass on the kitchen table. *"Remember?* The early study class? The *science* test?"

"Right. And Mia's going to—"

"Yeah. She's—actually, I think she just pulled up." Lily peeks out the kitchen door and holds up one finger for Mia. The soft whine of a song drifts from the car, and Dorrie wonders if Michael the science nerd will be in study class, his light hair slightly ruffled with sleep, unguarded and alluring at this early hour. She kisses her daughter, holds her just a second before she releases her to fly out to the driveway, to wave her small gloved hand as the door swings shut behind her.

Dorrie watches as they pull out of the driveway. The sky is pink and gray. Samuel squints toward the Keurig, pats down a cowlick with the palm of his hand.

"By the way," Dorrie says. "I've been meaning to ask you. Have you seen my black glove?"

Samuel appears to be mesmerized by the swooshing of the Keurig. "Nope."

"You sure?"

He shrugs. "Not that I remember," he says, but he doesn't turn around. "Why?"

"Well," she says, "I *lost* it. Why *else*?"

"I don't know. You sounded worried," he says. "Like it was a big deal or something." He waits for the Keurig to finish spitting coffee into his mug. "Why don't you just buy another pair?"

"Yeah," she says. "I really should."

It's Wednesday, the one day of the week she actually knows where Karen will be, at least if she's kept up her old routines and Dorrie thinks she probably has. "Karen's such a creature of habit," Joe used to say. "All her traditions, her holiday dinners, and her . . ."

At that point, Dorrie had stopped listening and tuned him out, having absolutely no desire to know the ins and outs of Karen's family traditions. She remembers this one, though, that Joe's wife and her best friend always got together on Wednesdays, whether Karen was at work or not. It was always at the same place, midafternoon. Something to do with the Tarot. The King of something. No. The *Queen*. The Queen of Cups.

Occasionally, Dorrie thinks about her impulsive drive down Karen's street. Ridiculous. Crazy, really. But there was some reason she was there; something pulled her across town to Joe's house. And it wasn't only curiosity and closure, if she's honest with herself. It was answers. She is impulsive, has always been. But not scattered as people think. There's usually a reason she does the things she does, even if not even she knows what it is. There was the time she felt she had to drop everything and visit her grandmother the day before she died of a sudden unexpected heart attack or the time she felt compelled to leave the dinner table in the middle of dessert and walk around the house to the backyard, where she discovered Purrl, apparently abandoned, half frozen, her beautiful white fur matted with dirt. It was her mother, Dorrie always thought, who put these thoughts into her head, flicked her magic wand and disappeared.

Karen was the last person she wanted to encounter while Joe was alive. Yet Karen, Dorrie knows on some level, has the answers she needs to pull the puzzle pieces together—possibly even to save her life. And all this time, all these scattered thoughts and trips to nowhere, all these scanned bills and dredged-up e-mail addresses, spying on the company, on Edward, even on Joe, and now, his widow. It has all been to find answers, to keep her small, imperfect life intact.

The drive to Waltham was a bit extreme, but eating at the same restaurant, sitting in the same public space, just happening to be there at the same time as her dead boss's wife—that wouldn't really be so strange. Coincidence, at the very most, if Karen were to see her, if she even noticed Dorrie there at the back of the room with her hat on, dark glasses masking half her face. "Oh," she could say on the off chance that should happen. "Karen! Lovely to see you! I've been meaning to call to ask how you are, to see if there's anything at all I can do to—" To what, exactly? No she'd leave that part out, stop at meaning to call. And then she'd simply leave with a brief but empathetic hug, a sad little wave, make her way down the cramped aisle. Unless there's more. Unless Karen looks at her and says something that makes sense of all this crazy stuff that started on the night Joe died. Or, really, months before. She'll know, Dorrie tells herself. When she sees Karen, she will know.

She takes the train to work. She sits at her desk, does the usual obligatory things, but she feels restless, as if she's at the very edge of something. Again, she thinks about Karen. It's probably been a year since Joe mentioned his wife coming in to Boston on Wednesdays. For all Dorrie knows, she's switched to another day. There are six others, any one of which Karen might find more convenient than Wednesday, even if she does hate change.

Dorrie glances at her watch. One thirty. She puts on her coat. "I'll be back in an hour or so," she calls to anyone who might be there to care or even notice that she isn't at her desk. "I have a couple of errands to run." She has the vague impression of an answer floating up the hall from Francine's office, but she isn't sure.

Nor is she sure she can even find the tea shop. She's only seen it driving through downtown with Samuel. She'd glanced up once, just as they passed the medieval-looking sign. She knows it's on Tremont in the middle of the block, but which block? She walks quickly to the train. The day is freezing. Clear, but freezing. In time the cold will give way to spring, and snow will fold itself into the fecund ground. Soon the flowers will nudge their way outside the cold earth. Dorrie pulls her coat more tightly around her. She isn't ready yet for spring.

She finds the tea shop with the painting of a Tarot card over the door. The Queen of Cups is a bustling, cheery place with yellow walls and framed oil paintings of éclairs and pink-frosted doughnuts. Dorrie orders coffee at the bar in front, two cinnamon buns—one for now, one to take home for Lily. She makes her way to the very back of the tea shop, where she sets her meager lunch down on a small wood table and slides into a bench beside it—a place for one, a small, dark nook on the way to the ladies' room, where she is basically invisible.

She stares at her nails, where the polish has chipped off, where the edges are ragged and uneven. She stares at her hands and thinks of Joe. And then, without meaning to, she thinks of Karen. Karen, the wife, who doubtless misses him even more than Dorrie does. Differently—in a less desperate, but a far more basic way. She sips her coffee. Again, she feels a sense of dread. A sense there's someone . . . She glances here and there around the small space of the room, the almost claustrophobic heat, the crowded clumps of chairs and tables. She feels trapped. Hunted. Threatened—but she can't pinpoint the source. Goose bumps stand out on her arms. Her stomach rolls. Her heart pounds. Voices chatter. Indistinct. A noisy hum. And then the separate, clearer voice. Her mother's voice pressed up against her ear. *Be careful, Dorrie!*

The front door opens. Karen comes in with a woman who must be the old friend, and Dorrie is suddenly ashamed to be here, for hiding underneath her hat, the large dark glasses. She feels silly, like a spy, like a voyeur. She wants to get up and leave, but she doesn't. She can't. She feels again that she is somehow under scrutiny—the watcher being watched. The sense of dread is suffocating now, her mother's voice inside her ear, insistent, urgent, like the night she tugged her daughter from the car. Like the night that Joe died. *Leave!*

But Dorrie doesn't leave. She doesn't move. She barely breathes.

Karen sits at a small table, facing the cashier in front and two small windows that look out to the street. She sits with her back to Dorrie, leans over the table toward her friend, and Dorrie knows she won't ask Karen anything at all, not even how she's doing.

The tea shop is suddenly filled with people. Occasional shrieks of laughter punctuate a steady hum of voices, and Dorrie slides down farther in her seat, picks at her sweater, at the tiny balls of fuzz from too many washings, from her own laziness, from throwing it in the washer instead of dipping it by hand in the bathroom sink and hanging it to dry. Karen's sweater is green and smooth as glass and cashmere, as she and Alice huddle over what looks like a small pad of paper. They seem to be jotting things down. Figures, maybe. Karen shifts her chair away from the table and laughs. A small, light laugh. Refined. Her hair is pinned up in a twist. A few loose strands curl down around her face and the effect is perfect in its imperfection.

She is lovely, but something else. Elegant, but more than that. Human? Vulnerable? For the first time, Dorrie understands that Joe had deeply loved this woman, despite their problems, despite their differences. Sitting in the darkened alcove near the ladies' room, Dorrie sees for the first time that Joe would not ever have left his wife for her.

Karen tucks a strand of hair behind her ear and something in the gesture says she was the type of wife who never failed to get the garbage to the street on the right day, who paid the light bill before the due date, who took their dog for his shots at the proper time—someone who organized their lives, both hers and Joe's, someone who will never lose her keys—who never once lost track of Joe until the moment Dorrie bumbled through their lives.

Karen and her friend look around the room, and Dorrie stares down at her hands on the pockmarked tabletop. It's almost as if they sense her here, as if they feel her staring at them. They stand up, hesitating at their table, talking, and then they walk to the doorway.

Dorrie takes a long time with the tip, counts out two bills, which she sticks neatly under her plate. On the sidewalk, just outside the door, Karen and her friend stop and chat a minute longer. They take tiny steps away from one another, wrap their woolen scarves around their necks, and slip their hands into their pricey leather gloves.

They walk off in different directions, both of them moving fairly quickly along the sidewalk, and Dorrie struggles to keep up in the shifting mass of people, to keep Karen in sight, ducking now and then behind a crowd, tilting her head down toward the sidewalk, staying invisible, staying several steps behind. She adjusts her sliding sunglasses, wraps her scarf more tightly around her neck. Her hands are naked, chapped and red, and she shoves them in the pockets of her coat. She looks around, glancing at the faces of passersby, and, despite the irony, she still can't shake the feeling that she's being watched. Again she feels dread surround her like a shroud.

Karen turns in at the train station and heads down the stairs in leather boots that cling like velvet to her legs. Her heels are high, and for a second Dorrie sees her teeter on the concrete steps, but then she grabs the handrail and continues down and down until she's standing on the platform. Dorrie's close behind her, but there are so many people, and Karen is preoccupied, bending over, staring at her cell. Her slender fingers poke and scroll. The train arrives, and, without even looking up, Karen glides across the threshold, into the last car, where she stands for several seconds just inside.

And then, as the doors slide closed, as the train jerks and wheezes—at that exact instant when it's suddenly too late—Karen turns and looks straight at Dorrie. She reaches for the doors as if she can open them, as if she's changed her mind, as if she'll die if she can't get off the train. She looks up at Dorrie again, and her face is frantic. Small lines are etched beside her mouth; wrinkles crease her forehead. She's saying something Dorrie can't hear with the din inside the station, with all the arrivals and departures, squeals of brakes and echoed shouts. She points at something behind Dorrie and her mouth is moving, her eyes huge and distressed. She looks as if she's screaming. Even over the racket,

Dorrie thinks she can hear Karen's voice, but, with all the clamor, she can't make out the words.

Dorrie takes a step toward her and a slide show of streets and faces, voices and Joe's hand on the steering wheel—it all floods through her, electrifying. Shocking. She reaches out toward the train window, toward this woman who loved Joe, too, and lost him, who was loved by him. She reaches toward the window as the cars thwack and shift, and Karen's mouth is still moving, shouting, still screaming. *Run. Run,* she says, she mouths. She tilts her body to her right. To Dorrie's left. *Watch out,* she mouths, her lips wide, distorted. Her face is pressed against the glass. *Run!*

Dorrie gathers all her strength to dive toward the steps, and then she feels herself moving, as if a gust of wind were pushing her. A forceful, gentle wind, light, yet strong, pushes her toward the stairs to the outside, to Park Street. She feels her mother's arms around her, hears her mother's words, the words she knows are really her own thoughts, the rational and realistic side of her, her left brain kicking in to save her, the essence of a mother. The memory of a mother.

X L

K aren wakes up that Wednesday morning knowing this will be the day she turns her life around. This will be the outing that will change her. She knows this. It's time. She'll meet Alice at The Queen of Cups, as she's done nearly every Wednesday for the past ten years, and afterward, she'll be herself again. It's something she feels *in her bones*, as Lydia used to say. She'll simply decide to be back on track and it will happen. It's a choice, she thinks. To a large extent, happiness is a choice.

"Poof," she says, snapping her fingers, and Antoine barks. "Right, Antoine?" He barks again. Lately he's stopped growling at her, and when he starts to nip her hand, he stops himself before his sharp teeth actually connect with skin. They've bonded over the break-in, the smashed glass in the little downstairs room. They've learned to share the bed, Antoine at the foot and Karen with her toes stuck underneath the spot where his plump body warms the covers. She lets him out while she makes herself a cup of coffee and back inside before she walks to the bathroom to peer into the mirror again, to blend in her foundation with her pinkie. Working for Alice has been fun; it's kept her busy, kept her mind off everything that's happened. For years, it kept her mind off the blankness she had let her life become. But now she wants more. She wants Joe's place at the table; she wants her husband's half of the company. In essence, she wants to be who she once was—capable and business savvy. Respected.

She takes her time getting dressed. She stares at a pile of sweaters on the shelf she had Joe build for her on one side of the closet and decides on a green pullover. It's nice. It's cashmere. Soft. A Christmas gift from Joe. It hadn't been the most festive holiday this year, no huge tree, no enormous pile of presents. It wasn't a particularly memorable Christmas. They'd had the usual, the gift exchange—the things they'd bought ahead of time and stashed away, things Karen found on sale after Halloween, or in the summer. She sighs. The holidays went by so fast, were eclipsed by grief in the next weeks, so she sometimes feels as if it should be autumn and she should only now be dealing with the holidays, cheeks pink in the brisk wind as she presses forward toward Bloomingdale's and Macy's.

She props up her magnifying mirror and pokes at her eyebrows, scrutinizes her face. She still hasn't actually read Tomas's text. She's saving it. She'll relish it, the compliments, the admiration. She sighs. If only he were someone else, if only *she* were. Or if she were . . . something—younger, maybe, more naïve—if she could bring herself to think love turned the world, could make herself believe that she and Tomas could not only pull together, tight as magnets, but stay that way for more than just an afternoon. Maybe at some point they can. Or maybe that one afternoon is all that matters. She grabs her coat and checks her watch. If she hurries, she'll make the next train.

"So how's Tomas?" Alice says, and Karen looks up, slides her empty plate to the edge of the table.

"Fine," she says. "I guess." She looks around the small restaurant, cramped, now with brightly painted chairs and tables. It's grown since they first started coming here eons ago. It's so much larger, with the additions the owners have built on over the years. She looks around and feels a chill up her spine.

"You haven't seen him?" Alice tries to push away the relief in her voice.

"Not since the night of the play . . . How's *your* love life these days?"

Alice shakes her head, looks down at her hands. "Nil." She bites into a chocolate cupcake. "You were lucky to have Joe. I know at the end you two got off track, but you had all those good years."

Karen nods. And, for a minute, she feels the memories without remorse. She sees Joe, smiling in the hospital when the boys were born, sharing Belgian waffles at a diner up the street on lazy Sunday mornings, lying on the tarred hot roof of an ancient sixth-floor walk-up in the summertime, can almost hear the street sounds drifting through a propped-open window in the spring, the dip of a mattress, the smell of coconuts and ocean air.

"Listen." She leans forward. "I've been thinking about this for a while now. "Why don't we take a trip up the coast this spring? Maine. Canada. You could close the shop and I—well—I'll have the insurance money by then, and who knows when I'll be back at Home Runs. I've been thinking I might just work from home. Do what Joe did without going in town to the— I don't know if I'd want to be there, in that office, where Joe and his—"

"I *love* it! The idea of a trip." Alice takes her glasses off and then she puts them on again. "I really do! We could . . ." She stops.

"Then why don't we drive up the coast and see . . . *What?*" Karen says. Alice's eyes are wide, darting around the room. "What's wrong?"

"Don't you feel it?" Alice says.

"Feel what?"

"Like someone's watching us?" She backs away from the table; her chair makes scraping noises on the wood floor. Alice prides herself on sensing things that others don't, and she is nearly always right.

Karen nods. "Yes, actually." She gathers her things together, slips into her coat.

When they leave, they stand up slowly, cautiously. They stand in the small, crowded aisle and talk as if they're waiting for someone to come back from the bathroom or pull out a cell phone or make a sudden, unexpected move. They look toward the door, as if there will soon be a face in the window or a figure pushing in rudely, a customer they hadn't noticed throwing bills down on a table with a heavy, angry hand.

Outside, they talk for a moment more before they part ways. Karen pulls her coat tighter around her and ducks her head against a sudden unexpected gust of wind. She walks quickly to the Park Street Station, feeling someone there behind her, even in the crowds of people crossing streets and hailing cabs. She is not like Alice. She is not the least bit spiritual. Karen lives her life in black and white. And yet she feels a presence like she feels the cold around her, like she sees the snowflakes swirling in the air.

She walks faster down the sidewalk, nearly falls on her way down the steps to the subway. She grabs the railing, rights herself. She looks behind her at the throng of commuters heading home. She's stayed too late in town; the train will be packed.

She pulls out her cell. She could call someone. Edward. He's only up the street. He could be here in five minutes. He could drive her home. She thinks about it, but then the train is there, screeching into the station. The brakes squeal. She'll call Tomas, listen to his soothing voice, his compliments. She needs them now. She'll ask him about the notes. *Was it you?* she'll ask him, even though she's certain that it was, that he meant the message to be comforting, empowering.

She finds his number in her list of contacts, but the call goes straight to voice mail. She doesn't leave a message. She scrolls down to his work number, the one she added while she stood in his apartment, while he waited for her to join him in the shower. She smiles— that lovely afternoon when they made love. There it is—she's put it under "WORK." Anonymous enough, in case she loses her phone, too, at some point. She presses her thumb down on the number, probably for the nurses' station. She'll ask for Tomas. She'll leave a message if he's with a patient. Just this once. She doesn't even have to see him. His voice will be enough.

"Hello?" A man answers, someone with a heavy accent. There are strange sounds in the background, loud, banging sounds. "Hood's Garage."

"Oh," she says. "I'm sorry. I must have the wrong—" But they'd called him only days before. *Work.* He'd had the number listed in his phone as *Work.* "Does Tomas still work there?" she says. "Does he still moonlight there?"

"He is our best mechanic," the voice says. "Since he come back from Honduras, he is here more time."

"Oh," she says. "Really? Is he *there*? Can I speak to him?"

"Not today. He took the day off today. Personal business, he told me. I don't ask him what."

She ends the call. She doesn't leave her name. She scrolls to his text message from yesterday. *Call me!* And now there's another from this morning, when she was on the train. With all the noise, she hadn't heard it when it came in. *My darling Karen. I will tie up the loose ends to make sure you are safe and then I will go back home to Honduras but you will be always here with me in my heart.*

The heavy doors slide shut. She looks up and suddenly Dorrie stands on the platform, staring through the window of the train, leaning toward the door, her arms outstretched. And then she sees Tomas move quickly through the station, straight at Dorrie. *Run!* Karen screams. *Watch out! Run!* She beats against the glass. *Stop the train!* But it just keeps lurching, starting to move, and Tomas is heading straight for Dorrie like a charging bull. The impact alone will knock her onto the tracks. *I will tie up the loose ends.*

"*Run!*" she yells again, and she leans far over to her right, trying to make Dorrie move, get out of the way. In a split second she'll be—

The train lurches forward. *Run!* She yells it one more time, takes one last look as the train picks up speed. Suddenly a dark-haired woman, a young, small woman, pushes Dorrie, shoves her hard toward the stairs. And then Karen can see nothing. Only tiled walls and the darkness of the tunnel as the train squeals down the track.

X L I

DORRIE

orrie sees a strange man running. His heavy coat is open, flapping out around him. His hands wrestle with air, but still his body keeps moving, keeps pitching forward toward the tracks as if he is a crazy overburdened bird that still thinks it can fly. "It was for you, Karen! Everything! It was all—" And then something smacks into him from the side. Another body zips through space.

Brennan? She rams into him, knocks him down on the concrete several feet from Dorrie and only inches from the edge of the platform. Something flies out of his coat and falls onto the tracks.

Dorrie doesn't recognize the man. He isn't particularly large. He wouldn't look dangerous at all if he weren't straining against Brennan like a mad dog, his arm twisted behind him, if transit cops weren't running toward him. If she passed him on the street, Dorrie wouldn't even notice him. Good-looking, fortysomething, deep brown eyes that are, at the moment, narrowed at her, staring at her, filled with hate.

For a few seconds, Dorrie feels nothing but a sort of hollowness at the pit of her, as if she's watching this on a screen, as if it's happening in someone else's life. Not hers. She stands, not moving as everything unfolds around her, and then she feels an incredible urge to run. Her insides race. Her breath comes in shallow, quick pants; her heart pounds, and she shivers violently in the icy station, but she doesn't run. Instead she waits. She watches, unsure of what might be outside, of where the danger starts or ends. She stands in the shadow of the stairs as a policeman handcuffs the small angry man and leads him from the station.

"Are you all right?" Brennan stands beside her. She reaches out, touches Dorrie's arm, and Dorrie jumps. "Maybe you should sit down for a minute," Brennan says. "They'll want to question you, but I'll see if I can get them to skip the formalities and maybe get it over with faster." She walks off to talk to an officer still standing in the station, and Dorrie concentrates on breathing as she looks down at the tracks where she could easily have died.

A cell phone lies where it landed after it flew from the man's coat pocket. The small thin patch of plastic lies faceup on the tracks, and Dorrie takes a step or two closer to the platform's edge. She stares down at Joe's burner phone, this final thread connecting them, this last sad trace. She breathes. The phone lies sideways on the ties. For just a second, it catches the light from the station, flashes it back toward her, and then, as Dorrie holds her breath, the B train rumbles down the track and crushes it to dust beneath the wheels.

"Ever seen that guy before?" Brennan has returned with the officer.

"No." Dorrie shakes her head. "Not that I remember. But I wouldn't, probably. He's not especially—memorable."

"Any idea why he might want to hurt you?"

"No." So many thoughts are racing through her head. Karen. He did it for Karen, he said. Screamed it. Was he trying to kill her for sleeping with Joe? Was he defending Karen's honor? But that wouldn't make sense. Not now, with Joe dead. What, then? *I did it all for you, Karen.* She starts to tell them what she heard, but something stops her. Karen was trying to warn her. If she had wanted Dorrie dead, she wouldn't have acted the way she had, beating on the doors of the train, yelling at her to move out of the way. No. She won't drag Karen into this. She's dragged her through enough already.

"He was shouting at the train," Brennan tells the cop who bends to write something down on a small pad he's taken out of his coat pocket. "Something about Karen. Most likely Karen Lindsay, maybe—the widow of the businessman who died on Newbury a few weeks back. Suspicious death."

Dorrie nods. "Karen was on the train. The last car."

"Anything else?" The cop taps his pen against a little notepad. "You see anything that might—"

Dorrie shakes her head. "It all happened so fast. I was standing there. I was just . . . It all happened before I could really even—"

"We're good for now, Mrs. Keating," the cop says. "A detective will most likely be in touch. Later," he says. "To get a more detailed account."

"She was trying to warn me," Dorrie says. Her voice sounds fuzzy, very far away, as if she's in a storm and a squall is blowing it around her head, tossing it here and there. "Karen. She was trying to tell me. She was trying to warn me." She hears her words zipping repetitively in the air. Faint. Insubstantial. They sound like someone else's words. She wonders if she'll always feel like this. Mad like this.

"You'd better get yourself out of this cold," the cop says. "You're shaking like a leaf. Plus, you don't look so good. You sure you're okay? He didn't do anything to—?"

"No." Dorrie tugs on her coat, tightens the woolen belt, fiddles with it. Her hands shake. "He didn't touch me. He just—I just saw him flying toward the train—the tracks."

She walks out with Brennan and stands on the sidewalk in the cold. "How did you know?" She feels a little better in the sunshine, out of the cave of the station, away from the tracks. "How'd you know to be here?" Sunlight slants down, touches Brennan's hair as they stand on the cold street, turns it a bright copper.

"Once a cop . . ." Brennan shrugs. "It was pretty clear you were in danger. After the other night outside Starbucks . . . I had an eye out for you, is all."

"Thank you." It sounds so meager, considering all that's happened. "Really, Brennan. You saved my life. Again!"

Brennan smiles. "Glad I could," she says. "But to be honest, if you hadn't moved in just that split second . . ."

"Yeah. Thank God for Karen."

"But the *way* you moved—totally incredible! I have never in my life seen anybody move the way you did!"

Dorrie hesitates. "It was my—" She starts to tell Brennan about her mother, about how she is always there when Dorrie really needs her, the vision of her. She closes her eyes for a split second, sees her mother skating on the pond in Boston Common the day before Lily was born, young, beautiful, the sky bright-bright blue and thick as honey—her mother so graceful, so free. She skated over to the very edge of the ice and took Dorrie's face in her hands, softly, gently, like a breeze, like the brush of a butterfly wing.

She listens for her mother's voice, but there are only the sounds of the station, the squeals and whispers of the trains. Dorrie clears her throat. "So," she says. "Today. With this guy— Was it about Joe's death?"

"It'd be one hell of a crazy coincidence if it wasn't. They're getting a warrant to search his place right now. Tomas Ramirez. Ever heard his name mentioned? At work or anything?"

"No." Dorrie gazes out over the gray street. Everything is fading. Late afternoon is turning into night.

"Well." Brennan tugs her coat up under her chin, glances at her watch. "If there's anything there to find, they'll find it."

Listen," Dorrie says. "There's something I have to tell you. About the night Joe died. I was there. I just—I'd lost so much already, I—"

"Maybe you should keep that to yourself." Brennan tucks her hair under her hat and looks down the street as if she's searching for someone. "It's not exactly news, anyway, whatever it is you're about to *not* tell me. There's footage," she says, "of that night. But they've got all they need. The rest is just—"

"*Footage?*"

"Little bakery one street over from Newbury," she says.

Dorrie reaches up, touches the cut that's healed into a small white scar above her eyebrow, remembers the window, the cakes, blood seeping along the blue of Lily's borrowed hat. "Thanks," she says. "Really."

"I'm not sure what you're even talking about," Brennan says. "But it's freezing out here. Drop you at your house?"

"No." Dorrie isn't really ready to go home. Not yet. "I'm okay," she says. "I think I'll stop and get a cup of hot chocolate or something. But, really, Brennan. Thank you. For everything. You're a damn good detective."

"Not yet."

XLII

DORRIE

Through the large front window, Dorrie watches Viv rush down the sidewalk. She sees her slip and slide across a patch of ice, sees her coat fly open when she turns into the doorway of the coffee shop, notes her friend's unbuckled belt, hanging loose from the loops. She really did rush to get here and it really is extremely cold. Viv could so easily have said she couldn't come or just not responded. She could have said she didn't see Dorrie's frantic little text until it was too late. She watches Viv push through the door. Life is just too short to hold a grudge. Anyway, Dorrie needs a best friend, especially right now. She needs a confidante.

"I forgive you," she says when Viv gets to the table, puffing and fumbling with her coat. "I'm not mad at you anymore." She takes a sip of hot chocolate and wraps her hands around the cup as Viv drapes her coat over the back of a chair.

"Oh. Thank God!" Viv just stands there. She looks as if she's afraid whatever she says will be the wrong thing and throw their friendship back off track.

"Just stay away from Samuel."

"No worries there," Viv says. "Absolutely none." She walks over to stand in line and comes back with a coffee. "So your text," she says. "It sounded urgent. I— Am I even *dressed*?" she says. And she is. But badly. She's wearing a sweatshirt with something that looks like grape juice down the front, juice or wine, sweatpants that don't match. Her hair is a tangle of thick curls, and she's wearing only a little makeup that looks like it's left over from much earlier or possibly the night before.

"Yeah," Dorrie says. "Sort of. Not your usual glam." She takes another sip of her hot chocolate. "I was nearly murdered in the train station today," she says.

Viv goes pale. "Oh my God! What *happened*? Who was it? Are you okay?"

"I'm fine. I didn't know him. Never saw the guy before in my life. It was so bizarre. He came at me. That's all I know. Karen saw him from the train and warned me. And then Brennan was—"

"Wait. *Karen? Joe's* Karen?"

"Yeah," Dorrie says. "Joe's Karen. It was all so totally—*surreal*. I was kind of following her, actually."

"Why?"

Dorrie shrugs. "I'm not sure." She stares out the window, where night is beginning to fall, where streetlights come on, suddenly, like lights on a Christmas tree. "Curiosity. Closure, maybe. I'm just glad it wasn't Samuel," she says.

"*Samuel?*"

"Yeah, Samuel. My husband? Samuel, the anger-issues-guy-who-passes-out-on-my-friend's-hotel-bed-Samuel? I found one of my gloves from the night of the accident. I'd lost the other one and I only had the one glove. It was in the car, on the seat. It was in Joe's car the night he died."

"So?"

"So I found it hidden behind a bunch of Samuel's stuff in the garage. I never would have found it. I never even go near his stupid workbench, but I was looking for something to clean." She takes another sip of hot chocolate. "It doesn't matter. I found it. That's why I wanted to meet you that night, but then we got into that whole thing about you and Samuel, and I . . . Anyway, he must have been right there on Newbury Street the night Joe died. He must have grabbed my glove. And he *has* been acting creepy. And you said he was—that you thought he was dangerous."

"I got a little got carried away," Viv says. "Samuel is about as dangerous as Purrl, probably."

"Wait. You told me he was . . . 'Watch out for him, Dorrie!' Didn't you tell me that? *Several* times?"

Viv takes a sip of her coffee. "I did. I know. But I was a little down on men at that point. Well, at *this* point." She sighs. "I suppose I've got issues. And he *was* really angry that night. I mean, he really *didn't* seem like the Samuel we all know and love."

"Careful."

Viv fiddles with her napkin, folds it into a tiny square. "Maybe I exaggerated a little."

"Okay. Granted, you do tend to overdramatize. But there's still the *glove!*"

"Wait!" Viv bends over the table. Her eyes are bright in the overhead glare of the cheap lighting. "Was it a *black* glove?"

"Yes."

"Leather?"

"Yeah."

"You left it in my car," Viv says. She takes another sip of coffee.

"So. Wait. So how did *Samuel*—?"

"I gave it to him," Viv says. "The night he came up to my, um, to my room. When he was leaving, I remembered the glove. I hadn't seen you since you left it in my car. 'Take this to Dorrie, will you?' I said, and he told me he would. I guess neither of us thought about how he'd explain exactly *why* he had it, which is probably why he never gave it to you. He just must have stuck it somewhere and figured he'd deal with it later. He was furious with you anyway. He couldn't have cared less about your chapped *hands* at that point! And then he must've forgotten about it."

XLIII

MAGGIE

Two weeks later, Maggie stands up and straightens her uniform in the full-length mirror on the back of the bathroom door. She's meeting Hank at the diner up the street from the station. They aren't partners, but Maggie hopes at some point they will be. They work well together. They always have, but even though Johnson isn't Maggie's favorite person—or Hank's, either, apparently—he is Hank's partner, at least for now. Her own partner is a nice enough guy. Gus. Not much of a talker. Their rapport is fine at work, but there's no overlap the way there was with Hank. They're not really friends.

She never went back to work at the beige office with the wavy floor after the day in the Park Street Station. She wasn't a good fit for Mass Casualty and Life. She wasn't built to sit in an office, to push buttons with a manicured finger, to swivel on a cheap metallic chair. Maggie knew she was meant to do less passive

things, more hands-on things, and the day with Tomas only rein-
forced her conviction. She'd called in to give her notice that next
morning, but her boss had let her off the hook. "Just come by and
get your stuff," he'd told her, and she had. Even though she'd wondered since the incident in Chinatown if she would ever be all
right back in the field—worried that she might freeze again or
hesitate, that she would let her partner down or put someone at
risk—she hadn't. Not at Park Street. Despite her fear of making
the wrong choice, despite Iraq, despite everything, she'd come
through when it really mattered. She won't let anybody down.
She knows she won't.

The timing couldn't have been better. After the article in the
Globe—after all the accolades—they'd called her down to the station that next morning. Her old station. Her old boss. "Glad to
have you back, Brennan," the chief had said. No prying. No fan-
fare. That was the chief.

Really, this is not the place she wants to be, not forever, and
Maggie understands this now, accepts it. She can forgive herself
for wanting more, for wanting to make the most of every minute she has left. To pay it forward, this gift. This life. She'll take
the test to be a detective for the Bureau of Investigative Services
as soon as she possibly can, set things up herself this time, go
through all the hoops and channels, work her way through the
ranks, but she will take the test. And she'll ace it.

Sometimes she thinks back to her first date with Lucas, tries
to picture the guy watching her from the back of the restaurant,
but she never saw his face. Most likely it was Tomas. Most likely
he was stalking Dorrie that night outside Starbucks until Maggie
happened along, calling Dorrie's name, foiling his plan. Would

he have killed her then? That night? Would he have stalked her to the trains, shoved her down onto the tracks and disappeared?

Maggie pulls up in front of the diner. Hank's already at a table, already on his phone, gearing himself up for a new day. She can almost hear him smacking his lips, almost see him rubbing his hands together. Same old Hank.

"So?" She slides in across from him with a cup of coffee, and he sticks his phone back in his jacket pocket.

"So the guys went over Ramirez's place with a fine-tooth comb."

"Find anything?"

"Naw." Hank leans back in the little plastic chair, cheap, like a McDonald's chair. "Buuuut . . ."

"What?" Her coffee tastes like water.

"They didn't find anything *there*. Absolutely zip. Clean as a whistle. But they did find something in one of the cars behind the garage where Ramirez worked. He drove it on occasion, according to the owner—Buick with a bashed-in headlight out in the back lot. So, when the detectives searched it, they found an old coat on the front seat. These were in the pocket—the originals. I made a couple copies; knew you'd want to see them." Hank reaches into a case on the floor beside his chair and pulls out a few papers, marked with creases, as if the originals had been folded for a long time, folded and refolded, read and reread. Words are typed across the pages in twelve-point roman font.

"What's this?"

"Take a look," he says. "It's weird as hell." He wolfs down a doughnut; white powder sticks to his mustache. "This guy was being played big-time."

"By—?"

"No way to tell. No prints besides Ramirez's. Standard computer paper—no clues there. Total anonymity on this one. Whoever wrote these notes thought it all out pretty well."

Maggie reaches for the little clump of papers. There aren't many. Three or four sheets.

"Take your time," Hank says. "Bein' on second has its upside."

"Yeah." It isn't Maggie's favorite shift, especially now, with Lucas in her life. Still, Maggie knows that this is what she signed on for. And there's always day shift to look forward to. "You have got to be fucking *kidding* me!"

"I know. Right?"

Maggie looks down at the papers on the table. Most of them are only one or two lines. One of them is only three words. She isn't sure exactly what she was expecting, but it sure as hell wasn't this!

She looks at the first note: *Karen's husband plans to kill her. He and his girlfriend. He beats her. I have seen the bruises. She is two people, the Karen you know, yes. But she's a battered wife as well, and she will keep this secret because she's terrified of him. She will protect this cruel man until he kills her.*

Maggie thinks back. She tries to remember if Karen ever so much as *hinted* that her husband might be violent or abusive or even forceful. She shakes her head. Karen Lindsay didn't strike her as the helpless type.

She reads the second note: *You are the only one who can help Karen. She trusts you. She loves you. If she wasn't so afraid of her husband, she would already be with you. Don't tell her that you know. Don't ask her any questions. It isn't fair to put her through any more than she's gone through already. You must act alone.*

And then: *Last night they nearly killed her. He beat her senseless.*

And, finally: *Help her! Please!*

Maggie straightens the little pile. "So, Tomas thought he was saving Karen by getting rid of her abusive husband. Not the sharpest pencil in the box, apparently."

"No. 'Love doth make fools of us all.' Any idea who would do this?" Hank sticks the papers back in his case.

"Where *were* these? How did Tomas get them? Were they mailed to him?"

Hank nods. "To the shop where he worked. Hoods. No return address, according to the owner—anyway, the envelopes are long gone at this point. Seems the husband wasn't abusive in the least. They called the widow in and asked her about it. This was the first she knew. She seemed genuinely shocked."

"Yeah. Even Dorrie said Karen was—you know—trying to warn her from the train that day."

"So who would want Joe Lindsay dead? And what about the woman? This Dorrie? Who'd want *her* dead? Was she Lindsay's girlfriend?"

Maggie shrugs. "He was training her to take over the company finances, so she pretty much knew everything Joe Lindsay knew. I'm thinking Lindsay's partner, Edward, wanted them both gone, so he could cover up what he was doing with the business." Maggie slugs down the last of her bad coffee. "But proving it will be almost impossible." Someday, she thinks. When she makes detective, she'll take another look at this. She gathers her things, puts on her coat. She'll call Karen from the car—drive to Waltham straight from here if Karen's around. There's still time before her shift begins.

"When Tomas saw Dorrie in the station that day, right where Karen was—who knows?" she says. "Maybe he thought she was after Karen. The husband's whatever. Girlfriend or whatever." She glances at her watch. "I'd better get going," she says. "Thanks for keeping me in the loop, for showing me the notes. This is so— Damn . . ." She shakes her head. "What people do for love, eh? Hey, Hank," she says from the doorway, one foot already on the sidewalk. "What color was the coat they found? The one in the Buick?"

"Black," he says. "One of those heavy puffy coats. Down or something."

XLIV

KAREN

Karen is happily surprised when Brennan phones. She wants to drop by, she says, to tie up some loose ends. She won't stay long.

"Please," Karen says, "come on over. For once the house is actually clean. And Antoine will be beside himself." She smiles when she hangs up the phone. It will be good to see Brennan. Nice girl, Karen thinks. Too bad she's left Mass Casualty and Life—the company could use a few more people like Maggie Brennan, something Karen didn't hesitate to tell them.

"Ten okay?"

Karen glances at the clock on the kitchen stove. It's a Wednesday. She'll be meeting Alice later on. "Sure," she says. "I'll put on some coffee, or, I don't know. Name your poison, Brennan. Tea? Wine?"

"Coffee's good," Brennan says. In the background, Karen hears the blare of a horn, the screech of a train.

"We'll be here." Karen yawns, starts the coffeemaker, opens the back door for Antoine, who bounds in from the yard as if he's over-heard the conversation, as if he knows that Brennan's on her way.

"So you're back with the Boston PD?" Karen sets a cup of coffee in front of Brennan. A nice cup, one she found at the back of the kitchen cupboard when she started getting rid of things. She isn't packing boxes yet; she's not that sure she'll move back to Boston, but she is paring down. Just in case. Traveling light, she tells Alice.

"Yep. *Officer* Brennan now."

"So many titles," Karen says, "so little time."

"This one suits me better," Brennan says. "At least for now."

Antoine sticks his nose under her hand, and Brennan gives him a little pat. "How're you doing, Antoine?" she says and he pants in delight. God. "I read the notes."

Karen nods. "Horrible. So someone must have set them both up. Joe *and* Tomas. This is so incredible. Was it Edward? It had to be Edward, right? No one else really stood to gain from— But I can't really wrap my head around it. *Edward?* A *murderer?* *Joe's* murderer? They were best friends since college!" Karen sets her cup down. "Do you guys have any fingerprints or anything? Any forensics?"

"Nothing. No prints besides Tomas's on the notes. And I'm totally with you. It had to be Edward. Still. He took a big chance, banking on Tomas messing up your husband's car."

"The brakes, you mean?"

"The brakes, the missing airbag fuse, running him off the road. Tomas confessed to all of it. But what if he'd gone to the police instead? What if he'd reported this alleged 'abuse'?"

Karen shrugs. "He wouldn't have, though. He was Honduran.

Things are different there. The police are different. Tomas wouldn't have reported anything to the authorities and Edward was probably counting on that. He has this gift for sizing people up, figuring them out. He always has. Anyway, knowing Edward, how meticulous he was . . ."

"What?"

"Nothing. I was just thinking."

"Thinking that . . . ?"

Karen shrugs. "That he probably had a backup plan."

"Scary thought. Scarier still, Edward would actually be free as a bird right now if Paulo Androtti hadn't decided to come forward. As it is, Edward will be going away for quite a while. I hear his lawyer's trying to get a plea deal, but he's kind of the last one to the table on that. Paulo beat him to it when he turned himself in and outed Edward."

"Paulo was the crew leader?"

Brennan nods. "Paulo Androtti ran the jobs, ordered the parts, that sort of thing, and, man, he spilled all the beans, talked about how they always used top-notch supplies, the best materials. Hired the best workers in the Boston area. Cream-of-the-crop. But, then, he said, about a year, maybe eighteen months ago, Edward had Paulo meet him at a diner in Southie. Told him to start saving the old conduit, flex, junction boxes, all the electrical wiring and fixtures. Two-by-fours, that sort of thing, from renovations. He had Paulo purchase materials for the jobs, the usual stuff from Home Depots around town, but then he had him return them the next day. Apparently Edward pocketed the money—probably embezzled here and there, altered the books.

"Androtti said he argued with Edward about reusing old

materials—said he was afraid the insulation on the wiring would be dangerous as hell, but Edward told him not to worry. It'd be fine. No problem. So, really, Paulo knew they were using substandard equipment, but he looked the other way, too—gambled with their clients' lives. It wasn't until that couple burned up in their home that it really hit him—Androtti—what they were doing, what he was part of. He walked off the job—tried to get in touch with your husband."

"So Joe would have—"

"I think he was about to figure the whole thing out. According to Paulo, they had a meeting set up but—" Brennan stops. She takes a sip of coffee.

"Joe died," Karen says.

"Yes. Paulo said he panicked after that. The city inspector was in it up to his neck—used to walk onto the job sites, sign his name without so much as a look, and take off. Edward was a snake, but a fairly powerful one. Paulo and his wife packed up and moved—he got another job, decided to fly under the radar for a while."

"So it must've been Edward who broke in and took Joe's laptop. He wanted to destroy the evidence. Which Joe didn't have, actually, but Edward couldn't know that for sure."

"Broke in?"

Karen waves her hand. "It was awhile back. Someone broke into the house. A couple of things were missing, the laptop and—poor Antoine was totally traumatized. Edward probably kicked him or something. They never got along."

Brennan reaches down, gives Antoine a little pat. "That right, Antoine?" Antoine whines. "So," she says. "Tomas Ramirez. He worked on your cars?"

"Yes. And we were friends, he and I." She will never tell a soul they slept together. Only Alice knows—Alice and Tomas—and Karen is certain that Tomas will go to the grave with their secret. Even if he didn't, who'd believe him?

"Obviously extremely fond of you. Enough to—"

"And I liked him," Karen says. "He seemed so sweet. He seemed like such a gentle, sensitive guy. Jeesh."

"So he knew your car from your husband's."

"Oh. Of course."

"Any truth to the notes?"

Karen smiles. "Nothing could be further from the—Joe never even really got mad," she says. "He was very passive-aggressive. And, do I, um, strike you as particularly fragile?"

"Nope." Brennan sets her coffee mug down on the table. "So, 'Joe and his girlfriend,' it said in the notes?"

Karen hesitates, weighs the pros and cons of dredging up all the crap about Dorrie again and decides against it. Brennan probably already knows that Joe and Dorrie were involved, and, if she doesn't, there's no need to tell her—no need to muddy the waters at this point, no need to ruin any more lives. She shrugs. "Dorreen. They were working together," she says. "Closely. Joe was training her to take over the finances when Francine retired. And Joe was really upset about that house that burned. He was nosing around—a lot. Apparently none too quietly. He was bound and determined to find out if there was a connection between the fire and the work that Home Runs did. He had a hunch, and . . . it turns out he was right. Edward must have thought Dorrie knew everything Joe knew. Or that even if she didn't, she knew enough to figure things out."

"She kind of did," Brennan says. "She had the pieces; she just didn't know exactly how they fit together."

Karen looks up. "Well, then . . ." she says, but that's all. After a few seconds, she leans over to grab their cups. "So who pushed Dorrie out of the way? At the train station?" She stands up, starts out to the kitchen with the empty coffee cups.

"Who *pushed* her? I didn't see anyone."

"No?" Karen says. "*Really*? 'Cause I saw someone there, a small woman, dark hair like Dorrie's?"

"Nope." Brennan shakes her head. "Just Dorrie."

"Huh." Karen sets the cups down in the kitchen. "Maybe it was a reflection in the train window."

"Yeah," Brennan says. "Must've been." She gets up, too. She thanks Karen for the coffee and stoops down to pat Antoine, who sits resolutely at the front door as if to bar her way.

"He wants you to stay." Karen leans over to pick him up and he snaps at her fingers. "If you're ever in the neighborhood, give me a call. Or maybe we could get a coffee sometime when I'm in Boston— a dog-friendly place, of course. Antoine would never forgive me otherwise."

Maggie nods. "Sure," she says. "Just let me know."

"Will do. Thanks for . . . God. Thanks for everything." She waits for Brennan's car to back out to the street. "Bye, Maggie!" She waves Antoine's paw in the air. He struggles in her arms, embarrassed, and Karen sets him on the porch, where he takes up his deputy stance. Together they watch Brennan's car until it turns and disappears.

Edward. Incredible. He could have ruined the company. Possibly already has. And Joe— Still, Karen knows that they all had a part in what happened. She brought Tomas into their lives, let him love her. And she knew he loved her. She always knew. And then there's

Dorrie. If she hadn't been with Joe that night, sliding around on icy roads, who knows what might have happened? Who knows if things might have turned out differently?

In the end, though, Tomas is the one with blood on his hands, the one who murdered Joe and, nearly, Dorrie. And he had stalked Karen as well, making her life a total nightmare for months, even if he did think he was protecting her. He was there, at the edge of her life, at the corner of her eye, watching as Joe ordered her a Chocolate Café Noir with strawberries—ready with his note as she parked in front of Chips on Charles, lurking. She shivers. And he'd lied about his job at Mass General. If she hadn't just happened to spot him working that day at his friend's shop, she'd never have known he was back at Hoods. She grabs Antoine and opens the front door. Clearly, Tomas lied to impress her. Or maybe he did work at the hospital. Maybe he was just moonlighting at the shop in Waltham. Still . . . Karen shivers. He made her trust him. She can't forgive him for that.

Some nights, when she wakes up after only two or three hours, knowing she won't get back to sleep, wishing she had a few more Xanax in the kitchen cabinet, Karen tells herself she only wanted to be rescued. Saved. She almost makes herself believe she wrote those notes for Tomas so that he could be the white knight she'd expected Joe to be, so he could liberate her, set her free. It's so much better than the truth—that from the moment she first saw those e-mails on her husband's laptop, she'd been dancing toward this precipice, that a dark, and unforgiving part of her had wanted things to play out just exactly as they had.

XLV

MAGGIE

Maggie drives back to Boston in the midday traffic. You can't be totally covered all the time. But if you're smart, if you plan well, if you can step outside a situation and see it objectively, keep your emotions from clouding your judgment and clogging up your strategy, you might just get away with murder. If you can play on someone's passions, plant an idea he'll embrace as his own, an idea that propels him to do things he would not ordinarily do—valiant and barbaric things, done in the name of heroism, done in the name of love—if you can do this, you've planned things well.

Dorrie just happened to be with Joseph Lindsay when he died. She could easily have been killed in the same accident, simplifying Edward's life enormously. The strangest thing to Maggie, although she'll never say it, is that both these women were right there on Newbury that night—the widow and the other widow—and still Joe Lindsay died alone.

Shit.

It's getting late. Maggie looks at her watch, switches lanes. *Come on!* She feels anger sweeping through her, annoyance at the drivers around her. It's okay, though. She doesn't hyperventilate; she doesn't overreact. She merely feels the irritation, allows herself to feel it. She's learning how to do this day by day, moment by moment, meeting by meeting. She goes with Lucas and she listens. Sometimes she talks about herself, about Iraq, about that day, the Humvee, the snipers. She doesn't tell them she has PTSD. She's learning to adjust, she says. She's learning to accept what happened. She doesn't like labels.

XLVI

DORRIE

When Dorrie opens her eyes, Samuel is already up, rummaging for his jeans in a bottom drawer. He's starting on the bathroom project he's been planning for several weeks—the renovation that he's had to put off every Saturday on account of iffy weather. Today, though, is the perfect day—blue sky and not so much as a snowflake in the forecast.

"Gonna start while the girls are still sleeping so they won't be in my way all morning," he says, pulling on a sweatshirt and stepping into an old grubby pair of jeans. "I'll pick up some of that odorless paint. The low-VOC. Not sure I'll get that far this weekend anyway."

Dorrie sits up against the headboard, rubs her eyes with the backs of her hands. "You sure you've got the right swatch?"

"Yeah," he says. "The lightest one. The one you left on the window seat, right?"

She nods. She can hear Lily up the hall in her bedroom. Mia's in there, too, and another friend who slept over. Dorrie smiles. Probably they stayed up all night talking, so the last thing they'll want to do is get involved with Samuel's DIY project. He'll pretend to be relieved, but really he'll be disappointed that his little girl's outgrowing him.

She shuffles over to the window and tugs on the shade. It flies open, winds around itself, out of reach, flooding the bedroom with sun. Blinding, dazzling, it sparkles off the white snow in the tiny yard.

She never actually told Samuel about her affair. Clearly, he knows. Clearly he *knew*. And if he should ever ask her, Dorrie is prepared to admit to what she's done, at least a part of it. She won't tell him everything—she'll keep some things to herself, carry them with her to her grave. Their anniversary has come and gone, without a word about trial periods. He bought her a bouquet of roses, took her to dinner up the street, a little Latin restaurant with the music up too loud. They'd even danced.

She slogs downstairs in her slippers and grabs the morning paper from the counter, peruses a small article about Everett Lansing on page two. He's come forward to shed light on Edward's wheelings and dealings—admitted to accepting money for turning a blind eye to substandard wiring, even to not inspecting it at all. Because of his confessions, Lansing's sentence will be a little lighter, but he'll never work again, at least not as a city inspector. Paulo Androtti got a slap on the hand—two years' probation and community service, teaching at-risk kids to weld, which Dorrie thinks is fitting.

She thumbs through the want ads. These days she tries to keep an eye on what's out there, just in case something interesting comes up. Edward's gone and Francine's gone and, for the next few weeks, Jeananne is gone. Who knows how permanent or stable her own position really is? She's still there, at least for now, doing Francine's old job and, sometimes, designs, although these days, she's hearing far more from old clients than she is from new ones.

All the wiring installed within the past two years is being replaced. After that, when all the dust settles, who knows what will happen? Maybe the company can never live this down, or maybe the old clients will be forgiving. Bostonians are tough, but fiercely loyal. Maybe Karen will decide to pack it in, close Home Runs altogether, open a book store up the coast, the way Joe once said she wanted to. Maybe she'll reopen the company under a new name or maybe she'll come back and run things on her own. For now, Dorrie takes things day by day, minute by minute. She's working with a woman Karen hired from Connecticut to get the company back on its feet.

She misses Joe. In her heart, she grieves for him. A part of her will always grieve for him. A certain song, a certain place, a scent, will bring her back to him, to their time together, and when it does, she'll leave the room or turn away, bury her nose in a book, until the feeling passes.

She glances through the kitchen window at the barren yard, glimpses a few buds sprouting on the spindly branches near the compost pile, thinks about her tête-à-tête with Brennan a few days before when they met for a quick coffee at Mug Me. She was near the office, Brennan phoned to say. Could Dorrie get away for a few minutes? She was in her uniform. She looked happy—she kept glancing at her watch. Punctual. Organized. Brennan.

"I'm in a play this spring," Dorrie told her. "You should come.

You can bring your friend." Brennan nodded, blushed a little. Dorrie hopes she does come, hopes she'll bring her friend. Any guy who can make Maggie Brennan blush is definitely worth meeting.

And Dorrie has landed a great part, the lead in an experimental play. She's looking forward to the challenge, looking forward to starting over. Spring is just around the corner. Redemption is in the air.

For now, she's fine with the world being wrapped in snow and ice, with the naked trees, with everything stripped bare for the cold instead of the opposite, which would make more sense. Dorrie thinks it might be the same way with love. Maybe the only way to really feel it is to strip away the outsides, the layers that bounce us through our lives, to feel the tip of someone's finger running down the bones beneath your skin.